ROBERT RICHTER

HOMEFIELD:

SONATA IN RURAL VOICE

Larae,
In appreciation of
your class's work--all
for naught.
Best wishes
R. Richter
2/12/01

Many thanks to these supporters of The Backwaters Press without whose generous contributions and subscriptions the publication of this book would not have been possible.

ANGELS

Steve and Kathy Kloch
Greg and Barb Kuzma
Don and Marjorie Saiser
Rich and Eileen Zochol

BENEFACTORS

Barbara and Bob Schmitz

PATRONS

Guy and Jennie Duncan
Cheryl Kessell
Tim O'Connor
Maureen Toberer
Frederick Zydek

SPONSORS

Paul and Mildred Kosmicki
Gary Leisman and Wendy Adams
Jeff and Patty Knag
Matt Mason
Pat Murray and Jeanne Schuler
Anne Potter
Carol Schmid
Alan and Kim Stoler
Don Taylor

FRIENDS

J. V. Brummels
Twyla Hansen
Jim and Mary Pipher
Richard White

Also by Robert Richter

Something In Vallarta (Permanent Press, 1991)

Tiime's Song, San Blas

Plainscape (Plain Ventures Press, 1987)

Windfall Journal (Jelm Mountain Press, 1980)

First Printing 500 copies January 2001

Published by:

The Backwaters Press
3502 North 52nd Street
Omaha, Nebraska 68104-3506
gkosm62735@aol.com
(402) 451-4052

ISBN: 0-9677149-2-3

Library of Congress Control Number: 00-93558

Printed in the United States of America by
Morris Publishing • 3212 E Hwy 30 • Kearney, NE 68847

THIS STORY IS FOR SARAH AND CALEB
AND FOR THE GUYS
WHO LET ME BE PART OF THE GAME

ROBERT RICHTER

HOMEFIELD:

SONATA IN RURAL VOICE

The Backwaters Press

PRELUDE:

I found myself dealing real estate in Mazatlan when I received the news about Uncle Karl, and I realized that for a long time this was what I'd been waiting for: a reason to return. It was the final chance of returning, too, because now even the family ties to the place were all but gone—all gone but mine. How tight or complex those ties were, I still didn't know, but they were there and I was headed for the High Plains. Again.

I knew that standing at the mouth of the family grave would inspire memories, images and incidents like requiem hymns, and I would have to sing them. I knew that I would walk the edge of open fields, feeling the wind carry a chorus of familiar voices— the sideline lyrics at ballgames with someone telling his version of the story again, or one of Buckwheat's gusty, blustery solos long gone over a cold beer and a view of the river valley, or even my own voice in journal notes of family refrain written down and left behind so long ago. Fragments of that harmony had always been in the wind no matter where I tried to lose them, the haunting ballad of living on the land never reaching a last verse. I knew it never would be settled history until I stood in that prairie wind and went through all the verses again. So I was going back.

I packed and caught the last bus north that night, and

even that act brought on the first memories. It had never taken me long to get moving because I always traveled light. My baggage had never been physical, my destination never in doubt. I was going back again for some kind of rest and reassurance, just like the previous trip fifteen years before, and that's where it all begins for me—April 1975, standing thumb out at the side of the Interstate in an alien wind, headed in-country.

FIRST MOVEMENT:

TERRAIN

CHAPTER ONE: COMING IN

What I wanted then was to be away. Away from the
fatigue of movement, away from the useless rage and from my
own tireless tripping into nowhere, to be in hiding. Yet, there I
stood on another Interstate interchange ramp, thumbing at the
east-bound traffic, leaning into the cold, roaring windwake of the
eighteen wheelers blasting by. And it was another middle of
nowhere, this time northeastern Colorado, on a shoulder of
sandhill covered by sagebrush and soapweed and bunch grass,
treeless and desert-like. To the south the ground rolled out to
cool-blue spring sky. North, across the four-lane, more hills
bluffed the far bank of the tree-lined and sandy South Platte River
flowing west to east as far as I could see. From the interchange an
empty strip of asphalt ran down toward the river. Above the trees
on the far bank the steel water tower gleamed, and the headhouse
of a grain elevator loomed with the name of the town painted
across the tops of the bins, the letters too small and faded to be
read.

The sign I stood beside near the end of the merging lane
read, "Next Exit 12 Miles," and beyond it, in the distance down
river, another water tower reflected the noonday sunlight. The top
of another elevator rose in miniature above the trees. No matter
the names. I knew these towns, each a twin to its neighbor, lining
the river all the way to Omaha—four hundred miles of the same
silhouettes, the same little businesses under the trees, the same
family houses along the same dirt streets named Elm and Maple
and Oak, Washington and Jefferson and Grant. Mainstreet. River
City. Clear to the Missouri. I had to grin, thinking that one of

them was my destination. When the name matched the memory, I would stop. That would be the last ride.

For a while there was a spacious silence along the Interstate, any engine roar muffled by the hills and distance, and by the feeling of exposure and vulnerability so near the end of my flight. Then the Doppler drone of a yellow Toyota shot by, the driver giving me that instant survey before hitting the brakes and rolling to a stop four hundred yards beyond. I ran for it, taking time to note the Nevada license plates, was in, and rushed away again with a man's smooth face full of grinning, perfect teeth and reflector sunglasses inspecting me like a hot meal. A mutual and instant evaluation took place.

"Where you heading?"

"Only about seventy more miles down the road. Thanks."

"Oh. Almost home, huh?"

I laughed at that. "You bet," I said, smiling into the windshield.

"I'm going all the way to Atlantic City," the driver offered.

"Long way."

"Well, I'm grateful for some company. The drive has just been hellacious."

Anticipating the pitch, I slouched down to rest my head against the back of the seat and listened to the subtle hinting in the banter of the driver's feminine purr. He lived in L.A. and Vegas; he loved to gamble and give things away; he trusted strangers too easily, fell under their spell; he liked to party when he won big and share his wine and cocaine and luxurious living until it was all gone. And when he was broke, he begged and did anything for a friend. Right now he was riding a high, heading for the Boardwalk, a different scene, the East Coast kick. He wanted to find new friends. A cute, little traveler's tale.

I let him carry on a long time, nodding or making sounds in the right places. Staring down the highway, I was thinking about the first time I'd been picked up by a homosexual—a bright gold Cadillac pulling over between Mobile and New Orleans, a petite man in green lamé pants who caressed a toy poodle with a red ribbon for a collar. That driver had asked the same question—Where you heading?—and had bought me a meal at a Denny's, walking ahead of me through the door, swishing his ass like a woman. That had been the summer of '68. I was nineteen and headed for Chicago. It had taken me another year and another, more physical encounter before realizing that I'd been propositioned that time near New Orleans, too. Now it seemed like an old song, and I resigned to the inconvenience, thinking only of the few miles left to go.

"You don't seem like you would be from around here," the driver said, taking a different tack.

"Yeah? How do I seem?" I kept looking down the interstate.

"Well, not like a farmer." After a proper dramatic pause, the coy, almost swooning voice added, "Kind of ...rugged."

I barked a laugh I couldn't hold back and turned sideways in the seat, facing the driver with a body language accent, saying, "Sorry. I'm not your type. I get drunk and beat up my lovers. I draw blood." Maybe forty miles to go.

The driver sat rigidly gripping the top of the steering wheel with both hands, staring statue-like down the endless road until he said, "Do you want to get out?" sounding almost hopeful.

"I just want to ride about forty-three more miles, that's all, Jack. But some day you're gonna die doing this kind of shit. Doesn't it get old?"

He shrugged, and we rode in silence then, in separate worlds until the driver's manicured fingers turned up the volume as the news came over the radio. It was big news and noise, a reporter hollering over the staccato beat of helicopter blades and the panicked bleating of voices. The U.S. Embassy in Saigon was under siege by V.C. and North Vietnam regulars, and anyone with any fear was scrambling for the final flights to safety, cornered on embassy grounds like lambs cornered by wolves. The driver looked from the road and our eyes met. It was one wordless communication we could share: It's finished over there now for the U.S. Finished for everybody ever involved after a decade and fifty thousand American lives. The one thing we had in common—a bad war—finally ended. The driver muttered, "Thank God," and turned his attention back to the road.

I silently agreed. End of April, 1975. End of a war, end of the road, end of a way of life, I thought, except for the hunted.

A few minutes later I took pleasure in this private ending

of my own, trudging up the good feeling of walking my last exit
ramp. It was a conscious movement, getting away from the
highway, and I could see myself sleeping for weeks in the shade of
the yard trees I remembered on the family homestead. I took up
the hike with a satisfying sense of heading toward something
different, with no intention of ever seeking another ride, though
the farm was still twelve miles or more out of the river bottom
and south across the tableland of wheat fields and summer fallow.

Across the overpass a narrow asphalt ribbon ran north
toward the river and trees and the bluff beyond. At the top of the
ramp the sign read, "Revere, One Mile," its arrow pointing to
another water tower and the steel rims of grain bins nestled
against the low skyline between the river and the bluff. The
common outline—except that these bins had once been the tallest
buildings in my life, when my father had worked at the Co-Op
there. So long ago now memory of it was only a shadow from
another world, a flash of images triggered in the senses more than
in the mind: the feel of the west wind; the scent and sound of
cottonwood leaves in full shimmer, and the summer snow of their
cotton seed all along the river; the way mud dried so quickly the
earth caked hard and cracked; the burning taste of heat; the
locusts' screaming evenings. Other old scenes floated up: of the
years my family had lived in Revere, of loading into the old station
wagon with the back end left open, cruising out across the bridge
and down dirt roads, heading for the family farm, the swirling dust
giving shape to our speed, the car flying off the ground at every
graveled intersection and dropping suddenly through the pit of the
stomachs of sisters screaming and bouncing around in the back.

Beside me, the roar of the Interstate brought back the
present, and I turned south and began walking the long waver of
road rising onto the tableland. After a mile, the asphalt ended, the
graveled road climbed a hill's sudden shoulder, and from there
disappeared into a pinpoint in the distance. The endless land lay
flat forever, spreading farther than I had remembered. Windbreaks were shimmering mirages. The azure sky over everything
absorbed distance with a wind that pushed its pale shape against
the green wheat and hummed in the winter wheat stubble. A
tractor worked wet, black ground along the edge of a long span of
center pivot towers. It seemed too early for farmers to be out

working the ground. Winter still hung on the edge of the wind.

But shining on a three-mile, mid-afternoon hike, the sun soon wore off the chill. I broke sweat after another mile, and the straps of the backpack dug into my shoulders. Twelve miles began to seem farther by foot than I had remembered from the dusty childhood rides. Perhaps it had been farther. I could feel my throat drying and tightening with thirst. Images of the Great American Desert rose in my mind.

In the first hour of the hike, two pick-ups had gone by. The first driver had slowed and given me a questioning look. I had only walked a mile or so by then and had waved him on, graciously turning down what I thought was an offered ride.

The driver responded by reaching below his seat and rising to brandish a tire iron in his fist. Through the open passenger-side window, he screamed, "Get back on the highway, you scum! You're here when I come back by, I get the sheriff."

My guts tightened with the old, familiar feelings. End of the war maybe, but the personal skirmishes had only begun. He stomped on the gas and peeled out, spitting gravel on me, and I stood watching his dust cloud diminish in the distance. Just what I needed, I thought, to be jailed in the county I was born in, twelve miles from my last destination, for crimes committed in another lifetime that never made a difference anyway. I walked on, waiting for the inevitable.

I almost jumped to a panicked run when I heard the next engine roar at my back, but against the huge horizon there was nowhere to go. I turned my head to see another pick-up. The driver in his seed cap slowed to eye me suspiciously, and it finally came to mind what an oddity I might be, walking down a country road—a bearded and ragged tramp, refugee from the days of rage, wandering off onto the plains, down a dirt road where everyone knew everyone else, but not me. An amused grin grew on the driver's face as he accelerated a dust cloud into the breeze. No threatened beating, no curses. I wanted a ride by then but wouldn't go begging. Or maybe I would the next time, even if the cost might be another lecture on the failure of my generation. The morning heat intensified.

Finally, I saw another dust tail plumed on the road behind me. A white, bulk fuel truck materialized out of the spring heat waves and the wind carried the purr of its engine to my ears. When I was sure the truck would roar around me, I turned my back and braced for the blast of dust and gravel. But the driver braked and brought the truck sliding to a stop in the middle of the road just beyond me.

I moved up along the side of the truck, wondering what kind of confrontation this would be, but the gum-chewing Cheshire Cat grin of the driver motioned me up into the cab. I climbed in beside a man about my own age, dressed in the service blues of a gas station attendant. "Mike" was scripted on the white oval patch above his shirt pocket, and a green De Kalb seed cap was pushed back off his forehead.

"Climb in, climb in," he urged in a tenor drawl, the kind of voice that hides nothing and puts anyone at ease with its first light syllables. "Where the hell you hikin' to?" He continued to grin across the seat as he crammed the transmission into low and lurched off down the road. He took a quick glance out his windshield, seemed to give the truck its head as he worked up through the gears, and looked me over with a clear air of amusement. "You know where yer goin'?"

"For a while I thought I did. I used to," I shouted over the roar of the engine and the wind at the open windows. "I'm trying to get to Karl Goehner's farm. You know it?"

"Does a hen lay eggs? Sure. I'm headed that general direction. Didn't anybody drivin' by offer you a ride?"

"A couple pick-ups passed me. Not their kind of rider, I guess. One used his tire iron to kindly point the way back to the highway."

Mike's grin widened even more. "That's cuz they don't know ya. You don't exactly look like a neighbor, neighbor. You know? You look a little like one of those crazies that fall off the Interstate ever now an' then. Sometimes there's bin some ugly problems. Still scares folks some."

"So why did you stop?"

His grin swept back and forth from the windshield to me, letting the pause build to its intended effect. "Well, cuz I know ya, a course."

I grinned at the thought, repeating the absurdity of the idea involuntarily, "You know me?"

"Sure. Calvin Parsons, right? See? I'm right. You didn't think I knew you from the moon."

"Well, I'm amazed," I confessed, enjoying the irony. How far had I come? How long had it been? "So how do you know that...Mike?" I asked, giving the name patch on his shirt an obvious stare.

"Well, you know. Everyone knows what's goin' on around here. Ever hear the one 'bout the reporter asking the farmer, what's the best thing about livin' in a small farm community? The farmer says, 'Everone knows everone.' 'Well, what's the worst thing about livin' out here in the country?' He says, 'Everone knows everone!' Hells bells, I'll bet there's someone around here can tell ya how many times a day I stop to take a whiz—if you really want to know."

"But I'm not from around here."

"Well, sure you are, aren't you?"

"Not recently, that's for sure."

"What's fifteen years or so? I knew you right away, didn't I?" Mike was still enjoying the game as we turned a sudden corner, barely cutting speed, spitting parts of the road into the ditch. "Recognize that place?"

From the buried remains of a childhood scene, I recognized the silhouette of a windbreak forest on the top of a subtle rise, the windmill towering above the new, barely-green branches of elm and mulberry, its blades whirring in the afternoon breeze, its vane pointing out the direction from which I had come. No buildings could be seen through the tangle of trees and brush and their winter catch of tumbleweeds.

"Still one of the biggest windbreaks in the county. Everbody says your grandpa was tree crazy."

"God! You know my genealogy, too?"

Mike barked out his pleasant laugh at my astonishment as he turned the truck down the elm-lined lane toward the house. The farmyard opened up in a great cup of trees, with corrals and white outbuildings tucked in out of the wind, and I climbed down into the April air purring now in the tree tops. The windmill churned and creaked overhead, spinning its song. Higher yet the cottonpuff clouds streamed ever eastward.

Mike turned the truck around in the yard and pulled up

beside me again. "Well, see ya around," the gum-chewing grin hollered down from the cab window.

"If you say so, I believe it."

"Say, you got any baseball left in you?" The twinkle of his teasing refired in Mike's eyes.

"You mean you don't know about my winter season in the Mexican League? I'm disappointed in your sources."

"Well, I ain't checked 'em for a while. But I'll probably hear all about it by sundown. You'll be old news."

"When you do hear, check my batting average, will you? I don't think the last weeks' games were in the stats when I left."

"Okay, we'll do. See ya around, stranger. And take care what roads you walk."

He grinned off down the lane, leaving me standing by an open gate, the stranger told that he wasn't, smiling at my destination.

Wonder what I'm doing here, I thought then, and I'd keep on wondering even after I told the story to the only guy who understood the question.

Buckwheat solos:

"Naw, naw, for me it was more of a mad rush, 'specially cruisin' that last morning poppin' speed and coffee to keep awake and pushin' that little MG up around ninety. Seemed like the closer I got, the faster I wanted to get there like up there between the rivers that's the only place to be, and I got to thinkin' 'bout that ground, then about the river there, the North Platte, and the way it goes clear back up into Wyoming, and then I thought, what the hell, I'll just follow the river all the way home. Hit the brakes at Rawlins—cuz that's where I was—and headed off north there to where the highway hits a little two-laner that meets the river right by Independence Rock on the Sweetwater.

"You ever seen that rock with all the names and notes etched in? Thousands of people writin' that they passed by there and leavin' letters for family comin' up behind on the trail—the goddamn Oregon Trail, man. That's one thing I remember about from high school there in Revere. Did a research paper on it and read about it and got so goddamn interested in it I even did it for real, and even old Maude Jack, who taught there a hundred years and some, couldn't believe it. 'Course Sandy typed it and did the real English, but I know that damn trail. I could even find it there in Wyoming without a map and drive right to it.

"I blasted by that rock about dawn, and that cold, pink light was just comin' on. And it was the first time I ever saw that rock—hell, the only time. There was dates and names of all these people passin' by in another time, and it seemed crazy so many thousands goin' by and half of 'em sorry they ever came—and the rest of the trail the worst yet to go—leavin' signs and directions for whoever was crazy enough to come after 'em like they could tell 'em what it was like and make it any easier or somethin'. Hell, what's the point? Didn't change a damn thing. Even when ya do tell the truth of it, ain't a fuckin' soul to believe ya. Hell no. Wagons westward, or die doin' it. Shee-it!

"Well, I shot on around the rock and along the river really pickin' up speed and light—light speed, man—and didn't even know I was doin' it, just cruisin'. Followed the North Platte all the way for home, hit the Interstate at Casper still right along the river, crossin' it a couple times with the ice flowin' and the water look-ing' thick an' dark as syrup, and all the time I was thinkin' 'bout those wagons and carts and people pushin' over the hills, and what for. And so slow the goin', and still losin' parts of families, gettin' killed or drowned or sick from disease, even starvin' to death and eatin' each other. And still headed they don't even know where, or why, or what it's like, just some crazy idea that it's gotta be better than what they left. It all still sounds too goddamn fucking familiar.

"But the river and the trees and the ground along the river was fine, man, in that early mornin' light, sometimes just a blur of color in the speed I was movin'. Then I took twenty-six cuz it stays along the river. I don't even know how I found it, just ran into it runnin' with the water the way I wanted to go. It's a fine little road rollin' through the towns and trees—I can tell you that—and in the mornings clear and empty like no one lives there but you, and it's your road to wherever, like life's a dream. And it is, man, when you're just screamin' down the highway for three days and nights so high there ain't life beyond the window, like that's the world right there and welcome to it, nothin' but the brain tickin' down the distance. I'd wake up somewhere and look around, thinkin': Oh, I'm in Nevada. Oh, I'm in Utah now. Oh, I'm in Wyoming and headed for Independence Rock, just like I'd planned it or something. And what's the big deal? Might as well drift off again till ya get where they're sendin' ya.

"Well, I woke up again out around Torrington, so I stopped at a truck stop there and had a huge breakfast—steak and eggs and toast and hash browns and lots of coffee, thinkin' hell, it's on Uncle Sam. It's always on fuckin' Uncle Sam now. I headed out of there tokin' a joint to mellow out the caffeine and speed. My heart was like a drum poundin' in my ears, cruisin' that last two hours or so for home.

"When I was startin' to recognize things, I couldn't believe how it took me. That snow-white morning light was flashed across Scott's Bluff, and the valley ran east forever, the river still windin' in the trees, and the hills all along the other side rough and bare in the wind. It was fine cruisin', man, down along the meadows and ranches, through Lisco and Lewellen, lookin' into back yards and pastures at everything, the same old tractors and rusted car bodies pulled into the fence rows, same old wooden shacks and barns fallin' down and waitin' for one good wind to finish 'em—just like nothin's changed in four frozen years. Same old junk equipment in the yards, same old white-faced Herefords down in the trees breathin' up clouds, and ducks settlin' in outa the south. Then I thought about those old blinds being there at the end of the lake and took the north shore clear around to look 'em over, but I spaced it off somewhere thinkin' 'bout huntin' with the old man and thinkin' 'bout that time down on the river, you and me with our b.b. guns, and how we saved ourselves when that cut bank took us. Then I was just watchin' the curves and feelin' the dips and climbs in that little car huggin' the road. Just ridin', you know?

"I came across the dam, lookin' down the valley and 'bout ran off the road so stoned and starin' and thinkin' how clean and quiet and isolated down there the river is. Cut cross country then, just past the dam and up onto the tableland over the good old home roads, and they never felt so damn good, and I was thinkin' they're just the same, too, everything up here between the rivers like the years and the war ain't touched a thing. Thinkin' everything'll basically be the same—the homeplace, the fields, the chores, the old man, Sandy and the kids—only I didn't even know those babes. I hadn't been around 'em. Then I'm thinkin', the only thing different is me, doin' seventy or so down the gravel, feelin' the wheels come off the road flyin' over the little rises, driving a crazy MG, and my fried mind a huge hyped blur and buzzed out constantly for over a year. A fuckin' crazy person with an arm still stitched up from the last operation and kinda hangin' off my shoulder like the stick arm of a goddamn snowman and my left leg jammed up there under the clutch pedal cuz I still couldn't bend the fuckin' knee and never will what with all the shit they did—hell no, man, it ain't ever gonna heal. Over three damned years now and it still drains and oozes and stinks like a cesspool.

"And I could see myself followin' dad around the place just like Chester on Gunsmoke. 'Wait for me, Mr. Dillon!' Shit! I could hardly wait. The hoppin', crippled go-for. Shit! I let off the gas, thinkin', what the hell do I want to do that for? Where the fuck am I goin' like I was lost or somethin'? And by then I was even past the place I wanted to stop and park—right here—where you can look out over both rivers and get the feelin' lookin' west how those rivers come out of different directions of nowhere, and the other way ya see how they're startin' to come together and you're sittin' up here on the dry hard ridge between them, feelin' the whole thing. But so blitzed out and bummed about where I was goin', I was already turnin' into the home lane and everyone was rushin' out to see me and kiss me and cry and shit. I'm thinkin': I've just come all this fuckin' way and for what? And here I am, stoned and alone, and I know I ain't workin' with the old man."

Calvin's journal notes/spring, '75:

It's some day, mid-May. Must be Sunday for we are all resting.

Have not been able to write here lately as I have been

exhausted most nights or spaced away on the distance to the stars. This has not been as I'd imagined. For some reason I had assumed it'd be a leisurely part-time work week. I'd take my breaks to stroll the country, looking at landscape and thinking of trying to sketch again, tuning in to the wind and open isolation, being very "Zen" about everything and meditating like some contented Buddha while taking on the character of a country gentleman. But I have been moving around physically more in the last three weeks than I ever did thumbing thousands of miles cross-country. And for ten hours a day, sometimes longer, sweating all the time—even in the spring coolness—and aching for sleep by sundown. The soft pounds I gained on the road and while lying around in Mexico are burning off.

I'm awakened out of a deep sleep before daylight begins. Since Uncle Karl works for AgCo in Tyghe, troubleshooting mechanical and electrical breakdowns for every irrigator in the county, the only time I see him for a list of daily duty is just before sunrise or late at night. He works longer hours than I do, of course, and if it's always been this way for him, I don't see how he did the farming, too—taking care of cattle, summer tilling, cutting wheat, planting, keeping his own ancient machinery running. The reason I've been so busy is easy to see now. I'm tending to all those neglected jobs, repairing the weak and weather-damaged homestead, building back up what's run down or decaying—and all the time it seems something is breaking down or wearing out or is in need of adjustment.

The first few hours I was here were full of the relief and paradise I'd expected, moving into the bunkhouse, showering the miles of dust off, then sitting out under the budding elms singing in the winds over the housetop. Martha brought me a beer and dug in her flower beds, pulling her short, round body slowly around the yard as she talked on about the family, about mom and Uncle Karl, about Aunt Sophie and her family down on the river, and about hundreds of cousins and such that I barely remember. She sang off name after name, and I'd forget them and their connections to me as soon as she said them—as they say, you can't tell the players without a program.

Then I got to wander around the windbreak surrounding the farmstead, the forest I remembered from being here as a boy.

I went into the barn and the sheds and shop to see how much of the place still fired up a memory. Much of it did. It all seemed so fine to me—not my fishing village in Sinaloa, or Nathan's old cabin in the Canadian Rockies, but seeming just as cut off from the rest of the world—a beautiful, private windbreak forest miles out on the open plains with cattle grazing off north on the prairie pasture toward the river and wheat waving green in the warm, windy sunlight to the south. The whole sky absorbs any sound but the wind's—which is everywhere—and casts a quiet peace as far as the far edge of earth. So much open, empty ground, yet I feel I can hide here.

Got to walk my first long walk out into the pastures to ponder the wonder of being here, of being away from that last crazy cross-country ramble, that six months of wandering in southwestern circles and seeing who'd put me up for a while. I was always an inconvenience and an uncomfortable memory to old friends, or like an old piece of furniture people keep running into in their new lives till they somehow sadly part with it—but then are glad it's gone and not there anymore reminding them of the past. Too much intensity, and everyone just wants to rest and forget, so I finally moved on—on with the crowd, getting back into the flow to wherever...or to nowhere. Sad to think of all that wasted movement and everything changing but me.

But out on the field edges I got to be glad I was here, walking away completely from all that, out onto the wide-open, empty ground, with Tyghe's crystal-white elevators glistening like a cathedral in Oz off on the southern horizon. From a small rise on the north edge of the pasture I could just make out the shoulder of the tableland dipping down toward the South Platte river bottom that I had walked out of only hours before.

Walked back to the bunkhouse to move in—with what little I have—to relax, to browse through a couple of books, and to think about a private smoke later in a reverent sunset solitude that would soon be pouring in my open door.

—But, not to be! By five or so Uncle Karl was home— earlier than usual, I've since learned—and by sundown we were well into shoveling wheat in the granary, loading the old trucks to haul it to town, and I couldn't believe the ache in my bent back and the sweat pouring off and the sucking for air in the dust and the steel scream of the auger. In the glow of the truck lights I was leaning in the doorway watching the old man in his wild mane steadily sliding the wheat toward the auger, cleaning out the corners, moving the auger with a shoulder as he scooped—a seventy-two year old wild man who climbed all over the last full truck, pulling the tarp down, tying it in place, casually finishing up his late night chores.

I had expected old Karl to come tottering up the steps into the yard and...I don't know, talk about the family, too, have a beer, softly welcome me gratefully to the farm. But I greeted no weary, aging, back-bent German farmer in bib over-alls. It was the grey, wild mane and beard of an old Nevada prospector(or an aging hippie) with wrinkles like canyons around clear blue eyes. The tattered orange seed cap pulled down on his forehead soft-ened the lines of his habitual grin and made his thick, long hair flare out over his ears as if he'd just received an electrical shock.

He saw me sitting in the yard and said, "Well, Calvin, how do?" knowing me immediately even after so many years and seeming less surprised than I had been that I'd actually come. We exchanged about two sentences each after the "How you beens?" then Martha was at the porch door saying, "Well, you're home early." It was about five thirty.

"I got to be moving that grain. It was lookin' a little buggy the other day."

"Well, ain't it a blessing that Calvin come in today?" She chuckled with delight and called the coincidence divine providence.

We walked out to the wooden granary standing along the field's edge about a quarter of a mile from the house and yard. Karl said, "Well, I appreciate the help, Calvin."

I answered, "I guess that's what I came here to do," and the rest of the walk was in silence.

At the granary he handed me a scoop shovel and ex-plained the set of the auger that spiraled the wheat up into the truck bed. All we had to do was keep the grain flowing and the auger full. Karl roped the engine to life, put the auger in gear, and we watched the golden grain simply sucked away for about five minutes. Easy enough. Then the auger began clattering against itself with emptiness, and for the next three hours we shoveled grain.

He never stopped except to climb out of the grain pile and up into the truck to round off the load and tarp it. With the auger off, I lay down on the mountain of wheat while Karl moved the other truck into place. My heart was thundering in my ears. I could feel my eyes bulging and watering. My shirt was soaked with sweat, and the small of my back felt stabbed with a thousand needles. Then in two minutes we were at it again, Karl twisting rhythmically as he swung his shovel and pushed a constant river of wheat down the pile. I wheezed and grunted, dug and lifted, till he noticed all my wasted energy and showed me how to do it right—swinging and pushing the shovel like an oar instead of hauling it around full like a bucket. The method was noticeably easier, but by then there was nothing to forestall the aching exhaustion.

Karl said, "I'm awful sorry, Calvin, not thinkin' to tell you about it. I just don't explain things. What I mean to say is, even when I come to think of 'em."

In the dark I rode back to the house with him showing me how to drive the ancient, groaning truck, how to start it and steer it and double clutch the screaming transmission through the gears with a full load of wheat. So glad to be finally resting, I barely noticed the lessons. We stopped in the lane by the gate, and he stepped up and into the kitchen for a late, ready-made supper as if he'd been sitting in an office all day. I dragged in to a meal I could hardly fork to my mouth and felt myself nodding off while Aunt Martha talked at me like Dorothy's Auntie Em about fresh-baked bread and the butter she churns herself.

I went out to the bunkhouse and fell into bed without a shower, and before first light, before any breakfast, we were out there again, hauling the wheat to town—me trying to learn the gears again, how to stop ten tons of rolling, loaded wheat truck with mushy brakes, how to work the power hoist, and all the while with the old truck protesting in a roar of grinding gears, the smell of burning brakes and clutch, and the creaking sway of the heavy load ready to topple us over into the ditch. I swerved the truck into the unloading area at the elevator, sending a couple guys scrambling for their lives, dumped it too fast and spilled it all over the floor so they had to shovel and sweep it into the pit, and then I drove back out here to do it again with the other truck.

We had a huge breakfast first, we shoveled wheat, moved

augers, climbed truck beds, and drove those rambling wrecks to town all day. Karl's trucks, like the rest of his machinery, are museum pieces—two 1946 vintage GMC two-ton trucks with power hoists that groan to lift the load, screaming transmissions sure to explode soon under the stress, no shocks, barely any brakes, no instruments except oil pressure and gas gauges—older than I am and still running down the dirt roads and vibrating apart.

We did this for four days. Karl had taken time off from his job to help me—or rather, while I tried meagerly to help him. My shoulders ached from manhandling the trucks' wild steering. My back spasmed from the shoveling. My legs felt like rubber from the long continuous hours of climbing and standing. In whatever position I hit my bed at night I stayed until morning when he was knocking on the door to get me up and repeat the process. The whole task seemed effortless for Karl, every move slow and deliberate and without haste, never breathing hard, barely breaking sweat. He seemed so much a part of the process that it simply happened, like the weather.

Those were the first four days. Thank God the fifth day was Sunday. Aunt Martha says God rested on the seventh day of creation and so should we, but I was well ready by the fourth. I didn't even get up for breakfast, or lunch. I used the day as it was meant—I rested—and went to bed early that night.

Since then I have helped to do—or outright done by myself—the shingling on the water house, fencing in the pasture(the one task I've known something about on my own), excavating and plumbing repairs at the stock tank, and in the evenings I've been helping to tear out the innards of an ancient combine. When I've had moments between these tasks, Martha has usually been there with ideas of her own like weeding by hand the Buffalo Burr infesting the corrals—you have to wear gloves to protect against the fine thorns; or slaughtering fifty chickens to pack away in the freezer—I got to cut off the heads and watch blood drain from the twitching bodies; or hoeing in the garden in the mid-day heat. And, for Aunt Martha, I haven't done anything quite right yet. It's done exactly to her specifications or you're made to feel like a dog deserving of a good kick.

At any rate, always doing something, moving my body

toward the quick habit of fatigue. At dawn each day we set to work, or rather, Karl sets me to a day's work till it looks like I won't kill myself with the tools he's given me. Sometimes the lessons take a long time, like the surgery on the combine. We're removing something called the shaker shoe and replacing all the bushings and bearings—whatever they are. I have no idea what's going on. Karl's mind is the repair manual, and my body is one of his tools. I always apologize for making him take time off from work, but as with all things, he is truly unruffled.

"The work is always there when I get to it," he says. "Job don't go 'way till you see to it. If they're in an all-fired hurry, they can see to it themselves as best they can. Ain't nobody's crop yet gonna die for lack of water. Just some folks gotta fret like tomorrow's doom. They know I got my own place to tend to when I have to."

And that's it. Karl and his place. There is no separation of the two, sudden or eventual, that I can see where I become the farmer here and he the hanger-on. By twilight he's home, and still in his ragged service blues, he helps me with the work of whatever chore I'm on—the milking or feeding, the rounds to the poultry pens, or mechanic repairs under the trouble-light in the shop. He knows what's to be done on the place and when to do it, though I doubt he could list those tasks in any logical order or schedule if asked to. Karl merely tends to the project that springs up with barely any explanation of why now or how, and I troop along, awaiting instructions and gearing up to employ myself like any other machine on the place, fueling up at Martha's table, resting up in the bunkhouse bed, going on to the next milking, feeding, fence down, or tree-tending time. It's just as well. Left to myself, I would never see that there's so much to be done around this small forested farmstead on the plains—other than to just ease back listening to the windmill's creaking song, or the water's running in the garden, or the trees' chirring on the edge of the wind. But just in passing, either Karl or Martha can point out some unfinished farm duty to be done, and none of it is made-up work. It's there when he shows me: belt about to break on a compressor, stalls to clean, bales to stack, tools to tend. And we haven't even gotten to the actual act of farming yet—the job I expected and thought about on the long trip out here. No, we tend to the task as it comes up before Karl, regardless of where we are or what had been planned before or what time it is.

Like yesterday. It was Saturday, so Karl was home the whole day. We were going out into the fields finally with a tractor and the tandem disc to begin my first operation in the summer till. But at dawn, in the barn for milking, one of the cows kicked the stanchion to pieces. It had been slowly decaying in decades of dampness and dung and weather changes, and a high-strung Holstein—misnamed Mouse—finished the job when she got impatient with the way I squeezed her teats. So after I picked myself up out of the manure and spilled milk, we spent the next four hours rebuilding that part of the barn completely, gathering new boards and bolts and tools, measuring and sawing and drilling. Karl always has the necessary supplies on hand somewhere on the place as if he knew (and he probably did) long ago exactly what would happen and had prepared for it—the right lumber, the right tool, the proper repair kit to fix a tractor's water pump, rewire an electrical circuit, replace some old plumbing, or rebuild a rotting stanchion.

By around mid-morning we headed down to the shop toward the tractor, but we stopped along the corral to talk about the trees growing up in the fence—volunteer cedar and elm that I casually remarked on in passing. He explained, like a philosopher, that a tree in the wrong place, even on a mostly treeless plain, is a weed. So we got to chopping out these seedlings for fifty feet of corral fence before they did damage by uprooting posts or spring-ing boards off. But before doing this, we had to go to the tool shed for axes and spades and take them to the shop to sharpen blades and replace handles so we would be working with the best and most proper tools. We finished that job by nearly noon. Then we gathered up the brush and branches and as much other wooden trash as we could find around the yards and buildings, and we built and tended a bonfire. By then it was lunch time.

We went in with good appetites to meat and potatoes, iced tea and ice cream, and in little less than an hour we tried again to make it to the tractor and out into the fields. Got nearly as far as the shop but found a hose on the fuel tanks decaying and replaced that first. We actually made it to the tractor then and went to work on the battery, first meticulously cleaning the terminals and cable ends, reconnecting, then charging it (with the charger whose plug we repaired first). Every other moveable part slowly came apart to be cleaned, too: a fuel filter, the oil pan, distributor wires, plugs and points, and all the other stuff about which I have only a vague idea. Going through it, Karl overhauled each piece, describing each act as he did it, why it's done, what the part is called, how it's this way on a Case tractor, different on a John Deere or some other make, and imparting other information faintly related or not at all connected. It all flowed full of complete sense and simplicity from his doing and describing it to me. I clearly comprehended for a moment, then utterly forgot with the next instant and item.

In eight years of off-and-on again college, with one degree and most of another, plus traveling in circles in four countries, precious little I've done in the last few weeks was ever learned any place else. I'm still mostly ignorant, while a man almost three times my age who never finished eight grades and continually claims to know nothing, can construct and maintain anything mechanical or electrical, probably with his eyes closed.

By well into the afternoon the old Minneapolis-Moline "G," called Old Moe, was purring in the shop, warmed and perfect—or almost, that is. We adjusted the lights(which we won't use) and cleaned the hydraulic couplers. Then Karl showed me the gear pattern and how to kick the tractor into gear with the hand clutch, revved up full on the rpm's, and gave me the wheel, pointing the way to the tilling implements. At the first cattle gate a wire broke, and we returned to the shop for more wire, fencing pliers, and a stretcher. Went back and fixed the fence, returned the tools, and headed again for the disc and drills and other machines where they lay buried in a winter's worth of tumbleweeds. We gathered weeds a while and burned them, clearing out around the tandem disc, walking around to inspect and grease it. He backed up to it then and hooked up, tightened the drawbar bolts and replaced a steel pin, kicked the tires. No, it had to be pulled back to the shop to fill the tires, to work a jammed grease zerk free with a touch of torch heat, and to replace another stripped bolt. We cleaned and worked its adjustments while he explained how the disc works and why it's used. On and on.

By then twilight was coming on, and since this was the weekend, we knocked off early—that is, before dark, just after the milking. I was told that today we'll finally, actually, get out to the field, but as Karl says, "Seein's believin'."

—And it won't be before noon. This is Sunday. I even slept in again—till 7:am. Karl, of course, was up to do the milking, Martha to fry a bacon and egg breakfast. By the time I went into the house myself, they were ready for church as usual, and for the third straight Sunday I told them I wasn't going with them. They muttered, "Oh, that's fine. Whatever you want to do." But in Martha's voice there was this sound of resigned pity for a poor, fallen son. Karl seemed to give it no other thought and went back to his breakfast, and Martha, with a sigh for this heathen, went back to her reading.

It was the daily devotional reading, even on Sunday before church. I ate and listened and watched this old couple at their sincere prayer. It's a time they are elsewhere and paying no attention to me, or even to the business of their lives. They sit apart from the world, nearer heaven, with the words of the daily lesson, away from the light over the table, from the dishes pushed back and the scents of the morning meal, with their two chairs slightly facing one another, Martha bowed over the Good Book in her lap, Karl's head bowed too, eyes shut, slowly chewing and ruminating the words of God.

It's been at this morning rite that I have begun to see about them more than what they've been to me since childhood, to see them not just as old, respected members of the family, but as players on their own very real stage and not just as extras in my private little play. Strangely, only for these brief snatches of moments during their devotion, do I see and feel them to be one unit: they live their lives so separately and silently.

Martha, staggering slowly from word to word, away from her cooking and canning, away from the gardens and animals and her invariable routines, seems older and weaker. Her silver hair is thin and tired, the wrinkles like deep cracks in the round softness of her jowls. Her pale eyes water. She seems all of her seventy-seven years and as much a part of this place as the trees—or more. She's older than any tree here, but less flexible in the wind. Yet who would shadow me here if she fell?

In his unmoving pose of prayer, Uncle Karl is even more a distinctive entity than when he is steadily going about his work.

It was during their first morning devotion that I noticed his hands. They are the history and time-tellers of his life here. The backs of them, sun-burnt and weathered, come out of his shirt cuffs like gnarled tree roots, several knuckles like large knots where limbs have snapped off, cracked and broken and hideously healed as hard lumps under the skin. His fingers, as they fold through one another, are twisted askew or not there altogether. Parts of the first two fingers on his left hand he lost in the gears of a cement mixer, and the ring finger of his right hand was once pulled into a gear box and left with mangled tendons and the permanent twisted shape of a hawk's talon. The tip of his right index finger was chewed up by a bandsaw, half the nail gone forever and the part remaining a shining, black button. The skin looks as rough as alligator leather. Of all his high quality and tenderly cared for tools, his own hands are the most battered. Even the palms, when I've seen them at some labor, are callused and creviced with wrinkles and scarred clear across from when he clung to a steel cable in a collapsing silo and saved his life. It's a wonder those hands still function at all, but when he shakes your hand in welcome, it's a solid and sinewy grip expressing the spark of energy and will that guides them in their work.

Folded in his lap in restful prayer, his hands are a massive sculpture of his experience, and protruding from the dark sleeves of his urban-cut, Sunday suit of double-knit pin stripes and pressed creases, they look out of place. But their not belonging is lost in the wild statement of his long grey hair falling over his collar and joining with the full bush of beard. This is a gaunt and weathered, old dirt farmer in the clothes of a big-city banker, contemplating his daily prayers, as comfortable with it all as the wheat waving in the wind.

When they finished "The Lord's Prayer," I rose in the final silence and said, "See you at noon." Karl nodded and grinned me out the door, saying, "We'll get in the field this afternoon sure." Even though it's Sunday afternoon, he's getting me started so tomorrow he can get back to AgCo and see to everyone else's problems. Besides, it's time I learned something useful.

Mike McCormick's lyrics/

I mean, you got to admire Buckwheat's old man. The guy
never had a childhood of his own. My folks say he was only
sixteen when his own father blew a valve and kicked out for good.
It was during a wheat harvest, about a hundred and four degrees,
no wind, and a hail cloud mushrooming up huge and black-green
in the west. You could see it was gonna crash everybody's party,
and Gerry's dad was huffin' and puffin' against a pry bar, trying to
jack the concaves in the combine up out of the way so Gerry
could get a bolt back in somewhere and they could get back to
cuttin' wheat before the storm hit. He was gruntin' and jackin' and
screamin' at Gerry just like Gerry took to yellin' at Buckwheat.
Hell, all three of them have been the same damn way.

Down inside that combine it was probably another twenty
degrees hotter, and humid as a green haystack. Right in the middle
of a fit for scrapin' his knuckles, grandpa choked on a "goddamn,"
and his heart gave out. Nobody knows how Gerry Van Anders
pulled his father out of there, but anyway it was way too late to
save him.

The hail slipped off to the northeast and ran down the
lake and out into the Sandhills. The neighbors stopped everything, of course, helped bury the guy—he was only fifty-seven or -
eight, helped the Van Anders finish cuttin' their wheat before they
went back to their own harvests, and at sixteen years Gerry was
the man of the place—his mother a widow, two sisters—one just
reachin' puberty, and no one else to tend six quarters of wheat
ground and pasture that were nowhere near paid for.

So Gerry growed up in a hurry. Never went back to
school, never played ball though everybody said he would have
been damn good, and the farm and the farming's been his hard
work ever since. The outbuildings—barns, sheds, shop and all,
stand right where Gerry wanted them, and they hold all his
projects and chores, his tools and machinery. There's a fairly new
windbreak that he planted and had Buckwheat and the girls water
to life. The ground's farmed how he decides, and the harvest sold
when he thinks it's time. A regular farmer now, and he's been
doing it, what?, well past thirty years.

By eighteen he had married Eula—she's a Robertson girl, and she was already pregnant with Buckwheat of course. Ol' Gerry found time for that sure enough. That's one tradition that ain't changed 'round here. And he had three kids—Buckwheat and the girls, his mother, and the farming to take care of by the time most guys are just dippin' their wicks and learning to like it.

And like I said, all three of them Van Anders men have been the same—hot-headed and stubborn and too goddamn independent for their own good. They all got that thatch of black hair that falls in their eyes, too, and those eyes in ever one of them is that black-blue of a thunderhead's belly—eyes so tiny and dark it makes that Van Ander jaw look like a cliff. Buckwheat got named John after his granddad, and he named his boy Gerald after his dad, and his boy'll be the same damned way—look at him out there throwin' pitches just like his old man, and it'll just keep goin' around in circles. Buckwheat had Sandy pregnant before their senior year was over—earlier than his old man, and they set up house in a trailer on the homeplace there. But a blind man could have seen that wasn't ever going to work out.

Gerry could never let Buckwheat alone, could never let him do anything his own way, and Buckwheat was too much like his old man to ever take it without throwin' it back in Gerry's face. Jack Purnell, you remember, lives two miles east of the Van Anders' place. He swears he could hear them two yellin' at each other if the wind was right, and no one doubts it.

Well, Buckwheat tried that for two summers, and Sandy got pregnant again and she hated living out there in all that family feudin' and with a baby and another one comin' on. She and Buckwheat weren't getting on too good either then, and he was goin' off and gettin' drunk and playin' ball with the guys all the time, doing anything to avoid going home. So even though he didn't have to, being married and the only son of a farmer and all, no one was too surprised when he up and joined the Army—no one was surprised but his wife and his old man.

So Buckwheat was in boot camp by the time Nixon got into office—'69, I remember, because right after that he started takin' troops out of Nam and no one thought Buckwheat would see any action. But four years later he come home all shot to shit, and he was one bitter son of a bitch, but he wouldn't tell you a damn thing about it.

After he was home for a while, he'd come into Cody's Bar and a bunch of us would be sittin' around maybe, and he'd drink a few with us and sometimes get pretty blitzed and he'd talk about Okinawa or Tokyo or about whores in Saigon. He had some damn funny stories 'bout strange places, man, but anyway, he wouldn't ever talk about what happened to him except that once.

He was really drunk and old Boar—who else?—started asking him about killin' people, gettin' shot up and shit. Buckwheat got really pissed. He said, "You fuckin' want to know, you fat-assed, stinkin' pig?"—which pretty much describes the Boar to a tee. "I got fuckin' shot up by a son of a bitchin' draftee as stupid as you who was so goddamn scared of the dark that he shot at anything that moved, including his own men. He killed two—that's the killin' I got to see, but hey! I was lucky. He only crippled the shit out of me."

I don't think anyone ever asked Bucky anything more about it after that. That was the night he almost beat that Mexican to death outside the Holiday Inn in Ogallala. God knows how he even drove that far in the first place. He was still poppin' a lot of Darvon then, and when he'd drink heavy, he'd get really weird and violent. But after his dad got him out of jail that time, he settled down some and mostly stayed out to the farm.

Everybody eventually got used to seeing him around town, and you could pick him out from a mile away, like Mrs. Latham riding her three-wheel bike around the streets pulling that red wagon home full of groceries, or old man McMurray who limps around on that foot that got gnawed off in an auger. Buckwheat'd swing that stiff left leg out and around and rises up on it instead of the knee bending natural-like—swing, hop, step, swing, hop, step. And his arm kind of hangs off funny from the shoulder—you remember, but like Thompson says, it didn't hurt his swing for the fence none. Anyway, it all got familiar again. He'd changed some, but it was still like he never left.

Things were okay at home for a while, too. He'd come home that winter and just hung out, eating his mom's cooking again and getting to know his kids—sort of. Never got that used to 'em, I guess. If you don't grow up with them yelling and screaming, maybe you never get used to kids. But everything was all right with Sandy again, too. She was pregnant again in no time. Even his old man was going to treat him different. It was going to be an equal partnership. No more boss and laborer. Buckwheat was even supposed to take a couple quarters and farm 'em however he wanted. But I think he knew that Gerry wasn't going to change. First thing, he didn't like the way Buckwheat had tuned up the big John Deere, and they were in each other's face. Buckwheat could have cleaned the shop floor with his old man, but he just said, "Fuck you. I got a job in town and I'm takin' it." And less than a week later he was running Duncan's station out there on the Interstate.

Well, by now you know that job at Mel's Service there didn't come up by accident. That job was open for months and no one would take it. No one wanted it because of the way it opened up. It was that youngest Siever boy that opened up every day at five a.m., and a damn good kid he was, too, varsity football for two years, could talk your leg off about NASA and space trips and stuff like that. Wanted to be a pilot, and he had already signed up for that new delayed entry program.

But it was that April Sunday morning, and the first car in off the Interstate was a late model, yellow Cadillac, Florida plates, two black men and a white girl with them. They were drugged full of some shit—coke, I think they finally said—and they fumbled through self-serve and wandered into the station for the bathrooms, fumbling with the doors and acting weird. Finally one of them pulled a gun. They robbed the cash register and took the Siever boy hostage. When they thought they had gotten away, ten miles down the road they shot the kid in the head and dumped him on the shoulder. Didn't even bother to roll him in the ditch, just left him like roadkill, and they took off blowin' coke all the way—or almost—to Denver.

Albert Jenkin's widow was living in that first trailer by the station, where Buckwheat's family moved later, and she was always up way before dawn. She seen 'em drag the boy into the car and speed off, and she called the sheriff. State police chased them till there was a wreck that killed the white woman, and I guess tore the arm off one of those bastards. They were crazies from Miami— Jamaicans they were—totally loaded, in a stolen car goin' nowhere but on some insane spree. Didn't even fuckin' know what state they were in. The town went sick over that funeral. Totally senseless. Just another sick, sick waste of good, young life. No wonder the Interstate still scares hell out of folks.

Mel Duncan, he worked double shifts for a month, the boy's and his own, but he couldn't keep that up. Took to closing early except on weekends, but he just couldn't stay with it and he was losing good business, too. Hell of a good guy, Mel was, a lanky guy and with that laugh like a man twice his size. But he was short-winded, being a chain smoker and going on sixty to boot, and he was sick inside a month of seventy-hour weeks. Still, no one would work there on the Interstate.

You know Buckwheat had to be thinking it through for some time because he made a clear offer and drove for a bargain, and old Mel still jumped at it. Van Anders got that first trailer for Sandy and the kids—the Jenkins widow moved down to the resthome in McCook right after the killing—for managing the rest of the court there, and he worked the morning shift, got choice of overtime, flexible hours, and some say in the management.

So he used that first fight with Gerry to get off the farm, and you know he was glad to be going. I think he liked shoving it in the old man's face a little. Buckwheat had that dirty grin he can get on his face when he told me how his father stood up, hanging on to the grinder still going in his hand, saying, "Why, son? Why would you want to work where that boy was killed?"

"Cuz it's your farm, yours and mom's. And I'm tired of this shit already," Buckwheat says.

"But there's plenty here for all of us, son," Gerry says.

"Not damn near enough," Buckwheat says.

"But down there where that boy was killed. Have some sense, son. You already put your life on the line once. That's enough," the old man says. "If you think you got to go, take that job farmin' for Purnell then. They even got that house on the place."

"That still ain't enough room, and I'm tired of you tellin' me what to do. I'm goin' down to Duncan's, and that's it."

Buckwheat just left it there and walked off leaving the old man to stare after him. He went in and told Sandy to start packin', and that's the first she heard of it because Buckwheat never discussed nothing when he got his mind set. But she was so glad to be moving off her in-laws' place she had a car load of stuff to move before lunch. I think she was surprised how little stuff, other than the kids' clothes and toys and junk, they had together after five and more years of marriage and living with in-laws. Mercy's old lady helped her move in. They're still best friends, cheerleaders together, kids at the same time, same church, that stuff. Couple pick-up loads is all they had. His mother helped them load up, crying about it all the time like it was a cross-country move by pioneers instead of just eleven miles down near town. Gerry never left what he was doing in the shop to come up and help or say good-bye. I'm sure Buckwheat never gave it a thought. That night they had us over to the trailer for soup and grilled cheese sandwiches and beer, and the next day he stashed that service revolver under the counter and went to work.

All the new work kept him busy and he never mentioned the Sievers kid, but I think he was a little spooked till he got used to it some. He started out using military terms. This was a mission under his control. He was in charge of his own deployment. If there was going to be a firefight, it would be on his own terrain now—the station, the trailer court, along the river and the perimeter of town. His duty was to command the station, hold his ground, make a living, pay attention, and protect his own flank, nobody else's. And everything was a weapon to him—a crowbar, a wrench, a file, a piece of wire, whatever. He had that revolver and a sawed off twelve-gauge out in the service garage. He'd tell Sandy, "No one's gonna waste me."

But he got used to it soon enough, I think, the rising in the morning dark, opening by six, and by then there'd already be heavy traffic on the Interstate. Sometimes there was even a truck or a family camper pulling a boat parked out in front of the pumps, having got that far some time in the night before the gas gave out. As soon as the pumps go on they fill up, pay up, and head off again. The traffic never stops. Someone's always awake and going somewhere.

The stop-and-go pace kept him plenty busy. Even with self-serve there's plenty of gas to pump, oil to check, tires to change, money to handle. Everyone's got to come into the station to pay, and that way the movement's not so anonymous. The RVs full of families are familiar, the cross-country movers with kids

and clothes and no sleep packed into junk station wagons with
knocking engines, the truckers with all their bullshit, and drunks
and drifters, the whole raft-load of cars that all look the same.
They still ramble on like that, only worse.

     Then there's all us local guys that still stop in every day,
regulars who commute up to the power plant, farmers, local
truckers, all the Co-Op's vehicles. I always drive in, even though I
haul bulk for the station in town. Got somethin' to tell from
wherever I just been, which is to say almost everywhere in the
county. Still work my own place up on the south shoulder of the
valley there, but hauling for Newcastle, I always got to stop and
see half the population about something. At least to tell the joke
of the day.

     Ramirez always stops because he has his breakfast at
Buckwheat's coffee pot and the vending machine. Still got that
piece of crap pick-up he did in high school to clank around in.

     "Hey, man, when we gonna go out and get loaded, man?"
That was always Timo's first question—if no one else was around
the station at the time. Thought him and Buckwheat had a
common understanding since Buckwheat'd been some kind of
grunt and knew how it felt.

     "Soon, amigo," Buckwheat says, and I believe they did
smoke a little weed on occasion.

     "That all you ever do, Timo, get stoned?" I'd say to bug
the guy.

     "Hey, no, man. Today, I'm goin' out to my uncle's to cut
firewood. Gets a damn good price in Denver." Or he'd be out
driving a truck for Behrends, or hunting deer down on the other
river, or doing field work for someone else. This and that. Tomorrow a little of something, always a little of nothing. Timo
Ramirez scrounged a living nobody knows how and hung out at
the bars with the rest of the single dudes at night.

     And Thompson always stopped in because he loaded his
milk truck out behind the station. He'd have to get in some
statistic on the Cornhuskers we maybe hadn't heard yet—which
sport depends on the season. He hangs around twenty minutes or
so, leaning over The World Herald on the counter, talking the
point spread or someone's injury, and filing it in the sports ency-
clopedia that is slowly consuming Thompson's whole brain. You

wonder if in thirty years or so he'll still have room to remember how to feed himself.

That second spring Bucky's back, first morning Thompson smells mud from a good thaw set in, he picked me up and we went to talkin' softball line-up, getting a practice up, who's gonna pitch and stuff. We go out to Mel's Service because he'd been working this up most of the winter.

"You're gonna play this year, aren't you?" he asks Buckwheat.

"What kind of sport joke is that?" Buckwheat says, kind of surprised. "You want a cripple humpin' along out there? How 'bout center field? I can't even fuckin' run the bases."

"You can pitch," Thompson says. "We'll bat a couple punchers in front of you, and you can swing for the fence. You can still swing for the fence, can't you? Then we'll bat Ramirez right after you for his long ball, so if you just get on, he'll hit you around. May as well. Good a reason as any to drink beer all summer."

"I don't need a reason to drink beer."

"We need your bat this year."

"I'll look like a damn jerk out there hoppin' around like a kangaroo that's got to pee. Besides, you already got half a cripple out there with Chub Chatman. You don't need another one."

We had a good laugh on that one, then Thompson says, "Naw, you'll surprise 'em. You got ball control. You can still hit. Hell, slide into second with that stiff one up and take out the double play every time."

"You got it all figured out, huh?"

"Well, we got to shore up the infield, but we'll move people around. Hell, man, nothing else to do all summer. Get back into it."

"I'll think about it."

"Okay. But everyone wants you to play."

"Don't do the fuckin' cripple any favors."

"Do yourself one. You love to play—all-conference fullback, hot-shot hitter in Legion ball. You hated last year just watching us and not playing."

"Last year, I was fuckin' learnin' to walk all over again."

"At least come out to practice and see what you can do.

You want to play those jerks down the river. Beat their asses with a crippled pitcher. Old Rolf will stutter and spit all the way home, he'll be so pissed."

"Thanks for the starring role. I'll think about it."

But I think he was already convinced. He pitched all that summer and got where he could put that slow pitch about any-where around the plate he wanted. Hit a few out, too, and he'd lurch around the bases with that fuck-you grin on his face, and we really had ol' Rolf stutterin' one game. Then that next year you showed up outa nowhere—remember me pickin' you up out on the tableland? Scared shitless, you were, of rednecks—like old Bucky himself.

Nobody figured seein' your face out there on the field was gonna make him come unglued. But then, his old man was still houndin' him to do some of the farming. That fat-ass, Crighter, was always doin' somethin' to piss him off, too. Old Buckwheat, them days, he was gettin' along with the world 'bout as well as hot grease and water.

CHAPTER TWO: FIRST JOURNEYS

It didn't begin for Buckwheat and me at a ballgame played against traditional rivals, or in an ancient pick-up with words over a beer and a night view of the valley, but much earlier. The land and the sky began it, and the river flowing between. They laid claim to our young senses simply because we were there. Our fate was determined by natural circumstance and a kid's curiosity as unconscious and uncontrollable as the elements.

If we had been asked, we would have said the old familiar grove east of town, but it was the river that drew us. Old man Klosterman's cottonwood grove was only a quarter mile east of Revere and next to the highway, safe and convenient and park-like. But the river came out of the farthest reach of the sky to the west, ran hidden through the treeline almost a mile south of town, and stretched forever east to the other end of the sky. It was the edge of our world, and wild country, forbidden territory because of the well-known threats it held in the lives of adventurous ten-year-olds—wildlife in the thick cottonwoods and willow undergrowth, tall-grassed cutbanks, icy currents and backwater quicksands. There were springs unexplored by the inexperienced.

Those years there were still no dams back into Colorado clear to the mountains, and the South Platte still flooded. This year, it had risen clear to the incidental dike formed by the Union Pacific railbed that lay between Revere and the river. Even the Co-Op, where my father worked in the grain pit, had flooded, and he had taken my sisters and me as far as the tracks to see the running water. My sisters had been scared, but to me it was a wonder of natural power, a miraculous change in the nature of things, a tantalizing manifestation of infinite distance.

Instead of pasture and cornfields out to the far treeline, blue water glistened, running fast and cold. The blacktop out across the bridge and the road beyond had disappeared. Nearby, tops of fenceposts looked like stepping stones into nowhere. Dark objects bobbed in the far currents, the unknown being slowly carried down this groove in the plain—flotsam headed for the edge of the earth. It was awesome and uncontrollable, and alluring. It was a vision of the world as an unpredictable power, immense and mysterious, and there to be explored till you knew all of it inside you and you couldn't be moved any more. It called in its songless way to boys just beginning to feel how large the earth could be, not a noticeable call, but a subtle siren inside, a feeling without form.

Buckwheat had seen the flooded river, too, but from the school bus on the bluffs north above the river where his family's farm was. From there the river was a vast lane of blue down the valley as far either way as you could see. The tops of trees perched like lilypads in two lines, marking the normal banks of the river.

At school, like everywhere else, the flooding filled the conversations, affecting every aspect of life—talk of so much snow in the Rockies, where neither of us had ever been, of the sudden May heat, of where the waters would run and which catastrophes would result farther on, far away. It was something to know about. It beckoned, and we made secret vows to answer the call together.

This May the flood waters had been less and had withdrawn early, leaving dead limbs and driftwood, grasses and soggy tumbleweeds hanging in the barbed wire fences, the pastures and meadows between the town and the trees like luscious bogs. The last day of third grade Buckwheat stayed overnight at my house, and the next morning we sneaked across the highway and the railroad tracks, circling far out around the Co-Op to avoid detection, and hiked toward the river. We both carried air rifles at "ready arms," Buckwheat's an old Daisy Special his dad had handed down to him, and mine a Christmas gift Red Ryder. We trekked into the forbidden territory toward the river, ready and confident, courageous and controlled, young senses tingling with spring sensations on the silent march.

The damp earth sucked at our boot heels as they crushed up the scent of fresh spring mud and new grasses. Cool wind hummed in the barbed wire we climbed over. The morning sun soon had us sweating beneath our day-packs as we hiked. The sky glistened cobalt and clear. Young cottonwood leaves shimmered silver and lime in a windchime chatter we could catch as the treeline grew toward us.

We hoped to shoot any game that sprung in our path, and there were cottontail rabbits twice, a swatch of ground color suddenly darting, then freezing into camouflage, then bolting and cutting as we tensed in surprise, aimed, and fired. We cocked, aimed, and fired again, then again long after the prey had outraced us, and even though we knew our firepower would never bring down a rabbit even if we could have hit one. Blackbirds winged up from clumps of bunchgrass and freshly plowed furrows, too small and too fast for boys to ever bring down, but we pulled off as many shots as we could until the birds were as small-looking as insects. We continually pushed on toward the river.

Just before we reached the treeline, we stalked through taller grasses to a flood-filled pond. As we topped a muddy bank, a small flock of mallards flushed suddenly into the sky. Wings thundered against the open stillness. Our air guns popped, pumping buckshot one slow pellet at a time into the rising flock as exhilaration blossomed in our chests and pulsed to our fingertips in a great and natural rush as old as the river itself. The flock veered downwind, disappearing into perspective pinpoints of dark against the sky.

Our senses vibrated like taut wires as we crept then, the last two hundred yards, to the trees along the river, looking for deer. We were hunters now, same as the fur trappers we had read about that year in school, men who made their lives out of wilderness and unknown distance, who had walked the banks of this very same river a century before. I felt the presence of old ghosts as we quietly stalked. The tree tops cut off the sense of sky, and when we could hear the roar of running river water, still hidden in the forest-like growth, we stopped in silent agreement, listening.

There had been no words since beginning our hike, but

now as we lowered our rifles and moved to sit on a young, flood-felled cottonwood, Buckwheat cackled in a dry, unused voice, "Which way—"

With his words a sudden crash of beating wings roared from the silent grass at our feet, jolting us both to our stance with unconscious cries of fear and surprise as we clutched our weapons. A hen pheasant bolted into the air not ten feet above us in a furious flutter, leaning to take the wind. In reflexive instinct of defense and protection we each fired once. Fifteen feet above the ground the pheasant arced and spread her wings for its escaping glide, but suddenly, she crumpled limply and plummeted. We turned wide eyes on one another, realizing what had happened—an incredible shot. We sprang after the bird, leaping bunch grass and fallen limbs, hooting victory cries with our rifles raised over our heads, and found her in the grass. She was still, but seemed untouched. I picked the bird up, feeling it warm and light, feather-soft and limp.

"The eye, look at the eye," Buckwheat whispered.

A single bb had smashed into it, severing nerves, the only possible hit that could have killed it. Buckwheat took the bird from my hands and carried it into the trees to an open, sandy area beneath a cottonwood on the river bank. There, he placed it on a river-washed rock and began to dance around it, grunting an Indian rhythm, raising his air rifle over his head, and I joined the ceremony, circling the dead bird, shouting a garrulous chant, both of us farther back along the river than even the old trappers.

Suddenly Buckwheat stopped. "We have to eat it now. That's the way."

"I've got matches," I offered, slipping out of my pack straps.

"Firewood." We gathered it quickly and cleared a sandy circle, built a rock circle for the fire. We teepeed kindling and started it, lighting the cover of a Lone Ranger comic book Buckwheat carried in his pack. When the fire was burning well, Buckwheat said, "Now we have to clean it." I produced the hunting knife as we each looked at the other.

"Feathers first," I suggested, and he began plucking tail feathers that popped loose only with great tugs and with an ugly cracking sound.

"Dad just skins them, I remember," Buckwheat said, and he took the knife and ran the point up the bird's soft belly as I held it. Warm innards oozed through our fingers, and we glanced into each other's eyes, recognizing an inexplicable mortality. We bent intently to the grim task before us, pulling the guts from the body cavity, then Buckwheat grabbed the edge of the skin and ripped it away from the bird's breast and thighs, cut off the wings and head in a quick frenzy to be finished. In a new silence, I sharpened a green stick and plunged it through the bird as a spit. We mounted it above the coals of our fire then and turned it slowly as we fed the flames.

When we placed it on a table of river rocks and cut off the legs, the outside was charred and the inner meat was still raw and sinewy. We watched each other chew and swallow. The breast was mostly done and tasted of campfire smoke and wildness, but it was edible and gave us confidence and courage.

Up through the new leaves we watched a vee of geese, high above in the blue, winging north. Above the geese, great, white barges of clouds sailed silently south. The river ran beside us, full and furious, the music of its motion carrying mud and driftwood and uprooted trees and parts of old farm buildings with it to the east.

I said, "What we should do is take a canoe all the way to the ocean. When we get out of school, on our own, canoe clear to the ocean."

"I want to go that direction," Buckwheat objected. "The way the pioneers did."

"We'd have to paddle against the current."

"Then we can go to the mountains and start from there and go through every state."

"We can see the whole country. The way they saw it, the trappers and hunters and Indians."

We built our vision together until we had traveled the whole continent, by canoe and pick-up camper, working our way around the world, farther even than the river ran—boyhood dreams that rang in our imaginations and carried as a buzz into our bodies until there was no more being still.

We smothered the campfire, shouldered our packs and rifles, and took to the river's edge, westward, letting the rushing water flood our spirits as it did the valley. The smell of fresh mud, the music of running water, the spring-vibrant color of the undersides of leaves, the dapple of light through the limbs and shadows of empty, tangled country—all were absorbed by the unconscious senses as two boys scrambled through the trees and undergrowth, moving upstream as silently as beavermen. Only the lure of the unexplored, just ahead, pulled us on, capturing us completely. We stayed as close to the bank as possible, circling willow clumps and bogs, log jams of driftwood left high and dry in young trees, moving up river.

Coming silently and slowly around a willow thicket, we spotted a herd of deer—a buck, two does and their fawns, drinking at a sandy backwater pool a hundred yards ahead and upwind. We dropped to our bellies in new grass without being seen and watched the deer drink. Between us and the deer another grassy bank offered better, closer cover, and we crawled nearer, our sounds covered by the gurgle of current that swept out around the deer's pool and swung swiftly against the bank we inched over. Within us both, the feeling grew that we could get off a shot at the buck. Even deep in our game we knew the most miraculous shot wouldn't bring down the smallest fawn, but we crawled toward our target, the medulla pumping the most ancient of messages through the body, the senses sharp and tantalized, to get off a shot that would sting the flank of a four-point buck.

We moved together, signaling with our eyes and hands, each knowing the other's mind, each helping the other to unsling his rifle, inching out on the edge of the bank. We lay a moment facing each other, cocked our guns, and then rose simultaneously to aim and fire into the startled herd.

But we never saw our shots hit their target. The sudden shift of our bodies to kneeling positions collapsed the cutbank we were on, and we avalanched into the rushing icy waters of the river. In the current and panic and fear, we were swept back around the willows, clawing the muddy water for air and orientation. Our heads bobbed up for breath, and then suddenly we were sucked beneath the limbs of an uprooted elm.

The rushing water pulled us down. Buckwheat slipped completely under, then grasped the last limbs and pulled himself toward the sky. He broke surface, sucking mouthfuls of air, glancing frantically for me. I hung in the limbs where the currents dived under the tree, my pack tangled in the branches, holding me face down in the onrushing water. I slapped madly at the water, fighting to raise my head above the muddy waves, choking for retches of precious air.

The current pulled at Buckwheat's grip, his open jacket and pack acting as drag. One arm, then the other, he slipped free from both and let them sink and go with the flow. Then he dragged himself through the limbs toward me in an adrenaline panic for speed, tearing his jeans on broken limbs, gashing his forearm, but not noticing. Hanging out on a limb above me, Buckwheat grabbed the back of my collar and wrenched my head above the slapping waters. I was choking and crying, heaving muddy water and bile in guttural convulsions as my friend called over and over, "I've got you. I've got you. Get some air. We're all right," the sound of it slowly calming.

We hung in the branches and the cold rushing current a while, getting our breath and strength back. Buckwheat helped me out of the shoulder straps of the pack and threw it up on the bank. I clawed my way into the higher limbs, shivering and gasping and suddenly feeling the sharp, icy edge of cold wind. We both struggled through the branches for the shore where the elm's roots still held, pulling limbs away as we heaved and grunted and writhed for solid ground. Finally out on the bank, we lay face up to the sky, feeling the thunderous beat of our hearts against the ground and hearing it echo in our ears with our rasping breath. Slowly the sun's heat, the bird song, sounds of wind in the leaves and rushing water came back to me as we shivered and rested and lay looking at one another's eyes, alive, but barely.

After a while, we stripped and hung our clothes on branches to dry in the wind that sent violent shivers through our cold bodies. A few feet down the bank we climbed down to a sandy beach below the bank and out of the wind where the sun could warm us. There we stretched out like otters sunning and let the new season's sun begin its bake while we watched the icy waters roll by.

Finally I said, "You saved my life."

"Nah. You were up out of the water. I helped, but you would have got free once you got your breath."

"Maybe."

"It could have been the other way around. There's no difference."

Then we spent a long time telling each other our personal version of the fall and recovery, and the telling made it all more real: the shot on the buck, the bank collapsing, being sucked away in a muddy terror, the fighting for air, then being caught in the branches of a dying tree. It was stupid and dangerous and miraculous and heroic, the feat of warriors or frontiersmen, but we knew we could tell no one else. The river was forbidden territory, and now we understood why.

Buckwheat said, "We were lucky, man. Maybe we won't get out of it next time. If we would have died, no one would have known."

"Even when I couldn't breathe and I thought I was going to die, I was wondering how far the river would carry us before anyone found us."

"No one would find us alive, that's for sure." We knew that now.

When our shirts and jeans were almost dry, we redressed, pocketing our soggy socks and putting on wet sneakers. My jacket and pack were still soaked. My knife and canteen, ball cap, extra b.b.'s had all been washed away. Buckwheat had lost everything, and both rifles were missing. That would be hardest to cover up, we knew.

We walked back to where the bank had caved in with us. It was a roiling muddy current now, cutting a new ledge, but just downstream on the edge of the water we found my new air rifle. We searched in vain for the rest of our gear until the color of the sky changed and we had to head home. Before we left the river's edge, I gave Buckwheat my rifle.

"I'm not gonna take your rifle, man."

"Then we'll share it. It's all we got left of what happened to us. We might be asked about it some time, and we've got to have something to show. It's ours now, whatever happens, but we can't say unless we really have to."

Buckwheat solos:

"Man, I don't know what it was with you. After that, you were always so damn serious. Everything's got to be monumental like every act's something God's made special to happen. Yeah, I think that's where I got that attitude from—not that I got it that bad, but from you, thinkin': yes now, we're special-made, one of God's designs, and He's got big plans for us. Like we were supposed to be just that stupid enough to stand up on that cutbank and fall into the flood and almost drown and crawl out freezin' our asses off and suckin' air and thinkin' our parents were gonna kill us now, losin' those rifles and all.

"Course you had reason to be serious. You were gonna get your butt blistered for losin' that new Red Ryder in a place we weren't even supposed to be. Took me all afternoon to cheer you up, teasin' you about Nancy Stouffer always choosin' you for a square dance pardner in P.E., remember? We called her Shark cuz she had those two rows of teeth in her jaw. That jaw coulda been carved from Mount Rushmore, it was so huge. She never got 'em pulled—half of 'em, that is—till our junior year, and it was too late then. Her mouth was the size of Mammoth Cave.

"Then I got you to laughin' crazy about me puttin' corn kernels in Old Man Closbach's harmonica, imitatin' him tryin' to blow "Ol' Suzanna" in music class, remember?, his fat cheeks gettin' to be big red balloons and his bug-eyes lookin' like they'd pop out any second and that bald spot on his head just a sweatin' like a cold beer mug in a sauna. He finally looked into that harmonica like a monkey lookin' into a coconut and got so pissed off when he saw the corn, remember?

"When we finally got warm down there by the river, I spent the whole rest of the time climbin' up naked in the tree and shit, hangin' on the branches like an ape. I guess I was just damn happy we got out of that water alive. That was celebratin', I guess. Then it turns out, you don't need that much cheerin' up anyway cuz we found your piece there on the bank just downstream from where we fell in.

"But right away you're back to serious. "You don't say, 'Thank God, my ass is saved.' You try to give me the goddamn gun, and I wouldn't take it, but then you figured out how we were gonna share it, how I'd take it home cuz mom comin' in after me would expect me to have it and she couldn't tell the difference, and how if either of us ever had to produce it we could say it was at the other guy's house.

"You were always good, even then, with crafty kid schemes, and I guess it worked. No one ever asked us, and we never went out shootin' again. I'll bet you never picked up a fuckin' firearm again in your life, did you? I wasn't that fuckin' smart myself. Then by the next spring your family had gone for Colorado.

"I was always gonna give you that gun back. When Tommy Mercy had that going away party for you—you know, all the guys around town comin' over, bringin' gifts how they do, ice cream and football in the yard and all that, I was the only son of a bitch that couldn't come cuz I had the goddamn chicken pox. I cried like a baby. I was gonna bring that rifle and give it back, and I never could.

"Then after that, you wrote a couple of letters, I remember, about all kinds of TV shows you could watch there in Colorado that we could never get out here, and about how there were swimmin' pools you could walk to every day and a real football league you could play in that fall. All kinds of stories. And the mountains. It was a whole 'nother world, man. I used to think: there he is in the fuckin' Rocky Mountains, right up there where he can see where the river was comin' from. You got to go, and I was stuck for life.

"Pretty soon though, it was all just a long time ago, and we all got into other things. We'd hear stuff about you sometimes cuz your and Mercy's mom were always writin', but it wasn't like you were one of us anymore, just some kid we knew from another time. Like, you broke your arm in some kind of bicycle wreck, and you were a hot-shit high school baseball player, and you went to Washington, D. C. for some kind of Student Council leadership thing. You were some kind of debater or speech-maker and got a scholarship for being able to sling bullshit. You were goin' to C.U. All that shit that happened so fast and far away. It didn't even seem real.

"Here, we were just playin' ball in Revere like it's Super

Bowl every weekend and we're the center of the universe. I was world-class hot shit myself. Then I got Sandy knocked up, and we were, you know, 'in love,' like we knew what the hell that meant. I was gonna farm with the old man. That was it then—eighteen and the rest of my life laid out for me.

"I'd think about you sometimes, thinkin: he's gonna play professional ball, but I ain't. He's gonna be some shit-nose lawyer and go all over the world, but I ain't. You were out there where things were happenin', and so much was goin' on, the fuckin' world changin' right under our noses and we didn't even see half of it. You were in the flow, and me, I was up here on the tableland between the rivers, tippin' over our old International combine on that god-awful east quarter. So damn steep the water still runs off in gully washes, but the old man is still farmin' it. Corn now. Shit! And I'm a papa and my wife's a shrew I've known since second grade, and nothin' was gonna change for a lifetime or so.

"Two summers then I tractored over the fields, doin' it just like dad wanted, just so deep, just so fast, just to his schedule of days. I'd go in nights to Sandy and listen to her bitch about the baby, or I'd go in to play softball in town and get drunk and not come home till someone drove me, and the family'd be pissed about that for a week or so or until the next binge.

"That summer in '68 I'd ride over the fields so fuckin' hung over and so fuckin' bored, and I heard you were down there on the north river, just across the valley fixin' fence and hidin' out, but I didn't give a damn. Old Virgil Peters was pourin' beer in Cody's then—and still is, I guess. Now that's one alcoholic zombie that never went more than two blocks in his entire fuckin' life, but he's got stories of the world, let me tell ya. He had it that you were as wanted as the Chicago Seven, a regular Benedict Arnold, and we were all spittin' on your name. And I was pissed even more cuz I was thinkin': at least he's been to hell and gone from here.

"Then Thadd Mercy heard you went back to C.U. and was runnin' SDS which was all communists and psychos we all heard—and that shows you what a kick-ass good team sponsor he is, lettin' a guy play second base for us that in a former life was a communist, drug-addict loony. But really, everyone was sayin', oh none of that can be true; we know his folks; he grew up here; he was a regular fuckin' Cub Scout; nobody from here can grow up to hate the President and dump on America.

"Then that year Burns got drafted, and then Menninger, and McCormick went into the Air Force. I was thinkin: everyone's fallin' in the river but me. I'd come in at night and shake the field dust off my body and stamp around out on the front step of the house, and you know, that's where grandpa had that Bible verse number pressed into the concrete when he built the house. First and last Bible verse I ever looked up and learned. First Timothy 6:6—'But godliness with contentment is great gain.' Well, I didn't much care for the godliness around me, and I sure as hell wasn't never gonna be content. I had to get goin' and do somethin'.

"But goin' to Colorado and signin' up as a grunt in SDS wasn't my idea of patriotism. I didn't know much about it, just that it was against America and the war, and I was gonna show you you didn't know shit. I figured you were just a crazy son of a bitch doin' idiot things that didn't mean shit. I was gonna find the real action, show you what guts meant. God meant for you to be a traitor, and He meant for me to sign up in the Army and make a deal to play football in Japan. I'd see more of the world than any of you bastards. Travel more, screw more, party more, and play ball, too. —Oh yeah, and learn more, too, and I learned all right. The fuckin' hard way.

"But I had myself convinced, just like you, this is what I was meant to do, take off into the world. You were never so serious in your miserable life, but me, I was dead serious. I signed up without even tellin' Sandy or dad or even myself what I was doin'. Just went in and did it and felt damn good about it.

"I remember drivin' home from North Platte where I'd gone to make a deal with the recruiting sergeant, feelin' like I'd really gone and done something with my life. Just like Parsons, I was thinkin', who said all along he was gonna go out in that world across the river and do something and then went and did it. I went and did it, too, all right.

"I remember thinkin' then again about that time down on the river when we were kids and walkin' home with nothin' left but one rifle between us. We were warriors, we decided, remember? That's how we got to it, talkin' about Sal Mineo in the movie,

'Tanka,' bein' blood brothers with Crazy Horse or somebody. When we crossed the highway back into town, we found that broken bottle down in the barrow ditch by the culvert. We both slashed our right thumbs and mashed them together in a handshake, and then we were blood brothers. We were gonna take on the world back to back, and hell, man, ten years old, we could do it easy then, easy.

"But you were gone in half a year, and then for years you were doin' all kinds of shit that I was just hearin' about. So finally I said to hell with it, went over to the edge and dove right in. Drove home thinkin: blood brothers like hell, come New Year's Eve I'll be in basic. I'm gonna be in it, too, even more than you."

Calvin's journal notes/early-summer, '75:

Another profound lesson today, cutting down the windbreak elm. On the edge of the western field, my own father and mother planted part of the windbreak the year they were married—two rows of ponderosa pine, a line of cedar, and one row of elm on the far edge to shade the young pine. The evergreens have a tap root that drills deep to water, but the elm are shallow rooted trees that spread their roots wide just below the surface and take in topsoil moisture. While they once served a shady purpose, now the pine are grown, and the elm roots spread under the wheat ground and take crop moisture. It's evident enough if you look and focus. Wheat will grow thick and green right up against cedar, but growth is always spotty and poor a ways out into the field next to elm or cottonwood.

Just another subtle observation of the ground that Karl has pointed out to me as the reason he wanted me to chainsaw down that line of living elm today. Another reasonable, sensible task explained—once I asked about it. Our labors may seem inconsequential or a waste of time to me—like it seemed unnecessary to cut down a beautiful line of full leafed elm out on a plain where trees seem like scattered jewels. But if you ask Karl, there is calm, quiet rhyme and reason to every act.

So he checked me out on his sixteen inch Homelite and

left for work in Tyghe, and I began to cut the windbreak elm that my parents planted, their job now finished.

It felt fine to be out in the June light, the green smell of summer, the wind humming in elm leaves and whistling mountain sound through the pine. I fell the first five trees and began pruning limbs and piling them so we could drag them off to the pasture later for the cattle (they love the green leaves). For half an hour I got into the spirit of the job, thinking how now I can cut and cure the wood, install a wood-burning stove in the bunkhouse, and two winters from now use these trees as fuel to get a final warm comfort from a job my parents began, that the seasons nurtured, and which I will have completed.

During these spacious thoughts, the chainsaw sputtered and quit. I yanked on the starter rope; yanked again; again. Then over and over till my arm was numb. I fiddled with the choke and the throttle and the spark plug wire. I let it sit a while and sat myself on a new, wet stump and considered the wide western horizon, letting the chainsaw cool, the gas flooding subside, and any possible internal breakdown heal itself like a living body. Then I yanked a while longer on the starter rope for nothing but anger, sweat, and dull sputtering.

After an hour, I gave up, took it to the shop to await Karl's inspection this evening, and I let Martha put me to wetback labor, hoeing corn in her garden. I felt bad all day that I had somehow screwed up another of Karl's tools. But I wasn't about to break it down and inspect it because I know nothing about the internal mechanisms of a two-cycle engine. I could take it apart, not know what I was looking at, and never get it completely together again.

I settled gratefully for the hoeing (and did it just Martha's way), knowing that if the handle broke, I could at least fix that. While I hoed and Martha picked the last late strawberries of the season, I got to hear about how Billy Conrad was an ignorant and farm-stupid little boy when he came out to the farm here as a foster-care child.

Having only one, bookworm child, a girl (my cousin, Ann, who left the farm for library back rooms as soon as she could), Karl and Martha always had foster-care boys on the farm. I remember some of them vaguely from when I was growing up and we visited here. They helped with the milking and chores and field work. They got schooling in Tyghe and got religion at St. Luke's down the road, and they got to live unabused farm-lives for a few years. Billy Conrad was the last one in Uncle Karl's care.

He came out from Omaha at age fourteen with two felony auto theft charges and a body full of bruises from his old man's general beatings. This much I already knew through Mom from earlier times. What Martha told me was how quiet he was and how afraid he'd be when he had damaged some of Karl's equipment. He'd wait for a beating because a calf, already sick with scours, had died, or because a wheel had fallen off the tractor while he was disking.

"But you know your Uncle Karl ain't like that at all," Martha said. She had a soft pleasure in her voice, recalling the incidents with a mother's fondness while trying to reassure me in her way.

"I know he isn't," I answered.

"Billy turned into a fine young man, and he loved the farming, that's sure. He had a way with the animals. They truly seemed to like him."

She let it drift off. I, of course, wondered where he was now and why not here instead of me. I had to ask.

"So where is he now?"

"Oh, you know, the war. He died over there in that Vietnam. He was a rifleman. Joined up cuz he loved his country, and it was what he wanted to do—to get off of other people's hands. Though he was never any bother."

"When was that?"

"In 1967. He was nineteen. He went back to Omaha for his last year of high school, and we went back there for his graduation. June of '65, that was. Then he went into the Marines and got killed."

I let it all go then, sorry I had brought it up. After a while, Martha asked, "You was never in the service?"

"Not in the military."

"Some other service, or just in school?"

"A civil militia," I said.

"Like the National Guard?"

"I guess the National Guard was involved at times."

"But never with the war."

"Not over there," I said.

As a result, Billy Conrad was dead, and the ragged, old revolutionary hippie is here, hoeing corn all day, maybe hunted for treason somewhere if someone wanted to go to the trouble.

Martha said later—thinking of it, I believe, because I paused to tie a sweat band around my damp hair to keep it out of my eyes, "It wasn't long after that, your uncle started agrowing his hair long."

"Really?" Though I've seen Karl as an individualist, I never guessed him, a seventy-two year-old dirt farmer and handyman, to be one to make an anti-war statement.

"Yes, sir. You ask him about it. I think though, he's fixin' to get his hair cut now that there ain't no more Americans in Vietnam."

So when he got home tonight—well before dark for once, I apologized about the chainsaw, and then I asked him about his hair as we walked down to the shop.

"Aunt Martha told me you grew your hair because of the war and Bill Conrad."

"Oh, I guess. In a manner of speakin'," he said. Easy smile and a look off to horizon—no different a reaction than to any other question. "What I mean to say is, it's not directly cuz of Billy, but it's roundabout tied to it, you might say. I grew it for the state's centennial celebration."

He told it with a kind of soft, amazed humor in his voice, like someone surprised to discover how people can be. It seems that in 1967 Nebraska was one hundred years old, and part of the local celebration was an old timers' hair- and beard-growing contest. A bunch of the guys there at Ag-Co, where Karl works, all decided to join the fun, and this grey, wild mane of a grisly prospector became Karl's new, temporary look.

Which was all well and good in Tyghe where everyone knows him and knew about the contest. What did long hair and a beard on an old mechanical genius from an old, county farm family have to do with the outside world? Not much. Until he found himself one day in North Platte in his greasy service blues, battered ball cap, and a day's weariness in his bloodshot eyes. Then that mangy, wild look was that of a long-haired hippie freak freeloading down the Interstate, and possibly some kind of radical political firebrand. A gas station attendant on the Interstate wouldn't take his personal check for gas, thinking Karl had probably stolen the checkbook and wallet from some good redneck native son.

Karl was surprised at first, then a little upset. His name on a check had always been good and never questioned. Then the station manager came out of the garage and told the trouble-making, filthy bum to get out of his station—till he found out this old hippie had unpaid-for gas in the tank of his old pick-up and no cash. He called the State Patrol. They showed up quickly, looked at the truck with the Ag-Co sticker, looked at Karl and his license with a clean shaven picture, and called in for a theft check. They listened to his story, never quite believing him. Karl demanded that they call clear to Tyghe, to the head man, who described Karl and vouched for him. Finally, the station manager grudgingly took his check and told Karl that he was sorry, but that he looked just like those filthy, ragged radicals and drug addicts that were filling up more and more of the Interstate.

"I'm not sayin' I'm a whiz at thinkin', so I suppose I thought about that little meetin' most of the ride back home," he told me. "There those folks were, makin' some kind of judgment on a man cuz they didn't like the way he looked."

Uncle Karl had met the uptight, redneck establishment just an hour away from home down the Interstate. He assumed they were friendly neighbors, and they assumed he was a danger and a threat for standing out.

"What's the matter with these folks, I got to wonderin'."

Then Billy Conrad had been killed. Missing in Action first, then found—no doubt in condition beyond description. Another nineteen year-old American casualty.

"It did seem some pitiful waste, that poor boy," Karl said. "And what for, I couldn't figure. So people like that there in North Platte can trouble someone they don't think's got the same idea as them? You might even start to think that whole war is one sad and crazy mess for the likes of nothin' but that."

So he had slowly, informally decided after the centennial contest was over at fair time—he didn't win—just to leave all that wildness on and let people damn well think what they wanted to think.

He was slowly telling me the end of this story as he casually fingered the chainsaw and looked it over. I explained how it had just quit on me and how I kept trying to start it till I ached.

"Well, I wonder," he mused, staring at it there on the work bench, and I could imagine the whole machine being broken down in his mind, each piece inspected and considered mentally, then the whole thing being reassembled again. "I'd think it should run. Did you check the gas in the tank?"

There's no describing the feeling of being totally stupid— a fist in the face from inside the brain thrust outward. A numb stun. "I only cut a few minutes," I offered lamely, looking over his shoulder as he twisted the cap off and peered into the dry tank. Like the feeling in a dream where you are naked in front of a laughing crowd. No Billy Conrad.

"Jesus," I said, taking God's name in vain right in front of him. "Well, I only use a chainsaw while my brain is on idle."

Karl just grinned with all his teeth showing.

"It never occurred to me. I only cut a few minutes...."

"Oh, they use a lot of fuel when you really get goin', and the tank's smaller than a hospital pisspot."

"Yeah." But nothing could have stopped me from feeling like a total idiot. I've got the spirit all right, but not one practical bone in my educated body.

"Well, what did you say? You felled five trees and limbed 'em? That's a lot of cuttin' for twenty minutes or so."

"My brain was definitely on idle. Or in another time zone. Sorry."

"Don't worry yourself about it." He told me some other story of a time when he did something foolish—probably back before he could speak or walk, but I wasn't listening. I was thinking about Billy Conrad, rifleman, and me. All I ever did was burn out a Selective Service office, miss a New York apartment building blowing up where a friend of mine was making bombs for the Weathermen, and run for Mexico. Now I am out here, learning that it takes fuel to make a chainsaw run.

I took the chainsaw back out to the elm row and cut till dark. Didn't feel like going in for supper. Refilled the gas tank three times. Profound lesson for a profound student. A master's candidate in political science, a spiritual philosopher, and not one sensible skill, not one useful service. Just an idealist "full of sound and fury, signifying nothing."

Thompson's lyrics

Ask anybody in six towns and three counties and they can tell you how Buckwheat played ball—he played it right up over your face. That game in Arthur that last year in high school, we were both teams six and zero, blowed away everyone else in the conference, and we were goin' up in the Sandhills to play them damn bull riders. Ever one of 'em was a rancher's kid. They played ball in the fall and rode bulls the rest of the year, and they generally pounded shit out of the rest of the conference—still do, Revere included.

Buckwheat that year already had over seven hundred yards and twenty-six touchdowns from scrimmage, four more on kick returns. But those cowboys had given up just thirty-eight points all year, and they let it be known they were gonna wrestle steer all afternoon.

They had the field for it, too, let me tell ya, fenced off right out in the pasture by the school. Put a little water on it, shovel the cow shit out, mow it and put down lime, and they called that a football field. Well, hell, eight-man ball. Nobody makes a big deal out of eight-man ball but the guys playin' it, and their parents, and maybe the whole town if you're winnin'. But that year two counties drove out to that pasture game, pulling their cars in around the field, and Ogallala radio was up in the announcer's stand that looked like a tinker toy shack poked up above the field.

Their grandstands was a couple of bleachers made outa old fence, set up across from one another at the fifty yard line. Their side was packed full of ranchers a hootin' and hollerin' and shakin' cow shit off their boots, and Revere people were on the other, with Miller's old man and Buckwheat's old man ready to go bonkers like they always did. Those two guys—for four years those two went crazy at every ball game we played in the country, screamin' at refs like they were gonna kill 'em, cussin' down the

coaches if they didn't think they were runnin' the offense right or
if their boys weren't in the game for some reason, or ridin' hell
outa their own kids when they fumbled or whatever. I don't know
how Rob and Buckwheat could stand to play. Their fathers would
embarrass a buffalo humpin' a heifer.

If we lost, they'd threaten coach's job with the school
board, or they bawled out their own sons like it was their fault
alone. But if we won, it was their kid that did it all himself. Well,
especially football that year, that might be hard to deny, but I don't
know how Rob and Buckwheat could even stand their fathers
actin' like lunatics. They were the joke of the county. But then,
we were winning, too, so everyone lived with it.

And that was just like Buckwheat, too. All that was out of
his world. For Bucky it was all in the game. There wasn't nothing
else, nothing but winnin'. He didn't know you could do anything
else, and when you were playing with him, you didn't know it
either. Like up there at Arthur. Coach figured we could out shoot
'em—sprint out passes and quick pitches outside. After the
opening kickoff, Rob calls what coach wanted: motion, twenty-
nine pitch—the flip outside to Buckwheat trying to outrun the
end.

But Bucky said, "Naw, run the twenty dive. And you
damn well better kick some ass in there," lookin' right at Mercy
and Chub Chatman and me. "It starts right now," he said.

Rob bellied it to him right up between us. We just kinda
screen blocked, and he popped through there like a two-ton steer
shot outa the chute, and he streaked for the sideline before those
cowboys even blinked. He had two steps on 'em and was turnin'
up field, and he could have gone all the way. But instead, he
looked down his shoulder, cut off his angle, and turned the run
right back into the two d.-backs. The first cowboy Bucky fore-
armed down on his back and ran over his face, and they carried
him off the field for the rest of the day after the play. The other,
Buckwheat liked to put a stiff-arm through the guy's chest like a
spear. He was out of the game for a while, too. By then two more
cowboys hit him, and Buckwheat dragged them fifteen yards
before he went down.

I can still hear coach screamin', "Around 'em, Van Anders,
not through em," wavin' his clipboard over his head like some kind

of signal. Buckwheat, like he always done, would kind of dumb-stare back at coach like, who, me? I do something wrong? Meanwhile, Arthur is carryin' their guys off the pasture. So okay. Rob calls the motion, twenty-nine pitch again and looks at Buck-wheat to see if it's okay this time. Bucky just shrugs it off like it's no big deal to him, but you looked in those thunderhead eyes and they were shootin' lightning.

I mean, they were always on fire whatever game we were playin', but up in Arthur they positively arced out. We'd go up to the line, and I swear you could see it already the way they got down in their stance across from us. Bucky beat 'em on the first play, and from then on it was just plain fun. Next play, Bucky in motion, Rob pitches to him right on that rocket step he had exploding out of there, and he was two yards outside before the defensive end came out of his three-point. I looped upfield, lookin' for a block on his cut back into the pack, but he gave a left shoulder juke to the D.B. that made the guy backstep down on his ass, and Bucky was gone on the outside, untouched and all the way. Six points.

The rest of the game we spent just knockin' shit out of those cowboys. For years they come down outa the Sandhills and mauled ever team. But that year we brawled back, just poundin' on 'em, lettin' 'em get up, then knockin' 'em down again. And everyone of us knew what was goin' on. We were givin' them a taste of their own game. We didn't care that the game stayed seven-zip till the fourth. We knew we could score any time we wanted, and so did they.

But Miller and Buckwheat's dads were crazy-ass screamin' for scores. "Run it up! Run it up!" They wanted blood revenge just their way. Coach thought it was just a hard fought, intense game that could go either way on the next turnover. No way. We were just waitin', and come forth quarter, we started rollin'. Buckwheat's kinda bent over, hands on his knees, and pantin'. He says, "Okay, I'm gonna break one."

I said, "Let's trap that bastard on the left end." Rob called it, I pulled and laid the shit stomper out with a shoulder high shot. Buckwheat cut up behind me and was gone. Forty-two yards, that one.

From the early fourth on, we passed and trapped and

swept, and Bucky'd run over one or two of them on occasion to keep 'em reminded, and it was thirty-five to nothin' at the gun. Buckwheat just kind of strolled out of that pasture to the bus like it was just another no big deal to him.

And basically, it was. I mean, he really wanted to beat up on them Arthur County bull riders, and he did, but the way he played the game was the same as always. I don't know when it started happening—eighth or ninth grade, I suppose. But when you got in a game and John Van Anders was on your team, you knew you were gonna win. You knew because he knew. He knew whatever side he was on, they were gonna win—whether it was a pick up game with choosin' sides as kids, or facing Arthur for a league title.

It wasn't that we always won. For a long time there wasn't enough developed talent around him to win much, but the wins were his wins, by himself. Football, basketball, baseball, you name it. We didn't start winning all the time till we were juniors in b-ball, but Buckwheat always played like we were winning—and would win absolutely—through the final play. When he finally got the rest of us convinced of it, we started playing ball like that, too. And when we started playing that way, Buckwheat started playing with us instead of just along side us. He knew natural how to set up your block on a sweep. He knew when to pass it off on a fast break to the basket and make us all look sharp instead of just shining himself. You'd get a hit for the first time in ten games, and he'd drive you in on a three-two count, two outs. Then we were winning the ones he couldn't win by himself, and we got all hot and wild and lived it up to the full. Beer and parties and girls and cars, goin' crazy. It was all teamwork, I tell ya. Buckwheat's team.

But playin' softball that first year Buck was back was another world, I mean to tell ya. Of course he hadn't played any kind of ball in years, and he weren't no high school body no more, God knows. But even as a 'Nam cripple he had more goin' for him on the ball field than Chub Chatman or Tumblin' Tommy Mercy ever had in their prime.

I'm not sayin' his eyes shoulda got crazy again like up at Arthur, cuz none of us, especially Bucky, was kids anymore. But he wasn't playin' attitude ball like he used to either. Mostly I thought that he just had to get used to pitchin' and that's what he was thinkin' about. Or that he was just plain burned out inside, and that'd be understandable.

But he got into the games. He gave a hundred and ten per cent through the last out pitched, but the energy most of the time was just kind of burnt-off wasted. I couldn't tell what it was till that last game against Rolf's. Buckwheat was out on the mound droppin' 'em in on the wrists, jammin' them batters, and darin' 'em to push the ball back by him. They'd slap it at him up the middle, and he'd corkscrew out of the way like a busted windmill, try to stab it, lurch around, and make the throw to first—if he stopped it. Well, they were doin' a better job of slappin' 'em than Bucky was of stabbin' 'em. He'd knock it down, and they'd get on before he could scramble it down. Or he'd knock an easy infield grounder off line, and it'd dribble by our infielders. And Rolf's team, them a-holes, they were lovin' it. Well, Buckwheat was tryin' to do it all by himself again. Win by himself. He plain forgot the rest of us out there.

When it hit me, I called time out—fourth inning, two out, two on. Tumblin' Tommy had just errored another grounder that Buck had knocked away. I came in from center and told Buck-wheat, "Why don't you let the rest of us play? See Ramirez out there in left? Get his fat ass movin' after a fly ball. Too late to matter now if it goes over the fence. At least we'll get the pleasure of seein' him earn his beer for once."

I figured it'd piss him off, and Bucky was already pissed off—stampin' and a fumin' in there on the mound, cuz they hit him for three runs at least every inning, and he'd be thinkin' the whole damn thing was his fault. Which it was. It was just like when we were kids. He'd be a pissed off asshole out there because he wasn't winning it by himself and nobody seemed to be helping him.

Well, he just kinda blinked at me like I just came into the game. He rubbed off the ball, said, "Yeah," and turned back to the plate. Next guy put a fly out to Ramirez, and he sprinted like a barge on sand, made a snowcone catch, and bitched about the effort the whole bottom half of the inning. Next inning, Buck-wheat started spreadin' it around the plate, making 'em pop up and ground out foul. We held 'em for the last three innings but couldn't catch 'em with our bats. Lost to them jerks again anyway.

Later, I got to thinkin' how Buck got the same way in a couple other games, but in different ways. Like when Lox was on first against The Coffee Shop—the winning run. I was on third, tying run, and one out, last of the seventh. We needed Buckwheat to go to the opposite field—punch a single or fly deep to right so I can score. But he goes up there blasting for the fence and pops up into shallow left. If he'd been half thinkin' the situation, he'd of done anything else. But he was dead-set on blastin' it. Buckwheat versus the pitcher. Another game, he's on first and we're down one in the last, no outs. Ramirez up behind him high flies to center. Buck knows he's not gonna outrun the throw to second, but Collard, that fat banker on Bunke's team, is puffin' away in center. Bucky thinks the guy is a Twinkie anyway, and he's gonna make the guy hit the throw right on the money.

So Buckwheat tags and goes hop-draggin' down to second like a deer with a broke leg, his old arms flappin' like a turkey that ain't ever gonna fly. He does a perfect Pete Rose slide for the inside of the bag, but Collard burned one in for once in his chintzy life. Never happen again in ten full seasons, but there it is, and there's the game. Two outs on the catch and the throw, no more base runner. Brownie gets up and triples for nothing, and Chatman chokes and pops up to end it.

Buckwheat started downin' Bud Light and shit-cussin' Collard. He wasn't pissed that we lost, and I don't even know if he knew. He was pissed cuz he hadn't beat the throw. Pissed he hadn't carried it all himself and won. That's Buckwheat for ya.

CHAPTER THREE: CLOSE TIES

On Sundays even now, voices in the wind are congregational, real and not merely memory, still chanting familiar litanies and family tradition. I made the necessary pilgrimage to St. Luke's only days after returning from Mazatlan because it is still the simplest way to announce one's presence in the county. The greetings were much the same as ever, warm and condolatory, but fifteen years before it had been so much easier with Aunt Martha arranging it all.

By Aunt Martha's decree, and the Lord's, there was never any work on the day of rest. Even that first, short Sunday afternoon when Karl took me out on the tractor for the first time, the experience for both of us had been more pleasure than work, and Martha cut it short by declaring an early supper. For me it was time to myself. On the previous Sundays, I had strategically slept in, just missing the usual six a.m. breakfast—and also regular service at St. Luke's where I would have had to face a hundred new neighbors, both strangers and distant relatives. Those Sundays, after Karl and Martha had left, I spent the days walking across all the land I was going to farm, filling the time with my own personal kind of rest.

But during the next Saturday evening meal Martha set out her Sunday plan along with the rhubarb pie and coffee.

"We'd sure love to have you share church service with us tomorrow morning, Calvin. Then we could just leave from there and go down to visit the folks on the river. We knew you'd want to come along and renew some family ties. We'll just do that tomorrow if you'd like." Karl looked up from his dessert, chewing

calmly, watching his wife go on. She glanced at his unblinking
stare and went on. "Well, you've been here near half a season
now, and they all want to see you and find out what you've been
doing these long years. And how everyone else has been—Jo and
your sisters. And you haven't seen David in years. Why, you two
used to play together all the time, teasing the girls and riding the
calves in the barn."

I watched Martha, too, wondering if she thought my
cousin and I would go off playing hide 'n' seek in the chicken
coop. And I wondered what I could tell them I'd been doing
"these last long years," as Aunt Martha called them. I'd tell them
I'd been a traveler and a scholar, I decided, not a radical provoca-
teur, not a political refugee and road tramp.

"Why, Aunt Sophie hasn't even seen your mother for a
year of Sundays," Martha continued. "And no one's seen your
sister since her new husband took her to Maine. They've been
asking after you all. And you know how hard it is to leave the
ranch down there on the river with so much to do all the time.

"It's just so good that David has come back from school
to help Uncle Eric, though it would have been nice to have
another preacher in the family. But hayin' just started up, and you
know they won't be going nowheres now to August. Why, I'm
sure they could put you to good use, too, for a time, if you'd care
to."

That was enough for Karl to finally say, "You do go on at
times, woman. They git along fine down there. Calvin here don't
need to be thinkin' 'bout their work. There's plenty here for him
to tinker with."

"Well, I was just remembering how he helped them out
those years ago when he come through. And if they get in a fix—"

"They ain't gonna git in some kind of fix they can't handle
themselves. They bin doin' it for years."

She turned her voice back to me. "Well, Sophie did ask
after you, and we did think we should go down for a visit tomorrow."

"We did?" Karl asked as if it might be true.

"Well, we did talk about it. And Sophie did call. She's
expecting us for dinner."

Karl turned his weathered face to me. "'Course, you're

always welcome to come along, Calvin. But if you got other ideas, don't let us slow you down none. They ain't goin' anywhere down there on the river that they won't be there a day from forever."

"Well, she did ask after you. And you were always her favorite after her own brood. They want to see you and you ought to come," Martha finished up, going back to her pie. She'd never been one to let life flow of its own free will, I remembered. The last days of doing chores her way to her satisfaction had brought that back clearly.

Karl was saying, "As for church..."

"What time do you leave?" I asked, deciding to get certain, unspoken obligations finally out of the way, to integrate on the brief and superficial level now and let the novelty of my being there blow over as quickly as possible. It would pass, and I would be secluded at the farm again soon enough.

The white steeple of St. Luke's Lutheran Church could be seen just three miles east of the farm, and it seemed to gleam more radiantly and grow larger as we drove toward it Sunday morning. Aunt Martha sat sideways in the broad front seat of the Buick, talking back over the seat about the church's history and its members. It stood at the intersection of gravel roads in the middle of the open prairie for ninety years, on a piece of homestead ground that my great-grandfather had donated to the parish. First it had been sod, a single room with a wooden cross at one end, then it was a rebuilt, clapboard, country school house, and finally it became the classic steepled structure we drove toward with its stained glass windows, the bell in the alabaster tower ringing as we approached as if announcing my return.

Karl parked in the ring of cars circling the church, all the car bumpers almost touching the foundation. Getting out of the car, my aunt and uncle greeted other folks moving toward the open, double doors. Organ music welled up and vibrated through the white walls and into the clear June air. Voices chorused the opening measures of a familiar hymn.

I felt a smile barely crack my lips. Too much, I thought, too much. Like a movie. Like folklore. If I were stoned, I'd be a smiling fool. Just like going out with the fishermen on Matanchen Bay, or celebrating Quebec's birthday in the city's streets—local color, and this foreigner's eyes.

I felt conspicuous but barely noticed as we slipped into a pew. An usher had greeted me by name, and an old couple climbing stairs to the choir loft had said, "Good morning," as if actually glad that it was. Standing with my aunt and uncle, I took up the hymnal and the final verses of the hymn. I'd grown up singing these songs and still liked to sing, regardless of the words.

Then the worship began, the order of service unchanged since my childhood. I remained silent through the spoken liturgy, but sang out the familiar responses, enjoying the music, feeling all the voices ring out into the high rafters, filling the morning and pouring out into the fields beyond the open windows. In place of the Holy Ghost, a past came rushing to consciousness on the wind, flashes from a forgotten time, random scenes with a sense of seasons and years and the long time since living it.

I had grown up Lutheran, even after my parents had moved us to the front range of Colorado. Governed by my mother's prairie-grown reverence, I had gone through confirmation and had taken communion. I had been baptized in this very church, had attended my sisters' baptisms here and family feasts, marriages, my grandfather's funeral. My god-parents also lived near the church. As I sang, I wondered if I'd recognize them—the couple climbing to the choir loft?

I listened intently to the sermon, pleased to find it speculative in nature rather than doctrinaire, or fire and brimstone. It concerned Saul's conversion on the road to Damascus and the theme of being "open to the Lord"—anything could happen to anybody. I felt no conflicts here with my own beliefs. How many times tripping on LSD had my spirit opened up and flown for the face of God? I smiled, relaxing, surprised to feel comfortable with the ceremony and service after so much time away. It was generational, the same thing happening every Sunday, the families gathering, chanting their parts of the litany, secure in their places and roles, with their fates as farmers and the children of farmers, never having to question what exists for them.

Utopia, or basest subjugation? I was drifting, feeling myself floating in a diversion of personal questions as the bene-diction was bestowed and the congregation stirred with the sense of conclusion. I was lulled to rest and totally unprepared for the post-service announcements: no Sunday School next week; choir practice Wednesday night; Lutheran Laymen cleaning the church grounds next Saturday. "...And we extend our greetings to our visitor, Calvin Parsons, the nephew of Karl and Martha Goehner. Most of you remember Calvin's parents, I'm sure. Calvin is going to be with us this summer, and possibly longer. So please welcome him," the pastor called, and the organ crescendoed into the closing hymn.

Now everybody knew. I was reconnected, family-tied, of some certain limb of the tree—Anna Goehner Parson's boy, grandson of Max Johannes Goehner, who married the youngest Kauphtmann girl, daughter of one of the county's earliest homesteaders. Everyone would already know that, too.

Standing in one of the small groups of men outside the church doors, I felt more isolated as an oddity than inherently connected to the conversations. There were the weather to ask about and conditions in the fields, the brief introductions to a hundred German-sounding names. All the women, standing apart in their own circles were built alike—short and stocky, grey-haired and grinning eyes. All the men wore suits and ties, looking more like greying business executives than farmers, except for their boots and weathered faces and mangled hands.

I responded to the expected common questions, many of them asked more than once. How was my mother? Fine (I supposed). How long had it been that my parents lived on the farm? About twenty or twenty-one years now (I had been told). Enjoying the farming? It was certainly new (and probably enjoyable if I ever learned it). What brought me out to God's country? I liked the outdoor work (the isolation, the privacy, the lack of politics). What had I been busy with these past years? Graduate school and travel abroad (and burning down buildings before that, running from the draft). Think you'll like being a farmer? I thought so, I told them, would try to fit into it (try this disguise a while).

But then, among the Sunday suits and the J.C. Penney dresses fluttering in the breeze, there was no fitting in. I wore an off-white shirt, open at the collar, the long tails hanging out over worn corduroy pants. I shifted weight uneasily in my Mexican huaraches and stirred the dust slightly. In a crowd of clean faces, a few moustaches, mine was the only beard. Other than my uncle's grey mane, I was the only one with hair cut at shoulder length and tied back in a short tail at the base of my neck. I felt relief that my old uncle had chosen to break that cultural ground, and I endured the neighbors' curious inspection like a foreign diplomat or the only gringo in a Guatemalan village. I was used to it, I told myself. A younger woman, introduced to me by Martha as another of my mother's cousins, mused innocently, "You certainly do look comfortable this morning." No crafty irony behind the smile. Smiling back, I lied, "I am," and looked away into the wheat fields across the road, wanting to be moving on through the day.

Finally in the car once again, heading north toward the two rivers, Aunt Martha began reciting a directory of the people that had spoken to me after church—what family, where they lived from the church, giving a short biography or relating a family trait a particular person carried. Like Harry Alford, of the Alfords farming just north of the church, of the Alfords who came in on the county's first train stop, of the Alfords who had a cousin that was county treasurer. With the men of the family all prone to that round belly they could never button a vest across; with the whole lot of them full of the gift of gab.

I vaguely wondered if Aunt Martha were somehow related, and with the next family file, from Alfords to Zinggs, I gave scant attention with voice and nods and let my mind go to watching the countryside glide by the car window.

The county highway took us off the south tableland, over the South Platte and into Ogallala, where a sign proclaimed the town "Cowboy Capital" of the west. I got that story from Martha, too: stop on the Oregon Trail, rail head for Texas herds and cowboys, though I knew that story already. From there a gravel road wound quickly onto the table between the two rivers and ran for the North Platte valley, through more winter wheat and fallow fields. Here, the ground was rolling and rougher than the south table, with a different color and texture to the land and the summer light falling over it. The sense of it seemed un-changed, familiar again, and agreeable—another way the old station wagon had gone, full of my parents and sisters in the back watching our dust tail, headed for the ranch and wrestling calves and girl cousins, having the run of the ranch with Davey and his sisters, swimming summer away in the shallows of clear creeks trickling down from Sandhills springs, feeding the river. The memories were still idyllic. I felt sure that it couldn't have been so, yet it had been, and it was why I had run there just seven years before.

Aunt Sophie stood at her kitchen door in the shade of giant cottonwoods that overhung the ranch house, open-armed, looking shorter and wider and greyer, more weathered than I had remembered. But her blue eyes glistened with the same simple meaning as they had my previous visit: glad her sister's son had come again, welcomed to the fold like another of her brood hen's chicks.

"And how are you this time?" she asked, holding me at arm's length and looking up into my eyes for truth, the smiling sound of her voice concerned and sincerely wanting to know about the child she once knew in me.

I had covered a lot of ground and had reached again the ranch on the river. It was easy to say, "I'm fine," because now, being there, I was again.

The last time I had answered that question, my aunt had been looking up into battered eyes, stitches across one swollen brow that hot end of summer, 1968. I had just hitched and hopped freight trains from Chicago and the Democratic convention where three days before, police had attacked Grant Park with tear gas and clubs and the chant, "Kill! Kill! Kill!" Running and suddenly cut off in the strange city, I'd gone down in the hysterical response, "The whole world is watching," and woke in the emergency ward of a hospital, surrounded by other bloody victims. The next day I'd fled the city with headaches and dizzy spells, afraid and confused and nurturing a growing, unacknowledged anger. Two Californians, driving on speed and pot for another confrontation in San Francisco, had dropped me off in Ogallala where I'd hidden the night under a picnic table in the park before making the long walk out to the ranch.

Aunt Sophie had let me sleep for two days, and then Uncle Eric had put me in the old jeep with fencing pliers, barbed wire, posts and diggers and fence stretchers, and I spent the next month mending fences in the Sandhills. Some days I took a sleeping bag and food and spent the nights out in the frosty open air, hiding, resting, mending fence, thinking. A month later I returned to the Boulder campus and joined SDS, and a new trail was taken—the one I was now trying to end.

"I'm fine," I reassured her. "Better than last time."

"At least you haven't been fighting with Chicago's finest again."

I leaned over and whispered, "No. Only with Aunt Martha," and Sophie clucked her warm laugh and ushered us into the kitchen full of Sunday dinner scents.

The afternoon went easy. Of my seven cousins, only the two youngest girls, still in high school, and Davey, were home. The others had married and moved on to lives in Colorado cities. We all talked family and they listened to my stories of Mexican villages and the desert Southwest. Toward dusk when my aunts and uncles sat playing pinochle, Davey and I slipped off in the blue battered jeep, driving up into the northern pastures to chase coyotes across the hills.

Cousin Dave seemed the same—blond, blue-eyed, laughing, and wild with the jeep in open country. Five years younger than I, Dave had always learned first and then taught me—how to ride, how to drive, how to raft the North Platte, how to fix fence and herd bulls. Davey had always sworn that he hated the ranch and couldn't wait to leave. He'd gone to seminary for two years at St. John's in Kansas, but was back now in partnership with his father.

"So what happened?" I asked as we rolled home in the pastel twilight, the Sandhills empty and pristine and silent around us, the open sky absorbing our slight sounds and movement.

"I don't know. Tried to do too much at once, I guess. Greek and Latin and the rest of it, too. And I tell ya, I never met more crazy carousers than at seminary. But this I can do on my own." He waved a casual hand at the silent Sandhills. "Then Carol came back, and you know we're gettin' married. This is the place for kids. It was the place for me. It doesn't seem so bad here now."

We talked as if the years had been only days. The ride was calm and filled with cool summer light.

"What about you, man. From graduate school to wheat farming? Come on, tell another story."

"I wasn't going to cut it as an academic. I didn't kiss

enough ass. Besides, it's just ideas no one believes in anyway."

"But out there with Karl and Martha?"

I stared out across the hills toward the deepening sunset, the shadows darkening in the pockets, the colors more brilliant shades of red and gold and silence.

"About four months ago I was down in Sonora again," I said, "In Hermosillo, seeing old friends, wondering what I was going to do, getting drunk too much and doing nothing but letting time eat up my life. I was in bed one night with a prostitute, after some binge or other. She was lying against me afterwards, and out of the blue she asked me what I was doing there.

"Contigo?" I said. "Here with you?"

"En Hermosillo. En Mexico."

I said, "Looking around, I guess. Looking for a place to live."

"You have no home? Where are your parents?"

"They live in Colorado. But it is their home, not mine."

"Ah, sí." She understood that. "So you are here with me." A little later she said, "There are many as you are."

"They all come to you? You must be very busy." She pounded on me a little, in a teasing way.

Then she said, "You need some place else to go." I asked where all the others went. "They go back to their families," she said, though she didn't really know. "Yours are in Colorado, verdad?"

I said, "No. In Nebraska. I'm 'el hijo prodigo'—a prodigal son." She understood that, too, a bible reader. A lot of them are.

She nodded and smiled. "Where is Nebraska?"

I tried to describe this country, but it didn't matter much. I said, "It is a great plain with many farms and ranches. Very flat"—though it isn't. "You can see a long way."

She sat up. "Your family has a rancho?"

"There is a farm that was once my great-grandfather's," I told her.

"Well then, you can go there," she said.

"It's not so simple."

"They would not welcome you?"

"Yes, but I don't know that I could live there. And there's not enough room."

She couldn't believe that. "Not enough room on the land?"

"To make a living. To make money."

"But there is room to live?"

I said, "Sí. Room to live."

"But they would welcome you onto the land?" she asked again, not seeing any kind of conflict.

"But I'm not from there."

"Sí, you are from there. From many other places also, but there is still the land of your family. Many people have no land. My family has no land. That is why I am here with you," she said. "Perhaps this is the truth?"

"Perhaps this is the truth. Anyway, here I am."

It was something Buckwheat understood, too, when I told it to him.

Buckwheat solos:

"Yeah, well, you can guess I left for all the fuckin' right reasons, too—gettin' away from the family feud, gonna see the world, buyin' a change of scenery, and of course football, fame, and fortune. Not to mention different sex. I was gonna do up wild eastern Asia, you bet. Those butts even had me believin' it was the right thing to do, too. American duty, you know.

"So I did basic in Georgia, then went to language school in California—fuckin' language school, man. I can't even get my own tongue right, but I was gonna learn gook talk. And I did. Twenty-one months later I was in Japan workin' word puzzles in Vietnamese and runnin' fullback screens for some base team. I'd unscramble what the gooks were sayin'. The army'd send them bombs and napalm on the Ho Chi Minh Trail, and they'd send me out in the flat for a flare pass on Saturday afternoons. Seemed like an even trade to me.

"Oh, they'd slip some dude into my room some nights to see if I talked in my sleep, but that seemed reasonable enough.

They bugged a house in Osaka to make sure I didn't like my oriental sex too kinky—and it's nice to be taken care of. And they long ago looked me up enough at home to make sure I shit good on Sundays or said the pledge of allegiance every day in school. Hey, just write home. Everyone knows ol' Buckwheat. I'm a good Nebraska boy who's never been beyond the end of the river, and I got the attitude they're after. Besides, they're takin' care of me, and I'm playin' ball ten thousand miles from home. What else is there?

"I got in three good games. The fourth game, two fuckin' sets of downs, man. Six plays, then some Navy nigger rolls up my leg and puts an end to my career stats. Twenty-nine carries, a hundred and seven yards, two receptions, no scores, no Armed Forces Fuckin' Hall of Fame.

"But, hey! That's life, right? Ol' Buckwheat can adjust. I still got attitude. There's always good old God and country. So man, I'm Corporal Van Anders. Top clearance, 525th Military Intelligence Group, new promotion. Hell, why not? Those 'few good men' they're always lookin' for were gettin' harder to come by all the time—'specially when they're bein' blowed away so fast in the rice paddies. I already knew shit only three or four others in the whole fuckin' world knew, including the president, man. They weren't fuckin' gonna send me home for a football knee.

"That was early '71. The stuff I was breakin' down was heavy shit, man. The Ho Chi Minh Trail was like that Interstate down there, only the gooks weren't just wanderin' around the country like those idiots down there. They made a huge logistical move into Laos and Cambodia just before the big rains, and of course we bombed shit out of it, but that didn't do diddly. If you could believe the numbers I was gettin'—this was from direct radio communications right from the fuckin' road, man—someone was in for some heavy shit. Ten years of Oregon Trail travel in about four months, and all of it military supply and gooks on bicycles.

"Then there was Lamson 719. You know, "Vietnamization" of the war, right? Shit, man. The Intelligence brass, they got all our numbers, and numbers from wherever else they got 'em—CIA and NSC and shit—and the poop was it would take four U.S. divisions to go in and clean 'em out. But you know,

this was after 1970 and Kent State. U.S. troops couldn't go into
Laos and Cambodia no more—without bein' caught at it anyhow.
So they got Thieu to send in the ARVN—mostly green draftees,
man. I knew that, and only two batallions maybe. This was
against parts of maybe two whole goddamn divisions of NVA and
VC regulars—combat veterans. I told the brass that. I told 'em
what was there—the first time I ever raised a stink that mattered in
my life—and they didn't give one diddly shit.

"Well, the ARVN got trapped at this Tchepone, about
twenty miles inside Laos. NVA artillery had 'em pinned down for
weeks and was chewin' the shit out of 'em. Well then, Al Haig
flew in there to check it out—I knew that cuz the fuckin'
Commies already knew it—and it turns out that Haig calls for
"orderly retreat," right? But the ARVN just up and ran for it.
Abandoned all kinds of equipment. Lost hundreds of men. But
hey, it was only ARVN, and by then nobody gave a shit about
them anyway. They couldn't fight and didn't want to, and everybody in CINCPAC and MCAV and even out in the bush damn
well knew it. Fuck it all.

"But hey, ol' Buckwheat could live with that, too. I told
'em, didn't I? Then a week later, fuckin' Nixon comes on the tube
and says—you know how Nixon talked— 'Tonight I can report
that Vietnamization has succeeded.' Fuck man, maybe that's when
I started thinkin' everything ain't like they always said it was. But I
was too damn stupid still to even know I was thinkin' it. I was just
doin' my job, man, servin' my country. But somewheres in there
I'm startin' to think maybe we don't know what the hell we're
doin'. Maybe nobody knows what they're doin', and it shoulda
been plain a fuckin' long time ago.

"Like, look at that down there, man, all those people not
knowin' where the hell they're goin', just goin', flowin' right on up
that Interstate one direction or the other. Right up the South
Platte, just like they headed up the North Platte a hundred years
ago or so. Still ain't none of 'em know where to hell they're
goin'—not even back then, but at least back then them wagon
riders had some sort of vision, some far-fetched dream of a
Promised Land and the freedom to actually go there and see for
themselves what it was really like. They had God and families and
every material possession packed up in a wagon to wander across

Indian Territory.

"Fuck it, man. School and the Army had me believin' it was still like that, the good old American Dream. Of course it forever wasn't gonna be what any of them pioneers imagined either, and it ate 'em up left and right. Chewed 'em up, and that big idea of theirs. But at least they got to go for it. They knew where they were goin' and why they were goin' and what they were gonna do when they got there. It was their trip.

"Those people down there in the valley, those lights cruisin' the Interstate, headin' to California and headin' for New York and headed for every-fuckin'-where but right where they are—they don't got a single clue where they're headed or why. Yeah, they might think they know—just like the fuckin' Army— but ain't one crazy cruisin' loony down there on the highway can tell you certain what he's gonna be doin' a year from now.

"They're all chasin' stuff that don't mean shit, man. Stuff, and the bucks to buy it with. If they're drivin' west and stop in say, Big Springs, the middle of nowhere, and they hear of a better chance to get stuff drivin' back they other way, they'll right there turn around and head back east. All they got goin' in life is wheels, man.

"Now, maybe that's all pioneers had goin', too, wheels, and what they could pack aboard. But they were goin' somewhere, even if it was just to a dream. They weren't just ramblin' around the country cuz they didn't have nothin' better to do. Neither did the goddamn VC, haulin' ass down their own trail. But us guys, shit, man. There wasn't nothin' over there for us, not even a fuckin' dream, though those bastards tried to make us believe it. For God and country, right? Shit! Guys went over there to Nam and got their bodies blown apart and came home in bags, or like Frankensteins—like this!— all sewn back together or parts missing, and what for? Just so those fuckers down there can go on ramblin' up and down the Interstate with no fuckin' reason at all. Fuck that.

"Course comin' home always makes a difference. You bet. Like ain't everything changed just peaches and cream. And, you're a man now, son. Yes, sir. Like I got pedigree papers like that Angus bull of his.

"The old man'd mosey into town and march down the

street to Cody's or into the bank just beamin' like, hey! he just gave his son in The Big One. Like it's still high school, man, and we just won another game cuz I sunk it at the buzzer again. Nobody's got anything on my old man. No, sir. Is he class American, or what?

"And it's gonna be different at home now, too, son. Just you see, he says. The hell with that. Instead of tellin' me what to do, he starts askin' me if that ain't just right what we should be doin'—isn't it, son, don't you think? You bet, pa! I'll just lurch on over and get started on it just like you say.

"Well, I went along with that about as long as the Darvon lasted. And that was the rest of the winter, and I laid around the house most of that time, spaced out. Mom was easy to live with cuz she ain't got a clue to real life. Long as yer eatin' her cookin' and clearin' yer plate, the world's just like God Himself intended. She's got her clubs. She's got her church cleanin'. She's got shoppin' and the meals and home keepin' and her grandchildren. And she's got her baby boy back home—maybe a little worse for wear, but that's okay. Moms don't care if you're a little fucked up as long as you're alive and eatin'. The rest can be taken care of with prayer. Well, you know, I did get back up over two hundred pounds. Healthy as a feeder pig, and that's the way she sees it.

"With Sandy it was okay. Better than okay. We screwed our eyes out those first weeks I was home. That's why Junior came along. Buckwheat Junior. Just started walkin', and grandpa's got a ball of some kind in his hands as soon as he sees him. Junior's gotta be just like daddy, and grandpa's gonna make sure. Sandy, she don't care, long as someone's payin' him attention. I bitch about it, and she whines, 'He's only a baby.' Junior's gonna shit in his pants another year, and that's all she's got time for. That and the girls and school and babysittin' half the trailer court kids and tryin' to get the rent out of Sauer before he drinks up his railroad check every two weeks. Sandy's on the ragin' go so goddamn much, you'd think life's gonna end if the goddamn groceries don't get bought sooner than yesterday, and tomorrow's already too busy to make time for it.

"Hell, it don't matter. Great sex for awhile, then she's pregnant, then it's just a regular marriage again and there's too fuckin' much else to get done. We might screw some Friday night if we remember it, and if one of the kids ain't throwin' up, or McCormick don't drop by to bullshit.

"Meanwhile, I got the job at Mel's station cuz the Siever kid was KIA, and I spend all my time fixin' Thompson's van or Ramirez' piece of shit pick-up and pumpin' gas in all those Interstate cars so those assholes can be movin' on down the road. That's what I live for, man, so everyone can go on truckin' down their fuckin' roads to nowhere. Hey! That's what I'm here for."

Calvin's journal notes/summer, '75:

Been out on the land three days now at the helm of a growling barge—Uncle Karl would say, "At the wheel of Old Moe." And Martha would say, "At this God-given duty" —working up the summer fallow with an open-air Minneapolis-Moline tractor, model GB, 1951, (only three years younger than I am) that is pulling a sixteen-foot tandem disc (even older yet). This is the second cruise across the open ground—Karl would say, "Doing the second operation," and Martha would say, "Doing another chore to be thankful for" —navigating under an endless sky filled with a fleet of clouds sailing endlessly east.

The ocean-prairie spreads to the circular horizon, its rollers and waves frozen in the form of solid dunes, the wind and water changing its shape and motion, only ever so much more slowly. Yet it is like being lost at sea, with no orientation but the surface itself and the brilliant sun passing over and changing the color of the light. It's like sitting in Enrique's old fishing boat so far off the Mexican coast that the land can't be seen, and the only other human life is other fishermen, dark specks bobbing on the sun-sparkled horizon. Here in the fields, Old Moe, named like any worthy vessel, crawls across the ground, and the only signs of civilization are the hazy green tops of the windbreaks tucked in the folds of far away fields and the dust plumes spiraling up where another farmer works some fallow roll of land. In the waters off Punta Mita in Jalisco, in the fallow wheat fields of the west Nebraska High Plains, the voyage is the same—out on the open surface of the vast face of the planet where vision is limited only by my individual perception and where space is an absolutely

private possession. —This is me, here, a part of nothing else, just
a rider on the face of the globe, watching the weather fly over the
particular distance I see on this passage. Yet I feel part of it all,
too, the cycles of change, Ecclesiastes' chant, "To everything there
is a season." A time to till, a time to drift on the ocean-plain, my
wake only a dusty scratch on this edge of the earth as I cruise
through time and space and life and the awareness of it all.

Fine feeling.

I'm floating free, out away from everything else, on my
own and indefinable by anything other than this place—the
ground I cover, and by my vessel—Old Moe. For a while, long
hours at a time, I am actually a farmer and nothing else. I ride,
doing my job, and watch the light of the world change.

Guiding a tractor across the field is actually more comfortable than being on the ocean. Bobbing on the waves in five
hundred pounds of cracking fiberglass and rotting wood pushed
around by a sputtering, smoke-belching Mercury outboard,
hovering on some random spot of sea, gathering in gill net and at
the mercy of the weather, I never felt relaxed. If the boat ever
broke down, reaching land and survival would be pure chance and
a matter of will power. Standing on the deck of Old Moe as he
roars and rolls steadily forward, tacking back and forth till every
inch of one marked and solid quarter of land is covered, I don't
feel at the mercy of the weather. If the tractor breaks down, I
take a walk to the windbreak, breathing easy—something I have
already come to do comfortably. There's rest in the work.

Being out on the tractor for the day is also more comfortable than being around the farmyard and Aunt Martha's ways and
means of spending time and labor. For her, time and labor are
one in the same. There is no life without labor—except for those
morning moments of devotion, and Sundays, of course—which is
fine if a soul needs that. But Martha also assumes that what task
is right for her is right for all of us in the immediate vicinity. And
not only is the specific task the proper desire and duty of us all,
proper also is her specific method of accomplishing that task. No
doubt she received her instruction right from God, or at least
from an angel, and it is surely carved in stone somewhere.

Some days ago (already the sense of particular days—

excepting Sunday—is falling away)...some days ago before this last
Sunday, before getting out into the fields again this week, I began a
morning by sitting out under the elms in the yard with this journal
and some books around me. I was going to read what Wendell
Berry has to say about agricultural America, and I planned to start
Willa Cather's *O Pioneers!* Uncle Karl had left me with no particular chore for the day, though the float in one stock tank needed
looking after and some window panes in the tank house still
needed replacing. But I could get to them any time before the
coming field work, and it had just showered the night before. (I
took in the late night dance of lightning, watching from my west
window.) So I figured I'd break the pace of days. Why not?

Because it's not Sunday, that's why not. At least that was
Aunt Martha's explanation after she saw me from the kitchen
window and came out to ask me what I had in mind for the day.

"Mornin'! Whatchya doin?" A regular, casual greeting
from her.

"Reading some, I guess, and I don't know...writing letters
to friends?"

"That's Sunday doin's," she informed me. "I sure could
use your hand cleanin' out the chicken coop this morning. It's
gettin' so bad even the critters can't stand it. I bin pittin' cherries
all morning,"—it's only 9AM or so— "standin' over that sink.
Like to wreck my back. Just can't be pushin' on so much no
more," she said as she stooped to pull a renegade weed from her
flowers along the fence.

"Well, take it easy some. You ought to rest when your
back starts bothering you," I said in a friendly, more gushingly
open voice than usual. —I am at that moment stoned on a
precious pinch of pot I brought from Colorado—an old hippie at
ease in the sunshine.

"Oh, I don't have time for that. There's always so much
to get done. You know, there's always plenty to be doin' 'round a
place like this."

"There sure is," this stoned hippie agreed with eagerness,
smiling, knowing what she was driving at. Things to do like
enjoying the morning business of birds, or watching the clouds
form and change, or letting country light fill the spirit, I thought,
but I didn't say it. These are activities Martha is aware of in the

greater world, but not in the one she experiences, unless it is Sunday. The old hippie held his tongue. What control.

Now, the chicken coop has probably needed cleaning for years—a couple feet of dung heaped under the roost, the roost itself and the nesting boxes in rusty-nail shambles, the chicken wire fences broken and sagging since even my own childhood memories. And Martha had announced the night before that it was bread-baking day in the morning. But suddenly, with me sitting out on my ass in the morning summer sun in cut-offs and sunglasses, stretched out with a book and morning bird song, it was time to clean up the coop—Martha's time, which is to say any time that I look idle and drifting.

So sure, why not? After all, it's also a single, loving concern of hers that I be a part of whatever occurs around here. So I put my things in the bunkhouse and climbed back into grimy Levis and sweaty T-shirt, trooped to the barn for a pitchfork and shovel, and we started in on the chicken coop just for Aunt Martha's peace of mind—never mind her back now.

I started scooping and hauling from under the roost. But, no, Martha insisted that the front nook with grain bags and ancient, rusted feeders and waterers and brooding equipment be cleaned up first—even though we'd just dirty it again tromping through with chicken shit and dusty, indeterminate filth later. Looking over the decayed and damaged equipment from distant decades, Martha lamented the sin of throwing anything away and allowed how that night in my spare time I could fix it all up at the shop and start a chick brooding business immediately, sure it should be another life's calling for me—poultry rancher. I showed her in detail how ninety per cent of it wasn't even high-class trash, and she mumbled some kind of disappointment and went on with the cleaning.

I began loading old grain sacks with the ammonia saturated refuse of a hundred generations of broilers and pullets and old roosters. But Martha decided that she wanted it all scooped into an ancient toy wagon, shovel load by shovel load, so she could drag it off herself. Doing it her way took twice as much trouble, dust, sweat, and stench, and twice as much time. She mulched half of it into her flower beds and piled the rest of it near where she was sure I'd want to plant a big garden next spring.

When the coop was finally cleaned out, I rebuilt nesting boxes and the roost—again, according to Martha's specifications. Occasionally, an old hen out in the pen would cluck up an impatient, indignant racket of assent to Martha's orders. Hard to tell a difference in the voices, the hen's and Martha's. That task took up the rest of the morning.

In the process we found a dung encrusted, paint stained gate-leg table in the corner of the coop. Just another hideous piece of junk to me, but Aunt Martha assured me that it was a fine piece of heirloom craftsmanship, passed down the generations, lost and just now rediscovered, for me to take apart, refurbish, and reconstruct as a shining family emblem. She proposed that I take the rest of my self-claimed day off and learn furniture refinishing—under her tutelage, of course. This was in case I failed as a poultry rancher, I supposed.

By that time, I was far from being a stoned, hideaway hippie. I was just a tired, annoyed peon, letting his resentment show for la patrona—in this case, Aunt Martha. I just said, "No," less enthusiastically than I had started our morning conversation. "I have some things to take care of this afternoon. I'll be busy."

"Oh, well, if you have something to do...." she mumbled off, as if she couldn't imagine it. With Martha you must wrestle the moment away from her, or she will use up all you have. She went back up to the house then to fix us a late lunch.

It would be, of course, the usual great lunch—hot leftovers from the beef feast of the night before, fresh garden salad, homemade bread and butter, and a cake and fruit dessert. While we ate, I was treated to a seminar lecture on how I'm related to the widow Ester Roessler who lives just a half mile east of us and who never lived more than four miles from the soddie she was born in. We got onto her lineage because I commented on the sweetness of radishes in the salad to show that I hadn't meant to be curt and insulting the hour before. But before I could know where the radishes came from, how, when, why, and in what condition, I first had to know the history of the garden ground they were grown on, and that, of course, involved the intermarriage of the offspring of local homesteaders and the ensuing biblical who-begat-whom's that made us third cousins, once removed, or something equally blood-joined. Therefore, we were eating family radishes which made them all the more significantly tasty.

The Heritage Hour was interesting, if not completely clear, and I only had to eat and rest and fog off mentally. And I didn't have to make up plans of afternoon activity to suit her. After lunch, I finished cleaning up around the chicken coop, washed off the scarred gate-leg, antique table and put it in the bunkhouse for a night stand.

Then I hid out in the bunkhouse the rest of the afternoon, reading what I had started that morning. Martha chose to work in her flower beds between the main house and the bunkhouse, bending her tired spine in the heat of the June day, stooping for weeds, pruning the roses here and there, mulching the soil around her mums. She'd occasionally straighten up to wipe the sweat from her wrinkled brow and to fan herself with her broad-brimmed straw hat while one hand crooked around to massage her lower back. Then she'd bow again to her labor with the slow, stiff deliberateness of the aged, looking every bit the worn-down farm woman getting to another neglected, necessary chore. It was a far cry from the baking she had intended earlier, and her laboring had its intended effect. The flower garden looked fresh and peaceful in the evening twilight, and I was distracted enough and feeling guilty enough never to enjoy what I wanted to read.

It was almost a relief when it came time for the evening milking. It is a labor approved by God and by Aunt Martha. No doubt the four old Holsteins agree, too. ...But tomorrow I'm out on Old Moe again, and glad of it.

Mike McCormick's lyrics/

I'm the one that was there so I can tell you what happened no matter what anybody else might tell you now, cuz you know me, I used to stop in at the station a lot passin' through. —Had to check up on the competition, didn't I? I always parked down past the station and out on the gravel toward the river—you know Newcastle, he never thought two different gas brands better be seen on the same lot. Why, the whole county might think we're price fixin'. As if him and Duncan didn't just do it over the phone every other midnight or somethin'.

Anyway, I was there and damn glad I parked out back by Thompson's refrigerator, cuz once that guy's car blew I never even thought about how it coulda blown my truck away, too. Then we all woulda been nothin' but flamin' bits, and probably half the trailer court, too. And it blew just like that, too, whoosh! Kapow! We were even damn lucky they was at the far pumps the way it exploded the windows in on us and blasted us against the wall. All kinds of crap fell in on us, oil cans, candy bars, new tires, and shit. It rained glass, and we got all sliced up.

I saw Buckwheat kinda pushin' things off himself, and his shirt was all rags and his arms bloody. He looked at his arms and then at me lookin' bloody some, too, and he shouts, "Oh fuck, man, we're hit! Jesus!" Then he starts shoutin', "Medic! Medic!" and crawlin' over to me on his belly. "Where you hit? You okay? Stay down! Stay down!" Yellin' crazy things.

But I was already gettin' up off the floor to see what happened. I didn't get the full force of the blast because I was mostly shielded by the wall and the Coke machine. I was up in maybe, I don't know, thirty seconds, but whatever, it was way too late to do anything for anybody. It was the goddamn Towering Inferno! There was nothin' left of the guy pumpin' gas. They guess he was drunk and smokin', pumpin' high octane into that Chevy Blazer, and kapowee!

The woman somehow got out of the vehicle, on the other side of the fire from us. I couldn't see her, but she was a ball of flame, I guess. Ol' Henry Reuther was comin' by the station, headed for town, when it happened. The percussion of the explosion blowed his pick-up right off the road, but it didn't hurt him none. He turned around and seen the woman come screamin' from the explosion all afire, and he run her down with a blanket and rolled her in it, but it was too late. She was dead before the trucks pulled up, and they had to treat ol' Henry for shock afterwards.

Me and Buckwheat were the only other ones there, and I guess that's somethin' to be thankful for, or it coulda been worse than that. As it was, the pumps were all on fire and roarin'. All the windows were blowed out, and even one of the garage doors was only half hangin' on its track. And Buckwheat was totally gone, I tell you. When I come to what had happened, I started diggin' for the telephone and found it under the overturned counter. I called down to the fire station, but it had already been turned in—that fast—and then I could hear the sirens comin' clear across the river and over the fire roar.

I looked around for Buckwheat again then, and he'd crawled on his arms and belly right past me and into the garage. When I saw him, he was layin' half way through the doorway to the garage and reachin' 'round into the cabinet for where he keeps that sawed off twelve gauge. I ran over to him, yellin', "Jesus! Whattaya doin'?" and he's yellin' back over his shoulder, "Get down! Get down!" rollin' over and pumpin' shells into the magazine.

His ol' eyes stuck out like a bloodshot bug, I swear. Where that huge jaw of his wasn't speckled red with glass cuts, he was white as a ghost. And blood was runnin' down his neck, and he looked back at me, breathin' heavy-like—more like pantin'. I was plenty shook up before, but I about crapped a ton there. He looked crazy!

I started yellin' to him, "Buckwheat! What the hell ya doin'? Buckwheat!"

Well, he's not even hearin' me for a minute there. The fire's roarin', the truck sirens are blastin' up, then I think one of the pumps made a small explosion or somethin'—another loud blast. I hit the floor, and Buck was all curled up beside me with his arms pulled up around his head. I crawled up over him—and he's like a small hill a layin' there—and I got the shotgun off the floor. I thought I better get it away from him cuz I wasn't sure he really knew what was goin' on. I could just see him blastin' away at the firemen or something. It was spooky as hell, him layin' there in a bloody mess, too. I didn't half know what I was doin' myself.

He'd let go of the gun anyway and was still coverin' himself and mumblin' again about medics and "Where are they? Where are they?"

I was crawlin' to my feet when some of the guys came runnin' in—Mercy and Smokey Johns. I got the hell out of there then, out the garage and between the fire trucks, while those two checked Buckwheat over a second, then picked him up under his arms and half dragged him outa there to the ambulance. I didn't know ol' Mercy could move that far and back without fallin' down himself, let alone carryin' someone else. Just shows you what good healthy fear can do for you.

But I hadn't realized how stunned Bucky was. The blast must of really throwed him against the wall. He was totally out of it at the ambulance. They got him down on a stretcher and washed off some of the blood, and worked on his cuts, checkin' his pupils and heart and all, and shootin' him up with somethin'. But they didn't take off till they had one of the bodies in and the fire was about out. They got it controlled real fast. Buckwheat, he never knew what happened. They had to tell him.

And I had to tell them—or as much of it as I could. They checked the scene out later and guessed the rest. The guy was some kind of insurance computer guy, him and his wife comin' out to the lake for the weekend from Omaha. You know, it's late Friday afternoon. They got their Bayliner with the big Mercury outboards. They got their dog and their camping gear stuffed in the back of the Blazer. 'Bout a half a case of Coors just behind the front seat. The rest was probably drunk as chasers to Jack Daniel's. They found the burnt up bottle up front.

They were both smokers, and they were probably both loaded to the top of their eyelids. The dumb bastard was probably smokin' and not even knowin' it while he's fillin' the frickin' tank. Balooey! Instant crispy. They only found parts of him. His wife died of the burns before the trucks ever got there. The dog fried up in the back of the Blazer. It was sick to look at, I tell ya.

Ol' man Reuther was in shock, like I said. It's a wonder his old ticker didn't stroke the final hour for him. I was cut up some, but the wall and the coke machine saved me. Buckwheat's face and arms looked like measles, and he had a gash enough for ten stitches in the back of his head. He musta hit it on the desk behind the counter when the blast threw him.

They kept him at the hospital in Ogallala for observation, but they let him go Saturday afternoon when it was clear he was gonna kick the door of his room in if they made him stay any longer. Sandy was supposed to keep him quiet and in bed for a couple days, but fat chance. He started tyin' one on that night in

Cody's, drinkin' J.D. shooters and beer chasers, same as that damn
fried drunk was drinkin'.

I came into Cody's about ten that night, and Buckwheat
was at the bar hasslin' one of them pipeliners from Louisiana, just
givin' him shit about his accent and about how all those ditch
diggers were givin' gonorrhea to all the local women who fell for
their slick bullshit. Ramirez was there with him, and that southern
boy wasn't crazy enough to give 'em any shit back. Ol' Smokey
was there just eggin' Bucky on with that howlin' coyote laugh of
his, but Chatman was in there, too, and Jimmy Lox, trying to get
Buckwheat to ease off.

When I got in with 'em, we started talkin' 'bout the fire
again, and we got Bucky over to a table and a little distracted so
that pipeliner could get the hell outa there. We drank and shot the
bull a long time, and Buckwheat downed them J.D. shooters like
Kool-ade for another hour. Burns and the Boar were shootin'
pool, and Bucky started harrassin' them, and they weren't smart
enough to let him be. Had to give him some smart-ass lip. So
Bucky, of course, goes over to show 'em how to run the table,
right? Gets 'em to bet that he can't get all the balls down in one
turn. Dumb asses. Bucky just up and lifts the corner of the table
off the floor, up to his chin, and all the balls roll down to the
other end and into the pocket or off the table.

Virg Peters, he's behind the bar. He comes all unglued
and starts to ring up the sheriff, and Buckwheat gets pissed. He
gets even more pissed when Burns and the Boar won't pay up, and
he starts throwin' chairs around the bar. Man, everybody's
scramblin' then. For once we were lucky Bucky was so far gone.
We got him cooled down some and outa there before the Deputy
come cruisin' around, or we woulda had our hands full cuz Bucky
hates that stud son of a bitch, Crighter. About four of us carried
him out in a big joke and got him in my pick-up and gone. He
puked all over my cab window, the sick jerk. We hauled him home
and carried him into the trailer. Sandy just bit her lip and didn't
say nothin'. She knows Bucky.

He was totally blitzed. He was singin' and wailin', totally
forgot about Cody's and all that. He was moanin' about R & R—
"No more ball for me, boys. It's R & R—rye on the rocks."
Anyway, he wasn't gonna play ball at least for a couple weeks, and I

guess he was never really gonna get over it, the fire and all. I think about it now and again, you know, thinkin' we coulda done something. But even now, how do you ever really know what's happenin' to your lousy life?

CHAPTER FOUR: HOMEFIELD ADVANTAGE

I believed then that what I needed was out there on the open ground, in the silence surrounding the emptiness, and I wandered the farm's four quarters, seeking solitude like a medicine. It was restful and spirit-settling time, a spell when all the weight of past losses and the failure of ideals shed from my back like an old skin. The war and its counter-culture were finished or fading. The rest of the American world would settle back into its petty self-absorption, but I would walk on the land and tend it.

My walks were also a temporary escape from Aunt Martha's minutiae of homestead routines. She sought as much of my free time as I did, filling it with her private trivia—transplanting house plants, repairing an ancient garden hose that should have been junked years before, or cleaning out the loft of the garage where several previous generations had cast off their obsolete hardware and tools. It was as if she were afraid of bad consequences in leaving me alone to myself.

One morning, unaccountably left to myself at breakfast, and in a kind of desperate impulse to be away, I scribbled a note at the kitchen table: "Took the Speckled Pony into town to take care of some personal business." I fled the house in a casual panic of escape, got into the ancient pick-up, and raced down the lane for the open country roads.

The Speckled Pony was a 1940 Chevrolet pick-up splotched in various shades of worn-through paint jobs—bright yellow, sunrise red, a splash of sky blue over the big round front fenders. In certain light the pick-up looked afire. In any light it looked ready to collapse from old age. But it was just another machine Uncle Karl preserved in perfect running order, the machine that had carried the old man around the country a couple times and had finally brought him back to the farm for good in 1943 when all his brothers had gone off to the war. Now the pick-up was an anachronistic burst of rattling color on the farm and was used mostly as a field and fencing truck—another old farm implement. But for me it was the only vehicle available that gave me access to the rest of the country.

Its obnoxious coloring and round, lumbering lines, the bulbous headlights like insect eyes, and the way the engine hummed had immediately appealed to me. The body creaked and rattled over the country roads and would take me anywhere and back. I had been wanting to get out and see more of the rolling land, and the Speckled Pony was my single chance. There had been an early morning shower—perhaps the reason for this chance to break away—and the gravel roads were soft and slick. The morning, June air was scented clean and fresh. The wheat was pale green and glistening, waving with a soft shush in the light piercing through the clouds that were breaking up into dense, grey-white puffs and drifting eastward with the wind. Across the horizons, rain curtains hung in wisps like blue gossamer skirts. The land spread and rolled in a sea of earthen colors mottled bright and muted soft by the changing sky. It was beautiful, and suddenly, I was out and moving again, cross-country.

I hit dry roads where the rains hadn't reached and drove among the rains curtains, ranging miles in all directions, circling and cutting through fields of young corn and sorghum, wheat and oats, zig-zagging and following REA poles toward pinpoint perspective. I stayed on the tableland south of the South Platte, gradually moving off west and north toward the river valley with its towns and highways. There was no other traffic on the country roads—a pick-up's dust in the distance once, a single cattle truck, a mile over and heading for the highway. There were tractors in dry fields here and there, and men working on machinery at fields edges who looked up and waved at my colored, fly-by blur and dust trail.

In the isolated middle of nowhere, I stopped the pick-up and got out. Off to the southwest a small, black thundercloud rumbled against the ground, lightning piercing its towering white crown of cumulus boiling up in the morning sun. All around the dappled light raced over the ground. Wheat leaned and waved in the southeastern windsong. I pulled a joint from the lining of my jacket and smoked it there on the empty road, viewing the endless land, the changing sky, the emptiness. I sat up on the truck's hood, leaning against the windshield, and looked out to the horizon, letting the earth's dynamics slowly fill my thoughts with pleasure.

I had celebrated the earth's beauty this way in many places—Colorado mountains, the Southwestern deserts, Mexican coastlines, Caribbean jungles. But this was Nebraskan high-plains prairie, a land of my forefathers, of my own roots, and I waved in the wind like the wheat. Here was a private and personal beauty. Time broke apart like the sky, and I drifted in thought like a cloud.

When a plume of dust rose toward me on the road, I scrambled down and drove off toward the shoulder of the river valley. The unfamiliar road suddenly dipped into gullied ground and wound down drywash toward the tree-lined river. I caught glimpses of the Interstate in the river's wide cradle, then the view was blocked by steep, narrow ridges. The road suddenly plunged, then horseshoed sharply into one last blind curve into the valley. In a tuck of shallow canyon, the road dipped across another joining gully, this one full of rushing water—tableland run-off that carved these gullies and rippled across my path. I braked hard, and tires ground in loose gravel and kept sliding until the pick-up splashed into the water with a sizzle and spray that killed the engine and left me dead in the water.

I panicked, imagining a great wall of water pouring over me, and I grabbed at the door of the cab, slamming it open and jumping from the running board to the far side of the water. As I touched the ground, the over-reaction left me, and I stood looking at the silly scene: the flaming, rust-colored pick-up dead in the muddy waters that rushed and foamed at the tailpipe and running boards. Had I known the road, been paying attention, I could have easily slowed, eased through the shallow run-off, and gone on without a thought but for its wild beauty. Where was it coming from? I wondered. The road had been dry.

Beyond the pick-up, the gully broadened and leveled out. The water S-curved against another shoulder of clay bank and eased around a small farmyard tucked under giant cottonwood trees, then ran behind a worn wood barn and a trailer house with a fenced-in yard. There were tractors, a truck, and cars scattered around the small outer yard. A few head of cattle nosed at the water running through their pens.

Not wanting to face the embarrassment of having to go ask for help, I waded back to the pick-up, climbed in, and tried to start it. The engine labored but wouldn't fire. I knew I couldn't leave it on the blind curve until the distributor dried out, so I resigned myself to going for help. Trotting the few hundred yards to the trailer house, I found a young girl swaying in the swingset in the yard, her blond ponytail bobbing with her ride. A small dog barked just inside the gate.

"Hi! Is your daddy home?" I called out in my best friendly voice.

"Nope." She kept her swing swaying.

In the pause to recover from such an abrupt end to my attempt at communication, the door of the trailer opened, and a woman leaned around the screen door to inspect me. I suddenly felt the strangeness of my appearance. The woman wore a red bandanna tied around her head so no hair showed. It accented the fine lines of her cheek bones, delicate nose, and the blueness of her eyes. In blue jeans and bulky sweatshirt and the shadow of the doorway her size and shape were hidden. She could have been between twenty or forty, a farm wife, a sister to my aunt.

"Hello. I ah...my pick-up. Well, is your husband home?" Words were sticking to my dry mouth.

"No, he's not. He's working in town this morning."

"Well, I ah...kind of blew it coming down through the gully there. I didn't see the water in time to stop, and the splash killed the engine. I kind of need to be pulled out."

A big grin infected the lady's face, making it come to life with a beauty I hadn't noticed at first. The eyes sparkled with a light laugh. No sister to Aunt Martha, I thought. Like no farm wife I'd yet seen.

"Kind of need to be pulled out, huh?" she repeated in a rich, taunting voice as she opened the door wide and moved lightly down the steps. She was lithe and long legged, tall and graceful. She came through the gate beside me, still showing a teasing sort of smile as she glanced at me. I caught the scent of lilacs in the long blond hair that fell out the back of her bandanna.

Over her shoulder she said, "Jaime, honey, you stay here and swing now, okay? Mama's going to help this man with his pick-up. Then I'll be right back." The swing never slowed its rhythm. The lady led the way across the outer yard to an old John Deere with a front-end loader, parked beside some fuel tanks. "You must not be from around here," she said, still grinning over her shoulder, glancing at me again.

"Well, no. Well, I guess I am now."

"Oh?" she said, turning to face me as we reached the tractor, showing surprise in her blue eyes. "I have to jump start it with the charger. Then we can start it up and pull you out."

She disappeared into a small garage and came back trailing electric cord and a battery charger on wheels. I stood watching her hook up the clamps to the battery terminals and turn the machine on, feeling suddenly embarrassed, ignorant, and helpless again, like none of this should be happening this way. She climbed up into the tractor cab, and the diesel engine clattered to life.

I stood with my stoned mind reeling with the unexpected. This was no squat farm wife of scowling Germanic stock with the suspicious stare at a stranger with ragged hair and shaggy beard. No disgruntled farmer in over-alls reluctantly dragged away from his chores to help some freak. Here was a beautiful woman, snickering to herself as she eyed me, taking on the task like an everyday routine, handling the tractor like a common toy.

She yelled down at me, "Want to get the charger out of the way?" I scrambled to turn it off, undo the cables and move it out of the way in an attempt to show some kind of competency. "Climb on up!" I climbed up into the open door of the cab, and she backed it away from the tanks, shifted, and headed it out of the yard.

In the engine roar she leaned toward my ear and yelled, "Got a chain in your truck?"

"I don't know."

"There's one in here, I guess. Is Jaime still in the swing?" She looked back over her shoulder and waved, and the child waved back, still swinging. As we rumbled down the road, the lady glanced at me several times, still smiling. I could only shrug and grin sheepishly, looking away.

When we reached the gully, her grin widened. "That's some pick-up," she hollered.

"It gets me where I want to go."

"Yeah, it looks like it," she said. "At least you won't lose it in a crowd."

She down-throttled, shifted, and backed around to the water's edge. It had already receded enough that the belly of the Speckled Pony no longer dragged in the current. I climbed down, dragging the chain, kicked off my huaraches again, and waded in to attach it to the front frame. After I was in the pick-up, she slowly brought the chain taut and pulled me out, watching over her shoulder as she dragged her load up onto dry ground. I shifted to second, popped the clutch, and the engine sprang back to life.

The woman climbed down from the tractor and helped undo the chain.

"Thanks. Can I pay you anything, or...?"

"Of course not. I didn't mind at all. It was fun. I didn't mean to be giving you a bad time."

"You didn't. Well, you did, but I deserved it. I never even thought of the possibility of the water being there."

"Didn't you come through that big storm off south there? It was pouring like crazy over there this morning and bound to be run-off."

"It slipped off behind me. I guess I wasn't even watching it."

"How could you miss it?" She laughed again. "Lookin' at the scenery?"

"Yeah, I guess so." I felt like a fool.

"When they get a big cloud burst up on the table there, we always get some run-off down here. The pastures on the hills don't soak it up like the summer fallow does. They talk about putting in a bridge here, but it hardly ever happens or lasts for long when it does rain. And everyone knows about it when it happens, and they just take another road a while—well, most people know."

"Now I'm one of them."

"I hope so." Then there was a silence, and she cast her eyes away as if all this should quickly come to an end, as if the time should not be spent this way if the job were done.

"How far am I from Revere now?"

"You are a stranger."

"Well, I have a general idea. Give me a break." I started warming into the situation now, smiling, reacting before thinking too hard about it.

She pointed down the road past her house. "About a mile and a half down you'll come to a T with a paved road. Turn east. It goes all the way along this side of the Interstate. Four miles, then there's the overpass into town."

"Okay. Thanks again."

"I was glad to help."

"What's your name? I'm Calvin Parsons."

Now the air of embarrassment and hesitation seemed to shift sides, but she controlled it enough to meet my eyes and smile.

"Karen McCormick."

I wondered if I should have asked, but was relieved that it was a familiar name. "Related to the guy who drives a big fuel truck?"

"My husband," she said, surprised.

"He gave me a ride to my uncle's place when I first got out here. A couple of months ago."

"Oh, you're the one! He did mention that." And the lines of a delighted curiosity tightened around her eyes again.

"Yes. He was as much amused as you were. Now I owe you both something."

She blushed, looking away, something changing behind her eyes again. "No, really you don't. Well...."

"Yeah, well...."

It faded again into an odd silence. I turned back toward the pick-up, climbed in, and drove around her with a wave.

She stood by the tractor to wave with a slight smile—a look of relief to see me gone, I wondered, or am I still just stoned? What a fool I make of myself. "My reputation, Iago, the immortal part of me." Well, I thought, it will be country news with a splash, no doubt.

I found the road into town and idled the old pick-up across Highway 30 and down Revere's one paved street for this

first time since I had lived there as a boy seventeen years before. I
gave no thought to the mid-morning coffee drinkers in Mac's Cafe,
who all noticed the Speckled Pony purr by like a rusty neon sign
lighting up the drowsy morning with fresh speculation and jokes.
I glanced toward Mac's, but only to note its unfamiliarity. It hadn't
been there next to Newcastle's station when my family had lived in
Revere, when I had been in grade school. That time seemed like a
dream now.

   The old red brick post office on the corner across the
street had always been there, but now it looked abandoned. The
run-down house next to it had been old man Mason's place, a
cobbler's shop, but that early memory stood empty now, too, the
old, bald man with white hair growing out of his facial moles no
doubt long dead. But the bank, next corner, opposite side, had
been the newest building in town in 1958, and it still stood,
looking weathered into the fixed scene of the village's downtown.
Next to it was Pickner's, once part Woolworth's with cheap
department store goods, part grocery, butcher shop, and bakery.
Empty, too, now, and I sensed that family of old, penny-pinching
brothers and their wives gone completely now from the town.
They had always taken in too much of the town's money and spent
it other places to ever be liked. Their children all moved away as
soon as they had gotten out of school, I remembered from the
clannish gossip of a distant childhood. The store had died with
the economy, the population, and the last brother left to run it.

   Across from Pickner's now stood a new, metal pre-
fabricated building with grocery store window front and painted
sale item signs pasted up, open for business under a plastic sign
that read simply, "The Store" —a small town 7-11 mock-up.
Beside it was the old drug store where I had gone with each week's
allowance to buy comic books—red brick and boarded up, another
business that had died with the past. Across from it was the
Community Center with a bulletin board outside its door, tacked
full of notices—maybe some of the same ones from my own time
there, I thought.

   On down the street was Mercy's Hardware, a cornerstone
of the town's business life, still there. I remembered going to
grade school with Tommy Mercy, stocky and slow, redheaded and
freckled, with teeth and cheeks like a squirrel when he smiled and

with an older brother who always beat up on Tommy's friends. Across from Mercy's was the old fire station, doors closed down, but projecting an air of regular use. Beside it, the eternal auto body shop with rusted parts scattered about in the weeds of the empty lot next to it. My earliest memory was of thinking that old, dead cars were buried there in the shade of ancient cottonwoods with the rusty fenders and hub caps as their tombstones.

From there, on north, the street was lined for two blocks with frame houses and flower beds under shade trees, then the village park—a full square block and still well-kept and cool green shady in the summer light. Kids played around the swings and merry-go-round. The vacant lot across from it was the scene of my first football games. Beyond that, the Lutheran church, tennis courts, then the school house, the traditional, classic three-story square of brick and windows with the playground around it, conjuring another flood of memories.

Beyond the school were two more blocks of trees and older clapboard houses; rising behind them, the steel water tower bearing the town's faded name; then the edge of a cornfield and the sudden lift of tableland between the South and North Platte river valleys. This had been my first world, and a montage of images, scents, and nameless faces flooded my mind. At the end of town, I turned down the last crossing street and began a slow passage back and forth along the dirt streets, looking at houses and trees and churches, the small shops and weedy lots, newer apartment buildings and other scattered, small-time businesses marked by weathered signs on garage doors or the kind of junk piled around them. I worked my way back toward the highway, passing the big salvage yard—forever the town's eyesore, then the ballpark beside it, green and well-groomed and the town's symbol of civic pride and sports tradition. Out along the highway were the lumber yard, Newcastle's station, Cody's Bar & Grill, the Co-Op and its grain elevators across the tracks.

This had been my childhood territory, this town and the wild ground down to the river. Everything seemed smaller now, closer together, less surprising or awesome or curious. In my fading, marijuana high, the free association of memories and feelings seemed simpler and more pristine than the town I now found. It seemed more peaceful than the most recent years and

territory that I had traveled through. I thought again about how
the small river valley villages like Revere lined the little highway all
the way across the state. The only real difference was that this
one, Revere, had been my world.

Distracted by time and old images, I found myself back
where I had rolled across the tracks and into town. The scenic
tour hadn't taken long. I parked on Main Street and got out to
cross the street to Newcastle's station, summoning up a mental list
of things I needed at the farm. The door of Mac's Cafe flew open
and a heavyset man plodded aggressively toward me, suddenly
yelling, "Hey, you goddamn hippie!"

I froze in mid-stride in the middle of the street, feeling
knots in my stomach tighten, thinking, no, how can this still be
happening?

"What the hell you doin' cruisin' this town? Lookin' for
somethin' to steal? Lookin' for Woodstock? You're in the wrong
goddamn state, buddy." Behind this large redhead, another man
came out of Mac's and sauntered toward me in a ball cap and
service station blues, grinning at this harangue.

"You one of them communists, buddy?" the redhead
continued, almost up to me before a buck-toothed smiled flashed
on and off his freckled face. His jowls hung slightly and looked
vaguely familiar.

The man's laughing tenor voice behind him hollered,
"Give him hell, Mercy."

"I'll give him hell. —How the hell are you, you hairy
son of a bitch!" Tommy Mercy, sixteen years older and much
larger than the last time we'd played together, sporting a chip-
munk's grin, thrust out a red, plump hand . "Scared the shit outa
you, didn't I? It was McCormick's idea." He jabbed a thumb back
over his shoulder at the man coming up behind them, grinning.

"Hiya, stranger," said the man who had given me the ride
out to the farm, skinny and long in the body, making his bowed
legs look like short stumps though he stood over six feet. "At least
you recognized this ugly puss," he drawled, poking Mercy in the
ribs.

For a while then, in the middle of the street, it was easy
laughs and reunion, old times, the where-you-been's, the what-are-
you-doing-now's, with my saying again in so many vague words, a

traveler, a scholar, an urbanite. My grade-school pals had grown up in Revere, had gone off to college a while, or to the service, had gotten married somewhere in between, had returned home to make businesses and families of their own out of what they'd come from. Mercy ran his father's hardware store now. McCormick raised a few cattle on what was left of family ground and ran Newcastle's bulk fuel truck. I would have graduated from high school with them and become...what, I wondered as we talked.

"Hell, we saw you drive into town through the window there. Think anybody's gonna miss that ugly thing?" They moved over to inspect the Speckled Pony and talk about Karl's reputation for keeping ancient machinery in perfect running order.

They'd taken up the conversation as if I'd never left them in grade school, and neither one seemed to have much else to do but stand in the quiet street and catch up on someone long gone and back now. With no bulk orders to run today, Mike was in town waiting for some kind of tractor part. I didn't bring up how I'd just met his wife, who had pulled me from the gullywash. It was a slow time at Mercy's store, and his wife was there in the stockroom if anybody came in. A couple of pick-ups idled by us, headed down main street, and we all waved between words.

"So, see any changes in town?" Mercy asked.

"There are a few."

That brought on some construction history and the who's-moved-where's. I'd been right about Pickners. And the auto body shop. Old man Mason was dead, too. They talked other names at me as my aunt had. I recognized some, others meant nothing. I asked about John Van Anders. When my world was only Revere clear to the river, we had done all our exploring together, had hunted rabbit in the grove that still stood east of town, had seined bait minnows in the river for money. I had learned to bat left-handed in my first game of baseball because John batted that way. We had both made our first flying tackles on the first day of the second-grade game, Tackle-the-Guy-Who-Gets-It. We were going to see the whole world together in a pick-up camper—that had been the plan for life.

His confidential tone muffled in his soft jowls, Mercy said, "Buckwheat got the shit shot out of him in Nam, and he's a mean bastard about it too, let me tell you. You think I was givin' you a hard time a while ago. You remind him of that shit, and he's like to take your head off—especially if he's got a little beer in him, which is usually the case. He's a hell-raiser, that guy.

"He don't talk about it, but his own guys shot him up with M-16 tracers. He 'bout didn't make it out of that."

"Can't be too bad if he can raise hell," I offered.

"Oh, he can still tear up a bar pretty good if he feels like it," McCormick grinned. "Right after he got back from California, he turned the pool table over in Cody's one night cuz Vern Keller run the table for fifty bucks, but Bucky's gettin' mellower. Last week he only lifted it off the floor to sink all the balls in the corner pocket."

"Last year he beat the shit outa Joe Sanchez in the parking lot of the Holiday Inn in Ogallala," Mercy offered, and Joe's the best Mexican in the county with a knife. Bucky just pounded holy hell out of him, I think cuz Joe laughed at him. He thought Buckwheat was too drunk to stand up, but he ain't made that mistake lately. Of course, Buckwheat was all forgive and forget the next day. Even went up to apologize to Joe—in the hospital. No hard feelings, you know?"

McCormick interrupted the history, pointing across the tracks at a refrigerated van with "Meadow Gold" painted on the side, rolling into town. "Here comes Thompson. He ever get hold of you?"

The van stopped in the middle of the street, and the driver got out, grinning. Thompson was lanky and loose boned and swayed as he walked, his cap pushed to the back of his head and a mop of straw-like hair sweeping down across his forehead.

"Know this guy?" McCormick asked him, shrugging toward me.

"Not to look at him. But I heard you were around." We shook hands. "Well, they ask you yet?"

"About what?"

"About playin' ball. I called out at your place a couple times. Your aunt ever tell you? We gotta pick someone up since Buckwheat ain't playin' for a couple weeks. How 'bout it?" I shrugged. "Slow pitch. Sixty-foot bases. You still run a four-six forty?"

"That was a while ago. I might have a four-eight forty left in me."

"That'll do," Thompson laughed. "Second base and bat lead-off?"

"For as long as I've played. How'd you know all that?"

McCormick said, "Told you all the stats on you'd be out before I seen you again."

Thompson said, "Two Colorado state records for stolen bases, right? All-state senior year? Our moms were best friends, remember? They wrote letters for years. Did you really play ball in a Mexican league?"

"Oh, yeah. They play good town-team ball down there. Strictly baseball though."

"Ojeda on the Pirates came up to the pros from somewhere down there."

"Where's he get all this stuff?" I asked. The other two rolled their eyes. "I haven't played ball for a long time."

"That's okay. These guys ain't for shit anyway, and the line-up can use a change." Turning to the others, Thompson said, "We can bat Brownie behind him and drop Loxie down as second clean-up. What do you think?"

"There's someone in the store," Mercy begged off. "I ain't puttin' up with his broken record this morning. See you Sunday, Calvin. I'll tell dad to get out another uniform."

McCormick had retreated toward his own pick-up, too, saying he had to run down that missing part all of a sudden. Thompson ignored them and turned back to me. "Remember Tim Ramirez? He's playin' in left. Billie Chatman? We got him catchin'."

By the time I drove out of Revere, I had a brief history of the team, the twelve-team Ogallala softball league, an injury report on the Packard rivals, and a place in the next game's strategy—member of another ball team, in another country, another time.

———————————

Buckwheat solos:

"I can tell ya Thompson would talk stats at his own mother's funeral—NU, Lakers, NFL stats. Whatever you want—

or don't want. Drives you nuts with that shit. He could give you play-by-play of last year's post-season tournament. I don't even remember who we played or where we came in. I was just playin' the damn games. —But we weren't first, I can tell you that.

"But Thompson, he's movin' players in and out of the line-up like he's Tommy Lasorda, messin' with the battin' order, tellin' us where to hit the ball, moanin' 'bout Ramirez' slump or Chub Chatman chokin' in the seventh all the time, poppin' up with runners on. He wants you there two hours early or stayin' late to scout the next team we play, figurin', of course, that it's your whole life, too.

"It's part of why his old lady's such a fat rag. If she wants anything, it better be sittin' in the bleachers with screamin' kids for another hot night of softball. She's always bitchin' and moanin' to Sandy. Thompson won't take the girls to their dance lessons. Thompson won't fix the garage door. —She calls her own husband by his last name just like everybody else. He'd rather be readin' a sports page than lookin' at her face, or catchin' whatever NU game's on the radio instead of listening to her screech and the kids cryin'. Trouble is, they're all girls, all four, and Thompson hates girls' sports. Who can blame him? He's cursed.

"I couldn't stand it myself, I know. I help the poor cuss out. I say, 'Maggie,' —ol' 'naggy Maggie,' we call her, but not to her scowlin' face—I say, 'Maggie, we gotta have Thompson runnin' the show. The team falls apart if he don't do it.' And that's true, but there ain't one of us to truly admit it to him because the fact of it is such a damn pisser. Besides, you say anything to him, and he turns on that goddamn almanac brain of his, kicks the motor-mouth in gear, and that's all you hear.

"But ya know, he knows the game and he knows the players. Probably delivers milk to everyone's house in the whole goddamn league, and sneaks a look at shoe size and school annuals. Hell, you wouldn't find this milkman screwin' your wife. You'd find him checkin' your closet for illegal cleats. He knows who can do what with a bat or a glove and when to do what with the ball. He pays attention to the game and knows what's goin' on. Of course, that's all he knows, too.

"But that's more than you can say for the likes of that fat ass, Chatman. That guy ain't got a clue what's goin' on in any game. All he knows is gettin' to the plate and hittin' the long fly. A few go over the fence, usually when there's no pressure and you don't need the runs. He's best at long fly outs, and if he ever hits it on the ground, he barely runs it out. Like it's almost too much trouble and shame.

"Chatman wants to be the Babe, but about all he's got is the Babe's body. Shaped like a blimp standing on end, and that sloppy, saggin' walk of his, it's like he's too weary to carry that dough-boy body of his around all day. Makes you sick to watch it cuz he doesn't even know he's a lazy son of a bitch.

"Hell! If he'd ever just try to make a play at the plate some game. We'd all die of shock. It's like his whole attitude is whining, 'Oh,well,' —standin' in that little feminine hitch—'they're just gonna score anyway, so why bother tryin' to smother it in the dirt and make the tag?' He fuckin' probably deals insurance that way, too, and that's why nobody buys it from him but his old man and his old man's big-operator friends out east of town there. He lives on their farm policy commissions and stuffs his fat ass in that chair of his in his shady, air-conditioned office and sweats over that stack of Playboys he keeps in his bottom desk drawer.

"No shit! A while back, me and Smokey Johns—we were drunker 'n' shit—jimmied a window one night and tacked up about two years' worth of pin-ups all over his office with a staple gun. God, he was madder 'n' shit for weeks. He called in the sheriff to show him what vandals had done. Only beforehand, he dumped all the mags and never mentioned the pictures were his to start with.

"A fuckin' joke. He rides that Harley piece of shit, you know, in his black leathers. Shee-it! Wait till he starts tellin' you about the women he picks up at biker bars in Colorado. Revere's own Hell's Angel, who also sells Mutual of Omaha. God's gift to women, and to Mercy's softball team.

"Hell, you could almost overlook all that piddly shit if he'd just make one good play at the plate or hit it over the fence when he's supposed to. He's choked in more games than a dog does chewin' on chicken bones.

"It's the difference between him and Ramirez, who's an asshole in his own right, as everyone can tell you, but at least out in the field Timo makes the play for you. He'll gallop like a buffalo clear across left field to make a catch, and he ain't shaped that much different than Chub Chatman. Difference is, he's mostly muscled where Chatman is mostly fat. Timo has to work—when he ain't too fucked up. When he actually goes out and makes a living, he's Revere's beast of burden. If you want bales stacked, call Ramirez. If you want feed bags moved, call Ramirez. If you want salt block hauled, or trees trimmed, or ax-split wood, or if you need a good back up in a barroom fight, call Ramirez.

"Hell, call him if you just want him to take a short fly ball in left. He'll sure as hell try. He may be pretty wasted when he does, cuz Timo's usually wasted, or about to be, on somethin'—pot or Coors or too much sun or somethin'—but he's in the game to play, and he puts that ball out of the park as much Chatman does. Everybody knows it—except Chatman—and everybody hates it, too.

"And what else everybody hates is that smug son of a bitchin' look on that Manchued Mexican face of his, like shove it, assholes, I just beat your white little butts with another round tripper. What a fat-lipped smirk he has standin' there along first base line, watchin' it sail over the fence, then givin' the bat that Reggie Jackson flip as he trots off grinnin'.

"Nobody gets another team pissed off at us faster 'n' that guy. He'll ride opposing pitchers or a guy that makes an error, screamin' at 'em all game till they're throwin' at his head when he's runnin' bases. Then he comes up pushin' 'em around like, Hey! What'd I ever do to you?

"Ump makes a bad call, Ramirez is there screamin' at him, hoppin' around, throwin' his glove down and kickin' it, cussin' and threatening the guy's mother. Rest of the game, all close calls go the other way. If it's the other team that's robbed, Ramirez is laughin' at 'em. He'll take a cheap shot slide at a guy coverin' second, or run down a catcher dumb enough to be standing in the base path when Timo trucks his two hundred pounds over the plate. All in the heat of the game, of course. Trouble is, he is the heat of the game.

"Yeah, we love him a lot. Single-handed he's got teams so pissed off, they come from fifteen points down to beat our butts, and we have to live with that. He'll come off the field, cryin', 'I hit

it over. I made my catches. Whaddaya mean, I gave the game
away?'

"But hell, I don't care. I never minded playin' with Timo.
He does everything he can to win—even if it's the wrong thing,
and the game's always interesting with him in it, asshole or angel.

"But I'll tell ya who the real angel is, and that's ol' Brownie
playin' third. How old's that guy? Almost as old as Smokey Johns,
and a hell of a lot healthier cuz Smokey never stopped drinkin'
and chain smokin' a minute in his life. But there was a time ol'
Brownie could keep up with him and drink him under the table.
He was playin' third for Bunke's then, even before the rest of us
were all outa high school, this was. He'd be so drunk he couldn't
stand up out there on the field. The other team'd drive shot after
shot down third base line and knock him down with the ball and
get a hell of a laugh from the stands.

"He was teachin' special ed. in Ogallala but about to lose
his job cuz he'd call in sick with the D.T.'s all the time. His wife
left him for Arizona. His father committed suicide. He lost his
license for DWI. His own dog abandoned him. He was the pits,
and at thirty or so the guy was an absolute wreck and due to be
dead any day. You coulda bet an office pool on it.

"Then he found God or somethin'. Old Brownie and Job.
That's what McCormick claims anyway, though Brownie never laid
any Christian shit on me, thank God. He turned it around anyway.
He worked a time for Mercy's old man in the store, and then he
started playin' ball for him, too. No one else would have let him.
Well, he ain't touched a drop since '68. Lost twenty-five pounds,
lost all his hair, grew a beard, got a teachin' job again, clear in
Wyoming, and now he comes back summers just to play ball—
seven or eight years he's been doin' that. It's nuts, drivin' thousands of miles to play ball, but he don't want to play nowheres
else. And that guy can slap a line drive down the line eight outa
ten times he comes to the plate—even when every third baseman
in the league knows it's comin'. And his own glove...I give four to
one you'll turn more double plays with Brownie at third than you
will with Chatman's little brother at shortstop. The guy's solid and
fundamental to hell and back. No situation's gonna rattle Brownie.
You'll get your throw to the base.

"With Little Chatman you never know. Natural athlete,

but no one ever showed him the fundamentals. And you can bet
he'd never get 'em from his fat-assed brother either. He's okay as
long as it doesn't matter, but he muffs one and the skinny little fart
is down on himself right away. Like he'll just never be good
enough to play for the great Mercy's Hardware of Revere, with all
the superstud, high-school legends he grew up worshippin'—
Mercy's Hard-ons. Like it fuckin' even matters at all. He even
thinks brother Billie's a star, for God's sake.

"Two years outa high school, you'd think the kid would
grow up. 'Course, his brother never did. It runs in the family. I
don't think Jeff's ever been out of the county—still on the farm
with the old man, doin' all the shit jobs Billie-boy was always too
fat-ass lazy to do. So he does everything he's supposed to, and his
dream comes true every Wednesday and Sunday, playin' shortstop
for Mercy's. And he kicks his glove and hangs his lip low enough
to step on and feels like hell when he blows a grounder, thinkin'
Thompson's gonna bench him for life, and you gotta practically
beg him to handle another grounder all night. He whines that he'll
never play ball like his heroes.

"Jesus! I kick him in the ass when he's standin' in the
dugout cuz it's just what he needs. Sometimes it'll stun some sense
into him. It don't matter that old Smokey is a goddamn drunk that
ain't got three good teeth left in his head and can't say a fuckin'
sentence without the fuckin' word fuck in it. It don't matter
Tumblin' Tommy can't stay on his feet long enough in right field
to ever make a catch look easy, or that's he's got six kids to feed
and his wife's probably humpin' the postman again just like in high
school. It don't matter I'm a fuckin' cripple, and Timo's a criminal,
and Little Chatman's own brother's a lazy asshole.

"We all get out on the field, and Mercy falls on his face for
a catch, and maybe Ramirez runs into a light pole for a two-out
foul with the bases loaded, or you and Brownie turn a tough
double, or me and Ramirez and Chub Chatman put three shots in
a row over the fence. It's great! The kid's in fuckin' heaven, I tell
you. Hell, maybe we all are. Our lives may be full of shit and
nothin', but we win one lookin' pretty goddamn good out there,
and what else is there, man, but friggin' Sunday softball?

"I got to agree with the kid. We're all for a while just shit-
grinnin', heaven-bound heroes."

Calvin's journal notes/summer, '75:

Despite Aunt Martha's sulking silence of disapproval, I drove the Speckled Pony down into Revere again last night to play a game of softball. The second one in a week, and for Martha, young men doing such things borders on the frivolous—which may be why she "forgot" to tell me about Thompson's telephone messages way before the season ever started. As I drove out, she was kneeling in the twilit yard, digging dandelions, and she looked up with a sad resignation that the young were abandoning the aging and their labors. I waved. She wiped her sweating brow and bent back to her never-ending chore.

Feeling the intended guilt, I cruised across the tableland for the river valley to go play games—with guys who were boys just learning baseball when I was, sliding into mud-puddle bases and learning to get the glove on line-drive grounders with sandlot bad hops. These are guys I know now only by what they were like learning the game as boys, not by what they've become. They still call Tom Mercy "Tumblin' Tommy," and he still can't stay on his feet. Timo Ramirez still won't shag fouls and still throws his glove at grounders that roll by him. Chub Chatman is still Chub Chatman, or Billie-boy, pouting like a spoiled baby.

Most of the others I only vaguely remember, or don't recall at all. I don't yet know much about what they do for a living or how they live. But just like at St. Luke's, everyone seems to know who I am. And they know me, I suppose, as whatever I was back then. I could play infield, I know, even at eight and nine years old. I got picked early when sides were chosen up. Now I get to play again, almost twenty years later, on the assumption that I can still play. What I am now, or have been since, doesn't matter to any of them—except to one.

I drove in last night and finally got to meet John Van Anders—Buckwheat, the weed—for the first time since being back in this territory. Totally different reaction to me than the others, and I knew him once the best. We were best friends and blood brothers.

I drove in and sat on the bench to put on my shoes. Most of the others were already warming up or out catching fly balls.

Thompson was sitting there, making out the line-up. Van Anders was sitting there, too, sucking on a Budweiser, hunched over on his elbows propped on one knee, watching Ramirez hit flies.

When I sat down, Thompson said to him, "Remember this guy? The only other left-handed hitter in third grade."

He looked over at me with a bloodshot, mean-drunk scowl. "Fuck no. Looks like a fuckin' hippie to me."

Tom Mercy's greeting last week had been a joke. This one wasn't. Thompson yuk-yuked anyway, sounding like a contented hen. Van Anders went back to watching the others catch flies. I warmed up, throwing with Little Chatman, who kept swinging around as he threw to glance Van Anders' way as if something were going to happen.

Finally, it did.

Everyone came in off the field. Ramirez went out to home plate with the umps to flip for home team advantage. Others were swinging bats and joking around, getting ready. I was out on the grass, getting ready to lead off, and McCormick was on the bench already ribbing Mercy, batting second, about having maybe one hit all year, saying something like, "They send Parsons up from the Mexican minors, and he goes three for three in his first game. That's your career total hits, ain't it, Tommy? I hear Thompson wants to send you down to the farm club in Toledo in exchange for a dwarf who knows how to bunt."

Smokey Johns screams out in his rocky voice, "They teach you how to catch fuckin' fly balls without getting grass stains on your fuckin' face down there, too." Everybody had a laugh on Mercy.

"Who's gonna buy the goddamn beer if I go down. Not any of you cheap assholes," Mercy continued. —Just a lot of friendly banter. Someone asked me then about old hippies knowing how to bat.

"It's Zen meditation," I said, "I do mantras. I close my eyes and start moaning, 'Om'." Just being silly—one of the guys, that's me.

I get some laughs. Johns yells down the bench, "That right, Buckwheat? You know that Asian shit. That Zen shit you learned?"

Van Anders was dragging right past me on the way to the

beer cooler again. He said, "Fuck Zen. This guy don't know shit."
Then he suddenly wheeled around on me and screamed something
in my face. Some kind of question. It had to be Vietnamese. I
just stood there like a fool, looking at his red face and his drunk-
dulled eyes not even seeing me. He screamed it again and put a
short jab of a finger into my chest. It shocked the hell out of me,
and I dropped the bat and backed up a step. He yelled something
else and pushed me down on my ass.

It was then all instantaneous—adrenaline fear. He lurched
another step toward me in his gimp, but before he got close, I was
up. Two steps, and I shoved him two-handed in the chest, yelling,
"Fuck you!" and that sent him over on his own ass—no small feat.
The guy is over six feet, two hundred pounds, and built like a brick
wall. But he was drunk and surprised. I spit out, "Whatever your
fucking problem is, I didn't make it, man. Leave me alone."

It all brought everybody else up on their feet and gathering around, getting ready to grab Van Anders and trying to calm
him down, getting between us. Mine was just a fear response. I
stood there panting, ready to run. I wasn't going to tangle with
Buckwheat, even if he were drunk.

I thought he'd come raging up at me, and so did everyone
else, I think. But he just sat there on the grass, shaking his head
as if he was trying to clear his vision, almost like I'd stunned him
with a knockout punch. It all happened in about ten seconds.

Everyone kind of rushed in around us and picked him up,
making half-funny jokes, half pulling and carrying him toward the
beer cooler in the back of Mercy's pick-up behind the bench.
Thompson and Lox and a couple others whisked me off toward
home plate, saying, "Jesus! He gets crazy sometimes." "Don't let
it bother you. He's just drunk," and things like that, apologizing
and trying to disarm the situation. "He's still fucked up from that
accident." "You okay? You okay?" Oh yeah, just fine. The other
team was out on the field, staring over at us like, what the hell is
going on with these guys?

I said, "Yeah, I'm okay," but I got up and fouled the first
pitch up right to the catcher. The game was on. They had Van
Anders cooled down and sitting in the back of Mercy's pick-up. I
sat down the bench as far away as possible. Three up and we were
three down. No more jokes. We headed out to the field.

Ramirez was pitching, and some kid was in his place in left field because Van Anders hasn't been playing since an accident a couple weeks ago at his gas station. First pitch, I got the first ground ball at second, an easy roller, and I muffed it. Thompson called time right away and came in from center. We stood around second base a bit and discussed it while I dusted off and pounded in the pocket of my glove. They tried to excuse Van Anders some more, but it was just my own psyche-out. I thought, I'm not going to let that bastard get to me.

Next batter came up and lined a hard one-hopper to Brownie at third. I can still make the turn at second without thinking, and we got the double play. That helped to change the flow. They got a single, then a force out at second. We got up again, and Ramirez drove a homer to left on a three-and-oh pitch and smirked around the bases while we all lined up along third base line to touch hands. Chatman got up then and pounded a liner over the rover for a double—an inside-the-park homer for just about any other runner. The rally was on then, and we got six runs in, batting around.

That got everyone focused on the game—even Van Anders, if he could focus on anything. He hollered some, but not at me, and he was gone before the game ended. Thompson said later that his wife had come around and hauled him home.

We played well the whole game—everyone felt the need to, I think. Good defense. We turned another double play. McCormick made a couple of catches against the fence in left-center, and Mercy even made a catch without "tumblin'." Everyone seemed to know where the ball should go, given the score, the runners, the number of outs. There was pleasant hint that this team really knows how to play ball. We got them—an Ogallala team—twelve to two in five innings.

I was glad Van Anders wasn't around wanting to continue some drunken, imagined dispute after the game, and the rest of the evening was cool, summer pleasant and low-key. Most of the team, half of them toting their families, went out to McCormick's, south of town, and set up a beer-drinking camp in the yard in front of his trailer. His wife, Thompson's, Mercy's, and others, laid out a picnic of cheeses and chips and venison sausage, watermelon and pies. A feast, and all of it basically provided by

Thaddeus and Ardith Mercy, Tumblin' Tommy's folks, who own the hardware store and have sponsored the town team ever since their first son had played, and now, clear through number three son, Tommy.

"One of the penalties for being on this team," Thompson said, leaning back in a lawn chair, full-bellied, his hat pushed back, a beer in his hand, "you have to eat, drink, and have a good time. Thadd's the best sponsor in the league, and we're the envy of every team. It's one reason they like to beat us so much. Of course, we enjoy it more if we win—which ain't been a helluva lot. But with you on second now...." He just grinned and drank.

We all sat around drinking and bullshitting softball and Kansas City Royals. Thadd Mercy came around to slap us on the backs and make jokes about Tommy's standing catch. There was talk about jobs and gossip about people I still don't know except by name. They asked me how I liked the farming and about what I'd been doing, and I gave the basic answers. We talked about how bizarre Van Anders had acted and how he and I had been best friends and how the war and his wounds had changed him. They still call him Buckwheat, the nickname I gave him in third grade, over sixteen years ago. I made it up to mean he was a weed in every other team's field, a nuisance, a pain. Now maybe it means in his own field, too. Too bad. They all assured me that he wouldn't even remember what happened.

McCormick tossed in the humor—if you can call it that. "Hell, you got nothin' to worry about. When Joe Sanchez tried to knife him, ol' Buckwheat kicked holy shit outa the guy, and then apologized to him the next day—when he visited the Mex in the hospital. Bucky promised he wouldn't even file charges."

A lot of stories and laughing and beer in the summer evening. Mostly Thompson's softball stories and McCormick's jokes and Smokey Johns' gravel-voiced cussing. Kids ran all over in the dark, playing hide and seek, screaming and laughing in the outer yard. The women sat mostly off to themselves with babies on their laps or floated around, putting beer and food in their husbands' faces. Pleasant company on a mid-summer night. Beyond the yardlight you could look up into countless, cool stars.

I'd driven out to McCormick's feeling somewhat of an intruder, but I was made as comfortable as if I'd played infield there forever. After four or five beers I could even ease back, feeling like part of the background, feeling governed only by the history and politics I had to have there—just like in Mexico: that I played second base, and I played it well. What else matters? Part of the hiding, the disguise—draft-dodging terrorist hippies can't play ball, but I can, here for Mercy's Hardware.

Another beer, and I had to find the bathroom. On the way back out of the trailer, I ran into Karen McCormick in her kitchen, slicing pie and watermelon. Her back was to me at first, her long, blond hair loose and thick down to the middle of her back, square shoulders in a man's small blue work shirt tucked into her jeans, narrow hips, nice ass, lean legs. She heard me and glanced over her shoulder, smiling, and turned around to face me. My first thought was that I shouldn't have too many beers around her. My first urge was to touch, and I felt as if she could see it in my eyes.

I said, "What are you doing?" and walked over close.

"Cutting pie. Want some? There's plenty. Maggie Thompson and Sue Mercy brought them. They're still warm." She fluttered around after paper plates and plastic forks like a nervous bird trapped uneasy in the corner of her cage.

Too close? That much beer and I wasn't judging distance too well, but only floating free, maybe a little too easily . I offered to help carry things out.

"You'd do that?" She grinned at me as if I'd suggested a practical joke.

"Oh, is that ladies' work?"

"Well, you wouldn't expect those guys out there to offer, would you? They'd starve before they thought of coming in here to get it themselves."

There was a little more silly banter, but I wanted to keep her talking, and she didn't seem to mind. Too pleasant. She wouldn't look too long at my eyes though. I felt drunk and over-bearing.

I said, "You must not have mentioned to Mike that you pulled me out of the gullywash."

She looked at me then as if she kept all kinds of pleasant secrets behind that moist blue of her eyes. She cast them off somewhere, still smiling. Nice eyes, all kinds of expression there.

She said, "You know, he come home for lunch that day and mentioned he'd seen you in town. And that he put Tommy up to scaring you in the street. But he didn't mention that you'd stopped for a visit here. I thought maybe you didn't want it brought up." She was enjoying where she had me. So was I. I was thinking, does McCormick know his wife is this beautiful? Does she know it? I remembered from that foolishness with the pick-up, but maybe I'd been too embarrassed to really look closely. I was staring plenty last night.

I said, "It just slipped my mind to tell the whole town what a fool I am."

She was still grinning, glancing at me, dishing out pie, smelling like the apples and cinnamon. "Oh, you weren't such a fool. Just not paying attention and thinking of other things than you should have, maybe."

"That's it. I'm always thinking things I shouldn't." I said it before I thought it. It meant right then and there, too, and I think she could have finished the thought for me. There was an obvious silence. It was time to get out before I made a total idiot of myself. I said, "Well, I better leave you to woman's work. Just to be fair, I'll try not to make you do any more tractor work. You should leave that to men—if you can find one."

"I'll try," she said.

I went out the door just as Thompson's wife, Maggie, was coming in. It's strictly one-at-a-time when she goes over a threshold.

More beer and talk. The women came around with pie. Karen McCormick handed me a plate and said, "Now pay attention and don't spill it."

While we ate and drank and hung around in the night, I watched her across the yard, trying not to stare, just glances now and then. Sometimes she'd see me seeing her.

I started thinking, man, you better go while you still can find your way home. You're letting the crazies build up. So I wound the Speckled Pony down the gravel roads through the peaceful night on a pleasant alcoholic high, thinking about a married woman and about how messed up and out of their lives— all their lives—I really am.

Today, I worked off a hangover, paying for the night's

sins, rebuilding a corral gate. Aunt Martha looked it over in the evening and was almost pleased with the work. Even told me I'd sleep well tonight for it—as if that would be a change.

Buckwheat solos:

"No, hell no, they ain't no kind of uncommon couple. They're like all the rest of us—work your ass off at your job so you make enough bucks to take care of the kids. Kids, man! McCormick's got three. Everybody's got kids. That's cuz that's what we were doin' in high school. Now they got dope and religion. Back then it was still just beer and screwin' for us. "If you were a hot-shot athlete, you could get the best lookin' ladies. The year we were seniors and went to state play-offs, we all did okay. We were into bein' fuckin' jocks and bein' cool. I was makin' love to the finest girl in school—ya gotta admit Sandy still looks fine when she wants to. And back then I was gettin' it on with another chick in Ogallala even and all kinds of irons in the fire. Thinkin' myself one big fuckin' deal, man, and not knowin' nothin' 'bout the real world and that goddamn war.

"McCormick did okay. And Miller and Mercy, too. Even Ramirez. McCormick's cousin or someone like that introduced him to Karen at a game in Hyannis. Now she's a beauty, no doubt, but man, she's from that cattle country, up around Whitman. Ya ever been down there yet? It's way out there on the prairie where completely nothin's happenin'. What they got to do out there but screw? And even that pastime was a while gettin' there. She was a shy lady, and he was horny as hell, wantin' to get into her pants so much he was never any fun after that, goin' out, drivin' country roads, drinkin' and shit. All he'd be moanin' about is how beautiful she is and if he doesn't snatch her up, someone else will right away. And finally the first time he does, they're pregnant sure as shit. That fixed that scene.

Hell, Mercy got his wife pregnant before they were married. So were Menningers, and two girls in our class by guys from somewheres else. They all have a thousand kids now, too.

McCormick joined the Air Force and got stationed at

Lowery in Cheyenne most of his time. Spent his years as a partyin' copter mechanic, gettin' drunk on weekends with his buddies. Karen was havin' another kid, lived on the base and took care of 'em. That's what they all do. They're fine beauties for a couple years, then they're worn-out mothers. Hell, my Sandy was a worn out mother in no time, and not likin' it one bit, livin' with my folks and never goin' nowhere, just tendin' bawlin' babes. We were fightin' all the damn time. By the time I went to boot camp, I was already a combat veteran.

"Mercy, and McCormick, and some of the others, I suppose they had their own shit, too. The women were livin' their own lives. They got these babies around all the time, see. That's what they are—mothers and cleaners and cookers and sewers and washerwomen. Farm workers. They ain't school kids no more, and most of them wish to hell they still were, or they won't think a thing about it, just go on and on bein' a wife and mother like their own mothers.

"Some of 'em love it! They're made for it. That's what they are. Life's nothin' but a flow. They turn into their own mothers and glad of it, and they don't think a thing about it. For some it ain't so easy. There's some ladies so beautiful they're dangerous. Everybody could fall in love with 'em in a look and one encouraging word.

"Beauties have to know and say a sweet hello to everyone or they're snobs and bitches. Beauties can't be talkin' too long in private with a guy or she's probably screwin' him. A beauty's got not to make any social blunder or else she's a bitch. And if she gets down with child, Lord beware! She's a shamed wench sufferin' hell for those powerful passions everyone suspected were there all along.

"Beauties got to be careful. That's why they're always married early out here or a downright bitch. Once they adopt the accepted roles of wife and mother, then all is forgotten. Meanwhile, all the regular dog-face girls are goin' out with lots of guys, havin' regular good times with everybody, gettin' drunk, partyin', and finally findin' someone themselves as ready—or not ready—as they get, and they get pregnant and marry and have their babies, too, and it's just, 'Oh well, it happens to everybody.' That's their life out here. Then all of 'em get real serious and moral, become busy women, devout mothers. They don't party or get carried away. They sit in separate rooms to themselves and talk baby shit and baby puke and baby words and crap while we drink beer and generally fuck off.

"Yeah, well, life goes on. So we're sittin' here in Revere, and it's how many years? Seven, eight? And we got our jobs and we've got our houses, and the kids are gettin' in school and growin' up, and we're buyin' cars and boats and drinkin' beer after softball games and just hangin' out bullshittin'. Like this! Only not all stoned out and starin' off into the valley like this here. All that damn traffic, all those lights, goin' and goin' and goin'. And down in Revere they're not thinkin', 'Hey man!, we're these families doin' this and that, and just buzzin' through the motions.' No, they're buzzin' through the motions all right, but they're not thinkin' anything 'bout what they are. What difference does it make anyway? If things are flowin' fairly smooth, let 'em go and damn it, get on with the next ball game. Then wash it all down with another beer."

Calvin Parson's lyrics/

Fifteen years later I stood watching those babies play ball. Same field, learning the same game, and becoming teammates in the process. I came wondering if I'd see my own features, and their fathers', in the look and style of their play. Right away I recognized Van Anders' son on the mound—his father's build and cliff-like jaw, the black wing of hair falling from the cap down over a dark eye. In the pre-game warm-up, I recognize no one else and know I'm not interested in the actual game. It would be their version of play, personal and private, just like ours was. And what I'm seeing is Buckwheat on the mound so many years ago, before that first game following his attack on me.

I had driven in late, watching the thunderheads boiling up on the western horizon and the blue deepening beneath them, hoping that the game would be rained out. I wanted to avoid any kind of confrontation, any kind of intense, personal involvement. It was why I'd come out to the farm in the first place, but I was falling into such a situation again.

Besides unfinished business with Buckwheat, there was the rivalry that would be rekindled in the game. That had been the major topic of conversation over beer after the previous Sunday's win—the game with Rolf's Bar from Packard, a town downriver thirty miles or so. Mercy's Hardware and Rolf's Bar had always played their most serious ball, no matter the sport, against one another. Rolf's had dominated the league along the South Platte for years. Mercy's was usually a third or fourth-place team, but had always given Rolf's the toughest games of the year, had played the spoiler and upset Packard's high self-esteem more often than any other team. And no player to grow up in Revere ever conceded that Packard teams could play better ball. Packard players were of the exact opposite opinion.

This mid-week, mid-season game didn't have to mean that much to either team, in regard to the league standings, but both teams hated to be beaten by the other. Perhaps half of both teams had played against one another since they could pick up a bat. Even I had been aware of "that other town" when I had been a boy growing up in Revere, Packard deserving of spite and disgust for some vague reason of history and honor. These town teams and their high-school versions had tangled for innumerable seasons, had competed for many trophies, and had also been in more black and blue disagreements in the heat of a game's closing moments than any one could clearly remember—except perhaps Thompson. The breaks of the game and the umpire's calls of a thousand games were tempered in the coals of personal, particular games.

Through the seasons, the moods and make-up of both town teams fluctuated like the weather, with players, attitude, and talent shifting to younger brothers and sons and the occasional new kid in town. Perhaps Packard had generally dominated play. At least, that was the attitude of Rolf's Bar, and in tough games they didn't stand for any change in the league's pecking order. They won the Ogallala League championship and the post-season tournament more than their share of the time. They liked to pretend it was easy to win, but Mercy's usually made them earn it, and usually with hard feelings all around, no matter what way the game went.

It was a full-blown rivalry, and nothing much would change until the line-ups changed somewhat. Team attitude altered only slightly with the talent and personality already on both teams. Thompson believed the attitude would begin to change that night with me in the line-up and because Buckwheat would be playing again for the first time since his accident.

The bright ring of lights around the ballpark already glowed above the trees of the town like a season's ornaments when I drove in across the river and pulled into the crowded line of cars parked down third base line. Far more spectators than usual. The field was already full of players warming up, shagging flies, and throwing.

Thompson was sitting on the bench working out the line-up when I sat down to put on my shoes, but he didn't look up. There were some greetings as I warmed up, but the level of stern quiet was noticeable when the team gathered at the bench. Rolf's had already won the coin flip for home team and had taken the field.

Thompson, the way he started off every game, said, "Listen up now," and read off the line-up, ending with a game plan pep talk. "We're set up to hit and run tonight, so damn it, hit and run. That doesn't mean try to blast every damn ball over the fence. Make them throw the ball around on us tonight and make them error, and when they're up to bat, let's not us be throwin' the goddamn thing all over the field chasin' base runners. Look 'em back to the base and back up the throws. Get off your fat ass behind the plate, Chatman, and catch the goddamn ball when they throw it to you. Mercy, stay on your feet for one goddamn, measly game. Good throws, guys. Calvin, start us off, man. Sock the shit outa the ball."

Rolf, himself, for years pitching to Mercy's Hardware, didn't recognize this lead-off batter—just some character in a short pony tail and full, clipped beard, compact and lean and with a jock's walk and a casual attitude settling in on the left side of the plate. He pitched me a challenge first, a good arch, right over the middle of the plate for a called strike. Then he pitched me careful—a couple balls deep and outside. One on the outside edge then, barely a strike. With the two-two count, Rolf tossed a high floater meant to die on the front, outside edge of the plate where the batter would have to stretch away power to hit it at all. But the pitch was a little strong, outside but deeper than he had wanted, and I slapped a slow grounder toward third.

The game's first play and the sense of my speed shocked the third baseman into fumbling the ball from glove to throwing hand after a slow charge for the grounder. His throw was a stinging slap, but three steps too late. Waiting on the next batter, the whole Packard team shifted stance and readjusted to Mercy's: new lead off hitter with a pair of fast wheels. Next up, a designated hitter—new twist for Mercy's, and not a power hitter, but old Smokey, Revere's one city laborer for decades already and a player longer than that, still running down outfield flies on stork's legs and still in the habit of punching singles to the opposite field or down the line to left. Rolf's Bar made their adjustments.

The first pitch again came down the middle for a called strike. The second was low and outside, and Smokey golfed it over the second baseman to shallow right. I rounded second without looking back and was into third, standing up before the throw came in from the outfield. Runners at the corners, no outs. That brought the Revere bench to its feet. A few car horns started to sound off. "Start on 'em early. Let's go! Here we go!"

Buckwheat Van Anders gimped over and erected himself in the batter's box with a stance and a sneer that Rolf, and everyone else, was familiar with. The blazing eyes said, "Put the first pitch down the middle, you bastard. I dare you." Rolf did, and Buckwheat nailed it to center, a low liner, and rambled to first. One run over, Smokey to third, runners still at the corners and no outs, and that got the hometown fans in the game early. More horns, some catcalls now, a few beers drained quickly and others opened.

The clean-up hitter. With just enough beer in his belly, a run in and runners on, Ramirez came to the plate under his favorite conditions. He watched a couple of balls with his smirk, called time out just as Rolf was ready to deliver the next pitch, and knocked imaginary dirt out of his cleats; settled back in. He blasted a three-one pitch to deep left and slammed the plate with the bat when he saw that it would be caught against the fence. Smokey scored on the tag, but Buckwheat was too lame to even think about trying for second. Chatman came up, and more to go one up on Ramirez than to keep the rally going, he powered the third pitch over the left field fence and chugged around the bases, slapping teammate's hands all the way down the base line to home.

Mercy's four-zip, but Tommy and Thompson both flew out to the rover, and the Packard team came up. Buckwheat checked his defense from the pitcher's rubber and delivered the first pitch. Their lead-off lined a shot at Brownie, chest high, and Brownie stabbed it. The second batter grounded one between first and second that should have been a hit, but I dove full extension to my left, short hopped it, came up to my knees, and made the throw. The crowd around the field sounded off, and Mercy's turned team spirit up another notch, putting early momentum on our side. The next batter put a clean single into short left, but their clean-up hitter bounced one right back to Buckwheat, who held it and made the batter run clear to the base before throwing him out. Mercy's came off the field full of fire.

Brownie lined his automatic single down third, and Little Chatman moved him to second on a single over the shortstop that fell in front of the rover. McCormick flied to center to move the runners. One out, runners at second and third. Then Jimmie Lox swung from the left side of the plate and flied out against the right field fence. Brownie scored, and Little Chatman moved to third.

Lead-off up again with the home-town bench wired and fired and heaping inspired taunts on the Packard team. Thompson yelled in my ear over the din, "Single 'em to death, man. They hate that. Let's go, let's go!" I remembered the first pitch Rolf had challenged me with and hoped to see it again. Rolf delivered it, and I stroked it up the middle. Another run, horns and voices going off, and the game was quickly slipping from Packard's control—you could tell, McCormick had predicted, when Rolf's starts stuttering, yelling at his infielders.

But Smokey grounded out to end the inning then, and Packard stiffened for the next two innings and scored two in their bottom of the fourth, threatening to blow the game open. Bases loaded, one out, clean-up hitter to the plate.

Buckwheat let him settle in the box, then called time out, turned directly toward me, and walked over. I felt my stomach tighten with expectation but kept my eyes on Buckwheat's. Buck said, "I'm gonna make him come your way. You gonna handle it?"

"I'll handle it. I'll crowd the bag and move on the pitch. What if he comes back to you?"

"You got the bag for the double."

"Might take me too long to get there if I'm moving. Hit me where I stand, and I'll get the tag and the throw."

Buckwheat went back to the rubber and dropped in three consecutive high floaters on the outside front of the plate. The batter punched the third one right back to Buckwheat. He made the throw to me in the baseline, and I made the tag, then the throw to first to kill the inning. That pumped the crowd up again, and someone set off the town siren.

Too early to celebrate yet, I was thinking, coming in off the field. Three innings to go. But there was a collective groaning and wild cursing going on all around.

"Not now," Thompson was howling, "Not a goddamn fire now," throwing his hands in the air with exasperation. "We got their asses in a sling, and there's a goddamn fire! I don't believe it." He headed toward the other bench with his head hung.

The Chatmans were first off, spitting gravel with their pick-ups as they left the ballpark, carrying three or four others in the back, heading for the fire station. The bench cleared around me. The concession stand behind the backstop began to close down, and other cars that had pulled in to see the game began to back out and head home. Ramirez sat down on the bench, popped the top to a Coors Light, and guzzled it.

"Hey man, might as well have a beer. Damn!, but we were beatin' their butts good. I like that." I couldn't tell if he meant the beer or the winning.

Buckwheat came back to the bench from his pick-up with a can of beer, too, and sat down. The three of us watched the angry pantomime at home plate—Thompson and Rolf throwing gestures and exasperation at each other while the umpire looked on from a step back.

Buckwheat said, "Like old hens scratchin' over a piece of fish gut. We beat their fuckin' asses, and they know it. Only they ain't gonna let us get away with just four innings."

Thompson came back to us, kicking dust, slapping his cap against his thigh. "Assholes!"

"Told ya."

"They're gonna make us finish the last three innings when we go to Packard to play." He shook his head at the beer Ramirez held up to him. "Naw, I better go and see where the trucks went and man the radio." Buckwheat took the beer from Ramirez and tipped it back.

Rolf's team was picking up their gear and pulling out of the park, laughing and relieved, and by the end of the second beer the still-lighted field was almost deserted. When Ramirez brought three more cold ones from his pick-up, I asked, "You guys aren't firemen?"

"I'm a fuckin' cripple, man. I ain't gonna go hoppin' 'round some fuckin' fire. They come and pull me outa them, I don't go walkin' into 'em."

I shut up, not sure what talk would lead up to with this guy. Buckwheat went on, "And Ramirez is a frickin' Mex. We ain't gonna let a frickin' Mex handle our city equipment—even if he wanted to. He might take it out and water his pot farm and then sell the truck in El Paso, ain't that right, Timo?"

"You're the one with the pot farm, amigo. Fuck an A."

"We're the fuckin' town degenerates, man," Buckwheat continued between gulps of beer. "Us and old Boar over there, the town's fuckin' fat-ass wino. Nobody's gonna trust us with a hose. We're certified psychos. —Ain't that right, Boar!" he yelled out across the field to the guy in over-alls rummaging through debris in the other dugout. A huge belly of a man bobbed up, looked over at us, and started shuffling our way. "Oh, shit! I blew it. Here he comes."

Ramirez said, "Shit, man," in the slight Mexican lilt he gave the language, "look what you done. He'll come hang around till all the goddamn beer is gone. I didn't buy tonight so the fuckin' Boar could get drunk."

"Then you better take the hell off with it, man. Hey, wait! Leave us two more."

Ramirez tossed us two more Coors and scrambled into his pick-up and drove off before the Boar reached the bench. Buckwheat looked at me, saying, "Yeah, when the fire whistle blows here, all the good citizens head off to save the fuckin' world. Only degenerates with no civic pride and duty are left." He took a long draw on his beer. "I notice you're still here."

"I've been called worse," I said.

"Yeah, I'll bet." Then loud enough for the man approaching to hear, Buckwheat said, "Us degenerates guard the town. We patrol it, ain't that right, Boar? Ol' fuckin' Boar here, he's our vigilante. Ain't you, Boar? He's got a whole goddamn arsenal in his pick-up, ain't you Boar? He don't let no shit go down in this town. He's Deputy Crighter's right-hand man. What you doin' over there in the dugout, Boar, lookin' for beers they might not of finished?"

The grizzled old man he addressed was wider and rounder even than Chub Chatman and a good head shorter. He wore railroad boots, and his grease-marked Oshkosh over-alls might have doubled as a hot air balloon. The tails of a flannel shirt hung out, the sleeves and neck buttoned though it was July. His ball cap read, "Caterpillar." His bulldog cheeks had three-day whiskers, and one of his eyes was askew and focused off into space somewhere so you couldn't tell if he were looking at you when he spoke. He grinned yellow teeth at Buckwheat.

"Aluminum, Johnny." The Boar held out the plastic trash bag in his hand.

"Bet you drain 'em down your throat, you old fart."

"Oh, no," as if it were a serious accusation. "I don't do that sorta stuff."

"Not you, man. You don't suck nothin'. Them cans, that good money? Buys you some of that good Kentucky shit, huh? I bet you got some right now, tucked somewhere in that tent you're wearin', ain't you, Boar? Yeah, yeah, I can see it in your face, Boar. You can't fool the old Buckwheat, you know that. Ol' me an' Boar, we're regular drinkin' buddies, ain't we? There you go!"

The Boar had fished a pint bottle, still in its brown bag, from a hip pocket, his yellow grin wider. He handed it over. "That's my man!" Buckwheat wiped off the bottle mouth with a flourish and said, "To you and me, Boar. We're two of a kind." He took a long swig and passed it to me. "Wipe off the bottle real good. Ol Boar's got a mouth like the plague." I took an oily, burning swallow and handed it back to Boar, who made chug bubbles as he tilted it back. He looked around for the ice chest.

"Sorry, man. We ain't got beer chasers for you. Ramirez took off with it. We're all goin' over to his place after the fire. He said, 'Tell old Boar to come over for a beer—if he ain't too fuckin' dirty. But you do gotta smell tonight, Boar. You been sleepin' at the dump again?"

"I don't sleep at the dump," he said, after another swig.

"But Smokey Johns says he sees you out there all the time. What you doin' out there, Boar, lookin' for things to kill?"

"Rats."

"Fuckin' Boar makes search and destroy sweeps of the dump, man, killin' rats. That's great, Boar. Somebody's gotta do it. I bet the town don't pay you nothin' for it, do they? You fuckin' kill all the rats in the county, and you don't get your civic credit, do ya, Boar? But you know, you do stink, Boar. Don't you ever wash? Ain't it about that time of year for the family wash day?"

It was like watching a coyote yipping at the hooves of a buffalo, Van Anders taunting with cutting praise and joking insults, and the Boar's stray eye trying to focus on the sense of what Buckwheat was jabbering at him.

When the beer ran out, so did Boar's distraction. Buck-wheat stood up. "Well, Boar, we gotta be goin' after some beer. See ya later at Timo's."

I took the chance to leave, too, and we moved off toward our pick-ups. Buckwheat said, "Let's take that fuckin' old fire bush you're drivin'."

"We going to Timo's?"

"Hell, no. Just the Boar. We'll grab a six-pack and drive up on the north table. That's the county entertainment 'round here. You drive around in the country drinkin' beer. Or gettin' loaded. You done your share of that, no doubt. You gonna turn down a little pot here tonight and claim some kind of conver-sion?"

I said, "I'll buy the beer."

"I'll let ya."

After the stop at Cody's, Buckwheat said, "Go through town to the T and take a right. It winds up on the north table." In the country, Van Anders lit a joint, and we passed it back and forth as I drove, Buckwheat muttering directions with held breath. Gradually, the world beyond the windshield closed down to only a short stretch of rolling gravel road the dim lights of the Speckled Pony could pick up. A few turns and curves and my sense of direction was gone.

"How the hell do people know where they're going in this country in the middle of the night? No signs, no landmarks."

Van Anders was staring out at the summer night blowing by the cab window, feeling the buzz come on, sipping a beer. He leaned his head back against the seat. "There's subtle marks. Dips and rises, and knowin' about how far you already come. People here been over these roads their whole fuckin' lives. They could drive 'em in dreams."

A moment later, he said, "There's a place up near my folks' where we can see back down into the valley, 'bout from Ogallala to North Platte down the Interstate. You'll get your sense of ground back. The ground don't change much."

After that night, most of the home games ended for us like that, a late-night drive, beer in hand, and stoned conversation at the dark edge of the river valley with traffic lights tracing the flow of the river down the prairie night.

INTERLUDE:

The wind was picking up to a soft wailing in the wind-break when Grady Standers helped me push back the doors of Uncle Karl's shop. We peered into the dusty shadows at the dark forms of steel dinosaurs, and Grady sniffed and clucked and scratched at the grey stubble on his sagging cheeks.

"Like them trucks in the barn. This junk ain't gonna bring much. 'Less we get a couple antique dealers biddin'." Grady came from a country family of horse traders and had been calling auctions since the droughts of the Great Depression. He stepped over and ducked his head into the framework of the ancient combine and blew a cloud of dust off the engine head. "Bet it still runs though, knowin' Karl Goehner. What'd he call her?"

"Mrs. Harris," I said. Ghosts sighed in the deep shadows of the old shop.

"Mrs. Harris, that's it. She done cut her last load of wheat, I reckon." He came back into the shaft of sunlight created by the open doors and jabbed a thumb over his shoulder at the dirt-covered form of the Speckled Pony parked askew on flat tires. "That, too. Don't reckon it'd be worth even showin'." He'd done a good job of ignoring the vintage pick-up. "I could maybe spring for a couple hundred outa my own pocket for it. Your cousin said she wanted to get rid of everything."

"Uh huh."

"Ain't like the land, you know. Land holds its value. Everybody wants the land. You talk her into sellin' the land and I can get you some money for that. But this here junk.... Who knows?"

"Don't be worryin' about it, Grady. The pick-up's mine. Inheritance, you know? I'm thinking about a restoration." The memories and voices had already been revived. It was just a matter of time and patience.

SECOND MOVEMENT:

SKY

CHAPTER ONE: HARVEST LIGHT

Down on my back, I pulled myself under the belly of the old combine again to make sure of what I saw, of what I thought I saw. I knew another inspection wouldn't make me any more sure, but pulling myself along by grabbing parts of the frame and braces, I positioned myself up behind the low-slung engine to get a backside look at the end of a drive shaft fitted with a sprocket and pulley. Roller chain and a V-belt looped off in opposite directions, and behind the congestion of moving parts were two hidden grease zerks, in a cast iron housing which held a bearing that held one system-within-a-system in place for friction-free, high-speed revolution. These were only two of the one hundred and twenty-three grease injection zerks on the entire combine, a 1947 Massey-Harris 21A self-propelled small grain thresher.

There were one hundred and twenty-three places on, in, out on, under, around, and up behind that required daily greasing so the bearings, or sprockets, or shafts, or augers kept running fast and free. I had counted that many zerks to hit with the grease gun the first day Karl had shown me where they were. But I hadn't yet memorized where they all were located. Each day since harvest maintenance had begun, I'd finished the greasing two or three zerks short of the total, the ones missed being different than the day before, I'd realize, when Karl pointed them out on his own inspection of his antique machine.

The two zerks that I craned to see as I squeezed my body into position I had not missed. It was how the grease had oozed out between the ball bearings and the housing that had made me wonder, but a cramped peek at the innards of the unit revealed nothing new to me, as I knew it wouldn't. I squirmed to readjust into position to work a hand back into the gears, trying to grip and shake the unit to see if something were loose, but there was too much slippery grime on my hand to exert much force. I felt into the grease again with my fingertips, along the smooth round surfaces of the steel balls in their casing.

I couldn't see what I was feeling, only being able to project an idea of it behind my closed eyes by the touch of my fingers. "You gotta use that third eye," Karl had told me the month before when we were putting the shaker shoe back inside the combine and bolts to some housing on a brace that had to be threaded and locked down in a tight nook using only the blind touch of tools and hands. It had seemed impossible, and Karl had had to climb inside the machine where I was and handle it himself like a patient Houdini.

I now moved my fingers to another nearby bearing and tried to feel a difference in... something—textures, edges, symmetry, something. The task only added more grease to the grimy supply that already filmed my whole body. I felt the slick, thick goo of dirt and grease in my hair and beard as I extracted myself from the steel nest of belts and gears and levers. The grime was embedded in the cracks of my hands and under the nails. It coated my forearms, and my pocket T-shirt was streaked everywhere I had used it as a hand towel. Where the grime had marked my Levis, chaff and dust stuck and ground in because of my crawling around, over, and under the machine. I dissolved the filth from my arms and hands with a gasoline-soaked rag that burned tender skin, and the smell made my head swim in the morning heat.

Karl was on the other side of the combine, crouched in under the feeder chain housing, pouring oil into the engine, a flathead Chevy six-banger that purred with constrained energy—the heart of the whole machine pulsing with power. He seemed comfortable, folded into what open space there was there, not spilling a drop from the oil can as he poured. I noticed that my uncle's sinewy forearms, protruding from his perpetual service blues, showed barely a mark of grease, though he'd been working around the machine all morning, too.

"There's this bearing on the other side," I started, "I don't know, it seems different—not that it looks broken, but maybe you ought to look at it."

Karl climbed out of his steel cranny, and we moved around the red behemoth as I tried to explain where the bearing was because I didn't know the names of the parts I was describing. Karl ducked down behind the left front drive wheel and snuggled in against the frame to crink his neck and look behind the sprocket. He pulled back and twisted away, snaking his arm in among the belts, examining the bearing and its housing with his own mangled fingers. Then he slowly extracted himself and moved back to stoop and stare a while at the outside of the whole unit, his straight arms braced on slightly bent knees, his blue eyes moist and shifting in concentration.

He finally turned his head over his shoulder and said, "Put the machine in gear, but leave the rpms at idle. I've got my jewels out of the way." He waved what fingers remained on his left hand behind his back at me.

I climbed up on the open platform and sat in the driver's seat, slowly leaning down on the lever that moved an idler pulley into place and put the whole threshing mechanism in gear. In slow motion, the combine rattled and shook to life, belching a cloud of dust and straw out the back end. Even at idle, the old Massey 21A vibrated with the controlled chaos of counter powers, the rising pitched howl and whine of belts, the jingling whir of chains, the growl of forced air, the rattle and clang of age and labor.

Karl sat back, out of the way of the shivering, roaring machine and motioned me down beside him. When I leaned in to look at the whirling belts and chains, Karl shouted, "Can you hear it?" I shook my head, not even imagining what Karl meant. "A high-pitched scream right in there, and a rhythmic scraping, like chickens scratchin'."

I turned my ear and tried to separate the overwhelming roar of the whole, vibrating, red machine into different tones of shiny squealing and rusted decibels of clatter, the wavering hum of motions and blurred shapes. It was like trying to pick out the individual sounds of an orchestra in tune-up cacophony. I tried to focus on the sound of the gears I was concerned about and thought maybe I heard what Karl described, but even so, I didn't know if that were good noise or bad.

"Look at the end of the shaft," Karl said into my ear, "See how it's jiggling back and forth some? Even with them belts and chains holdin' it in place. Supposed to be steady."

I could see it and hear it now that the details had been pointed out to me. I stepped back from the machine with an overwhelming dismay. There were thousands of places like that on the combine where something was bound to go wrong some time. How would I ever be able to tell?

"Shut ol' Mrs. Harris down. All that's got to come off, I reckon, so we can get at them bearings," Karl said, waving the talon-finger of his right hand in the general direction of the wobbling gears.

I wondered why Karl would grin about it. The second breakdown in five days, another part of the old machine rattled to death, another day of harvest lost to repair. Even I could tell by now that it would be at least one long day for repairs. That's if parts could be found. No one carried parts for machines twenty-eight years old and obsolete. We had spent one day in June "robbing parts," as Karl had called it, which meant driving to a graveyard of ancient machinery by a town way up the North Platte River and stripping useable pieces from a wreck there that was similar to Karl's bright red antique 21A.

"Glad you found that before we run on it, Calvin," Karl said as he hauled the first needed tools out of the shop. "Would of been worse to run on it till it tore apart."

"Lucky," I said. "I don't know what I was looking at."

"And payin' attention. That, too, is good as grease sometimes."

Under the glare of the drop light, that night we finished snapping the connector on the last roller chain back into place on the repaired unit. We had torn it down piece by piece with Karl's mind as the instruction booklet, examined the broken bearing on the naked end of the shaft, replaced it, and rebuilt. The bearing had been so basic a part that it was in stock at the machine shop in Tighe. Only a brief trip to town was needed, but under Karl's patient and detailed scrutiny, it still had taken more than twelve hours to complete the repair.

A vast array of tools as common as pliers and as special-
ized and unfamiliar as a percussion-drive bearing puller were
needed. Karl had them all, and two stories about the combine that
came up in the course of discussing it's repair.
     The first was about its name, Mrs. Harris. A farmer who
lived between the rivers had given her that name one season when
Karl had cut wheat for the man after the death of his wife. The
farmer, named Kruger, had lost his wife in a car accident coming
home on the Interstate one night just before harvest. She had been
bringing parts home for repairs on their combine. The Krugers
were members of St. Luke's congregation, and most members had
gone to attend the family's grief. The women had all brought food
and had seen to the bereaved family's needs. The men had
brought their combines and trucks and finished Kruger's harvest
for him.
     One Sunday after church soon after, in a conversation of
quiet thanks, Kruger had recalled to Karl his neighborly help. He
said, "Seems like every time I got up from my chair to look out on
what God had left me with, there you were on old Mrs. Harris,
dumpin' another load into the truck. Old Mrs. Harris, always a
goin'."
     Karl finished the story as the wrench in my hand slipped
from the nut I was tightening. I rammed my knuckles into the
bolt, scraping back skin and bringing blood. I jerked back, shaking
my hand and grunting, trying not to curse in front of my uncle. I
sucked on the knuckles a while, examined them again. "Damn and
to hell with it! Shit, damn, and everything else!"
     Karl commiserated and examined the damage. He was
experienced in hand bashing. When I finally picked up the wrench
again, Karl asked, "You okay now?"
     "I'll live. Damn, but Mrs. Harris isn't as cooperative so far
this season," I spit out as he moved back into position to work.
     "She's more stubborn and finicky in her ways now, that's
sure. That's why she takes a lot of care. She's cut a load of wheat
in her day. Come 'round her and look."
     We stopped our work, and Karl led me around to the
front of the combine to stand before the big reel and cutting bar
of the fourteen-foot header.
     "Look down under there."

I bent down to examine the steel underside of the header just below the sickle bar that scissor-cut the straw.

"See all them little grooves down long there?" Karl asked, and I focused on the long row of small grooves that gave a serrated look to the edge of the header. "Those are all worn there just by the straw stubble rubbing against it. She cut thousands of acres over a lot of years. Old Mrs. Harris was part of the Harvest Brigade. You remember that? No? Well, a bit before your time. But these old Massey-Harris 21's were really the very first, efficient, self-propelled combines ever made. Maybe you seen old newsreels, ten or fifteen of 'em cuttin' together to bring in the crop for the war effort.

"Without these machines we never could have fed Europe after World War II. These Masseys freed up a whole lot of farm boys to go fight Hitler. This whole brigade of machines cut wheat from Texas into Canada just so's the world could eat bread during the reconstruction of Europe, and Mrs. Harris has been helpin' since '47. Now you won't see maybe a half dozen runnin' in the whole country today."

Karl had bought Mrs. Harris off a machinery lot in 1955, the header full of blow dirt and weeds, the round grain bin robbed off, all the rubber V-belts brittle and broken or gone all together. He had run a good bargain with the dealer, who threw in any parts Karl might need to make it operative, and he had rebuilt the combine from the ground up. He kept her shedded in winter and he had tended her inner mechanisms for two decades like a doctor serving his finicky patient. As a result, Mrs. Harris still ran around the wheat fields, "cutting many a load" while all the other farmers had gone on to newer and fancier, bigger and more costly machines with deluxe cabs and electronic sensors and high-tech parts, and the ability to clear a field in a fraction of the time it took Mrs. Harris.

"You get to know her ways," Karl remarked after we had resumed our work in a long silence. "Like an old wife, I reckon. You learn to know what to do to keep her happy, and she don't really cost you much to keep around. Old Mrs. Harris will still cut a load or two tomorrow. You'll get to see."

Promise, or prophecy, or educated guess, whatever it was, it happened, and I got to see.

"Why don't you run her awhile," Karl said after we had checked and tested our repair and made a few minor adjustments to tighten belts. "You can break open a new land."

I had ridden along the first days while Karl showed me how to run the combine, standing over the steering wheel on the open platform that nested behind the header and above the left drive wheel. He had demonstrated how to control the chaos of the mechanical beast with levers to raise and lower the header, to adjust the over-the-ground speed to the density of the wheat stand and the capacity of the header to cut it off and feed it up augers and elevators and into the raging bowels of the combine where the grain was threshed and separated from the straw and chaff. I had taken the driver's seat and the wheel and learned the feel of the beast. At first Karl stood beside me, helping run the levers, telling me what to look at, what to adjust to, as the combine crawled over the field. Gradually, I had taken over all the controls, and Karl only talked about what the gauges revealed about the machine, what pinpointed sounds were from, what to look for in the one tiny mirror that showed the straw and chaff being blown out and spread behind the back end of the machine.

Alone at the controls for the first time, I drove the combine into the field, put the threshing mechanism in gear, throttled up to full rpm's, and began cutting wheat, taking a swath off the eastern edge of the field. The reel gently pushed the laden stocks forward, the sickle scissored them off and began to gorge the header full. I watched the auger feeding the cut wheat to the center of the header where the whirling front drum fingered the crop into the machine. I could see it in my mind, the wheat fed up the housing to the threshing cylinder spinning in a fast blur, crushing the wheat heads from the straw; see the heads mashed against the sieves of the shaker shoe, the mangled straw shaken and blown out the back, the wheat shaken and blown and augered, threshed and shaken and fanned again, then elevated up to the spout.

Looking over my shoulder, I saw the golden-red grain begin to appear and pour down the spout, running with a golden chime into the round tank that sat behind me. Suddenly, it seemed incredible, miraculous: the combine moving over the standing wheat, the roaring threshing mechanism revolving, spinning, and shaking in a myriad of counter powers and screaming gears, sprockets, bearings, augers, belts and chains, all holding together against the centrifugal and centripetal forces roaring around me, and then the billions of clean wheat berries spewing into the bin.

That it all worked, that I controlled it, adjusted and inspected it with levers and dials and wheels; that I cut down the growing wheat to be trucked to flour mills; it seemed unbelievable, an awesome combination of design and precision parts and human ingenuity and craftsmanship.

I worked the machine south, across the edge of the unmarked sea of wheat, feeling the combine tremble with speeding parts and barely contained energies, then I turned right, driving up the south side of the field next to the summer fallow—the bare ground I had worked three times already, getting it prepared for the coming fall planting. In the roar and rattle of power, I began to worry about the machine's containment and endurance. Something will go wrong, some piece fall apart, I thought. So many different, running parts, so much energy and speed, so much contortion and counter-action, heat and stress, how can it hold together? How can it? Yet it had a roaring life, a name and a history and a character. And it got the job done year after year. An American machine, I thought, like a nation of peoples at war with itself, how does it survive?

I guided the small machine up the south edge of the field, always glancing back into the bin, checking the gauges, adjusting the speed and the feed of the crop into the machine. When the bin seemed half full, I turned back north across the field, cutting a virgin swath through the golden sea of wind-waved wheat, and an indescribable beauty rushed my senses. Endless amber waves rolled toward the horizon, broken only by distant dark strips of fallow ground and green stands of young corn shimmering in the heat waves of the July afternoon. I cruised across a vast land framed and domed only by a glistening, clear azure sky. At the lowest western edge of horizon, white billows of cumulus began to build, boiling up like silent emotions. The beauty simmered through my senses and soul, deeper than words and ideas.

At the far northern edge of the field, I turned back to the east to finish the round, constantly checking the bin to see if it would overflow before I reached Karl, who stood on the parked truck, waiting. The wheat stand was thicker here, and I slowed the combine to a crawl, listening to it growl full-mouthed and furious. I worked the controls of the machine and watched the constant action, forgetting repaired parts and violent forces, nations and names and histories, private feelings of freedom and beauty and the satisfaction contained in the single soul. I pulled up to the truck and augered the load into the box. Then, for a time, I wheeled the antique combine down the field, round after round, a 1947 Massey-Harris 21A of the old Harvest Brigade, a machine named Mrs. Harris, cutting an endless circling swath of new wheat, nothing else abstract or uncertain, simply a part of the process.

It took concentration and careful maneuvering to pull out of the wheatfield, shut down the thresher, and steer in by the truck to auger out each load. Wheat poured into the truck box, and Karl, standing on the dented cab and leaning on the scoop shovel, would reach out for a handful of grain, letting it run off his fingers as he examined it, smiling. A few kernels he would pop into his mouth and crunch as he reached for another handful. As the auger rattled empty, he would give a thumbs up and a widening grin.

"Go get some more," he yelled once over the engine roar. "Old Mrs. Harris wants to cut another load. It's out there."

_____

Buckwheat solos:

"To hell and history with that shit, babe. No more wheat harvests for my old man. He's gonna cut corn now, that's where the big bucks are. His fat little banker in Ogallala—that Collard that plays centerfield for Bunke's and can't make a pick-off throw to save his ass—he showed the old man the future, punchin' up the numbers on his little calculator like he's a goddamn gypsy with a crystal ball.

"Ever see a fat banker out sittin' on a tractor? Hell no, but he knows all about makin' money, and he's gonna make the old man a fuckin' truckload of corn money. Now, he don't know the ass-end of a tractor, but he damn sure can add all these little long columns of numbers, and if this X here equals five and Y here equals ten, why then Z is gonna equal a fuckin' zillion.

"Now, you ever see a farmer behind a bank officer's desk? Hell there, too, but dad's got this big investment plan for this modern farm that's gonna grow dollar bills next to the ears of corn. He couldn't tell interest on loans from capital gains, but if he grows a hundred and twenty bushel corn, and if the price is two dollars a bushel, he's gonna buy that package tour to the Holy Land mom's always wanted, maybe buy a new pick-up, too. All kinds of wonderland dreams.

"Of course, if X equals two, or dad grows one hundred and ten bushel corn, or maybe Y is six and the fuckin' price is a buck eighty, well then, he's got problems. But hey! that's what your friendly fuckin' banker's for, see? Cash flow gets a little tight, he's gonna advance you a few thou—at the usual interest of course, and carry you a year, or five years, or fifty years maybe, till it all pencils out in his little column of figures.

"But that's all down the road, see, and circle irrigation is the life-blood of today's farming and tomorrow's big profit. Yeah, right, and the old man thinks mom is weird prayin' to the Virgin Mary. But the banker is two years out of business college and the fuckin' prophet of the plains.

"Of course, the old man's got to reveal this big decision to me, but he can't just come straight out and tell me. He calls me up. 'How about a little help with the harvest this year?' He doesn't say, 'with the last wheat harvest ever,' or anything like that.

"So sure, I can get Mel to take some of my hours at the station, and I blast out to the farm in the MG—and damn! what a ride. About the only thrill of the day. I turn into the drive, and out in the summer fallow east of the house there's a well digging rig from Tyghe. Fuck, I know what it all is right away, but I go up to dad ducked under the combine somewhere—this is so he can stage his big performance like he wants.

"I say, 'What the hell's goin' on in the east field?'

"'I'm gonna grow corn and make this place pay off,' he says. 'Both these home quarters, I'm gonna put pivot systems on 'em.'

"'This ground ain't shit for pivots,' I said.

" 'Lots of folks run 'em on steeper ground."

"I didn't say it couldn't be done. I said, the ground ain't shit for pivots, and I told him so again. Told him he damn well knew it, too. It's wheat ground up here between the rivers, rolling ground sittin' up on a clay butte that sticks up in the sky and gets more than its share of the nastiest weather. The rain patterns are best for winter wheat.

"Sure, there's plenty of water underground, surrounded by rivers. But up on the table it's four hundred feet down to it at least, not twenty like in the valley, not fifty and artesian like up in the Sandhills. Hell, I don't have to tell him all this. I fuckin' learned it from him, for Christ's sake.

"But he's gonna go in debt against the land, buy sprinkler systems, have wells dug, buy big Perkins engines to run it all, and do what so many are surviving at already. Pencil it out. You can be a banker, too. You can grow thirty bushels of wheat on an acre and sell it for three dollars and make ninety dollars an acre—and remember you only use half your ground because we summer fallow, right? Or, you can grow one hundred and twenty bushels of corn on the same acre and sell it for two dollars a bushel for two hundred and forty dollars an acre. Plus, you use all your acres because you don't use fallow conservation tillage. Big bucks, babe. Made the old man's eyes light up like someone stuck an arc welder up his ass and ran a bead. Maybe the banker, but oh yeah, he doesn't know squat about a welder either.

"The old man's rapping all this investment and tax incentive shit at me as his way of getting me involved in the family farm business again, see? He decides what he's gonna do, goes does it, and then justifies it in these planned little speeches. Sure, man, he can show it to me all in dollars and cents. He can even show me how I can be in on it full-time, too, and there's enough for all of us to live on. This is his idea of how to change things for the better, for the family.

"Hell, he don't even realize he'll spend more in one year just on fertilizer than he spends in an entire season on the production cost of wheat. And he's got to put up new grain bins to store all this new abundance, and up-date his tractor because all his machinery will have to be sold or traded to convert to row cropping.

"Then there's the minor detail that he—or me either—don't know shit about growin' corn. He'll just get the county agent to live out here and teach him how to do it. Or he can hire an agronomist consultant from the university to tell him about lab experiments and hybrids and how to spend more big bucks poisoning weeds and poisoning bugs, oh yeah, and poisoning the whole goddamn food chain in the process.

"Plus, he's gonna have to hire reliable, full-time help because he can't do it alone even if he is Superfarmer, and I sure as shit ain't puttin' in with any of his big ideas. Goin' in debt for a fortune, man, just to farm irrigated corn for maybe a few cents more profit. That's if interest rates stay low, and if corn prices stay high, and if fuel and fertilizer costs don't go up, and if hail doesn't smack the piss out of the crop.

"How can he believe that shit? I look at him tellin' me all this, I can't believe what I hear. 'Everything's gonna be different.' —Again. Everything but the old man.

"When I tell him I'll help with harvest but I'm stickin' at Mel's station, he screams his big reason. He's doing all this so he has something to leave his family. It's my guilt trip to take. He's doing it all for me and Gerald Junior, farming the ground like I'd never farm it, while he goes expansion broke workin' me like his crippled slave to get it done. Something to leave the family. He'll never leave the land except in a wooden box, or by eviction. When it comes time to leave anything, it won't be his to leave to anyone except the bank.

"I tell him that and he's really pissed off, his old craggy face like a rock. The bank says this, economists say that, the government throws in one of its phony fuckin' promises about prosperity. —I know all about their fuckin' promises from first-hand experience, and I'm yellin' back at him that he never farmed but one way and that was the way he had to.

"He had to farm because his own dad died, and there was no one else. He had to earn a living at it because he couldn't do anything else. He had to do it as sound business just like everyone tells him to, just to keep the place at all.

"It never had anything to do with farming the ground the best way. It never had to do with anything but a buck. And it don't fuckin' matter because that's all it is to almost everyone, or it's nothin' at all.

"There we are, man. I'm on the place fifteen minutes and we're yellin' at each other. 'You want to leave me something?' I say. ' What about the windbreak?' It's that original tree claim grove on the far east side of our ground. The daughter of the homesteader who claimed that quarter just by planting five acres of trees on it sold it to grandpa the year before he died. That stand of trees is only twenty years younger than those Oregon Trail ruts that cut across between the rivers just twenty miles west of here or so. It's the same part of history as the dream of havin' some place to go. There they are, a nice little shelter to build a house behind and live there.

"What about 'em,' he says.'

"So leave those ten acres to me while you still got 'em.'

"No way. They're gonna bulldoze those trees out so the sprinkler can run clear 'round and he can plant five more acres of worthless two-dollar corn. I already knew he had to do it that way, and he's gonna have less to leave behind than a miserable patch of homesteader's trees."

Calvin's journal notes / autumn, '75

On the morning of autumn equinox, I was out on old Moe, pulling the steel-wheeled drill down the field, seeding winter wheat, wondering how it will ever reach moisture and germinate. This is the culmination of the summer's field work. All I am thinking is, did I do it right? Is the moisture down there below all this dry dirt surrounding me? Each operation has been to destroy weeds and hold the precious rain water where the seed can reach it, come planting. Any day now the ground will tell everyone. There will be wheat seedlings, or there won't. Simple as that.

But even with the worry, the day was beautiful and I celebrated the equilibrium of the seasons. The morning was dark with fog and cold with heavy dew, but Moe roared to life and the John Deere drill, another antique, squeaked slowly around the field. By mid-morning the fog was burning off and the steam seemed the breath of earth.

All day I stopped only to load the drill box, shoveling the seed by hand from the truck. —And I stopped to dig behind the drill, looking for the seed to see (again) if it were packed in fine, moist dirt below the loose, dry, top layer. I took only my lunch and a jug of water and rode the day out, going round and round, following the marker with the front tire and watching the sky each direction change hue and texture with the sun's slow run for the horizon. By late afternoon the air was thick and still with a golden light. The shadows in subtle folds of ground were deep blue pockets, the windbreaks darker silhouettes.

I stayed out after sunset to finish the last field, out till the light was a long, red seam in the west where the edges of the universe looked sewn together with rays of golden thread. End of a season of learning this land.

I parked Moe and the drill at the field edge and walked into the yard, feeling I had accomplished something simple and right, and on a special day. But every day since then, I've been back out to the field, still wondering. Sometimes I walk a ways out and dig in a furrow. And find nothing, or maybe a single swollen kernel. Too anxious, even though Karl assures me.

"Set your mind to other things," he says, simply enough.

So I have. With the lull letting me think of comfortable relaxation and the coming cold season of hibernation, I decided to fix up the bunkhouse interior to my idea of cozy liking. I've been thinking of paneling the walls with weathered barn wood ever since I discovered a pile of it out in the corral. I also found an old, Hottentot wood-burning stove under a pile of junk in one of the outbuildings. Karl says it's the original stove from the big house when it was just a four-room box out on this windswept prairie. I rescued it, buffed and polished it up some, and dragged it into the bunkhouse.

It's not hooked up yet, and I've only got about a wall and a half paneled, but the place is starting to take on a personal, homey feeling somewhere under the sawdust and tools and boards. Then yesterday, Aunt Martha finally had to come in to see what all the banging and pounding was about.

When I turned and saw her in the doorway, I thought maybe I had hit her with the board I was carrying. Her soft, round mouth hung open and she muttered, "My God!" and that's about as much of an expletive as you'll ever get out of Martha.

"Kind of shocking, huh?" I said while I watched her wide eyes dart from the walls to the wood pile to the stove and back to the walls. "Kind of redecorating." I could feel this foolish grin growing on my face, so I moved back to the job at hand.

It was the first time I'd ever seen Aunt Martha speechless. When she finally fished her tongue out of her throat, she said, "But why did you have to mutilate the house to do it?" Barn wood and wood-burning stove were evidently not Martha's idea of fashionable decor.

"You don't like it?" I asked over my shoulder. I decided to keep busy. "I kind of like the look."

"Where did you get the wood?" she demanded, as if I might have torn down the cows' shed or used some of her precious preserve of saved farm junk. I told her, and told her I'd asked Karl about using it.

She turned to go with one last glance of disgust, muttering, "Well, it may be your style, but it ain't mine." In a disgusted sulk she added, "I was going to ask you to help me do up another batch of tomatoes from the garden, but I see you got other distractions," and she was out the door, slamming it behind her.

Poor Aunt Martha. I continue to be a source of disappointment and failure to her. Come to think of it, not unlike I am for most of the rest of American society. The American Way, or no way. Aunt Martha's way, or no way. When I went over to the big house for lunch, I got a story of the American Way with my bologna sandwich and tea.

Did I know there was no electricity on these farms until after World War II? Farmers had to organize their own cooperatives and make a plan. They had to beg the government for funds to buy poles and cable, and then had to put it all in themselves. Before REA—that's Rural Electrification Association, I was carefully informed—there were only coal-burning stoves and kerosene lamps and windmills for water. No refrigerators, no electric heaters, no modern kitchen appliances, no irrigation.

At first I thought it was all just another part of her continued drive to pump me full of family history and local facts and all the values she thinks I should absorb and exude. But this was more explicit. How could I reject the modern, gleaming comfort of fine plaster walls for the rundown look of barn wood? How could I replace a modern propane heater with a stinky, filthy, troublesome wood burner? How could I think of refurbishing an old kerosene lamp just for atmosphere and fumes? In other words, how could I reject the conveniences and progress that others had worked so hard to have brought out to the country? It feels like an old, old question really. How can the younger generation, and me in particular, reject anything or any idea the older generation has given us through hard work, sacrifice, and generosity? They have given us "all this"—America as we know it—and then they feel justified in making judgment on the acts of the younger generation's use or abuse of it. It's as if we're not allowed our own personal decisions about what to accept, what to be thankful for, when to be obedient, while they decide what version of "The Truth" they think we should know "for our own good."

Yes, the Generation Gap. One of the catch-all slogans of our recent, sad history. And here it's served to me by Aunt Martha with a sandwich—which I guess is somewhat better form than a billy club from Chicago's finest. The expectation is for me to embrace all or nothing, which has been the very expectation I've always seemed to encounter since Chicago, '68. It was love it or leave it, wasn't it? One of us, or one of them; not simply someone with a personal conscience, someone who wanted to do right by interpreting and acting on the facts as he might come to know them.

Wasn't it finally frustration and rage against that unyielding attitude that set me to SDS politicking in Boulder, sent me toward Ted Gold in New York, incited me to burn draft files, and finally drove me surrendering to Mexico to hide out forever? Now I've come to the farm to hide out, and Aunt Martha has found me. I'm her personal project, no doubt assigned by the President himself, or at least by the FBI, to get me back on track in the American Way now that the war is completely over. I'm to be "re-educated" just like the defeated South Vietnamese.

This has been a setback for her, this wild restyling of the bunkhouse, but I can rest assured that she will continue trying. She thought that after lunch, maybe I could "leave your destruction site" for a couple hours to get another lesson in canning tomatoes. She was sulky and mostly silent while we scalded and peeled skins and stuffed jars full of ripe tomatoes, as if I'm barely worth the trouble to teach her crafts to. There is never any question about the value and necessity of the crafts themselves, or where and how exactly they fit into life, only questions about the apprentice and his approach and appreciation.

I've tried to maintain an accommodating attitude, but I've gotten impatient with the simple denial of personal style and perspectives. It's clearly a clash of personalities, and at times I wonder why I should bother. I can move on again.

But that's just it, I guess, the "again." The saddest observation about myself is the fatigue and the dying out of rage in me now. Only a few years ago I wouldn't have put up with her. I'd have shoved it back in the face of my antagonizer and moved on down the road as angry and independent as possible. Maybe the end of a long war has made everyone want to put it all down to rest.

The surprising observation about myself is that this rubbing raw of personalities with Aunt Martha irritates me. Why should I care? But it bothers me that she can't recognize in me any sense of appreciation for this place—her place, or for her history and skills. She wants it all to be for me just as it is for her, and it can never be. I have my personal history to deal with as well as hers, my own acquired perspectives and values, such as they are. I get angry that she can never realize that revealing them and channeling them into something as insignificant as barn wood paneling and wood-burning heat is a blessing and a concession. I get angry that her basic assumptions are simply wrong. I can appreciate her way of life, her values, her history because I grew up with them. But she will never know or appreciate mine because she never could have experienced what I have, and I will never be able to explain my own history because I don't know exactly what it's tied to except some sense of lost innocence and embarrassing naiveté. Nothing's ever been what I was led to believe while growing up. No untainted heroes, no fairy tale right to American might, no happy endings.

But none of the idealism inspired by resistance to an undeclared, unwinnable, unreasonable war—despite young spirit and indignant rage against this betrayal—has come to pass either. No new Age of Aquarius, no new and higher consciousness, no new world order.

    —God! What has any of this have to do with Aunt Martha? That she can conjure this uneasiness out of me bothers me even more. Just a stout and stubborn country woman, seventy-seven years of age, who still insisted on driving a couple of truck loads of wheat to town this July harvest—explaining that it's always been part of her job at harvest, but really making sure I was going to do it the way she would. A woman who was the last surprise child of an early homesteader, steeped in farm family life and never farther from her homeland than the state capital, a participant only via newspapers and gossip in one Great Depression and two World Wars, one UN Police Action, the Cuban Missile Crisis, and one Undeclared War (—no, she lost Billy Conrad in that one). A woman whose only relationships are with God, family, husband, and life on the land for the last three quarters of a century. Yet she can drive me up a barn-wood paneled wall.

    She has got her obstinate ways and ideas. Were they ever betrayed? Probably not by anyone she ever knew personally. She's got her own world. Has it ever been threatened or challenged? Only by the likes of me, who was of that old world once and was lost, who is only partly (or not at all) of that world anymore, who might forget or never learn the fruits of her hard and isolated labors, her loyalties, and her faith.

    But I have made my own independent ways in a new world. Were they ever anything but confused by a thousand influences? Only by most of what I've experienced. In making my own way, was I ever questioned? Only by everyone, myself most of all. Of what is that "Way" composed? I'm still trying to sort it all out.

    Martha has no doubts about hers, and she'll always go on telling me about it, afraid to the end that the labor is in vain. But she is of persistent, pioneer stock, and she had one last story to tell me about her and Karl buying this farm from my grandfather, or rather, about taking over his payments to the bank. Martha's father's land had long before been divided up between her much older brothers. She married a prodigal son, Uncle Karl, who returned to take over his father's farming because he was the only family member left to do it, having lost two younger brothers in

World War II and two sisters (including my own mother) marrying non-farmers who had moved out of the country.

There wasn't much to take over except the debt against the land. Their loan was with the Farmers Home Administration, and their agent, a cousin of Karl's, told them that if they could pay off the loan by making double payments for fifteen years, they could save almost half their costs in interest reduction. They made the obvious commitment and did it. That was when Karl began working for AgCo in Tyghe. Even Aunt Martha had to take a job in town to accomplish their goal.

For many years, I already knew, she had worked as a secretary to an insurance salesman in Tyghe. I silently pitied the poor man, who I assume is now dead, having been driven to an early grave by a meticulous, exacting secretary who, no doubt, eventually made him feel as if he were working for her instead of the other way around, which situation drove him to work harder than he had ever intended or needed to till she worked him to death.

A small human sacrifice. Plus the sacrifice of their own lives spent all the time at work—on the farm when it wasn't off the farm for someone else. Another sacrifice may have been the closer relationship to their own daughter, my cousin, who grew up rarely being with Karl and being dominated by her mother until she fled the isolated farm life for universities and a federal profession on the East Coast. But only four years ago, Martha and Karl did make their final payment on the farm. This land is theirs, not only spiritually and physically, but legally and financially, too.

And all this just so it could become the hideout of a young American renegade, who also happens to be family.

Most of this story I already knew because my mother didn't really neglect my sense of family history so completely as Aunt Martha assumes. But I listened to it all as the last jars of tomatoes were pulled from the hot water bath to cool. She concluded her history lesson by stating the obvious. "Hard work and sacrifice. That's what it takes, but then that's what the Good Lord put us here for. And the land is ours to pass on as we see fit."

I was glad, as usual, to get out of her kitchen, and I went out feeling again more as if I worked for Aunt Martha than with her. I made my daily walk to the edge of the field, and finally in the first furrows I can see it: the new delicate blades of wheat glowing lime green in the late afternoon sunlight. My first crop sprouting from the earth. —And from hard work. I had the urge to run in and tell Aunt Martha, "See? I really have been doing something right." But she'll see, herself, soon enough.

Thompson's lyrics/

   I don't know if Calvin here gets the credit or the blame—depends on how you see the stats, but you're the one that brought it out of ol' Buckwheat again, and Bucky always had a way of bringing it out of us. Changed the season around up there in Packard when we had to go make up that game when we were creamin' them at home and the fire call came in.
   Now, Calvin plays natural at about ten percent over full speed, and it ain't like Bucky didn't know it before, but Parsons here don't even know these guys we been bustin' our asses to beat for a hundred seasons since baby-ball, and you're runnin' bases like it's the World Series. It's the way Buckwheat used to play.
   We went up to their ball field way down flat. We could all feel it. Lox was late, out bangin' his boss's daughter, and Chatman was tryin' to sell Smokey life insurance, and half of 'em were talking farming like nobody wanted to be there in Packard cuz we knew what was gonna happen. Just a summer-night hassle. Rolf's team was cocky, of course. Their field, their escape of the loss, hot-shot infield warm-up, showin' off for the stands full of wives and girlfriends.
   So we started at the top of the fifth, right where we'd left off: Little Chatman coming to bat, score at six-two, our favor. Could have drove the nail home in the coffin first at bats, if we'd been psyched. Big deal. Two ground balls and a fly out to center. They get up, double, single home the run, then home run. It's six-five after five pitched balls, and they batted around, all but one, before they were done. Then it was eight-six, them. They were lovin' it, horns agoin' off, phony high-five shit in the dugout, shit-

eatin' grins.

But none of that stuff rubs off on Calvin, like it's always just him and the ball and the game you're playin'. You remember leadin' off the second—I mean, the sixth, and strokin' a clean single up the middle as usual? Smokey popped up foul, tryin' to go to the opposite field, and you tagged up. They were all yellin', "He's got wheels, got wheels," and you eased off your stance till the outfielder lobbed it in to Rolf on the mound. Then pow! The shot for second. Rolf caught the move outa the corner of his eye, dropped the throw, and couldn't even make a play on you. Plus, you took out McFee covering second with a perfect slide and had him spittin'-dirt mad in one play.

It's that kind of fire gets a team goin', and Buckwheat, like his old self, picked up on it. He knows McFee can't handle a ground ball if he gets mad, and Bucky laced a hard shot to the guy's right. McFee let it roll up his arm for a face full of line drive. He saved his life, but on his ass, no way could he make the throw even on Buckwheat hoppin' for first. Third baseman had to retrieve it, and Calvin stoled the open bag while Rolf was stutterin' where to throw it instead of coverin' third.

Okay. We're on our feet and goin'. Gotta get the old "mo"-mentum from somewhere, and there's Buckwheat sneerin' on first and Calvin dancin' on third. Timo tried too hard and popped the first pitch as high as the lights. Furtler's catch, two down, no advance. Timo beat on home plate with his bat—usual style. We still could have blown it back open if Chatman would have just run out his suckin' grounder. He's puffin' his big belly out, ready to hit the homer that Timo couldn't, and he dribbles it to McFee. Son of a bitch doesn't even run it out, and McFee choked and errored again. Calvin was scorin', Bucky slid into second, and Chub Chatman is standin' in the batter's box, cleanin' the plate with his lower lip.

Buckwheat came unglued. He charged Chatman like a ragin', wounded rhino, screamin', "Run your fat ass to first, you fucker! Run! Run it now!" And old Chatman took off down the base path with Buckwheat limpin' right after his ass, and Rolf's whole team ridin' and deridin' us.

Then Little Chatman—can you believe it?—he starts givin' Buckwheat hell for screamin' at his hero brother. Right

there on the mound while Buckwheat's throwin' warm-ups, sayin',
"Fuck you, man, fuck you." The whole town of Packard was
lovin' it, blastin' horns and screamin' while we held a conference
on the mound.

I'm tryin' to calm Bucky down, and Chub Chatman is
poutin', "What'd I do?", and little brother, then, started in on his
fat-ass brother himself. "You fat fucker, you make us all look
bad," and really ridin' his ass. None of us could believe it, old
Brownie lookin' at Lox and me like, can we get this show off the
field, please? Calvin was goin', "Let's play ball. Let's play."

"We damn well better shut 'em down here, or we'll never
git off this field tonight." That was my line, and I was believin' it
gospel. Well, Calvin got the first grounder at second—automatic
out, and that got Buckwheat settled back into pitchin'. They got
two singles, but he got two fly balls to leave the runners on.
Everyone came back into the dugout pumped up and pissed off.

Mercy got his usual ground out, but he run to first like my
wife was on his ass. I singled, and they couldn't stop Brownie's
shot down the line. Two on, one out, and Little Chatman stood
in, still steamin'. He was gettin' hoots from the stands, but his
eyes were in place. God, he creamed the crap outa that ball. You
knew it was gone when you heard it. His first home run ever. He
come trottin' around third base, lookin' at his brother, sayin',
"What you shoulda done, asshole."

Next play, McCormick gets called safe on a late throw—
their own hometown ump—and Rolf come stutterin' and spittin'
'offa the mound. We jumped his ass good, and there's the focus.
Nine-eight, our lead. Man on, one out, and we never looked back.
We got two more, held 'em with Buckwheat gettin' 'em to pop up,
swinging for the fence, and we beat their asses.

Thaddeus went for the first case of Bud, and we breezed
through the second game. Ten-runned 'em in five innings, playin'
sharp defense behind Bucky's pitchin' and poundin' the holy hell
outa that ball 'cause we knew we could do it.

Then we hauled over to Rolf's Bar after the game and
made him serve 'em up till closing. My momma shoulda seen it.
Only four of their team had the guts to show their faces in the
bar, and Buckwheat had to drink McFee under the table, doin'
tequila shooters.

I was thinkin', "Oh, no, he gets pushed, he's gonna bust up Rolf's place like it's a doll house." But his spirits were loose. We all were, and nothin' happened but a lot of suckin' suds. Me and Brownie, who still stayed off the sauce even over this, packed Buckwheat home and dumped him on the trailer floor about two a.m. We were talkin' that he'd never even make work at the station next day with the hangover he'd have, but he showed up at the Patterman auction next mornin'. You remember hearin' about that, Calvin?

Seems like Menninger and Berhends come 'round to Van Anders' trailer about nine or so and found Buckwheat more or less where we had left him the night before. His kids got the TV blastin'. Sandy was long gone, lookin' after her youngest and some other trailer court babies. Mel had opened up the station because I'd called to tell him about Buckwheat's condition. They got him up off the floor and poured some coffee in him and started stuffin' his hangover with that American Ag. Movement bullshit of theirs. They're the ones talkin' farm strike and minimum price support and tractor marches on Washington and that stuff.

They're all crapped up about Patterman's farm auction 'cause they're basically in the same sinkin' ship. They bought some of that high-priced land a few years back when the government was sayin', "We can sell everything you grow," and the prices were way up, and all these bankers were sayin', "Get bigger, get modern, get your tax break." Now the government's got so much grain it's rottin' on the ground, and the price ain't for shit, and the farmers still got to pay for the land and pay off the interest. This all means the cost-price squeeze is gonna kill 'em 'cause operating costs inflated with the boom price, but you know, they never come down when the prices do.

Well, Pattermans are only about two years of this shit ahead of everyone else. They borrowed, they expanded, then there goes the prices. And they had some bad breaks, like that one bin of corn goin' bad before they knew it. It was under loan and now it's worth pennies—if that—as bad feed. It can happen to anybody, but nobody's profit-cost margin can stand that on top of everything else.

So the FmHA told them to sell out, makin' Pattermans a kind of area example. You get spread too thin, have a crop failure

or a major breakdown repair, too bad, we're callin' in the loans.
Never mind it ain't their fault that the government told them to
over-produce, that they don't set grain prices, that the land is
priced crazier than gold and bankers say buy, buy, buy.

Lots of guys are gettin' pissed off, and you can see why.
It's get bigger and grow larger volume to make up for the cost-
price gap, or get squeezed out by being too small or being too
much in debt trying to get bigger. The government don't care if
they're killing off more farm families, and that's the Tabasco in the
soup as far as Menninger and Berhends and a whole bunch more
are concerned. They're just being driven out.

So they were going 'round that morning stirrin' up guys to
go out to Pattermans' and hassle the FmHA agent about the
farmers' troubles. Considering Gerry Van Anders' situation, it was
easy to see why they'd come 'round to Buckwheat. And there he
was, hungover and mean as a horny bull. And he's still got some
of the fire you stirred up in the game the night before.

Like I said, as for blessing or blame, I don't know. Buckwheat isn't likely to just put all that energy into our ball games. To
him, it's all just one big, long game with a lot of different parts to
it, a whole lot of different teams, and always a score to keep. You
know by now how Bucky played.

I was on my Thursday milk route, coverin' the places
between the rivers, and I knew the sale was on, so when I drove in,
I wasn't surprised to see lots of pick-ups lining the road and
packed in the yard and lot of neighbors wanderin' around. I went
up and stashed the milk in the refrigerator on the porch—they
didn't have to sell their personal property, and you gotta eat and
drink milk even when you're goin' out of business—and comin'
back to the van, I could hear Grady Standers startin' to call the sale
over his bullhorn.

The Pattermans were standin' around him—kids, too—up
on a flatbed full of the usual shop tools and old, leftover supplies
and parts and homemade equipment. Grady was giving the usual
opening speech about how everyone knows the Pattermans, and
how John's been a real good farmer who took care of his equipment and machinery, and how hard luck is sendin' 'em packin', and
we can all help out by givin' a fair price for all this bargain stuff.
And old Grady had a good crowd of neighbors and used machin-

ery salesmen and antique hunters down in front of him, even though it's a hell of a time of the year for an auction. That's usually winter business, but the yard was jammed with seed caps and sunglasses and red faces, and that's why I didn't see him before I heard him. But I sure as hell heard him the minute he started.

I heard, "No sale!" and thought, what's that? Nah, couldn't be. Grady was still goin' on, startin' to describe the junk on the trailer, and I'm almost back in my van, and then I heard it again: "No sale!"

Then someone else yelled it, too. Grady, he tries to keep callin', but it's Buckwheat all right, up near the front. "No Sale! We ain't puttin' him out of business. He don't deserve to be put out of business. No sale!"

Someone else yelled, "No sale!" Then someone else.

The agent was right down there in front—that Dunnelly guy out of Ogallala, and I could see him shiftin' and gettin' kind of bug-eye worried that this might get out of hand real fast. He climbed up on the flatbed and got the bullhorn from Grady to try and calm things down quick. Mary Patterman was startin' to cry into her husband's shoulder, and the kids were clawin' at their parents' legs like they didn't know what everyone was gettin' riled about. There was some more yellin', "No Sale!" and "Who's next on the hit list?" and the crowd murmur was growin' like we were comin' into the bottom half of one hell of an inning with the pitcher about to be knocked out of the game.

Dunnelly's shiny bald head was runnin' with sweat. He was sayin' things like, "This won't help nothin'," and "My orders come down from the regional office," and "This only prolongs the Pattermans' financial problems," and "I don't make government policy." But even on the bullhorn, he was gettin' drowned out, and there was old Buckwheat leading the rally. "No Sale! No Sale! No Sale!" Breaking the game wide open.

You could see things swinging the strikers' way. There wasn't gonna be any sale, and old Dunnelly was shaking his sad mug and pleading with Patterman, and the noise was starting to sound like cheering instead of angry buzzing. Then John Patterman got on the bullhorn, and he started thanking his neighbors by name, but his voice started to crack into a cry, and he stopped. Then the noise started to die down so he could be heard. Finally, he got his appreciation out, but then he said, "Folks, I got to sell. This only puts it off a few months more, and I guess I'm too tired to stretch it out any longer."

Well, it was a long and sad enough speech, all right, but he told them in the end to let the sale go on so his family could try to put it behind them and move on to something else. He just asked them to buy what they could for a fair price for the sake of his kids. The whole family was up there sobbin' by then, and some of the women in the crowd, too. Enough to make you think, what the hell is this country comin' to?

I supposed the whole scene was gonna get him some sympathy bids on some of his equipment, and you can always count on neighbors to help out, too, but no one was likin' it and the Ag. Movement boys were grumblin' in their beards but lettin' the show go on. That's when that asshole, Crighter, popped off the siren on the patrol car.

Big mistake.

Someone must have called it in when the commotion was just gettin' started, and Crighter, with that belly of his poppin' buttons and wearin' off the paint on the steering wheel, got sent up there. He had just eased into Pattermans' yard during the cryin' and speech-makin', and he coulda seen it was dyin' down. But he's got to push his role. He was seein' it as a chance to bust some heads—which is all he's good at. But that's drunk heads he likes to beat on, and he musta forgot it was broad daylight.

The whole crowd kinda jumped and split, and he nosed his patrol car right in there, up to the trailer, siren screamin', this shit-eatin' smirk on his flat face. He killed the siren and pushed his door open and hauled himself out, and there he is, face to face with Buckwheat and tappin' that goddamn night stick in the palm of his hand like he's Supercop.

"This asshole causin' you trouble, Grady?" he asks Standers without lookin' at him up on the trailer.

"There's no trouble now, deputy," Grady says. "We're goin' on with the sale."

Crighter shoulda left it at that, but he's got an audience now, and there's Buckwheat, lookin' six shades of green and growlin' under his breath. Crighter's gotta say, "You open that ugly mouth of yours here, and I'm gonna run your ass through the wringer and hang it out to dry."

Buckwheat says, "You couldn't hang out the laundry, Crighter, if your mother was Chinese. She had pigs instead of kids."

That's all it took. Crighter raised his night stick, and Buckwheat kicked him in the nuts. The whole crowd groaned, and Crighter's eyes bulged, and he sank to his knees. Buckwheat was over him in a split second and had the night stick. He woulda beat Crighter to a pulp, but Menninger and Berhends were on his back in an instant, pullin' him away. They coulda never done it if Bucky had been as drunk as the night before, but he was in pain, and Crighter can thank God for that.

The deputy was just curled up on the ground, clutchin' his gonads like jewels, moanin' like a sick sow, and then the laughin' started. A little at first, then more and more, and pretty soon it was a riotous belly laugh, watchin' that sick son of a bitch drag himself back into the seat of his patrol car and lay there callin' for back up.

Menninger and Behrends hauled Bucky out of there fast and stuffed him into his MG and told him to get the hell out of there. He was so pissed he was blowin' smoke, and he cut out, spittin' gravel. He musta pushed that MG up to seventy or eighty over those roads goin' home, so damned pissed off he was. He tried to take that first curve on Meyer's road, cuttin' back down into the valley, and rolled that MG to smithereens. It just laid him out on the dirt on the first roll over, a little cut up, and his thumb broke, but nothin' else hurt. The car rolled on through the pasture fence and caught fire. If he'd a been strapped in, he'd been dead sure. The fire blacked off half of Meyer's pasture there. The fire department had to come out and hose it down and haul that crazy bastard to the hospital again.

After they pumped him full of Valium, he calmed down some and simmered it off. Why he'd want to do all that, I don't know. None of it did a damn bit of good. Didn't stop a thing. Wrecked his car, cost him his weekends in jail for the rest of the summer, his wife wouldn't speak to him, Mel was pissed off at him, he was on Crighter's shit list, and there he is, same old Buckwheat, full of fire and nothin' to burn with it.

"Save it for the ball games, you asshole," I told him.

"Fuck the ball games," he growls, sittin' there behind the counter at the station again like nothin' ever happened.

"Well, what the hell else is there?" I asked him.

"Not a god damn thing," he says, so I knew he'd be there the next Wednesday night for the post-season tournament. At least it was not over the weekend. We got him to put it all into playin' the game and gave the whole damn league a run for that trophy, didn't we?

CHAPTER TWO: WINTER LIGHT

By mid-December of '75 I needed to get out and away from the winter isolation of the farm. For weeks the grey, icy edge of wind had moaned at the eaves of the bunkhouse, and I had listened. Hours of reading, hot tea by the warm stove, good hours of quiet. I had even tried to do some charcoal sketches of barren trees and snowdrifted fence line, empty horizons. But my first drafts were undisciplined and weak renditions of the images I saw outside and felt within. Out of practice, I had let myself fall into musing about how few lines there were to work with to capture the emptiness of the open, winter plain. Stir-crazy already, I thought, when I caught myself drifting, and not even to the winter solstice yet.

That's why, during an evening supper, when Aunt Martha had suggested that I go with them to a wedding and reception, I let her talk me into it. Their invitation came by way of family connections. After she had detailed the genealogical ties, Karl had summarized that since three Bachman brothers had homesteaded on the tableland south and west of Revere in the 1880's, and each brother had married and sired six or more children, now practically everyone in the county was related to them one way or another. Karl was related through his mother's side of the family and also by business. Although he barely knew the groom, Karl did all the repairs on the father's irrigation systems. Their farm's smooth operation depended on Karl's knowledge, and that was what had really put him on the guest list.

I once again benefited by association, and I didn't mind. The familiar Sunday faces at St. Luke's, that I had yet to match

with all the correct names, would all be there, and those who
would talk the weather and crops, too, being neighborly nice. Aunt
Sophie, Uncle Eric, and part of our own clan would be there, too,
to make me feel comfortable and connected. There would be
good food, beer in the barn, and a local band at the reception. I
half looked forward to the formal socializing and hoped it would
make me appreciate a return to my winter hermitage. In a half
wicked humor, I wondered how it could be a party celebration
since Aunt Martha was going to be there, no doubt running the
whole spectacle.

In the front seat of the big Oldsmobile, she sat partially
facing Karl at the wheel, smiling and urging him not to be late.
Her round, red cheeks glowed in the December cold, and her eyes
glistened. She had been to the hairdresser in Tyghe and had
bought a new hat for the occasion to match her fine, blue-white
permanent. Despite her reservations about the young couple to
be married, this was an acceptable celebration to Aunt Martha
because it was simply a local version of the Feast of Cana—even
Jesus had attended, and it was family-building. Her only misgiv-
ings were based on the age of the couple and the speculation
about the suddenly arranged date of the ceremony.

"Well, Ester Roessler heard from her cousin in Revere that
the Closterman girl is pregnant. Why else would they set a date so
close to Christmas? Instead of waiting for spring and a proper
season." The gossip had come along with the supper's dessert and
the invitation to attend.

Karl had ended it in his usual practical way, saying, "It's
not like it ain't happened in this county before. Won't take but a
few months, and folks'll be able to see for themselves instead of
hearin' it from Ester."

Despite Aunt Martha's urgency, we were some of the last
guests to arrive at St. Luke's, hurrying in through the cold wind to
be ushered into a back pew. Martha was escorted by a skinny,
acned boy in a tuxedo, with Karl in his Sunday suit right behind
her, removing his go-to-meetin' cowboy hat and holding it behind
him in a gnarled hand. I slipped into the pew beside them. In the
church crowd of suits and bright dresses and winter corsages, I
felt like an eastern bohemian, wearing the cream-colored alpaca
sweater I'd bought in Guatemala, my worn-down comfortable

corduroys, and the World War II Navy overcoat—an heirloom that Martha had exhumed from a family time capsule cedar chest.

But I was also grateful to feel that after eight months on the farm, I was no longer a curious object of special interest, even if I still looked slightly more eccentric than my wild-haired uncle. Attention was focused on the ceremony and participants, and I leaned back to enjoy my private observations and thoughts.

Above in the balcony, a single guitar was plucked alive, and a girl's voice began singing the first words of "The Wedding Song" while a line of black-tuxedoed, young groomsmen stepped out before the congregation from a side door. Then bridesmaids in shining, kelly green formals slowly marched up the aisle. Two of them, with curled long hair and glistening blue eyes, were pretty, and I was suddenly conscious of what my winter was lacking. But so young, I thought. Are any of them out of high school? I looked over the assembled marriage party as they stood smiling and fidgeting as the song ended and the organist hit the first chords of the wedding march.

Beaming and beautiful in satin billows of white, the Closterman girl came down the aisle on the arm of her grave-faced father. She was a blond child with soft, vulnerable lines of expression barely beginning to grow around her innocent eyes and trembling smile. Her father's serious gaze seemed almost as young as his daughter's. He was slim and dark-haired, age showing only in the weathered texture of his farmer's face.

I felt uncomfortably closer to the father's position than to the boy who stood grinning and waiting at the altar. Mathematics clicked through my mind. High school kids, maybe eighteen, nineteen, at the most. The father maybe married himself at that age, thirty-six now. At age twenty-seven, I lived ten years between them. By my age, these kids will have been a married farm family for a decade, I thought. In those ten years when they would be raising a family, what will I have done with myself? A thousand, crazy, unenduring things, I thought. Nothing matters.

Not knowing any of the participants personally, I watched the ceremony unfold, feeling it to be children's role-playing, the acting out of cultural fantasy, with everyone too young and inexperienced to understand the limiting finality of their acts. Yet it continued solemnly on, adults and other children witnessing the

ritual from the pews, affirming its sanctity with their presence. I
saw my aunt smiling, barely mouthing some of the vows as she
looked on. She and Karl—again—were an exception to the scene.
They had married late, I knew, when they were in their late thirties,
Martha considered all but a forgotten old maid. Karl had just
gotten back from roaming the Northwest to take over the farm
being left by younger brothers going off to war. Their age was the
reason they had only had one child, a daughter, long since moved
to the East Coast. In Martha's warm gaze at the couple, I could
read a satisfied feeling of her own life being reconfirmed and
enlarged again.

I thought then about some of the team members, guys my
own age, long since married and familied, and about John Van
Anders' stories about their lives. Their family situations seemed
settled and solid and content, the companionship taken for
granted, the relationships a timeless, unconscious aspect of their
personalities and daily routines. This ceremony imitated their own,
renewing the simple, intimate promises and dreams of what love
and life might become.

There was only a brief reception in the church basement
with neighboring farmers talking December weather and declining
crop prices while they filed through the line to shake the new
husband's hand and hug the new wife. I didn't go through that
formality, but hung at the back of the milling crowd, listening to
Karl and his friends, picking up on names and relationships and
local geography as I sipped coffee.

After the cake-cutting, on the long drive north up the
church road to the old Bachman place for the reception, Martha
recited the couple's social notice: the boy, Lane, would go into
partnership with his father; they would live on the old Crawford
place; the girl, Janice, would raise a yard full of more Bachmans
with plenty of help from the relatives. Their lives seemed happily
set, approved now by God and Aunt Martha.

In the fading rose-tinged sunset, we pulled into a farmyard
full of cars and pick-ups. Lights and the bass throb of music
glowed from a large Behlen quonset, its tall, steel doors open only
a crack to allow a flow of guests in and out. In the closing winter
darkness, the cold air was brittle and sharp, but at the doors I

moved into a warm, thick scent of barbecued beef, beer, and crowded excitement.

Inside, the farm shop had been converted into a vast hall, every piece of machinery and supply moved out except for the tools hung in neat order above the work bench and the John Deere combine wintered in the far, dark corner. In the other back corner, under a blaze of flood lights, a four-piece band played contemporary rock with a country-western twang. A sea of shadowed heads bobbed in the dancing, the bride's white gown flashing out to catch the eye. Along one shop wall, a row of tables served a smorgasbord of beef sandwiches and salads and sweet desserts. Women in Sunday dresses and cotton aprons served a winding queue of guests. In front of the work benches on the other wall, more guests sat at picnic tables, eating and drinking and talking. In between, the whole shop floor was crowded with small, standing groups and running, dodging children, dancers and neighbors hollering into one another's ear. The air rang with music and the cacophony of voices and clattering dishes, the constant susurrus of people moving and the sounds of celebration.

I was glad to melt into it all, and for a while I was an anonymous part of it, eating with relatives, listening to music, watching the mix of generations dance, gather to talk, laugh, hug, whisper, reunite as I had only seen in small Mexican villages. Behind the crowd noise, the band played fox trot and polka, rock and country-western. Dancers changed places with talkers and eaters. Kids ran pitchers of beer to tables and wrestled with friends.

Enough proper socializing, I thought, time to find the beer keg. I maneuvered through the crowd of dancers and cliques of gossip and jokes, moving closer to the band. In the shadows of the parked combine, near the kegs packed in tubs of ice, there was a covey of tables and folding chairs crowded with familiar faces. They spotted me as I filled my first cup with beer.

"Well, say now, if Martha didn't let him outa his cage! Come over here and sit your ass down!"

It was the McCormick's and Thompson at one table, the Mercy's nearby, a table of Van Anders and Chatmans and others. The men wore their suit coats open and their ties loose and crooked around their collars. Their wives were in best dresses, piled hair-do's. Everyone slouched back or leaned in, drinking and joking and partying as if the summer season hadn't ended.

Thompson dragged a chair up to the table, saying, "Where the hell you buy your clothes? What is this, military casual?"

"An international Goodwill on East Colfax in Denver. It caters to high class bums. Very exclusive."

Tommy Mercy called over, "Can you stand this much excitement?"

"I'll drink to calm myself." I lifted my glass in salute. There were other greetings and traded remarks around me, and Mike McCormick teased from two seats down, "You wouldn't be here looking for a woman now, would you? That's what these dances are for, you know."

I turned in my chair with some clever retort and looked into the eyes of Karen McCormick, seated next to him. Her look shot off into the crowd as my own moved beyond to Mike's Cheshire Cat grin. "We got to git the next Bachman marriage bedded down. There's still a sister or two left." His wife leaned back and elbowed him in the ribs for the malicious hint in his voice.

"I'm in favor of the idea," I parried, "It's just, they're all so young. How old are the two that got married?" Running nervously at the mouth, I was suddenly remembering why I had been glad to see the end of softball in September. More and more I had caught myself looking in her direction, standing near her, or taking an offered drink from her hand.

"He's almost nineteen. Janice Closterman, ah, that's Mrs. Bachman, I mean, she's two months pregnant. And a whole seven months out of high school."

Karen turned to him. "What were we, Michael, wise old folks?"

"I'm just tellin' Calvin here, that's why you got to get 'em young. If Bachmans have a girl, maybe you can get 'em to promise her to you, Parsons. Good farm operation to marry into."

There was more banter and beer across the tables, and the focus of the joking shifted to Buckwheat staying subdued and civilized.

"I'm always civilized, you assholes! That's what's wrong

with me." His wife pulled him up by the hand and led him hobbling and grumbling into the crowd of dancers. "Move it, you swine," he yelled back over his shoulder. "If Frankenstein has to dance, so do you!"

McCormick waved him off. "Not me."

"You're not going to?" I asked. "Seems like the only decent reason to get married—so you always have a dance partner."

"He won't dance," Karen said. "He's a creep."

"You dance," Mike said. He pushed at his wife's shoulder. "Here. She's an old one, but she'll do. Then I don't have to hear about it."

I looked to her for an answer.

"I never get to. All right," she said, putting her shadowed eyes on mine.

As we rose from our chairs, I asked, "You're sure this is okay?"

"It doesn't matter. It's just like you'll be dancing with Mike." In her ear I said, "No, not to me."

Then I followed her onto the dance floor to the swaying beat of an Eagle's song. Her dress was a powder blue of crushed denim that defined her lean lines. It had a modestly scooped collar and a slightly flared hem that swayed just above slim ankles. Her thick, golden hair was piled in soft, loose curls. She swung around to face me with a brief clear look and a slight, embarrassed smile, and moved to the beat of the music.

Karen looked beyond me as we danced and watched the crowd of dancers around us, casting only brief glimpses my way. I sensed her self-consciousness and leaned in close enough to smell the mild, clean edge of her perfume.

"I didn't mean to make you uncomfortable. If I'm staring at you, you should just take it as some kind of compliment."

She tilted her head toward me. "I thought I was the one staring," she said, rocking back and smiling at the dark floor.

When the music stopped, we moved together, clapping for the band. I said, "I don't mind."

"Everybody else might, though."

"Well, if it's just one dance in a lifetime, I'm going to enjoy it—as unobtrusively as possible. One more? I was just getting used to it."

"Sure." The band hit the first chords of "Rock Around the Clock." "Oh, but can you dance rock 'n roll?" she asked as though she didn't expect it.

"Sure," I said, taking her hands. We turned a couple of easy moves, then her eyes smiled flashes of light, and I led her through turns and twirls. I was aware of her rhythm and balance and the space between us, the shifting touch of fingertips as we moved to the music.

Then abruptly, the dance ended, surprising both of us.

"You must have a sister who taught you to dance," Karen said. We stood close, jostled and crowded by other dancers waiting for more music.

"Actually, my sister was too young. And I never had a social life. I took ballroom dancing as a P.E. credit in college. You know, trying to meet fascinating women."

"You didn't." I grinned at her, nodding. "Did it work?"

"I scared them all away. Too intense, or something. Maybe I just couldn't keep the beat. They thought I was crazy."

"Were you?"

The band struck up the sensuous tones of a love ballad by Alabama.

"Still am. I'm trying to control it, though," I said, putting an arm lightly around her waist and moving with her into the music.

For a while, we danced then, and I focused on the feel and shape of her in my arms, feeling that she let herself be held as closely as she dared. I felt a warm, electric tingle everywhere our bodies lightly touched. Her hair had the scent of vanilla and winter rain.

Finally, she drew back and looked up into my face with an animated social smile. "We should be talking about something," she said.

"The weather?" I offered.

"What about you?" I shrugged off a distracted smile. "Mike and Thompson tell some amazing stories."

"Everyone tells stories, but none of them are ever really true. I tell stories, but they're just about things I've seen. Not much has ever happened to me."

"To me either," she said.

"I don't know about that," I began, but the music stopped, and she backed away from me, saying, "Thank you," then moved quickly back toward the tables. I followed her cuts through the milling dancers, trying to keep up, feeling as if I'd done something wrong.

As we reached our chairs, Buckwheat shouted across the tables, "Hey, Parsons, get your ass over here! I knew you would be good for something someday." As I moved around the tables, he continued, "Take Sandy, and go dance. I'm sick of the monster mash."

Sandy Van Anders stood up and smiled. "My turn," she said.

"And keep your hands off her ass, Parsons, or I'm comin' out there after you," Buckwheat called after us as we moved toward the dance floor. His wife turned back and stuck out her tongue at him.

"Only if I scream," she hollered back over the music. Into my ear she said, "Don't mind him. If he really thought it, he wouldn't say it. He'd just do it."

We danced leaning toward one another's ear. "He's in a good mood tonight," I offered.

"Oh, yes, but he knows everyone's watching out for him, so he feels obligated to entertain them. Keeps them guessing."

"Not you, though?"

"He's on his best behavior. He promised, or I'll kill him, and he knows it."

She seemed genuinely sure and smiled at me dancing before her. She wore a dark wool skirt and a white, oversized sweater. A large pendant hung down between her breasts, accenting their pleasing shape. Her eyes were brown and narrow, and her light brown hair was cropped close above her ears and shagged down over the collar of her sweater. She was shorter than Karen McCormick, I mentally compared, larger boned. The round shape of her face, cheeks, and chin made me think of her as cute more than beautiful, different from Karen's fine, chiseled lines and lake-blue eyes that made me feel, more than think of, calming beauty.

I consciously cut off that train of thought and opened myself to enjoying the moment. The music was adequate, the atmosphere party-warm and lively, the woman I danced with attractive and a good dancer enjoying it, too. I was glad that Sandy Van Anders was so obliging and talkative. The few times I had met her during the summer, impatient disinterest had been the air she most exuded, as if wary of any activity or person that Buckwheat might be involved with. Quiet and stone-faced, she always seemed to be awaiting misfortune, ready to deal with it in resignation and with no nonsense. The wedding party, I was glad to see, seemed to lighten her spirits. She is like Aunt Martha, I thought, a younger version.

We danced until the band took a break and then returned to the table and full cups of beer, bawdy jokes, Thompson's retelling of the post-season tournament. I moved around the tables, trading a few lines with people I was beginning to know, consciously staying away from the seat I had started from. I shared a late beer with Thadd Mercy, who kept asking, "You're playing next year, aren't you? Damn straight, you are!"

I caught sight of Karl, who nodded toward Aunt Martha putting on her coat and wrapping a shawl about her grey head. The crowd was thinning—too soon, I thought. All the movement around me had to do with good-byes and departures.

I looked for McCormick's, but they had disappeared. Then Mike caught my arm as I was heading for the door. "Hey, once the holidays get by, come down to the valley for dinner some night."

"I shouldn't," I said. "Just putting you out for no good reason."

"Hell, yes, you should. You'll go crazy up there on the tableland, shut in with Martha all winter. I'll call you."

Out in the car Karl said, "Used to be, we'd come hard out of a dance, way back when, and we'd bed down in the wagon box. And if you left the doors open at home, your team would have you in the barn before dawn. These days, don't think I miss it though, with my bones. There's a storm blowin' in. I can feel it."

A light flurry of snow wisped through the night before the headlights on the road home. Martha turned to me in the back seat. "There now, aren't you glad you come?"

Buckwheat solos:

"Don't be messin' with that Nebraska Virgin stuff—which you don't even know what that is cuz I ain't been up here to tell you, do ya? Well, it ain't your virgin sister who's too young for it, or your never-been-screwed-till-she's-married virgin—though there's some Nebraska Virgins who still make a point to see that happens. And it ain't your Virgin Mother Mary either, though you might say most of 'em end up actin' like it. It ain't even your age-old, so-dog-faced-ugly-she'll-never-get-laid-til-she-dies virgin, though some of 'em end up lookin' like that pretty damn fast, too.

"Ol' Janice Closterman Bachman is on the way to bein' one herself now. First off, a Nebraska Virgin is married and has kids. She mighta been screwin' since before the blood ever flowed, and probably was pregnant the first time she ever passed an egg. Most of 'em you can get pregnant just by takin' your pants off in the same room with 'em. So it ain't like they never had sex. They coulda screwed every night of their high school lives in the back seat of the family wagon and still be a Nebraska Virgin because it's not when, or where, or how often that defines her. It's who with and how.

"Who with? One guy, the love of her life. They mighta played doctor in first grade and shared a late-night couch in eighth grade. They might not of ever kissed till prom or seen each other naked till their honeymoon, but it's this one guy. Probably knew him forever, and that's who she was with when all their hormones kicked in. Wham, bam! And wasn't that fun, might as well do it forever.

"So she's known the guy at least since high school, and she's probably all he's ever known, too, and whatever they learned, it was from each other, and all that ever was is makin' the beast with two backs. Ha! That's Shakespeare, man, the only line of Shakespeare I ever remembered—the beast with two backs. They never done it like dogs, never hangin' from a tree, probably never even ridin' the range with her on his saddlehorn. There's one way or no way, and that's missionary, my son. I know where of I speak. I had one once myself.

"Now, that's not to say none of it's good, 'specially if you

don't know nothin' else. Hell, even if you do—and I did—it's
nice. It's just I never seem to know it at the right damn time.

"Like with Sandy. I think about it, I know what that
Bachman kid went through. One day I'm sittin' in old Maude
Jack's class, and a breeze is comin' through the third floor windows, and the sun's pourin' in, and it's smellin' like the ground's
into March thaw. Miss Jack's scratchin' on the board, all lost in
one of those diagrams of hers, and everyone's asleep or pawin' to
get outside, throwin' paper wads and pen tips and scribblin' notes
to send clear across the room.

"I was watchin' Sandy comb out her hair in the back row
in a big bar of sunlight. She had it cut then, just at the ears and
kind of wavey down across one of those fawn's eyes. She was in
her cheer uniform and showin' her really nice legs, danglin' one
over the other. I could just see the profile of her face cuz she was
starin' out the window, too, that round nose and chin tilted back
and with like a doll's smile.

"God, the room started to get hot, and I could feel sweat
even startin' to trickle down my sternum, and my ears burned, and
my pants were pinchin' because I was startin' to get hard. I'm
thinkin' then, look how beautiful she is, look at those legs right up
there where they cross under the edge of her skirt, look at the
curve of her breasts. I was lookin' at everything about her and
startin' to boil and rumble at my desk.

"There it was, feelin' all that the first time, and I been
sittin' across from her, or next to her, or behind her or something
for ten years, pokin' her and hittin' her, and teasin' her. Square
dancin', for God's sake, and math problems and science projects,
and just hangin' out around her. And it had always been like we
were gonna be together in the world of Revere, America, because
she was the most beautiful in the world, and I was the biggest jock
in the world. That was naturally the match.

"Hell, man, if the world's a three story building, K
through twelve, with two hundred kids and a county full of
farmers, it's a fuckin' fairy tale come true. Oh, the world got a
little larger, maybe even three counties wide, but not much more,
and who the hell needed it? She was beautiful, and I was a ragin'
hero full of hormones. Great match, I'd say.

"It was like I couldn't wait to get my hands all over her. I mean all over her. In the halls we were always hangin' around each other, rubbin' around, teasin' and touchin' and grinnin' all the time, sneakin' off somewhere to neck, pet, get sweaty. And dancin' was nice, homecomings, or after movies, goin' out on the country roads and goin' crazy all over her—as much as she'd let me.

"It wasn't much at first. She had a strict bringin' up. The Millan's are fairly religious, and hell, her old man was the county sheriff at the time. She had to really watch her step for family's sake and politics, too. Not to say she didn't know what guys like me were after. She had her own sense of reputation, too. I hadn't even got my hand in her pants yet, and moms of all the dog-face girls and jealous guys are callin' her a whore. She wasn't like that. She wasn't gonna go all the way till it was anything but love.

"Course, what the hell does she know about love? She's fifteen, sixteen. Me, too. What the fuck do we know?

"So it's not until a little before Christmas our junior year. I was with one of my sisters, who was babysittin' at Purnell's on a school night. I drove her over because there was a storm brewin', and I was doin' homework there, watchin' TV. We heard a pick-up pull into the yard, and in a minute there's Sandy with three Boetcher kids in tow, standin' in the doorway.

"She was knocked back to see me there cuz she knew it wasn't our place, but she was lost. In fact, she was lost in a stolen pick-up. The sheriff's daughter, right?, with three kids she's babysittin'. She'd been takin' a Santa Claus suit out to Wayne Colson, who always plays Santa for the Lion's Club, but she's only got a vague idea of where she is cuz it's dark and there's flurries and the roads aren't familiar. Since she was baby watchin', she took the kids along in her mother's car, figurin' it'd take maybe half an hour.

"Well, toolin' along, she comes up too fast on an un-marked T in the road, couldn't make the turn, and drove right out into someone's field. She got it stopped without hurtin' anyone, but she was stuck. Fairly serious predicament with the storm comin' up.

"There was a yard light about a half mile down the road, so she bundled up the kids—the oldest was six, and she carried the two-year old—and walked to the light cuz, you know, whoever it is would know her and help. That's the way it is out here. Just had to make it to the light. They got there, but it was just Purnell's shop on his east section. Nobody lives there. But the old field pick-up, still full of alfalfa bales, was parked there, and of course had the keys in the ignition. She just started it up, backed it out, and come lookin' for help.

"Purnell's was the first place she come to, and there I was. Well, Sis kept the kids, and I followed Sandy in dad's four-wheel drive. We put Purnell's pick-up back, and I took her to her mom's car. I drove into the field and put my brights on, and we could see that she just had the front wheels jammed one way and had dropped down in a shallow irrigation ditch. I got the chain hooked up, locked in the four-wheel drive, and pulled her out.

"We delivered the Santa suit, came back to Purnell's for the Boetcher kids, and I rode with her to deliver them back home. Then we were a long time gettin' me back up to Purnell's. We parked somewhere up here between the rivers, talkin' about how we'd handled the whole situation, feelin' like we could handle the world together. The old heater in that Pontiac was blastin', and the snow was startin' to howl a little at the windows, and we were into each other's clothes in a minute, gettin' as close to each other as we could, and on fire, too. Musta been meltin' snow faster'n it fell for ten feet around. We were pantin', 'I love you. I love you,' like it's the only thing we could ever feel, and the physical feel then of it, too, was crazy-fine. The first time I ever felt what it's like to explode with a woman. Incredible.

"She cried, of course. I said, 'I'm sorry, I'm sorry.' Stupid things, getting dressed, embarrassed, afraid, even sayin' that we got to watch ourselves, wow!, like we were kids finally findin' out what it's like playin' with matches.

"We didn't say anything, ridin' back to Purnell's. I was drivin'. She was just pressed up against me, holdin' on. I was feelin' all kinds of things—good, and scared, and like I wanted to scream, and like I didn't want to show my face anywhere cuz everyone would already know just by lookin' at us together. I don't know what she was thinkin'. Sorry? Scared? Hurt? Now would I think she was a slut? But hell, we were already married from then on, really.

"We didn't even talk to each other for a whole week, wouldn't hardly look at each other. Everyone thought we had a big fight. I thought she hated me for wantin' it. She thought I'd throw her away and ruin her.

"We went out though, the next weekend, to a movie, and then went somewhere in the country but didn't do much. She cried some more. I said, 'I'm sorry,' some more. We said, 'I love you,' some more. And we really did, with everything we had, and pretty soon we were doing it again and making some kind of commitment to forever. This was the way it was gonna be.

"Whew! What a long ways back. After that, I guess, life was just a strut, man. It all just kind of changes the way you carry yourself and the way you look at life.

"That year, we were really startin' to win, too, more and more—football, state quarter-finals in basketball. I had the finest lookin' woman in the valley smilin' at my every move and as much love and fame as I could take. King of the fuckin' world. Senior year got even better, and Sandy and I were like glued together, talkin' kids and farmin' with dad and happy everafter shit. Crazy!

"I'd get freaked about it and chase pussy in Ogallala. Cock-sure, you know?, and livin' it up, King of the Plains. She'd hear about it, and cry, and we'd have fights and then great sex makin' up because we knew what we were gonna do for the rest of our lives, and I guess it all felt pretty fuckin' fine at the time."

Calvin's journal notes/ deep winter, January '76

Late night in the deep pit of winter. I can hear the flames flutter inside the stove. The lamplight flickers and casts shadows that hang in the warm air. I'm sitting here drinking too much Jack Daniel's again, going crazy, thinking I should go see her, talk to her, touch her. But I can't. It's been over three weeks now, and I still can't let it go, don't want to let it go, thinking: I can't even believe it could come to this depressing confusion and crazy desire.

I wasn't going to let it happen, didn't even imagine it possibly could, not with her. She's eight years married, a mother of two, a housewife and farm wife, a cook, a janitor, a servant, a family's beast of burden who's never known any other life, never been anything but defined by family and home and constant nurturing. She's a younger version of Aunt Martha—no, I can't push it that far, trying to be repulsed by it.

Because she's also incredibly beautiful—not just her fine lines, the graceful ways she moves; not just the soft lines around the inviting smile and the bluer than sky-blue eyes; not just her gorgeous straw-blond hair (done up in a French braid as thick as a hawser down her back that night). It's also an incredibly attractive presence, an aura made up of the feeling that she can look in behind your eyes and understand anything you might say to her, any need you can't even explain. The subtle light in her expressions, the open interest in her eyes, the easy way she laughs, the sense of calm self-acceptance in her unselfconscious responses. No, I wasn't going to feel a thing.

But for a free, night's meal in the middle of a black, bleak January, I entertained the McCormicks, sang for my supper, told stories about my life for laughs and the unusual. After they tucked their kids into bed (Tony, almost eight, and Jaime, just past three), we sat at the kitchen table over black coffee and whiskey, Mike telling about Lowery and the University, but mostly me, talking Mexico like a travel agent and SDS like an undercover reporter. She'd listen and laugh or smile or scoff just right, or gush a skeptical gasp and say, "You didn't," reaching out spontaneously to lightly tap my arm as if I'm an old and comfortable acquaintance. She made me want to tease and make her laugh, to entertain, to tell tales of my life as if it were Arabian Nights and not a lesson in American hypocrisy. It didn't matter how much of it was true and what it was really worth. The way she sat, leaning her forearms on the table, her blond tail like a rope thrown over her shoulder, the quiet attention, and the way her eyes would throw light at mine when we'd finally, briefly, make contact, all made me want to make her keep touching me and laughing, and it was happening without my thinking it or guiding it, just given up to going with the flow and the feeling of the night and her company.

None of it was conscious, none of it obvious. Out of my winter isolation I babbled away over whiskey. Mike told jokes, and Karen listened and laughed, poured coffee. I'd try not to stare too long at her with the lust pouring out my eyes, and she never seemed to notice it (nor Mike either), never really sending a signal, an offering, a clear feeling. Was it there in the air around her, or just me imagining? I didn't know, only knew that I wanted to be there with her, wondering how could it ever happen? Would she, could she ever let it?

Then it just did. The Bearcat scanner sitting on the TV crackled, and Mike jumped up to go listen, bumping the table with his thighs as he rose. In reaction I jumped my chair back a few inches and into Karen on the edge of hers. As Mike moved into the livingroom, we were frozen that way, listening to an ambulance call for a roll-over on the Interstate north of Revere—injuries, no fatalities. First, attuned to Tommy Mercy's voice on the scanner, we didn't notice touching each other. Then I did, and I just didn't move away. I could feel her realize it then, too, and not move away either—till Mike's footsteps came back toward the kitchen.

"I'm on call tonight. I gotta go." Of course, I moved to leave, too, afraid even to look at her. "Glad to have you over," he said. "Another time."

We got our coats on and were out the door with Mike trying not to rush me too fast. We got in our pick-ups, and he headed for Revere. I turned for the south table.

I didn't have my stocking hat. The night wind was raw, wind chill way below zero. The Speckled Pony has barely enough heater to keep the windshield from fogging over, and it's a long drive in the cold. I should have gone on anyway.

—Instead, I put it in reverse and backed up into the yard and to the door. She heard me because she opened the door before I knocked and stood there with my hat in her hands. I moved across the threshold and she backed up a step, watching me.

I said, "My hat."

She said, "I know," and held it out to me, and I grabbed her wrist and pulled her to me. I couldn't help it.

I kissed her, and she kissed back, and I just held her then a long, long time, stroking her hair and slowly undoing the braid till she pulled me by the hand back through the trailer to her bed.

She was warm and tender and giving. Everything. A release, a flood, an incredible surge and slow, soft eddying. Afterwards, we lay on our sides, facing each other. I dragged my fingertips the slow, long length of her, knees to forehead. Her cheeks were wet, but she wasn't crying aloud. I held her, and she nestled against me, trembling, while I half listened for the sound of a pick-up engine. Into my chest she said, "I never thought anything like you could ever happen in my life." I couldn't say anything, just hung on to her.

Then there was a night shuffle in the hallway, and she tensed against me with a gasp of fear. A knock meekly sounded on the closed door, and Jaime's sleepy voice muttered, "Mommy, why's the door closed? I don't feel good."

"Mama's coming, honey. Go into the bathroom. I'm coming."

She rose and was a slim, white flash to the closet where she put on a robe. She went by me and through the door without looking at me, and I was left grasping for my clothes in the unfamiliar darkness of her room. I could hear Jaime crying and gagging behind the closed bathroom door as I dressed faster than I ever have in my life and creeped out like a low-class thief.

I drove back here to the farm without seeing any of the road—my hat down over my ears. I never slept. Did she?

The next day I was already crazy and couldn't think of anything else. What did I do? What did it do to her? Is this love, just crazy stupidness? Should I go back there now? What if Mike is there? What if he already knows? How could he? What is she feeling? Should I go over there? —Round and round. I couldn't read, couldn't keep the fire stoked, sipping gallons of strong coffee till I was caffeine buzzing back and forth across the floor, thinking: Is this love? Crazy stupidness? Can't I go back now? Round and round.

I didn't go. The next day I restacked a huge mountain of bales in the barn without seeing one bale. All day: Should I go see her? What is she thinking? I want to, I want to. Will he be there? What would I say?

The third day I drove over. It was after nine in the morning when I came down the gulleywash road, saw Mike's pick-up was gone, and drove into the yard. When she answered the door, I could read a surge of thoughts in her eyes and the sad turn of her half smile. It was grief and regret and lost easiness and weary guilt. I looked for love, desire, need, and I know they were there, too.

Stepping in, I said, "I had to come see you."

"I knew you would. Every sound that went by for two days, I started to shake." She wouldn't look me in the eyes. Jaime sat in the livingroom, stacking plastic blocks and running into them with a Tonka truck.

I said, "I can't help wanting you...needing you."

I said a thousand things about need, want, love, beauty, loneliness, lostness, till she was crying into her hands, standing in front of me. I pulled her against me and held on tight while she tried to push away. She quit struggling then and just cried against me, sobbing, "I can't. Please, I can't. I want to, but I can't."

Jaime crawled over to tug on her mother's jeans. "Mommy, what's wrong?"

"Go play, Jaime. Go on," she answered quietly. Jaime went reluctantly with a pouting look at me.

Karen finally pushed away and looked at me, wiping tears away. "How could I?" she asked in a hopeless, despairing, soft sob. Even broken apart, she was so beautiful and desirable and needing. Everything in me wanted her, wanted to take her away. —Take her away where?

"Please, Calvin, you have to go. He only went to town for coffee," she said, rubbing her eyes with the tail of her blue work shirt. "I couldn't face.... I'm sorry."

I stood in silence awhile, watching her. She wouldn't look at me. I left then, feeling...empty, lost, cut off more than ever from everything. I couldn't go back to the farm. Just drove. Out to the lake and back, up the river to Packard and Rolf's Bar. Before lunch I was drunk.

That's where I've mostly been these last, late winter weeks— downing the sauce somewhere along the Interstate. Afternoons in generic Holiday Inn lounges, nights in the small town taverns—Rolf's, Cody's, even the Sip 'n Sizzle in Ogallala where the old-time alcoholics hang out, nursing cigarettes and afternoon beers and deadend lives. Sometimes I run into Ramirez, or Chatman, or other single guys whose faces look familiar. They're roaming the bars, too, looking for women that don't exist—slim beauties that might drop off the Interstate, looking for that perfect Midwestern man, or girls home from college, or restless secretaries and grocery clerks. Instead, what they—what we—find are overweight, dumpy, sad-eyed, plain-faced ladies so lonely they've got no place but being drunk at Cody's on a Friday night. Everybody's empty and filling the void with booze and stupid talk, waiting for winter to end.

Some nights I don't even know how I drive back to the farm. But I make it and pass out and somehow get up to milk cows every morning, just a raw, painful body going through the hungover routine. Yesterday I managed to puke in the milk bucket before I finished, the result of a particularly bad combination of way too much late-night tequila, no food or sleep, and the pungent stench of the early morning cow manure.

Is this a life?

I went back to bed for the rest of the day and didn't recover enough to go out again last night. I'm burned out down to the bottom maybe, and still there's so much more winter to go.

Aunt Martha looks in on me less and less, more and more disappointed, though she hasn't got a clue what's happening. I rarely make the evening meals anymore either. Karl's usually home early now—on winter hours at AgCo—and he does the evening milking. I'm usually long gone, always mentally, if not physically, too.

The oldest questions are coming back to me, the ones I've asked everywhere I've ever been: What the hell am I doing here? Is anything living up to what I thought it could be? Why am I failing the dream, the ideal? Did they ever really exist? And where can I go from here?

Mike McCormick's lyrics/

You got to give Buckwheat credit. Hell, he hadn't gone on a rampage clear since Patterman's auction when he sorta disarmed ol' Crighter in front of half the county. There it was almost spring already, and he'd been a sleepin' bear. But Thompson laid odds Bucky couldn't hold it in till spring ball. He said somethin'd set him off, and this did. —It's no wonder to me, really, I just happened to sit in on some of it, and it was weird shit even to me.

I was comin' back from a regional firemen's meeting in North Platte, and I figured I'd stop for a beer at Rolf's before drivin' all the way home. It was a fairly snookered Friday night crowd and even with some strangers' faces 'cause, what do you know, the pipeliners are back around the area. The ground's thawed, and they're finishin' that natural gas line up on the south table. They already got weekend money and nothin' to do but scratch where it itches and party.

Well, no big deal to me. I can be bought a beer by a pie-eyed boy, but it don't mean I have to eat his line of bullshit for it. You know, they tell a good story or two. They been to Iran. They been in Alaska. They met all kinds of wild people in all kinds of places who are rich from some scheme or shakedown, or will be soon, or were once, or some damned thing. They been everywhere and done everything.

Well, it's okay. They got a way of tellin' it, some of 'em do, and they all got that southern twang and style and phony down home, aw shucks sweetness. If you been out and about some, you can see that shit for what it is and maybe even look past it some, but I swear, the way it works on some women, it's enough to fry even my sorry ass. It ain't likely I'd introduce one of these slick bastards to my sister, let alone have my wife hang out with one, but that's about the story of that night.

I come into Rolf's and right away Buckwheat sees me and stands up, hollering his orders like he does, "Get yer ass over here!" So I go over, and him and Sandy are with Andy Bracer and his wife and these two other grinnin' guys I never seen before. One of them stands up and pours me a beer out of a pitcher he's just taken off the waitress' hands.

We go through the what-are-you-doin'-in-the-enemy's-bar thing, and it turns out that Buckwheat and Sandy are helping celebrate Andy's and Becky's wedding anniversary. It's like twelve, thirteen years for them, four kids, five years on the old Bracer place. Been here forever. Well, these other two guys are pipeliners, helpin' out, too.

They're old friends, see. That is, old friends of Becky's. And Sandy kinda knows them, too, see. That's 'cause way last summer Becky was workin' for a while in Ogallala, punchin' a cash register at Safeway because they weren't makin' ends meet with the farming. —What else is new, right? Well, she got into hittin' the bars a bit before goin' home nights, and it didn't matter much 'cause Andy'd be out doin' something in some corner of the farm anyway, and the kids'd have all the home chores done and be gone off to whatever summertime doin's were cookin'.

Beings Sandy and her are cousins, Becky'd come by for Sandy sometimes and haul her along. It's like nights Buckwheat's workin', or he's off playin' ball. He knows about it and don't care. Andy knows about it, and's too busy to care, or even to think too much about Becky bein' barroom buddy-buddy with these slick-talkin' southern tongues.

Well, that's the summer before. Becky, she starts tellin' me how great a time they all had, drinks and laughs and friends. Just innocent party-time life like Becky probably never seen since high school maybe. Her and Andy been married since then, and with farm and family for a dozen years, she just mighta forgot how a man can cuddle up to an unattached lady with the compliments and attention and the razzle-dazzle stories. She ate it up, was plain to see, from a king-size platter. She was even rattlin' on about how this guy, Cecil was his name, even came out to the farm for some home cookin' last fall, and the kids just think he's the cat's meow. Why, he's even a family man himself with a wife and two kids, but they're conveniently in Arkansas, and he's got nothin' to do but spend summer nights in Nebraska bars, keepin' company with Becky Bracer.

Now, I don't need no crystal ball to see disaster happenin'. Becky, she's just tickled to see this Cecil back around, and Cecil, he's grinnin' like the cat that ate the canary. But it seems way over Andy's good-natured head. He listens to his wife coo and chatter, and she leans all over this Cecil, sayin', "Now tell 'em all about that crippled camel seller in Morocco." "Now tell 'em about that Hell's Angel in New Orleans." "Isn't he a scream?"

So all this is goin' on while the pipeline boys are buyin' the pitchers of beer. —Hell, they ought to be payin' something for the privilege of our society. Buckwheat, he's takin' it pretty good really, 'cause Sandy ain't involved that much, though she's part of the "we" in some of Becky's tellin'. Him and Andy are talkin' ground thaw and fuel costs and seed corn and such, mostly ignorin' Becky and her buddies. Him and Sandy even got up and danced a bit. She pulled him out on the dance floor right after he says, "What bullshit," to the end of one of Cecil's little adventure stories.

I decided to pour another glass of beer, thinkin' about waitin' to see if Buckwheat was gonna clear up the social connections, so to speak. God knows Andy ain't gonna do it. And hell, maybe there wasn't much left to make clear anyhow that it would matter.

This pipeliner friend of Cecil's, he asks Becky to dance. She'd sure as hell love to! So I'm sittin' there with Andy and this Cecil, and it's nothin' but quiet. Finally, Andy starts askin' stuff like, "How many kids you got?" "What's their names?" Dumb shit stuff. Cecil's askin', "Now whaddaya farm?" as if either of them cared two turds.

Meanwhile, Becky's out there on the dance floor stompin' and wigglin' around like she is possessed of rhythm and nothin' pleased her more than the present goddamn musical moment. Becky Bracer—I seen her dance at a hundred dances maybe in our lifetimes, and she'd never moved around then like she was out there that night, 'cause if she had, it wouldn't have gone unnoticed for long. Not by me.

Women, you go figure. I sure as hell don't know what they want. One day they're happy and satisfied with what they do. They got it safe and easy in a home they've had ever since school days. They got family to take care of and the best place in the world to do it. They got town and country and everyone they've ever known livin' around them to do anything they want.

But there's always—or suddenly, either way—somethin' to bitch about. There ain't enough of anything, or there's too much of something else. Sometimes it's just fine that you spend thirty, forty hours a week workin' for somebody else, and another eighty hours keepin' a farm goin', and maybe even a few hours of sleep are okay, and you're providing everything just fine. Then some days you're just not treatin' her well enough, like you don't deserve nothin' yerself. Who knows when or why?

So there's ol' Becky Bracer out there wigglin' around to this country band playin' hard rock like butchers doin' surgery, and

her and this pipeliner are right around Buckwheat and Sandy, and
Buck's lookin' over his shoulder at Becky sometimes with a look
like, who is this person? They all come back to the table then,
Buckwheat hobblin' over like he does, and the stud kinda struttin'.
The women sit down, and Becky goes back to this "Tell us where
you're goin' to next" stuff with Cecil. Buckwheat downed a glass
of beer and poured another and said, "Drink up, McCormick,"
like he was havin' just one hell of a pleasant time.

Then this other pipeliner—he's still standin' up, bouncin'
to the cool of the next song—he's gonna spread his wealth. He
asks Sandy to dance. Hell, she knows him, they're friends, right?
He says, "That is, if it's all right with you, Sarh, she's your lady," in
this cool southern voice to Bucky, right?

Buckwheat says, "Hey, yeah, all right with me. But I don't
know, floor's kinda dirty out there. Maybe you oughta mop it up
first."

Dumb-Ass says, "Mop it?" When he gets it, he says,
"Hey, no offense here. Just bein' friendly in friendly country."

"No offense like a bad fart," Buckwheat says. "No one
can see it, but we all got to sit here and smell it."

"Fuck you, too, Jack." This guy, maybe six feet tall, a
skinny one-eighty, nothin' under that southern sun tan but a beer
gut, he thinks Buckwheat's just a fuckin' cripple.

Buckwheat puts his glass down and gets up slow-like, like
he has to with that stiff knee. He's grinnin', too, like he always
could, like the world's just a pleasant place. Then zap! He's got
the guy by the throat before he can even lift a fist. "Time to mop
the floor, fucker!" And let me tell you, Buckwheat took him
dancin'.

Oh Jesus! did he beat the shit outa that guy. Dancers
scattered like scared cattle, screamin' and stampedin'. Tables and
chairs started screechin' and crashin' together, glasses breakin'. I
got a glimpse of ol' Cecil sittin' there between Becky and Andy,
lookin' back and forth at 'em, wide-eyed, like hey!, would I want to
cause something like this?

Hugh Thayer was behind the bar. He comes leapin' over
it, and someone else rushed in from the back. Buckwheat was
hammerin' this guy's head against the floor, and they tried to pull
him off. One table nearby got knocked over then in the shuffle. I

grabbed Sandy 'cause she started to go after Buckwheat, screamin' and cussin' him, and I dragged her back by the arm.

With the crowd gettin' all shoved together, a couple more fights started up—pipeliners against townies, and bunches of people in between gettin' pounded around and headin' for the doors screamin' like scared kids. That's what I did, too, pullin' Sandy along. I don't know where Becky and Andy got lost. Cecil, he had his hands full with some guy from Packard poundin' his teeth down his throat.

Outside, people were scramblin' for cars 'cause the State Patrol wasn't gonna be too far away. Sandy went with me in the pick-up, sayin' to hell with Buckwheat, he was on his own. I pulled out and just headed up a side street a couple of blocks and parked because they'd be speed trappin' everyone runnin' for the Interstate. We just sat there and waited. Sandy was pissed, callin' Buckwheat every name in the book. Then she cried and cussed for a while, then she just went mad-steamin' silent.

Finally, she just said to hell with it, and I took her back to Revere, only we took Highway 30 instead of the Interstate. I defended Buckwheat and told her the guy deserved it. She said she didn't even know the guy. Buckwheat just wanted to get crazy, that it didn't have to do with her and that guy at all.

I said, "He was just tryin' to show Andy what he should be doin'."

"Well, Andy won't ever learn it, especially from John Van Anders, because he's got no idea himself. He's proven that his whole damn life."

Well, she knows him better than I do.

Anyway, I let her off at the trailer court and told her I'd find out what happened to Buck. I checked at Cody's first, then I called the sheriff's office. They wouldn't say about anything. Then I headed back toward Mel's station, and here come Crighter patrollin'. I flashed my lights at him, and we rolled down windows, and I asked what's up. He gets a charge outa tellin' what he knows. You gotta kiss his ass just right to get it, though.

He said they hauled four pipeliners into North Platte, and a couple guys from Packard, too. But he didn't mention Buckwheat, and he would have with pleasure if he knowed it happened. So I went lookin' for Buckwheat. Back up to Ogallala. I found

Becky and Andy in the Holiday Inn. They were havin' margaritas and openin' each other's anniversary present like nothin' happened at all. She got him this watch that he sure as hell can't wear anywhere but Sunday. And he got her this silver necklace thing, I guess that she can wear when she goes out dancin' with Cecil, I don't know. They gonna keep on like this? I sure as hell don't know that either.

Anyway, Andy said they got out with the crowd and walked over to a cousin's of his who lives in Packard. No clue to where Buckwheat went. So I drove around town lookin' for his pick-up to be parked in front of the other bars in town, but I finally found it out at the truckstop on the Interstate. He was in there chowin' down on scrambled eggs and steak like he was stokin' a hot steam engine. He was still pissed, just kinda grunted when I sat down in the booth across from him.

I said, "What the hell happened to you?" He had a big red welt up along the corner of this left eye. It was all bloodshot, and the eyelid had started to swell down on it where the pipeliner had got in one good punch.

"One punch," he grunted, and kept on chewin' on steak like an old coyote on a rabbit's hind quarter. He looked like he shoulda had that steak on his eye instead of chewin' on it.

"How'd you get out of there without the Smokeys gettin' you?" I asked him.

Well, he filled that whole jaw of his with a cliff of teeth, grinnin, and said, "I gave 'em the body."

For a second there I was sure he meant it like that, but then he says, "I just picked the guy up and threw him on Thayer and that other guy workin' there and split out the back way behind the bar. Fuck, man, I ain't stupid. I'm a survivor. I don't get nailed in that shit. Not anymore at least."

"You didn't have to cause all that crap," I told him. "You got a lot of people really pissed now, including your wife. You beat up a guy she hardly knows. You're gonna get yer ass sued for damages 'cause you're not exactly unknown in these parts. Plus, the law's gonna stick it to you."

"Anybody fucks with me, I'm gonna mop this floor with 'em. Let any of 'em come in here and give me shit."

Pourin' hot sauce on his eggs and eatin' and fumin', he

was like a volcano waitin' to blow. So I stuck around and got him tellin' about it and laughin' finally, tellin' him he shoulda been poundin' on ol' Becky Bracer maybe, as she's the one who got them pipeliners all to prowlin'. And I told him about Andy and her in the Holiday Inn.

He just shook his head. "They're all just fuckin' idiots, man."

After a while, he said, "Shit! Let's go get fuckin' drunk." But by then it was way past last call anywhere but Hawaii, and besides, his pump didn't need any more primin'. I followed him to make sure he went home. The lights were still on, and I could hear Sandy start layin' into him, screamin' at him the minute he opened the door.

When I got home, it was way after two, and Karen had the doors locked on me. Turns out then, she's pissed 'cause I'm so late without tellin' her or callin' her, like it ever mattered before what time I come in. Even when I tell her what had happened, she's more p.o.ed, screamin' that I'm takin' care of a friend, but not ever home to take care of her or the kids. So I got the same word bashin' that Buckwheat got, just for seein' the matter out. Now, Karen'd been on the rampage a couple days, and I was just gettin' the stone cold silent treatment like I wasn't even there.

Her thing was, I didn't care about things around home. I was never payin' attention to the kids. I wasn't thinking about the future. She'd been on this gripe ever since she told me she was pregnant again. See what I mean? You don't know what women are thinkin'. Karen was never so glad in her life as when she got Jaime house-broke out of diapers. Then she's actin' like a furrowin' sow again. Swore she never wanted to go through childbirth again. All of a sudden the family's got to get bigger. Bigger is better, right? Hell, who knows anymore. Women. You go figure.

CHAPTER THREE: STORM FRONTS

Turning the key and hearing the low, dragged-out growl of the engine, I cursed the brittle cold. My breath seemed to hang like a deadened spirit in the twilight of the cab. When does the cold end, I wondered. The starter of the Speckled Pony ground down again, and a wire of panic probed my stomach. I thought, I have to get out of here.

Before the depressing thought of my isolation could develop, I climbed out of the cab, and without hesitation, went around to the hood, popped it open, and turned to grab the cables of the battery charger. In hasty efficiency prodded by the pain of stabbing cold, I quickly had the cables connected to the battery and watched my breath dissipate in the icy air while the charger hummed. Then, moving back behind the wheel, I pumped the gas pedal, pulled the choke, and turned the key.

The starter growled with renewed vigor, and the engine coughed once, twice, and died. I tried once more and felt a grin of relief as the Speckled Pony finally began to purr again with life.

I let the engine warm while I stowed the charger and closed the hood, then I was out on the frozen roads again, headed for Revere. The last light along the horizon was pastel purple and crimson, washed weak and puny by the arctic edge of the wind. Spring felt like an unachievable dream. The darkening fields around me lay barren and desert-like, the browns and greys dying into shadow and night. Nothing but the wind howled across the tableland, and I drove, shivering, over the empty ground.

Nothing lives out in this, I thought. Nothing survives for long. What am I doing out in it? Where do I think I'm going? It seemed ridiculous then to have worried so about getting the pick-up to start. It didn't matter. There was barely any difference between getting out and staying hidden in the bunkhouse.

I've been doing this for eleven months, I thought. I had been on the farm longer than I had stayed in any one place since returning from Central America over four years before. But what difference had it made?

Seven weeks since seeing Karen McCormick, talking to her. That seemed an even longer stretch of time. Mexico seemed like a fantasy. School and SDS meetings and political cadres seemed like legends or fairy tales that turned out to be not true. I thought of friends as dead and as cold as the bleak country I drove through, bit-part players and fragments of history as vague as any other era defined, defunct, and left behind. The old ideals and vows had been livable only as long as everyone stuck to-gether, as long as an evil force like the war and all it represented hovered over us like a plague. There was none of that now, only winter, nothing and no one else.

As I drove west on the gravel road, the night closed in. I fought the urge to drive four miles farther on and take the turn that would take me into the valley past McCormick's. Instead, I turned north on the road that would take me most directly toward the Interstate overpass and the blacktop into Revere, picking up speed as the engine warmed and the heater tempered the cab air, thinking: all this time here, and all that's changed is that I can find my way down the dark roads.

Then the lights of Revere winked like gems in black ink as the road reached the shoulder of the tableland and dropped down into the river valley. A steady flow of vehicle lights cut the darkness both ways down the Interstate, and I found myself hoping then that I wouldn't have to go into the trailer house next to the gas station to get Buckwheat. I felt like a corruptive influence, appearing suddenly to lure John Van Anders away from his family's company and out onto the back roads for a cruising session of beer and pot. Sandy Van Anders never implied or accused me of anything, but she never looked me in the eye when I was there either.

I coasted across the overpass and in under the lights of Mel Duncan's station. Only a local pick-up stood at the pumps.

Inside, Mel leaned on the counter, talking to the driver, and I was relieved to see Buckwheat sitting on the window sill, watching the TV flickering behind Mel. When I hit the horn lightly, Buckwheat got up without looking and used a key on the Coke machine, opened it up, and pulled out a twelve-pack of Miller Lite. A wave to Mel's nod, and he was out the door and sliding into the Speckled Pony.

Buckwheat popped the top on a can as we pulled out of the station and handed it over. "About damn time, bird dung. If I didn't lock it away, I woulda had it all down my throat before you ever showed up." He sipped at his own can of beer. "First damn beer since I mopped up Rolf's floor with that fuckin' pipeliner. Sandy's got me under armed guard practically."

"I hope she doesn't think I'm wrecking your family life, pulling you away."

"Shit. By now, she's damn glad to see me go. Besides, it's what everybody else does. Guys all over the county are out cruisin' around the back roads, suckin' beer and bullshittin'. It's a regular goddamn tradition even Sandy understands. It's what you do cuz there ain't anything else. You go down to Cody's and everyone thinks you're a drunk. You cruise the roads doin' it, and you're a regular fuckin' Joe. Besides, then I don't get inspired to tear up the place. Very peaceful, this. But goddamn boring."

We drove over the river bridge, slowly through town, and wound up onto the tableland between the rivers. Buckwheat lit a joint and passed it. "And Sandy knows I never get into trouble with you. We just drink beer and do illegal shit. Only people we can possibly kill is our worthless selves. That's a comfort to her. —Here, try some of this," he said, holding his breath. "Picked from down by the river. It's not Thai stick, but it will get you stoned."

"Then I will get lost," I replied, greedily taking the joint.

"You already are, brother. Lost, that is."

We smoked the joint and opened two more cans of beer before anything else was said. Then Buckwheat claimed, "Hell, man, you don't know where the fuck we are, do ya?"

"Yeah, I do," I claimed, and I made the turn that took us toward the valley lookout. Another mile, and I pulled over, cutting the engine and lights. The wind howled at the corners of the cab.

Below, the traffic lights flowed through the darkness like colored bubbles on a strong, unseeable current. The invisible lights of Revere glowed up against the cloud cover far to the west. We drank silently, watching, drifting in private silences till Buckwheat said, "Damn and be Jesus! Say somethin', will ya? You ain't said shit since you pulled up. What the hell's eatin' you?"

"You usually do the talking."

"I ain't had enough for that yet, so fuckin' say somethin' before I throw your ass out into space and see if I can hit a truck down there."

After a while I said, "I was thinking about dead people."

"He's thinkin' about dead people. Great."

"People who shouldn't be dead. You ever hear of Billy Conrad?"

"The name sounds familiar. Naw, don't know him."

"He lived on the farm for a while, helping Karl. He left this and joined the Marines. He was dead inside a year, and he should have been here instead.

"Then there was a guy I met in Chicago in '68, named Terry Lyons, from some college in Massachusetts. Different kind of soldier. It was no great brotherhood. I knew him for maybe two days. We got stoned together in Lincoln Park, talking about Nixon and McGovern and some chick Terry was there with, named Haley Stars, who had picked him up hitchhiking and had screwed his brains out all the way there from Cleveland. Terry Lyons, screaming, 'Peace now! Peace now! Peace now!" just when everything was getting started, when the whole park started moving on the Democratic convention. I never saw him again once we got moving toward the Hilton. I didn't find out till I got back to Boulder the next fall that he was one of those who crashed through the storefront windows of the hotel during the clubbing. He cut an artery and bled to death. Fuckin' Terry Lyons. I was thinking of him when I was driving in tonight.

"And Ted Gold. You ever hear of him?"

"I never heard of anyone I care to remember."

"No? Ted Gold? He was famous for about a week in 1970. He came to Boulder to help us organize a delegation for the moratorium in Washington. Late '69, that was. Seems like a century. He was one of the inner circle, a Weatherman, who was going to bring the war to the American streets. It wasn't so much his politics—which were Marxist-Leninist with as strict an interpretation as a Baptist's with a Bible. But he had a smiling, confident, kick-ass attitude and style, like damn straight!, it can be different. It will be different, because, by God, we'll make it that way. Bring on the bombs, baby. He could make you believe.

"It was just after the Days of Rage in Chicago, and it did seem then like the revolution was here. We fought hand-to-hand in the streets. Six Weathermen were shot. Two hundred and fifty beaten up and jailed like political prisoners. When the C.U. contingent went off to march in Washington, Ted stayed behind, and the night of the march, we blew up the main entrance of the IBM plant with a pipe bomb. It was no big deal, really. There were a lot of bombings all over the country that winter, but I can't tell you how damn good it felt to strike back. The war really was home for some of us.

"For a while then, I guess I was crazy. The plan was crazy. I went to New York to meet Ted and about half a dozen others. I was going to join the rebels, that's what it felt like. And then five minutes before I reached their hideout, they blew themselves up in a Manhattan townhouse. Three of them. The others escaped. They identified Ted Gold by the print off a severed finger.

"I was stunned. Two months later, almost to the day, the National Guard shot those kids at Kent State. Everything and everybody was crazy. I wanted to destroy everything America stood for. I cried and got drunk and got stoned for three days straight. Then I sobered up, broke into the Boulder County Selective Services offices, and Molotoved it. Mostly to wipe out my own personal records, of course. Then I went into exile in Mexico, another deserter.

"That was Terry Lyons, Ted Gold, Kent State, Kennedy and King and Bobby Kennedy before that. And a whole bunch more no one ever knew or even thinks about, dead from their own bombs, or from riot control, or from drugs and doing crazy things because the world was crazy around them. Everybody was just going along with the ride, trying to survive any way they could."

After a timeless silence, Buckwheat said, "So you were there. You didn't have to kill anyone."

"No. I only had to watch them die for nothing. It gets

cold like this for so damn long, I start thinking of dead people.
Everything's dead. The ground, the sky, people I knew, the past,
anything to fucking believe in even."

Buckwheat belched into the following silence. "I don't
need to listen to this shit, man. Fuck it. Fuck the war. You need
to get laid."

I felt the urge to tell him about Karen McCormick, about
how beautiful and alive she was, about how vulnerable, how
generous, how much I needed her. I could burn that down, too, I
thought. I could have her. I could destroy that fine institution of
her marriage. A secret told once in this country is soon
everybody's secret. I could see what would happen. I said, "What
I need is to get out of here."

"Shit, man, and miss softball and wreck Thompson's life?
You're still nothin' but a bad-ass freak who ain't got a damned
thing to do. You lost the war. I lost the war, and we ain't got a
fuckin' thing to show for it. At least hand me that last beer before
you go. I know what to do about that. Time to get wasted, and
don't wake me up when it's over."

Buckwheat solos:

"Do some of this and shut up a while. Sorry I asked.
Besides, you're not goin' anywhere for now anyway cuz there's a
blizzard blowin' in. That's all you're feelin' is a blizzard movin' in.
All day today I watched the geese glidin' in to hunker down in the
trees along the river east of the station there. Lots more of 'em
than usual and lots earlier in the day than usual. They know it's
comin', and no one's goin' anywhere for a day or so. Not even the
honkers. Not even them lights cruisin' down the Interstate.

"Especially them. You watch. The wind'll pick up to
hurricane crazy, and even if it's barely snowin', it's a howlin' white-
out, total blindness, killer cold. And in about two minutes those
yellow brick roads down there are sheets of ice. Truck'll jackknife
off in the median, cars'll do doughnuts and get buried in the
ditches. And every damn one of them that's left comes crawlin'
off the Interstate to save their fuckin' lives, cuz if any of 'em get

caught out in it, they're too damn stupid about storms to know
how to survive. People get stuck somewhere they can't even tell,
and no one can see 'em passin' by, and they curl up by themselves
and freeze to death in the front seat or fall asleep to carbon
monoxide dreams. You watch. It'll happen. Especially when
there hasn't been a blizzard for a few years. Someone gets caught.

"The ones that make it into some town, they hole up
anywhere they can. Every motel for two hundred miles will be
full—from the Holiday Inns to the dives out behind gas stations.
Even some school gyms or town halls fill up, no one goin' no
damn where till the blizzard says so. They can't do a god damned
thing about it either, but go out in it and die, so they sit and wait
like helpless babes. Big plans, big trips, big dreams, tight sched-
ules, big-shot meetings—everything gets put on hold.

"It's like a permanent population down there on the road,
you know? It's just that it's always on the move most of the time,
thinkin' it's got life by the balls, but it's really just the weather lettin'
it happen, and weather will shut it all down, too. Maybe it'll just be
for the length of the storm—if there's not much snow and just a
bit of a blow. But if there's lots of snow, the country shuts down
for days. Even the highways take forever to get cleared, and
people just sit and wait, live with it or die in it.

"Don't bother the home folks that much—most of 'em,
that is. Only the really stupid ones don't think to stock up and
hunker down—dumber'n a fuckin' goose down in the river reeds.
Sandy went into town before lunch even and came home with
enough to feed an army for weeks. Everybody was toppin' off
their tanks at the station this morning, goin' into town for
somethin', restless as ants. They don't even notice that they're
doin' it.

"But there'll be somebody who's got to dash out into it
for diapers or medicine or milk or somethin'. They got to be
convinced personally that a blizzard is bigger than they are. And
somebody's got to be a technological cowboy and put tire chains
on the big, new one-ton four-by-four, hook up to the hydraulic
blade, make sure the winch is workin', and go macho out there in
the storm to pull stupid people out of the ditches, and to bust
through drifts, breakin' trail for stragglers, and just generally
provin' that they ain't afraid of the fuckin' weather and that they're

a damn sight tougher, too.

"Let 'em think that if they want to. It always worked for me. It's why my life's such a big son of a bitchin' success. I always know what the fuck is goin' on. But all it takes is one slip up, one let down, one miscalculation, and the blizzard takes you. Just like that.

"I remember about eleven, twelve years ago. —You were already long gone. Henry Reuther's brother was livin' out at their place south of town. They raised chickens then, lots of 'em, in cages in this huge building. Well, ol' Louis Reuther, he couldn't let them birds thirst to death, now could he? Besides, it was nothin' but a storm. Seventy-mile-an-hour winds. Already a day and a night of snow howlin' in and three foot drifts in the yard. But the chicken shed was only sixty yards or so west of the farm house. He could walk it in his sleep, and probably did a time or two, and ol' Louis set out for it just like always.

"Only he never came back. By the time it let up enough to see at all, and Henry went out to look for him, there were no tracks or nothin'. It was over a week before they found him. They figure the north wind pushed him off to the left of the shed, and he walked right on by it without bein' able to see a thing in the white-out. By the time he figured it out, he couldn't tell he was clear out on the edge of the field. Probably he panicked and wandered all around till he was exhausted and got caught up in drift on the lee side of a row of young junipers out along the road. That's where they finally found him.

"He couldn't have seen twenty yards ahead, and the storm just took him over. He lived out there on the place his whole damn life, and there wasn't a thing he could do about it. Fifty-seven, he was, when it happened, and he never did a god damned thing in his life but try and raise chickens. Nobody thinks it can happen to them, but all you got to do is go out in it, and it just gets you."

Calvin's journal notes/ late-winter, '76

I went out into it because I was desperate with restless-ness. Because, like Van Anders said, you don't think it can happen

to you. Because I was crazy with the powers of it raging and
raging relentlessly, the howl rising and swirling and screaming at
the windows and the eaves of the bunkhouse, the gale force of the
wind making the tiny cabin shudder slightly, the light outside a
single, solid dark grey-white fury, the frenzy of driven snow never-
ending.

It was beginning two nights ago as I drove home from
Revere, the first flakes flying through the yellow shaft of headlights in front of the Speckled Pony. Tumbleweeds streaked across
the roads, smashing into fence lines. The wind only purred
because I was running mostly with it the same direction, but at the
road edges I could see how it tore at the grasses and savaged the
tree limbs in the windbreaks I passed. Already it was raging to my
stoned mind.

I parked in the shop, and walking to the bunkhouse, I
could feel the sharp, driving edge of cold cutting my bare hands
and ears. The snow was already settling in the yard behind the
trees, and the windbreak roared in the blackness like the rabid,
angry growl of a wild beast. I could feel how easily the cold can
kill, and I ran the last few yards to the door.

Too wasted to deal with the hassle of building a fire, I
burrowed in under the down comforters on the bed and crashed
out from consciousness and the usual midnight depression. All
the rest of the night the blizzard built up a furious madness, and it
screamed in everything I dreamed.

I woke to Uncle Karl stamping in through the south door,
letting a cold, huge cloud of flakes swoosh in with the raw, grey
light. I shivered into my clothes, and I could see my breath in the
air because I hadn't built a fire the night before. Snow was already
shin-deep in the yard, but it had let up some, and it was easy
enough to get to the barn to milk and feed. With stacks of bales
and the cows and cats in out of the storm, it was warmer in the
barn than in the bunkhouse. Milking was routine, but the smells
of hay and fresh manure, milk and grain and animal heat, were
more pungent and enclosed with the storm raging outside. The
wind's roar off-set the purr of life inside the barn. The mood of
normal morning calm insulated us from the drive of the blizzard.

I had breakfast with Martha and Karl since he wasn't
bothering to try to get to work in town. I sat in on their morning

devotional and stayed for another cup of coffee and blizzard
stories. One was about the storm of 1888 that killed thousands
of animals and hundreds of fresh Nebraska pioneers. Any sod
house society that could survive that violence could withstand
anything, and did. And the blizzard of '49—shortly after I was
born—when the whole Midwest was closed down for weeks and
farmsteads had to be supplied by airdrops. Natural catastrophies
are part of the way of life. Certain times are defined by them, and
lives are changed forever by them, or taken away completely by
them. Survival is chance and little else.

Spring tornadoes (yet to come), summer hail storms,
autumn field fires, winter blizzards. It seems like any kind of fate
can fall out of the sky on you. And what can you do about it?
Not much—prepare as much as possible, be vigilant, protect
yourself, and when it happens, be smart, react and recover as best
you can, be resilient.

And what I should have done and could have done, I
didn't. As if the words were just words, that's all, as meaningless
as so many others. As if the storm in its monotony disguised its
true character and teased me.

The rest of the day I stayed, half hibernating, in the
bunkhouse, keeping the stove stoked, heating tea, reading some. I
had to have a lamp on all the time, the blizzard so deep the grey of
the day was darkness. The howl of the wind was a subconscious
song. Sometimes, I sat looking out the window into the white fury
in the yard, watching the dark shapes of fence and tankhouse and
barn flicker like mirages, details oscillating with the intensity of the
storm. Out beyond the corrals, the rest of the universe was
invisible, and the wind-driven snow that hid it had no depth or
distance, no substance or soul.

Night came early. The evening milking and then supper
seemed late in the slow motion tick of time and the quick darkness. The yard lights, one near the house, the other at the corner
of the barn, seemed unable to cast light. They were merely dim
globes of light smothered by the blowing snow. During milking,
Uncle Karl talked of a time as a child when they strung a guide
rope the hundred-plus yards between the house and barn so that
he and my mother wouldn't get lost carrying their buckets back
and forth through the blizzard. During supper we listened to the

radio tell us that the country between Denver and Omaha was virtually shut down and would be for at least the next day.

I retreated again to my house and stove and lamplight. The blizzard night was a prison. I daydreamed of Mexico and wanted to be there. I thought about what had first sent me running there, thought about Ted again, and Billy Conrad, and all the wasted lives and time. I thought about how I got here and the uselessness of it, the nonsense of it all. I thought of Karl and Martha snowed in with their Bible and their memories, of Buckwheat Van Anders snowed in with his kids, of the McCormick's lying together in bed in their trailer house, listening to the wind. It's just a long monotonous storm. I sat sipping Jack Daniel's and water, sobbing and crying at I don't know what, just wanting to be gone from it all.

Then today, I almost was.

Didn't sleep much of the night—too much napping around all day. The moaning wind was constant. I got up before the alarm to go do the milking. No problem, just a drag getting up in the dark and cold, like mid-winter again.

Didn't think about it, just pulled on jeans and boots and one of Karl's old, worn parkas, and stepped out into the storm as if it were just another day. I put my head down and trudged for the tankhouse, maybe forty yards away, but I couldn't see it in the dark and snow. Drifts were at least knee-deep, and the wind louder and more violent than I had realized at first, and the blizzard incredible and exhilarating in its ice-edged rampage.

I came up to the tankhouse almost before I saw its grey form materialize in the blinding fury of blowing snow. I wasn't at the corner where I had headed, but along the side, and I waded through drifts around the leeward side. From its southwest corner, I looked for the barn and yard light, but couldn't see them. A thousand butterflies took flight in my stomach. It seemed like a vast polar wilderness, an unexplored challenge, the rage of the storm an erupting thrill, and I stepped out into it as if it were a game, groping into thigh-deep drifts and wind roar and blinding snow.

First, an image of Louis Reuther frozen in a drift beside some trees flashed into mind, then the feeling that I was lost just as he had been. I had no idea how far I had moved. I stood in my tracks and tried to will the dark form of the barn into being while the shock rose in me that a story could actually become reality. Wind, not a word, but a violent, driving force, and cold, not an idea, but sharp pain against the edges of my exposed face. And the very real feel of death. Stupid, senseless death.

Around me, total white-out. Nothing but the blizzard's rage. So total and beyond comprehension. My senses simply stopped working—snow-blind, wind-deafened, numbed cold, nothing to taste or smell but the edge of pure emptiness. Consciousness simply blanked into blizzard, too. I was paralyzed. There was no direction. No difference between distance and closeness, earth and sky, and any move was the wrong move.

I suddenly acknowledged my helplessness, not even surprised by my careless disregard for weather's power, but awed by the truth of the overwhelming force of nature. Then another sudden thought from nowhere: I'm tripping. This isn't real. But the thought wasn't from nowhere. The blizzard suddenly seemed like a trip on LSD, the way it takes over the senses and mind so completely if you let it, forming its own dazzling reality, short circuiting the senses and receptors with hallucinated sparks and primeval shadows and unrestrained emotions, confronting you with everything you are and all your limitations and even your own sad, silly, insignificant death.

I was plainly and simply full of fear, standing there in a growing panic, straining to see into the roaring white glare all around me, looking for anything I could identify. I stood there feeling the cold snow drift in around me as if I were a fence post, amazed again that the storm could actually do this to me, that I could be destroyed by what was once only an idea.

I was like everybody else I've known who died or just gave up. I've been thinking about them all lately, and thinking there, caught in the storm, that maybe it was all just premonition.

All this emotional weight carried around so intensely and for so long, just to go out into a blizzard and die trudging to the barn to milk cows that had more natural sense than I did. It seemed supremely ridiculous. Then I thought: Simple truths, simple truths. I don't even know why I thought it or what it meant, except that I decided that I didn't want to die, at least not die by simply giving up.

I focused on the ridge of snow drifting now at my waist. Its crest ran a discernible line in the lee of my body, suddenly pointing out to me the direction of the wind. I knew it had been blasting from due north during the whole storm. That direction, I realized, was just off to my right. In my head I visualized the yard between the tankhouse and the barn. If I moved shouldering into the wind, it wouldn't matter if I missed the barn because the corral fence would be there somewhere to run into, and I could follow it to the barn. If I tried to move straight to the left, pushed by the wind, I could end up lost in the windbreak, like Louis Reuther. In my head I created an orientation out of the blinding snow and the force of the wind, out of the idea of this place.

Eventually, you have to move on no matter what, and so I did. I don't know how long I'd been simply standing there. A long, freezing time. I finally lifted my feet and legs and pushed hard right of forward through the thigh-deep snow, feeling a surge of energy rush into me, the body and brain powering up with lifesaving adrenaline.

I plowed maybe twenty feet with the snow getting no deeper. Then I thought I saw a dark form of something and willed it to be the top board of the corral fence. I pushed on with renewed energy. A new surging thrill rushed through me as when I had stepped out away from the tankhouse and into the storm. As I thrashed nearer, the form ahead darkened, too tall to be the fence. Then a massive wall of snow seemed to rise up just before me.

Even five feet away, it took me a confused moment to realize that it was the hay stack just to the left of the barn. The dark line was the leeward edge of the long stack disappearing back into the blinding white fury of the storm. A huge wave of relief rushed out from deep inside, a burst of joy. I turned due right and trudged to the south barn wall, invisible only about thirty feet away. Then I could see it, and in an instant I was standing in the shelter of the wall, and I moved along it to the snow-plastered, drift-hidden door at the corner where the wind and snow blasted past.

In the separating room I found the light switch and the most comforting warmth I've ever felt. I was soaked and shivering, and I stripped out of my coat and boots and jeans. My thighs were bright red and numb. I hung my jeans and coat above the propane heater, drew up the one chair in the room, and huddled by the precious heat.

I could hear the hammering roar of the wind at the ice-covered east window, and opposite, beyond the door into the rest of the barn, I could hear Old Mouse and the other three cows mooing impatient complaint about their painfully full udders. It was a beautiful sound. I listened, sitting there by the stove, for maybe an hour, warming up, letting go of a lot of things—old disappointments and resentments and angers and regrets. Not consciously. It was all just the raging blizzard, and I had gotten through it this far, and it felt good. Better than good.

Later, I redressed and went in to milk the cows like any other morning, except I was a little late. The smells of the barn, the cats mewing for milk, the cows stomping and chewing and swishing tails, the sound of warm milk foaming into the pail, the feel of life in the gushing teats, it all closed in snuggly around me, under the roar of the storm.

When I finished milking and tending, I got back in the warm room and took my time separating the cream and stowing it in the refrigerator, bottling the milk, breaking down the separator and washing it, putting it back together. It was all like a new experience again, but comfortable with familiarity.

Then I waited. I wasn't dumb enough to test the storm twice, and the waiting was easier than waiting has ever been. Storm accepted, as well as my own condition maybe. Sometime later, the grey gloom seemed to lighten, and I looked out the south window and could see the tankhouse and the windmill rising above it into the still raging snowblow above the windbreak tree tops. I plowed back past the tankhouse and to the bunkhouse in only a few moments of cold struggle.

It was almost noon, so I changed and went trudging to the big house for lunch. Not even Aunt Martha had thought I'd be stupid enough to plunge out into the worst of the storm. They both just assumed that I had gotten up there late and had just finished the milking, and I let them go on believing it.

Didn't stay for afternoon talk, but came back here to my fire and quiet contentment. I've read some and done some dishes, cleaned the bathroom—personal routines, living out the storm.

Now the snow has stopped. The sky seems higher, but a cold, dull steel grey. The wind has not let up, and though I can see to the tops of the far western windbreak pine where I could have drifted in to die, between here and there the raging wind whips up a blinding ground blizzard. No one will move until it has calmed. Then the whole country will begin to dig out. Karl and Martha both assure me that the real season will be here next week, melting snow away to new spring green below, just as if none of this has happened. That's the way with spring blizzards.

Gerald Van Anders' lyrics/

My boy, he got wounded there in Vietnam. —It was bad, as anyone 'round here can tell you. And it wasn't like he had to go. My John, he's the only son of a farmer who was an only son himself. Growin' food, we're already doin' enough for America. That, and family's all we got. He didn't have to even join up, but John, he wanted to serve his country, and I guess we're supposed to grow 'em up to be that way, and that's right and good and all. We all know that some times there's got to be sacrifice. We just don't want it to be us that gets sacrificed all the time.

It didn't seem right that John's got to be the one that gets hurt. I mean, first off, he told us before he even went to Japan that he would never be in combat because of the special job he had. We was proud he had special training and assignments. It was secret stuff, and they come 'round home checkin' up on Johnny before they ever let him in on it. He took language school and reconnaissance training somewheres near Seattle, and he was supposed to learn to tell 'em all that the Communists were sayin'. Then he got assigned to the —it's right here somewhere—the 525th Military Intelligence Group. They was never supposed to even go to Vietnam. But there John went anyhow, and we didn't even know about it till after he was wounded, and the shock liked to kill his mother.

You can say that I was angry 'bout this enough to write to Mrs. Smith. It was the only time I ever wrote a letter to Congress because I ain't good at such things, but I wrote and said, this ain't right. He wasn't even supposed to go to Vietnam, so how could this be? After that, I got some of this correspondence from the Army, sayin' that what John was doin' was all Top Secret because he was liaison personnel between this CIA field officer and this 525th Military Intelligence Group. And he had been ordered to this base, or village, called Dau Teng, which is in Binh Long Province, to find out first-hand if these intelligence reports he had worked up himself from intercepted Communist communications was true. That was April of '72. He was in Saigon some time before that, but not for long.

Then he was assigned to what they call a CRIP platoon, under this Major Waverly. CRIP means Combined Reconnaissance and Intelligence Platoon. It wasn't anything I knew about till we flew out to San Francisco to see John in the hospital there, and he told us. All the Army said was, it was a small scouting patrol that covered large regions on foot, moving real fast, to gather information from villagers and natives that might be useful to our boys and the South Vietnamese Army.

They didn't tell us that they kidnapped and tortured folks they thought was Viet Cong leaders for information, and executed V.C. tax collectors, and spied on villagers in enemy territory. Johnny had to go with them, and he told us they done those things, too, besides ask people questions. They were looking for this whole battalion of North Vietnam Regulars with tanks and supplies and ammunition that Johnny was sayin' was dug in in giant tunnels under this whole province. He wasn't supposed to tell us that, but when we seen him—just two days after more surgery on his leg again, he was all doped up and in a mood and state of mind I never seen in my boy ever before or since.

I thought, my dear God, what did they do to my son over there? He cried hard like I never heard him, there when we first come to see him, and he was ragin' mad like us Van Anders can get, but it was comin' out of his mouth as this big joke of how they got pinned down with this other patrol they run into. It was a First Cavalry company of light weapons platoons, and just like John, they were some of them green GIs in the jungle for the first time in their lives. And what they were pinned down for was because Johnny, he found what he said was there all along and they weren't believin' him—over three thousand North Vietnam troops and their whole supply support. This was the day he got wounded, April 13th. By the first of May, when we seen him, the papers were already sayin' this was the biggest Communist attack since the Tet Offensive of '68, and it come pourin' right down out of Cambodia and Binh Long Province.

Part of the first wave of action pinned down Johnny's platoon and this First Cavalry company on a ridge where two valleys joined together. They got mortared real bad and lost a lot of men. When he come back home, he had dreams about that for awhile, but we didn't let anyone know, and they finally stopped. Well, they got some air support, but it didn't help much. Helicopters tried to come in to resupply them, but they dropped the ammo into the trees, scared off by machine guns, and the Communists, they captured it and blew it up. They kept 'em pinned down till dark, and snipers picked men off any time anyone moved. After dark, they screamed and howled like Indians to scare our boys into thinking they'd be slaughtered, and the GIs could hear their own wounded, too—too far out to be covered, moanin' and cryin' and bein' shot one by one by the Communists in the night.

Then John went to sleep some time before dawn, and when he sat up in a dream, this GI shot him with his M-16, with tracers, and killed two others right beside Johnny.

John, he didn't even know he was tellin' us this stuff, I don't think. It was terrible, and his mother sat right there listenin' and cryin' in her hands, and he just went on talkin' about it anyway like it was the funniest thing in the world. He finally stopped when the doctors come in again, and we was there four days, visitin', but he never talked about it again, and never even when he finally come home.

I was thinkin' maybe it was the drugs they had him on, but I wrote to Mrs. Smith again and told her all what Johnny said— horrible things. Some two months after that, there was a letter from this Major Waverly, who was Johnny's patrol leader. It was like a report about the battle, and he told only some of what John told—the mortar barrage, the Communists attackin', the number of dead, including the wounded that the Viet Cong shot. He said that he couldn't tell me what happened to Johnny exactly because he wasn't right there when it happened. He said, in the hell and chaos of battle sad and horrible things happen, but there are also incredible acts of heroism and courage and honor. He said, thirty-seven American sons were sacrificed in that battle, doing duty with honor for their country. He didn't know, no more than any other man, why God allowed the world and war to be the way they are.

It didn't do no good to chase after it anymore. Johnny, he was one of forty-six wounded that got lifted out by helicopter the next day. The Communists went on around their position in the night, instead of slaughtering them all, because they were goin' after somewheres else more important all along. They're sayin', now that the war's completely over, that it's a war we lost, that it was wrong to be there in the first place, and that we're a country in shame. A man's got to wonder if it ain't so.

Since then, there's been Watergate, and Nixon, who got us out of that war, he resigned. Someone tried to kill President Ford. The oil embargo sent all the gas prices rocketing, and how can an honest farmer make any kind of living like that? Terrorists everywhere are killing folks, and what for nobody knows. Now there's talk about granting amnesty to draft dodgers and deserters. It's a country that doesn't know what to do with itself, and the families of all them boys that died, and soldiers like Johnny, who won't ever walk straight again, what do they have for all this sacrifice that was talked about and written about so much?

What's to show for all that pain? I got to think that all they got left is what they got to go home to. If it ain't the country they left to go fight for, when they come back, what's there for them in its place? Here, it was the farm to come back to for Johnny, and that never changed. "You can come back out here any time you want, and you know that. This here's your place, too." That's what I always told him.

INTERLUDE:

From behind the backstop, I watched the boy settle into the batter's box and cock the bat, a left-handed batter. Like I was. Lead-off hitter, and an infielder. Like I was.

He crouched over the plate and took the first pitch, a fast ball down the pipe, for a called strike. I had always liked the first pitch. He stepped out of the box and took signals from Thompson, coaching at third base.

—Thompson. No sons of his own. Now he coached everyone else's boys. I didn't know the signs, but I knew the bunt was on: fifth inning, his team down three to one, man on first, no one out, lead-off hitter up. The other coach knew it, too. He was yelling across the field to his third baseman, moving him down the baseline toward the batter.

"He's got wheels. He's got wheels." Like I did.

The batter dug in again and stuck his face out over the plate, the nose and chin like his mother's. The pitcher delivered, low and inside. The boy turned to bunt, hopped back a step, and still got wood on the ball, dribbling it down the first base line. He was two steps beyond it before the catcher moved. The pitcher was looking at his first baseman, who had hesitated—cover the base or go after the bunt? By the instant the pitcher had decided to go after the ball himself, the batter was half way to first. His foot hit the bag before the pitcher scrambled it down, turned and cocked to throw. No play. He turned to look at second. No play.

That brought up Little Chatman—son of Little Chatman. Had to be, I thought. He and his girlfriend were inseparable back then. Thompson had the bunt on again. The boy took two wild pitches before he laid the next ball out in the grass in front of the pitcher. The runners moved on the hit, and the pitcher had to take the force out at first. Runners on second and third now, one down. The next batter had that wing of black hair pressed against his forehead by his helmet, his cliff-like jaw set in a determined scowl.

"Recognize these guys?" It was Mike McCormick's voice behind me.

"That's got to be Buckwheat's last."

"Yeah. Named Kevin. Buckwheat's old man wanted him named after Bucky, but Sandy wouldn't even consider it. Thought it might curse him to be just like his father.

We watched the boy take a three-oh strike across the middle of the plate.

"More patience than Buckwheat."

"A Chatman on second base," I said. "Yours on third?"

Kevin Van Anders drove a line shot past the shortstop's out-stretched glove and into left-center field. Two runs in. Score tied.

Mike McCormick said, "Spooky, ain't it?"

THIRD MOVEMENT:

WEATHER

CHAPTER ONE: STORM DAMAGE

Driving in toward Revere for that first home game of the year, what I thought about was the gathering. The first pick-ups would be pulling in around the ball diamond, probably Thompson first, or Smokey Johns—always around town anyway, a fixture like part of the waterworks or the street maintainer he tended. He'd be sitting in the open door of his truck, setting down his first beer of the evening just long enough to lace and tie his cleats. As soon as another arrived, a ball would be in the air.

They would all come in from whatever they'd been doing out on the ground in their busy lives—driving deliveries, running tractors, doing business somewhere down the river. It was Wednesday evening, the first scheduled game for Mercy's, and everything stopped for the game. It was time to get together, hit the ball, and run the bases.

We had started the season rusty and ragged in the pre-season tournament the weekend before, losing the first game to an Ogallala team of graduated, high-school jocks—too many errors and wild throws, and too many pop ups to shallow left. But there had been good signs—two infield double plays to end rallies, and a last inning rally with the bats that ended two runs too short because of some dumb base running. With one game's practice under our belts and a loss to strengthen resolve, we had won a second game, and another on Sunday morning, before being eliminated just out of the trophies.

We had only lost the final game in the last of the seventh with a clutch hit over McCormick's head at rover, and we had all come off the field feeling short-changed and ready to pick up the level of play come the regular season.

"We make the good throws to the right bases sooner, we stop the cheap hits, and we win instead of lose 'em this season," Thompson had said as we sipped beer and watched from picnic tables behind the center field fence while Rolf's played Bunke's for the championship. Everyone had agreed, confidence reinforced by Coors perhaps, but I had felt it, too. We had team potential, and once again, this could be the season. And it had all felt especially good after the long, cold hell of a Russian-like Nebraska winter. We had all groaned and stretched and run like reawakening bears when we took field, had laughed and drunk and talked afterwards like refreshed survivors. Spring rites had been performed and the freedom of summer announced.

I welcomed the focus of my thoughts. I had always been able to lose myself for a while in the action of a ball game. It was a place to burn off emotional energy and aggression for clear and simple purpose—to score runs, to play well, even to reach some-times beyond the usual range and clearly contribute to a common win. In the anonymity of urban high school, and later in the pressure of difference in Mexico, it had been baseball that was the refuge. During the troubled years of SDS and the restrictions of graduate school, it had been handball tournaments. Then there was Thadd Mercy's softball team.

In my mental picture of the players I saw McCormick, then I thought of Karen. Would she be there? I had wondered the same thing before the pre-season tournament, and she hadn't come to any of the games. Looking for her had broken my concentration and colored the pleasure of the games. Just to avoid me? I wondered. I could feel the thought of her as an emptiness in the pit of my stomach and a dull uneasiness at the base of my neck. I hadn't seen her since—. I cut the thought off.

As I pulled up behind the dugout bench that evening , I saw Thompson and Tom Mercy standing out at third base, looking up at the sky. They glanced my direction as I cut the engine, then returned their gaze to the silent roil of grey-green clouds off west down the valley. I had ignored the building weather on the drive in, but now as I walked out onto the grass, I felt an eerie edge to the dull, grey color of the sky light. The air seemed thick, and it muted voices and dulled the slap of the bat on the ball and isolated the far-away, warning blast of an approaching freight train whistle.

Thompson walked up as I began throwing warm-up tosses back and forth with Jimmy Lox. "This is not looking good," he said. "Look at the color of those clouds."

I held the ball and turned to the west. The towering billows of cumulus were sacred satin white on the outer edges that still caught the last light of the sun already far below the horizon. But its deep heart was murky green going to black, and the underside, so close to the distant shoulders of the valley, a deeper-than-indigo blue.

"That might be hours away," I offered hopefully. "No wind."

"Yeah. No wind," Thompson responded in an ominous tone. "It's just swirlin' around up there. See? There's other clouds coming in from northeast, too, and the wind's been hard and hot southwest all day." He turned his eyes to each quadrant of the sky as he mentioned it. "All the ingredients for tornado. The fire department's got spotters out already."

"Are we going to try and play?" I asked.

Thompson shrugged. "As long as there's no lightning, I suppose so. But we better get on with it."

By the time the warm-ups had ended and the coin toss at home plate took place and Mercy's took the field, the edges of the cloud bank had become less defined, and the whole sky above the trees beyond the outfield was a solid, grey wall. The curtains of rain to the west were streaked and distinctive and closer. The sky above rumbled with first thunder.

No one's mind was really on the game. Buckwheat walked the first batter, and the next one rolled a slow grounder up the middle for a hit. McCormick threw the ball in from center as the first raindrops thudded on the infield, fluffing dust into the still, warm air. The sky behind us had gone deep black.

The raindrops were huge and random, like small water balloons exploding on the ground and the backs of players. Buckwheat tossed in a couple more pitches, then the sky broke loose. Suddenly, the field was the bottom of a waterfall, the air roaring with its falling rush, the town around us obliterated from sight. The players and spectators scattered fast for the shelter of cars and pick-ups parked along the field edges. On the heels of Little Chatman, I headed for the sideline in full stride.

I found myself headed toward McCormick's pick-up in the blurred line of vehicles and veered off, leaping the players' bench with Little Chatman and then splitting around his pick-up. Chatman was in on the driver's side, and I jerked open the other door. But Chatman's girlfriend and his dog filled the cab. I slammed it shut and wheeled around. It was Thompson's car behind me. I yanked open the driver's door and piled in on someone climbing out of the way. When I got the door closed and sat upright, I turned to look into the smiling eyes of Karen McCormick.

"This is Thompson's car," I said, immediately feeling stupid for it.

She kept her smile, but cast her gaze toward her feet. "I know," she said. "Maggie took her kids to her mother's car. We were talking."

The beating of the rain on the car was suddenly a deafening rattle. The windshield was running grey blur and beginning to steam over with the lengthening silence inside.

Karen said, "Enjoy your swim?" The inviting smile was still there. I was conscious of the water dripping from my hair and beard, the cold clamminess of my soaked jersey. Goosebumps suddenly burst down my arms, and I shivered violently.

"It's incredible," I offered. She nodded, and we tried to look out the windows, but only the grey, thundering rain and a sheen of wetness could be seen. In the rain-rattled silence I looked at her beauty again, the thick golden hair slung down over her shoulder, the fine line of her jaw and throat, the moist warm blue of the eyes she turned on me.

"I love you," I said, without ever having thought it. "I want to be with you."

"Oh, Calvin. We just can't." I watched the tears well up in her steady eyes as she faced me. "I want—" But she cut it short and dropped her gaze to her lap. "I've been wanting to see you because I have to tell you about the baby—."

"No, don't. It doesn't matter. I want to be with you."

She flashed a sad smile and a glance of tender pity for my

ignorance and asked, "What do you think we could do? Would we live with your aunt and uncle?"

"We could go away somewhere."

"Oh, Calvin." She reached out and touched my arm. "Where could I go? You can go anywhere because you belong everywhere in the world. But I'm only from here. And my children are here."

"We can find a place here then."

"And what? Will you live with my children? Do you think I could ever live without them? They need me. Do you think Mike would ever let me take them away? He's their father. His parents are their grandparents. Roy and Lana are my parents, too, by now, and there are my own parents. How could I ever explain to them, to any of them...? How do I take you to them?"

I held her hand in mine as she looked away again and fell silent. "What about your needs?" I asked.

Her eyes came back to me. "You are like everything in the world I could never have. You're so different from people I know, the guys here. The things you do, you do for different reasons than anybody else would. You're strong. You're so.... I think I need you, too, but I also need my family. And their needs are more important than mine."

"And more important than mine."

I watched the tears blossom again in the corners of her eyes, flashing pain and pity and love and the denial of love. She said, "Oh Calvin. Mike, my babies, they love me because they need me. You don't really need me, but you love me anyway. You can't know what that means to me."

We sat facing each other in a growing, aching silence then without noticing the diminishing rain. Then a blur of movement brushed against her window. The back door burst open as we started out of our private moment, and Thompson tumbled into the seat with Mike McCormick almost on top of him. I watched them, dripping wet, as they sat up, and Karen tried to keep her face diverted, turning to roll down the window and look out on the sky.

"Hey! These windows are fogged over like a steam room. What you two been doin' in here," Mike joked. Then a softball smashed against the windshield, starbursting it, and we all cringed in reflex. Thompson cursed as another ringing crash pounded the hood. Another shattered the back window as we all cowered lower in our seats, crying out. The hail stones crashed like ringing hammer blows around us, random, jolting, deadly bombardments.

"Jesus! The size of softballs!" Thompson shouted. "Stay down!"

I found myself lying over Karen, who had rocked over in the seat toward me. I gently stroked her arm and hair and felt her against my chest, shuddering softly with silent sobs. The sudden, random hammer blows changed to the sound of gravel pelting the car as the size of the hail stones diminished to marble size, increased in intensity for a moment, then stopped abruptly with the vibrating punctuation of silence. The music of dripping, running water gradually grew louder, and we slowly sat up in our seats.

"If somebody was out in that, they're dead," Mike said, and he and Thompson scrambled back out of the car into a light sprinkle of rain.

Karen sat wiping her eyes with the sleeves of her denim jacket. "Please," she said as I climbed out to survey the wreckage of the storm with everyone else.

Buckwheat solos:

"The whole place went raw winter again like there ain't a damn bit of sense to seasons. The weather does what it damn well pleases, and to hell with you. That infield looked like a glacier. Ice everywhere, and those big ones—like Thompson threw every softball we own over the whole ball park. The cars all around the diamond looked like a bat got took to 'em—smashed windows, hoods dented, lights knocked out. That speckled, flamin' forties pick-up got lucky cuz its windows were down and the windshield is so straight up and down. Only lost a headlight, and the dents fit right in with the rest of the look. But anyone with a real car, wasn't one didn't have at least one window cracked.

"Around the outside edge of the park, the tree limbs were all torn down and hanging. The sky was that cold steel grey and blowin' off northeast real fast. The air was super-cooled. You could see your breath at first. Maybe like Iceland here in town, but I knew right away it was gonna be hell on the home place cuz that's where it was all headed—right up over the north tableland, headed for the other river valley.

"Hell, I didn't even have to call. I just went up there the next day, and you could see it out there in the east field as you turn into the drive. His brand new, shiny sprinkler system was twisted and bent and spilled over on its side with the tires in the air. One of his big, new, sparkly grain bins was mashed over like a tin can, and the roof was heaped up in a wad in the field behind the house.

"I didn't have to say a damn thing. The old man's out in the shop, and I go out there. He says, 'Insurance covers it all. We just got to start over.'

"Fuck insurance. There's so much damage in the country, it'll be weeks before they get to his system. He'll plant it to corn anyway. About the time it's up, they'll come in with their equipment and kill a good section of it, and he'll have to do something else with that. It's just stupid shit.

"It'll need water before he can get his sprinkler back up, you watch. Now, he could go to Gaddis and beg to get his crew to maybe get him up and goin' sooner, but fuck no, that won't happen. Why? Cuz Jerry Van Anders don't do business with that bastard, Larry Gaddis, see. That's cuz maybe two decades ago, Larry Gaddis was chasin Jerry's sister—my Aunt Jannie, that is, in high school, and on a date he maybe put his hand up Jannie's skirt or something, and dad had to go defend family honor by beating the shit out of him.

"And besides, Gaddis' brother was in the pen a while for stealing cars in Omaha. So, hey! it's just a no-good family, and we don't do business with them even if it means saving a corn crop maybe by gettin' water on it two weeks earlier. Fuck no.

"Such damn petty shit, man. But it makes sense around here. That's business. It's like, Newcastle don't buy insurance from Chub Chatman because Chatman screwed his cousin in some kind of deal for that piece of shit Harley he booms around on. Mel Duncan thinks the whole Kelso family are a bunch of crooks cuz Vern Kelso never paid off a set of tires he got from Mel, though he can sure keep his bar tab at Cody's paid. Mel won't even give credit to the guy's mother. She probably put Vern up to it, see.

"We ain't givin' anyone a break, and hell, who am I to talk? That fuckin' Collard, man, got the prissiest, fuckin' fancy house in Revere, but he's an Ogallala banker. He's too good to buy his groceries here, or gas for his big Continental at Mel's. He even plays ball for an Ogallala team. But he sure as shit can tell my old man how to put his life in debt to every fuckin' business in the county. I wouldn't go into his goddamn bank if it gave away gold bars. I'd steal cars before I took a loan from him.

"See, man? We're just a dumb flock of ignorant, stubborn asses. Me, my old man, Mel, Newcastle, ever damned one of us. We got our good, legitimate reasons. Fuckin' petty games, man. We don't need a world crisis. We don't need a war. We can dick around with people's lives right here, and hell, why not? Nothin's gonna change. People don't change.

"Robb Miller's sister got caught with her pants down in a closet at school in eighth grade with Bobby Burns. Ever since then, she was a whore, probably went down on every male in Revere and made a fortune sellin' her ass in Ogallala. Of course, I never talked to one guy that actually ever did her, but they always knew someone who had. She's probably still like that in Detroit or Lansing or wherever the hell she ran off to to be herself. And old Timo. Hell, he's a Mex. His old man never spoke a lick of English except for liquor labels, so Timo's just as worthless. Everybody knows he grew up eating hard boiled eggs in Cody's. And if anything's stolen, he probably fenced it, since that's what Mex's do, you know.

"And old Boar. He's lived in a house without running water so long, you can smell him just thinkin' about it. And if you stink, you ain't got any class to speak of. He could take a bath from now till Judgment and people here could still smell him. The governor himself could appoint him Marshall, and Boar would still be a drunken son of a bitch who gets hot when Crighter waves his pistol around.

"We're all just sad sons of bitches who ain't gonna be anything other than what we grew up bein' in everybody else's mind. Menninger's always gonna be a goose hunter no one ever hunts with cuz he shot Harry Leggy's ass full of buckshot once.

Sam Berhends is always gonna be a farmer who never gets his crop in on time and always harvests too early. Mercy's always gonna be Tumblin' Tommy, even after he never runs another step or wins the Olympic hundred-meter dash. Chatman is always gonna be fat and lazy. My old man's always gonna be the stubborn kid who made the farm work when his own father died, and will never listen to anybody but his banker.

"And me, I'm always gonna be an old, hard-drivin' high-school hero who could just pull it out for the team but could never please the old man. We are what we are, by God, till we die of it and everybody gets to say, 'See? I told you so.'"

Calvin's journal notes/ spring light, '76:

Been out on the ground again! —as I write those words, they have the feel of an announcement, like that of a surviving explorer returning from a torturous expedition. I climbed up on Old Moe, hitched to the one-way disc, and took to the field for a four-day journey. Like sailing home on the simplest of vessels, except that my destination is not some distant place. The trip and the destination are the same thing. I was not getting to some other place, but intricately going over and over—or in this operation's case, round and round the same ground, each lap a subtle distance shorter as I spiraled slowly in toward the center of the field, following the pattern of an earthly galaxy.

I stood on the open deck of the tractor, steering across the land, feeling the mid-May sunlight on my face, smelling the ground turned up for the first time this season and the scent of young, green growth mulched into the moist dirt. The hawks were hovering and diving for mice turned out of winter nests by the disc. The sky behind them was streaked with fading contrails. The horizon seemed farther away than during the winter. The clouds that blossomed as the day warmed had the clear-edged, roiling shape and brilliance of warm-season clouds.

Just simple spring beauty and the human feelings it stirs.

I don't mind being without an air-conditioned cab and stereo and power steering. Standing on the back of Moe, I was right down where I could even hear the discs scything through the stubble and new, young weeds. Behind it, I could see the way the ground broke open and how different the texture and moisture content is from what I remember from last year.

Out on the ground again! —Simple revitalization being involved in clear and simple ways with the natural process of the season coming on and with the land to prepare for another sowing and harvest. Out in the field I am involved and productive in the elemental processes, but at the same time, I am out away, just cruising at a distance from everything else.

Off on my own voyage, I can't be reached by the rest of the world, nor it by me. Out there on the ground, I'm not the turmoil in others' lives, nor they the turmoil in mine. We're all busy with our own being. Aunt Martha can rest, at least a little, content that I am doing something positive again with my life and time. Uncle Karl is keeping summer hours again now at AgCo, and except for more and leisurely lessons in maintenance and attitude, the farming is trusted to my hands. Neighbors are out in their own fields, too, self-absorbed. I can see their dust plumes and pick-ups moving down the roads. Thompson's off on his milk route, thinking about the lineup for our next game. Buckwheat's at the station. Mercy's in his store. McCormick's out in his own fields, too. Karen is at her chores and duties.

I spent too much of that cruising time thinking about her, about being around her, about making love to her, about lying over her in the front seat of Thompson's car, caressing her and feeling her against me while the hail pounded down. I think: I've got to change this line of thought. And I'd get back to looking at the sky and wondering what weather the wind will bring in from the west. We need some rain now for the ripening wheat. It would be nice if it stays warm tonight for the game. ...But pretty soon, I'm back to seeing images of her smile, the flash of her hair in the light. I think: I've got to give this up.

She's right, I know. How many lives can I—can we—change because I need her, want her? How could she stand it, and how could she stand me for making it happen?

I think: what about my needs? Winter was an icy, lonely hell of bleak, grey silence. How do I endure that without her? Or even now, how do I cope with being around her and wanting to touch her?

So there's the old urge again—why stay around here? Move on. What's to stay for if you can't have her, can't even be part of it all comfortably? Hit the road. One more season of softball, bring in another wheat harvest, plant once more this fall for Karl, and then head south for the winter. It could happen. I'm used to the road, and being unattached is just a part of that way of life.

Uninvolved. What does it matter if it happens here, or out on the Interstate? At least here, out in the field I am productive. Uninvolved, but more than merely drifting. How could I be as productive on the road? Perhaps by going to trade school and becoming an itinerant appliance repair man, fixing a few toasters in Cincinnati, refrigerators in Phoenix, air-conditioners in Louisiana, moving on now and then to ever-new, suburban horizons till I'm attached somewhere and meet the urban woman of my dreams. Sounds as promising as going round and round the fallow field waiting for what can never be.

These are thoughts from tractor time. Every once in a while, I come back to the present, check my gauges, listen to the roar of the engine, look over the one-way disc trailing behind. No matter the feeling, the distance the mind travels, the ground gets worked. Eventually, the field is worked and ready again for weather.

When I came in that last afternoon, after getting the ground done, putting the disc away and servicing Moe, I was looking forward to a nap before supper and getting ready to go into Revere for the game tonight. It would have been a pleasing and easing way to get out of the mood of fieldwork, but Aunt Martha had other means of doing that.

She was behind the bunkhouse, pruning limbs and watering in the blossoming orchard of cherry and plum and pear trees. As I came up she called to me to bring a step ladder so she could trim in the highest branches. When I saw what she wanted to do, I did it myself rather than endure the guilt trip of leaving her to climb up there herself while I showered and rested.

It didn't matter. In the late spring light, the blossoms were sweet-smelling, and petals fluttered down as I sawed. Bees worked their duty, too. The song of running water was symphonic and soothing. In a slow-rising creak, the windmill's wheel turned in the cooling stir of breeze. I didn't mind her trimming orders or her lessons of when to water and how to put moth balls down by the base of the trunk to keep worms away.

When we finished with the last light, she told me that Karl would tell me what to do with the piled branches when he got home tonight. Wanting to be off to the game, I asked her if she knew when that might be.

"Oh, you know," she said with a tired sigh, "he's pretty much gone for the season now. Late, most likely." She was bent over, gathering her saws and pruners and packages. I don't think she actually realized the sound of her voice, but the obvious finally struck me—she misses him.

"He puts in a lot of hours," I said. "It's too bad he has to stay away from the farm so much."

"I reckon the Good Lord feels that other folks need him more than I do. He's got to keep their machinery going, or what they going to do about their crops?"

"It's a lot of time here alone, too, Aunt Martha."

"I go to my friends when needs be," she said, starting up through the trees for the big house. "And I have family."

She stopped then and turned to look back into the orchard, and when she spoke, it wasn't really to me. She said, "There's times, I know it ain't easy. Hours and days. If I didn't know sometimes when I'm walking in amongst the trees that the Good Lord's walkin' there beside me, I don't know that I could make do with it. You got to have faith that there's reason enough for what comes your way and that He'll help you bear it."

Then, of course, I felt completely unworthy and helpless as the younger generation, as the ruthlessly irresponsible family member, as an incompetent companion. I didn't want to tell her, "Well, too bad. By the way, I'm off to play softball with friends. Have a nice day." But then she let me off the hook in a most gracious way, as if something like that might happen for me, too. We started back up the path again, and she said, "I'll have a supper ready for you in a minute so's you can be along to your ball game. The weather's been good for that at least."

So, I said that'd be great, and that's where I went. It feels good, too, to come in out of the field and go into town for a ball game, to take a different kind of field and play the spirit out.

We're doing well. Won again tonight, seventeen to nine. The guys are hitting well. Van Anders has such control with where and how he puts the ball across the plate. Thompson and Timo and McCormick are silently competing to make the best, most accurate throw from the outfield, gunning down runners. I've helped to stabilize the infield, and I like to lead off and run the bases and burn the energy off. There's an unarticulated confidence when we come off the field. We know we're going to be hard to beat this year.

For awhile, the rest doesn't matter. You can put your heart in the play, and it's a safe place to be. Afterwards, beer and bull about the game, the plays, the players. A decent time under the lights.

But it didn't last too long tonight as a new line of lightning was flashing along the western edge of the night. Driving home cross country, I watched the prairie light show close in and felt the wind quicken. Everyone was apprehensive because of the recent severe weather, but there were no warnings out.

The storm line broke on the farm just as I drove into the yard, but it was only a short, furious shower of soft rain, almost misty. There was only enough to scrub the spring air clean coming now through the open bunkhouse door. There's a dripping music at the eaves. The ground will be wet enough to render some of today's disking useless, and I'll soon have to go over it all again. Not wet enough to do the growing crop much good. We wait on a heavier storm. We watch for it. Out here, life goes the way of the weather. Simple enough for now.

Tom Mercy's lyrics/

It's one of those times you look back at, and don't ya wonder if maybe you coulda done something to make things different so they wouldn't turn out the way they did. I'll think back to meetin' 'em there at the Holiday lounge, and it'll be clear as the day in front of my face, but back then I wasn't noticin' nothin' because there I was, thinkin' I maybe gotta move the wife and kids to Denver; thinkin' I maybe gotta take this job they're offerin' me

there managing the True Value store in Littleton. Lots more
money. Big new schools. New house. Big opportunities to move
up. Big, new place. Maybe I got to move like so many others.

You know dad's store, it couldn't support him and mom
and my family, too. There just ain't the business anymore, not
enough people around just to come in needing hinges or paint or
hammers or somethin'. Families move out. Families barely makin'
it don't buy nothin' if they can scrounge up a piece of junk and
still use it. Tough times. The oil prices, they skyrocket. The crop
prices and the calf prices, they drop so low you can't stoop to see
'em, and the farmer, he puts off paintin' the barn another couple
of years. The calvin' barn ain't gonna get reshingled. The house
ain't gonna get re-wired.

What you gonna do? You gotta feed your family, give 'em
somethin' to live for. At the same time, I don't really want to leave
where I grew up and where my own kids are growin' up. Hell!
Give Thompson an excuse to find another right fielder? And it's
pretty easy in the store, you know. I get out to the lake to fish
most ever when I want, kids get to play ball. I'm down at the cafe
most mornings, finding out what's goin' on. I like the fire duties at
the station and the Lions Club work. And dad couldn't run that
store forever by himself. Who else was gonna do it then?

You know, I was thinkin' all this stuff and went in to
down a Budweiser over it some more. Guess I was surprised to
see Buckwheat in there because he wasn't usually done at the
station that early, and he don't usually drink at the Holiday. But he
was with that vet he met that rode in off the Interstate that
afternoon on his Harley, headed for the East Coast. How they got
to talkin', I don't know, but they was bosom buddies by the time I
showed up, and lit up like a carnival, too.

Bucky yelled me over to the bar, bought me a Bud, and
showed me this K-bar—a combat knife the guy had just given
Buckwheat as a present. Buck said, "Here's another good service
man. Served his country to the hilt, huh?" —That was some kind
of joke about the knife, I guess. Right away I thought, "Uh oh,"
but it was no big deal. When he introduces me to this guy, I see
they been talkin' about all that stuff. He says, "This here's Corporal McNamara, USMC, '65 to '69. Wounded only once."

The guy stuck his hand out to shake. "Like the Secretary

of War," he says.

"To the Secretary of War!" Buckwheat shouted out, and lifts his mug, and McNamara lifts his, and they toast, "To the Secretary of War!" So I lift my mug, too. They were talkin' Saigon stories.

I was always state-side, but you know. I still get together with guys sometimes and talk about those times. The mood can get to ya, I guess. But hell, they were in good spirits, those two, talkin' about this Chinese hooker named Sue Tong Mai—Sue the Tongue, the head madam somewhere, on some Saigon street. And they weren't really talkin' so loud as to be out of hand neither. It was that pipeliner and some welder from at that new power plant down river.

That, and maybe the thunder startin' up. It was rollin' in when I finished up that interview and headed for the Holiday. It'd crack like cannon and then roll down the river valley. The thunderheads were really boilin' up there to the west, but not so fast, I didn't think, to get severe again and pound us. It was just loud and sudden and all happening up in the sky. No lightning was touchin' down anywhere I could see up river yet. But even inside the lounge, you could hear it roll. It'd stop conversation, even for Buckwheat and his friend, and people'd listen.

This McNamara said, "Bombardment," kind of Vincent Price haunted like, and Bucky said, "To bombardment, my specialty. I'm sorry I can't give you a cluster bomb in return. That's what I killed with. But you can't strap one to your belt."

"To bombardment," McNamara said again, and waved it off, and they chugged another toast. I drank to it with 'em. Like I say, I'm thinkin' this job thing and wonderin' if we'd play that make-up game with the thunder rollin' in. And thinkin' I'd probably have to tell Thompson that Buckwheat ain't likely to show up for it, at least not in condition to play.

That's when this asshole at one of the tables near the bar says, "Why don't you sad, sorry vets just fuckin' let it ride. The fuckin' war is over."

I guess that's when I started noticin' things clear then. This guy with Buckwheat, he's Bucky's height, but not his size, got hair like Buffalo Bill, but brown colored, and a big, bushy moustache the same color. He had on this rawhide jacket like Indian scouts used to wear and logger's boots. Plus he's an ex-Marine, two tours in Nam. Jesus! And there's Buckwheat. They both turn on their stools and look down on this table of union boys from the power plant, sittin' there with these two pipeliners.

You know those guys. They blowed in from all over the country for a while, chasin' the big contract jobs. Shit. Just glorified bricklayers and electricians and carpenters who can't keep steady work. Some of 'em druggies and thieves and ex-cons. The pipeliners you could tell by that Looziana drawl. It was Friday after work, and they always kicked off early for the weekend, and it ain't exciting enough, or fast enough, or cool enough, life here in the sticks. They got to be livenin' up the action right away come the weekend.

There they sat in their work boots and greasy Levis and pocket T-shirts, leanin' back in their chairs like gamblers and gunfighters, behind a table stacked full of empty Pabst cans, lookin' back at Bucky and this Marine. —And at me, too. Then I was thinkin', this may be Buckwheat's kind of pleasure, but not mine.

It was the longest goddamn silence I think I ever sat through in my life. This clap of thunder boomed and rolled away, musta seemed like for half an hour. Nobody moved.

Finally, this vet says, "Aren't you the faggots that came in on those Japanese pieces of shit out there. Was ever there a faggot that didn't like to straddle a Kawasaki?"

Well, Gracy Barker was behind the bar. You know her— as wide as she is tall, and jugs the size of cantaloupes. She's got forearms that make Popeye look like a wimp, and's always got a smoke tucked up behind her ear. She's been behind the bar long enough to serve the whole Nebraska Navy in more ways than one, and long enough to know a fight before it ever gets started. She comes right down the bar from where she's washin' glasses and gets the phone in her hand like it's a club.

"See this, boys? See this?" she says. "I'm callin' the sheriff right now." She knows Buckwheat and brawls, and she's dialin', lookin' back 'n' forth from him to the table.

"Get them fellas to pipe down," this southern boy smiles out.

"Fuck you," this motorcycle vet says back.

Gracy's sayin', "It's ringin' now. Hello?" She holds it out so we all can hear the dispatcher sayin', "Hello? Who's calling, please?" Gracy yells over at the table, "Git movin' your asses to the door, boys."

Well, they started shufflin' up and givin' Buckwheat and this Marine tough stares, like they don't even realize they're gettin' away with their lives. —Almost, that is. As soon as Gracy hangs up the phone, and they're all out the door but one, the last one says over his shoulder, "Too bad that piece of shit Harley you boys rode in on just fell over in the lot."

That's all it took. Buckwheat and his new friend headed for the door.

I turned to yell for Gracy to get the cops, but she was already doin' it. It was time to head for home, but fast! By the time I was out the door, two of them power plant boys were already down and bleedin' between a couple of parked cars, and Bucky and this vet were workin' on two more. I thought for a second that maybe Buckwheat went real crazy and used that knife on the two that was down, but I could see it stickin' out of his back pocket. The last two power plant boys was runnin' for the river, smart enough to see they were overmatched.

Runnin' for my pick-up, I yelled for Buckwheat that the cops were comin'. He was runnin' this guy's bloody face into the door of a Buick, and he didn't pay no attention to me.

I yelled at him again as I backed out of the lot, but he was in another world by then. But the Marine guy, he heard me. He threw off this other dude like a rag doll, stepped to his bike and picked it up, jumped it alive, and took off for the Interstate. Got clean away, I guess, cuz no one seen him after that, that's sure.

In the roar of his Harley fadin' out, I could hear a siren comin' from over the viaduct. Then that got drowned out by another boom of thunder. I saw Bucky cringe at it and look up at the clouds rollin' in. Then he just looked at this limp guy in his hands, and he dropped him right there. He saw his vet buddy disappearin' over the interchange on his Harley, and Bucky just up and climbs one of those Kawasaki's layin' there, kicks her engine up, and takes off, too. In my rearview mirror I seen two of them guys they beat up drag themselves up and stumble for the riverbed to hide. Two of 'em weren't goin' anywheres without medical assistance.

I pulled into the Standard station right next door to the Holiday there to gas up like I never been anywheres near that lounge or a beer in my life—or at least in the last ten minutes. I seen the sheriff's car come blazin' onto the river bridge, and Buckwheat shot by 'em in a blur, headin' the other way into Ogallala. They radioed after him, squealin' around the station, and skidded into the motel parking lot to pick up the bodies.

The cops never even looked my way, thank God. I seen one of 'em go in to ask Gracy Barker all about it, and there I am, pumpin' gas and listenin' to it thunder, back to wonderin' if it was goin' to get to rainin', thinkin' it probably wouldn't with the air so dry like it was and August gettin' drier by the day. I'm thinkin', it's shits for the farmers, this weather, and that means the shits in the hardware business, too, and what the hell am I gonna do with my life and my family. I'm thinkin', it's the dog damnedest thing. One minute I don't know what kind of life to go for, and the next minute I'm thinkin' I maybe got to defend what I do have from pipeliners for the sake and the honor of some ex-Marine's Harley Davidson with Buckwheat Van Anders who's this guy's best buddy because they been somewhere near the same battlefield once. Now I got to go home and explain it all to my wife, and catch hell for bein' anywheres near there.

Damn if it don't beat all. It's like they say about this Nebraska weather, if you don't like it, wait five minutes and it will change. Buckwheat and the weather and what you do with your life—can't predict it, can't control it, can't even be sure it ain't gonna get you killed. I was wonderin' if he was gonna stay out of Crighter's way, and all I knew for certain was, I was gonna go to the game later and tell Thompson that Buckwheat wasn't gonna probably make it.

CHAPTER TWO: CHANGES

Again that season I found myself on my back, staring up into the gears and guts of another machine. Only this time it wasn't the combine, but one of the old, 1946 Chevrolet grain trucks that after only thirty years of service, hauling tons of wheat by the two-hundred bushel-load, had cracked a sprocket in the transmission. Uncle Karl had surmised the problem as soon as he sat in behind the wheel and worked the shift stick like a probing sensor while trying to put the truck in gear.

We had towed the truck into the shop, had crawled beneath it and begun tearing the machine down, disconnecting the drive shaft and scraping away the oil and mud grime to get at the bolts that held the transmission in place against the clutch plate. The whole transmission had to come out, all eighty massive and bulky pounds of cast steel housing and forged and machined gears and shafts in their oil bath. It was awkward, straining to be twisted up on one elbow while working overhead with the other hand, muscling the ratchet and socket that worked the big bolts free.

As we worked in the shadows and the stark brightness of the drop light below the truck, the decades' accumulation of caked dirt and weed seed, oil leaks and engine grime drifted down on us, sticking to our hands, and matting in our hair and the sweat of our forearms, falling into our eyes and mouths, and grinding into our clothes. The anchor bolts protested their loosening. The years of constant jolts and vibrations and temperature changes had crystal-lized their permanent tightness. Karl and I squirmed and struggled in a chorus of grunts and guttural growls, positioning and bracing, gripping and prying and pressuring the tools, gradually working the bulk of the transmission free in an afternoon's exhaustion.

Our teamwork was natural and unconscious with Karl twisted up under the truck beside me, supplying the directions and explanations of how the transmission worked and how it was held in place, pointing out which bolts to work on and which tools to use, lending the third and fourth hand and a new angle of pry and pressure where needed. I supplied the major muscle power to the tools and applied the suggested techniques, responding to Karl's directions.

"I think the other direction there, Calvin. Counter clockwise to loosen em, right?"

"Oh, yeah. Well, I was just trying to make it more of a challenge."

"Well, let's try a little W-D Forty and give the head there a good whack with the hammer, and see if you can shock the rust free."

"A hammer I understand. The motto behind my profound mechanical experience—such as it's developed in all of a year or so—is, if it can't be fixed with a hammer, duct tape, or baling wire, it can't be fixed."

"There, she's comin' now. Go easy on those bolts here at the end. She's just hangin' there now on the last threads. We got to get a jack in place and rig something up through the floor of the cab so she just don't fall out of there like a nut out of a tree."

As we crawled out from underneath the truck, I said, "That took forever. It's a good thing we started well before harvest."

"You never know mechanic jobs. What looks to take five minutes can end up takin' five days, and what looks to be a major overhaul sometimes turns out to be just the turn of a screw. If you need the machine, I reckon you do the job and keep on doin' it till it's done. Time is just what it takes to do it right."

We sat a while in silence, leaning against the front tire of the truck and wiping ourselves down with shop rags, letting the muscles relax. Karl closed his eyes and leaned his head back. He's thinking it out, I supposed, as I watched more sweat bead on my uncle's forehead, form a rivulet, and run down his temple and into the blond and grey peppered tangle of hair. He was ready to get on with it.

"Where do we go from here?"

Karl sighed the silence out the shop door, blinked open his eyes, and looked around the floor in front of the work bench until he spotted the scissor-arm hydraulic jack.

"We need to get that jack positioned under the transmission and cranked up all the way. I don't think it will quite come up to where we need it. Couple inches short or so.

"It's awful heavy, Calvin. So I'll get in the cab, and we'll sling that there chain down and up around it, and I'll try to hold it up while you loosen those last two bolts. Then I'll try to ease it down on the jack as it comes away from the engine, and you kind of balance it and guide it down where it belongs. Then we'll jack it down and pull it out from under there, open it up, and look inside."

I got the chain and jack while Karl climbed slowly into the cab and tried to kneel over the transmission that showed through the open floor. Karl dangled the chain down; I caught its end and snaked it under, around, and back up to Karl. Then I pulled the jack in beside me and pumped the arm with its steel palm up toward the base of the transmission. While I was working the bolts loose with one hand and using the other, palm up on the bottom of the steel housing, to guide it down, Karl pulled the chain snug and strained to lift on it, easing the pressure on the bolts.

Through clenched teeth he grunted, "Don't be too long about it. I ain't got all my old strength."

I worked one bolt out, and the transmission swung slightly, balancing on the last bolt as Karl grunted above me. Then the last bolt. One minute turn, and it suddenly hung free in the chain.

"Cal—!" Above, the warning was cut off by a cry of knifing pain, and the load fell to the jack in an instant and dull crunch that sent a surging scream of agony exploding from my fingertip, through my arm, and out my mouth as the air rushed from my lungs with the shock. "Ahhgghhgg! My God! My God!" I clenched my tortured left hand in the violent grip of my right, pressing it against my stomach as I writhed and jerked with pain, banging my head and shoulders and knees into the truck's frame.

But none of that pain registered in my mind over the acid fire charging from my wounded hand.

I held it up to my eyes, screaming, seeing nothing there where the top half of my index finger should have been. It was a red, oozing stub of mangled bone, torn flesh, and meat. I gripped it to my chest again, howling.

"God! It's gone! It's gone! God, where is it?" I twisted and crawled on an elbow toward the jack. The transmission had toppled off toward the right tire, and in the droplamp light I craned to look into the steel palm for my cut off finger, thinking cool and slowly through the pain that they can sew them right back on these day—just ice it down and take it to any old doctor. But in the cup there was nothing but blood and small bits of mashed flesh. The falling weight had splattered my fingertip, not severed it, like a hammer hitting the end of a hot-dog, and had sprayed it across the jack and the shop floor and onto my face and shirt.

My hand being there, instantly pushing away on the bottom of the falling transmission, had kept the load from crashing down on my face and chest, but I hadn't realized that yet. I only felt the throbbing blast of pain in my hand that was para-lyzed now with shock, a raging fire at the end of my arm that seared into my brain with more intensity than I had ever felt. My breath whistled between my teeth. My heart drummed thunder in my ears. Clutching the fist of pain, I pushed myself out from under the truck with my legs, striking out with adrenaline kicks against the ground, responding only to the animal urge to flee the pain, the synapses of every nerve firing short circuit and uncon-trolled, my muscles snapping and releasing, flexing and shivering.

I found myself on my feet then, stamping and jumping to the explosion of pure agony, crying and groaning in low, breathless gasps of air. Then turning, I saw my uncle collapsed in the cab of the truck.

"Uncle Karl!" I rushed to him. Karl's legs stuck out under the steering wheel, his boot heels tangled with the pedals. His body lay half up on the seat, his head toward the passenger door. I raced around to the other side, the pain momentarily dulled in my curled hand.

"Karl, what happened? What happened?"

I tore the door open to hear my uncle's slow wheezing, see spittle dribbling across the seat, his eyes closed tight into the wrinkles of his leathered skin.

"Can you hear me? Uncle Karl!"

"It's some bad pain, boy."

I reached for him with both hands, and the left one twitched in pain as I touched him, and I screamed out again. Karl groaned as he moved, the breath rushing from his lungs.

Clutching my wound to my chest, I ran across the yard to the house, shouting for Martha. She came swaying through the porch door, rubbing her hands on an apron stained with cherry skins and juice and as red as my shirt. Her eyes were round and wide and moist with fear. Her face was flashing with emotion and questions.

"Sweet Lord, what did you do?"

"It's Karl," I yelled, running up to her. "He needs an ambulance. Fast!"

"What—?"

"Now! Now!" I screamed, panting up to her, and my desperate voice sent her careening back into the house, with me right behind her. She fumbled at the phone book, suddenly a jitter of helpless nerves with shock taking over. Then she let it drop to the floor and dialed.

In an age of silence she stared at me slumped in the kitchen chair, bowed moaning over my crippled hand, then an answer. "Ester! Thank God. I can't think what to do. Please call an ambulance right this minute. Right here. Both Karl and Calvin are hurt. Hurry!" She hung up. "I couldn't think who to call. Ester will do it. Where's my Karl?"

"In the shop. In the cab of the truck. He's just lying there. He's breathing. He's alive. I don't know what it is. I tried to move him, but he's hurt. I couldn't with this."

"Your hand?"

"I'm all right. Go! Go on."

Martha scurried out the door, leaving me sitting hunched over, rocking with the roaring throb of pain in my hand, feeling the slick, warm blood dribbling down my wrists. It's just gone, I thought. Part of me is gone. God, it hurts. God, it hurts.

I rocked, stamping my feet on the kitchen floor till the low wavering wail of siren rose slowly toward me from beyond the window. Finally, I thought; then: It didn't really take that long to get to be a farmer, did it?

Calvin's journal notes/ spring darkness, '76:

Just came from seeing Uncle Karl in the hospital in Tyghe. They cut off his hair, and his cheeks seemed hollow and his sun-baked face is as pale as I've ever seen. His shoulders under the hospital gown looked boney and frail, and it was like seeing another person lying there. Except for his eyes. There was nothing weakened there, so my initial surprise was softened, and I don't think it showed on my face.

And of course, the first thing he says is, "I'm awful sorry about your finger, Calvin, Lord knows I am. I been prayin' thanks every minute I didn't do you no worse. I hope you'll forgive me." I thought he was going to cry.

I said something like, "No, no. I could have gotten it out of there. It just happened. Things just happen."

"No, no," he says back. "I thought I could hold it up, and I knew I was feelin' poorly. I just shouldn't have tried it and risked your life."

That gave me a chance to jump in and give him hell about not telling anyone, and worse, not doing anything about it. Here's a man, a mechanical genius, who keeps his antique farm machinery purring perfectly, but he lets a ruptured hernia go because more important things needed doing, like trying to hoist a truck trans-mission with two handfuls of chain.

Martha was right there by the head of his bed with an open magazine in her lap. "I've tried to get him to have it taken care of for years, but I never could."

It seems that he's had this problem for years, but you know, "It don't bother me too bad, if I ain't doin' too much climbin' around, and then that girdle always did the job of holdin' me together," he says. —Except finally, the day before yesterday, the bowel finally fell out of its distended cavity. And he couldn't even wear the girdle then without pain, but he's got to be out in the shop under a truck, pulling the transmission because the job needed doing and it was a two-man job. So, when he's hauling up on a chain full of truck transmission, and it lets loose, the stab of effort made him pass out with pain. They had to operate on him almost immediately, and everyone was amazed, incredulous, that he'd been doing the things he was doing—and I don't mean just yesterday, but for years, with a condition like his. Talk about running a machine till it breaks down. And he'd never do that with a single piece of farming equipment.

So. He's sorry now about my finger, but I'm sorry that I didn't see a thing. I don't see a frail, half-crippled man in his mid-seventies, in need of a hernia operation, having trouble getting around, looking a little grey-faced and sick. I just see Karl, a man I know, a close relative, who has always been here on the farm, going about his business—shoveling grain, running Mrs. Harris, pulling transmissions, milking cows, climbing other people's sprinkler systems, making things run smoothly, getting the crop planted and harvested and a thousand other things. Always just there, doing it, and it has nothing to do with time and age. He's as basic to the place as the windbreak trees, but all of a sudden, something happens, and it's clear he doesn't last as long. His limbs aren't as strong. It just seemed so to me because I don't know any better.

I've never seen him as someone who really needed my help. I knew I could be handy, in the same way a tool can be. Sure, I'm younger, have more strength and agility and endurance. But I've never done anything he couldn't have eventually done himself. On the contrary, I can't do anything around this place without him because I'm practically stupid. Not of much more use than a hammer, or a plow, or an engine.

Now, at the least, I'm a much more needed tool, and quite possibly, it's necessary now to start thinking on my own. Maybe I can, for once, be more helpful than helped, more useful than using.

But no, no, he wouldn't blame me a bit, he said, if I wanted to leave and do something sensible with my life. We've talked about it some, my still thinking of leaving, maybe going somewhere to teach. I was kind of preparing him for the possibility because I wouldn't have wanted it to seem to come out of the clear blue. But even if I'd had some definite destination come this fall after the wheat is planted, how could I simply head off for the horizon again, leaving Karl in this condition? Besides, when have I ever done anything sensible with my life before?

But not to worry, he'll be long gone better by then, he says. This is only the end of June, and though he doesn't look so great after emergency surgery, he's no feather in the wind. It's still his work and most of it he'll still be able to do—if he's more sensible now about his limitations.

"And besides, you know, Calvin, there's a hundred fellas out there that would be more than happy to rent that ground. Of course, they're good neighbors and friends, and they've most of them been by to wish me well, but I can tell you, if I was dead tomorrow, there'd be a dozen of 'em camped on the doorstep, waitin' to see if the widow will rent 'em the ground."

Yes, I know things can be worked out, but right now, here I am. I might as well do the work. I don't mind doing it. It's clean and simple and productive. Of course, I don't know diddly about it, and I confessed my ignorance to him for maybe the ten thousandth time.

"You do fine, Calvin, and you know there's no mystery to it. You're just takin' care of the ground, and if you pay attention to it, it pretty much can tell you itself what you should be doin' to help the process along."

Simple as that. Except for the going through of the actual process, keeping the machinery running and working at the proper time. Karl tries to tell me that I don't need his expertise as much as I think. There are neighbors and friends, and that's what ag services are for—repair men, advisors, suppliers, an extra hand if you're in a jam. And besides, it's not like Karl is going away. In fact, after he's out of the hospital, he'll be around even more than usual because he won't be going back to work at AgCo for a long time. Maybe never, though hundreds of customers will come begging for his help and time. For sure, he has to be quite careful for a good, long time. No harvesting this year. I'll be running Mrs. Harris, and Aunt Martha will be driving the trucks again with Karl riding along, and we'll haul all the wheat to the elevator in town this year. Cutting the crop by myself—but Karl will be there to tell me how to put back together anything that falls apart.

We can always get neighbors to help if we find out we need it. Fred Menninger, who mechanics in Revere, and the Alfords, who live just north of the church, came over to the farm after they heard about the accident, took the truck transmission to Fred's shop in town, and had it fixed and back in the truck by late last night. No big deal. It's ready for harvest. Folks just happen to be around if you need them, that's all.

It was an unfinished job that I couldn't have done myself even if I were physically able. For more than two days now, I've been carrying my left hand around curled against my chest, still a constant fire of pain even though I've been drugged to the max on Demerol. As Buckwheat had to call up last night and say, "The god damnedest things we do to get good drugs, huh? Remember, you can only do that eight more times."

Once is enough. At times I can distinctly feel my lost finger. The severed nerve endings still tell me it's there, and it keeps on hurting savagely. I can hold my hand up and look at it and see that the end of my finger is really gone, but in my brain it still hurts right there where it isn't anymore. And no drug in the world can stop its hurting. If I let my hand hang, it throbs till it feels like it will burst with pressure. If I try to use the hand, the new, raw fingertip—they just filed the bone end down, cauterized it, and pulled shreds of skin over the new end—is stabbed with a thousand white-hot shots of electric shock. God, it hurts. It still hurts, and that's all I've been thinking and saying now for almost forty-eight hours. Right now, right where it should be, but isn't, it silently screams pain. How long until those nerve endings in my brain finally burn out?

How long until those other nerve endings die out in my head? —The ones that feel her.

Coming out of Karl's room, I found the McCormick's out in the hall, waiting to visit Karl, too—Mike, Jaime in his arms, Tony's hand in Karen's. She's showing plain and clear now that she's pregnant with her third.

Mike had the usual joke ready, of course.

"When Thompson heard you got a finger cut off, he says, 'My God! Which hand?' I told him, the left, and he says, 'Oh, then he can still make the throw to first.' He didn't know where he was gonna play another cripple. I'm supposed to tell you that we play tomorrow night."

I told him I didn't think I'd make it to the games for a while.

I grinned through it, but I didn't have anything else to say. Mike stood there swaying a little, asking about Karl, saying the things everyone has—that it was terrible, that we were both lucky, that Karl is an incredible, and crazy, person. His kids then were trying to poke each other around his legs, restless in the sterile, quiet hospital. Karen sat in a chair, at the edge of it. I could feel her watching me, but when I'd glance toward her eyes, she would look away to the floor.

I stood for a timeless, floating moment in a fog, thinking how beautiful she was just sitting there quietly, her kids teasing and coming up to her for comfort and attention, her husband at ease and joking and concerned for his friends, their lives taken care of and full of good love and good life. He has everything, but does he know it? He goes home to her company, her meals, her warm bed. His kids cling to his legs, ride on his back, laugh him happy. She's there taking care of them all till she's like Martha some day sitting beside his hospital bed, reading to him from Family Circle, giving him full and quiet comfort.

Mike said, "Say, you look really spaced. Are you sure you should drive back to the farm?"

I said I was fine, just sleepy. He volunteered Karen to drive me home while he stayed to visit Karl. It was the only time her eyes stayed on mine, trying not to show the feelings flashing across them. "If you think you need a ride...," she said. Is there comfort enough there for me, too?

She was clearly relieved when I said that I could make it myself, and I did. Came back here. Alone. Now it is dark. Harry Alford came over to do the milking. I didn't feel like going out and showing off the new contours of my hand.

I fixed a peanut butter sandwich, one-and-a-half handed, in Aunt Martha's kitchen. She's stayed in town both nights, sitting late by Karl's bed and then sleeping at the house of friends there.

I'm out here by myself at the bunkhouse door, looking outside for any weather that might come up and cover the blazing stars. Washed down my dose of Demerol with a bit of scotch and water. The night out there is huge and silent. Even full of stars, the sky is empty, and the dark ground beneath stretches out forever. I'm just sitting here, getting drunk, looking out the door for lost parts of myself, and getting used to my new dimensions. No help for any of that from anyone.

Thompson's lyrics/

There's some that say trouble comes in threes, and it sure did for these folks.

The way I picture it now, there she was, up to her knees in the harvest, a wadin' through the wheat heaped in the back of that old truck, leanin' on her shovel, and lookin' out for Calvin to bring in another bin full. They were cuttin' wheat on that quarter just across the road from St. Luke's there, and she waved when I drove by, her old straw hat flappin' in the breeze. Karl was sittin' there in the open door of the cab, takin' it easy because it was only some two weeks since his operation. He wasn't even supposed to be movin' around yet, but how you gonna keep him out of the harvest field? Calvin was out in the field on that antique Massey, cuttin' away on a pretty good stand of wheat. They were just workin' on their harvest like most everyone else.

It was perfect harvest weather, too, climbin' up toward a hundred degrees and a dry, hot wind wavin' the wheat and scatterin' the chaff. The afternoon fields were full of folks, trucks and combines just purrin' away. The sky was about as blue and clear as it gets in July.

It was my Wednesday route up on the south table, and I was turnin' north up toward Alford's. Harry and Arla were about the only ones I delivered to out there in those parts 'cause most folks around were still getting their milk and cream from Goehners. They're the only ones here about that still kept a few dairy cows cuz Karl still didn't believe in one crop farmin' even if the whole world goes to it. So neighbors bought from them, and who can blame them? Arla is my mother's cousin is why I delivered out there to them, and the only other farmsteads on the route are the Catholics.

Well, I drove in and delivered the usual—two gallons of

two percent and a block of cheddar, and we were standin' out there in the yard visiting. Else-wise, neither one of us would have probably heard the church bell start up. It rang out a couple of slow, long bongs, carried north on the wind.

Arla said, "Well what's that, you suppose?" and she kind of cranked her head to look through the trees down toward the church. "There's no funeral today, is there?"

I said I didn't see any cars parked there when I come by, but the ringin' kept up and was takin' on a steady, slow rhythm ringin' out over the fields. I said, "Field fire?" but we couldn't see no smoke anywhere in the sky. We looked at each other with shrugs and scrunched up faces, and I said that I'd run back down that way and see.

I jumped in the van and covered the mile in less than a minute and fishtailed around the corner of the church as I braked up. One of those old grain trucks was standin' there. The ringin' had stopped by then, and Calvin come flyin' out the basement door. Almost ran into the van, but he stopped up against it and flung the door open.

"Martha's up in the back of the wheat truck. I'm sure she's dead. I got to get back out there."

I yelled, "Get in!" and we headed down the road toward where the trucks and combine were parked on the edge of the field. Calvin just started ramblin' about it, sayin', "I just didn't see her in time to do anything. I was way out in the middle of the field. When I came up with a load, Karl was tryin' to climb up over the cab, and then I saw her sprawled out up there on the wheat. I told him not to climb up, but I couldn't stop him."

Calvin had got up to her first, but her lips were blue and her eyes were starin' straight up at the sky, and she was gone for sure. He said that Karl came climbin' up over the hood, a callin' for her, and when he got up there and picked her up in his arms, Calvin left him sittin' there holdin' her and cryin' to her, prayin' and rockin' her when he came down to the church to call for help. And as we drove up, we could see Karl still up there on the truck, kneelin' in the wheat, and cradlin' his wife in his arms.

I stopped on the edge of the field, and we ran across the stubble to where the truck was. Calvin leaped up there in one spring like it was a toy. He was up there with his arm around Karl when I crawled up, and he was tellin' Karl, "Somebody's coming, but it's too late, Uncle Karl."

Old Karl whined, "I know, I know. We talked that it would come some day, but I just wasn't ready, Lord. You know I just wasn't ready. Why do this, Lord? Why?"

It's the most helpless feeling there is when there's nothin' you can do for the dead or the suffering but sit and wait with them. There those two guys knelt, holdin' on to her, Karl prayin' and moanin' soft-like, and Calvin just starin' off across the fields. You feel like chaff in the wind.

And there was Martha Goehner, about as headstrong and healthy as an old woman can be in these parts, finally finished bringin' in the sheaves. A seventy-eight year-old woman who wasn't about to allow her husband to hire some high school kid to do a job she could still do herself. If there's a harvest to be brung in, by God, she'd truck it to town herself. Probably would even scythe the wheat and shock it if the combine broke down, too. But this one was the last harvest for Martha.

You got to feel for the family, but for Martha Goehner, you know she wouldn't have wanted it any other way. Up to her knees in the harvest when the Good Lord said, "The game's over for you, lady." How else would you want to go?

Well, pretty soon, though it seemed like a long and silent time, I could hear the wail of the ambulance and see the flashing lights turn off the highway and come down the road toward the church with a deputy's car right behind. They drove right down into the ditch and up to us in the field, and jumped out with oxygen and a heart jump-starter, but it was clear it was all over. Karl had closed her eyes. All they could do was finally pull him away and help him down and then bring down the body. Karl and Calvin both went off with her in the ambulance for town.

By then, other folks was startin' to show up, comin' in out of their fields when they seen the ambulance and the commotion in the field there. I was left to tell what happened, and Arla had followed up, too, and was tellin' how Calvin rang the bell till we noticed. Inside an hour there were four combines in that field, too, and more trucks than they could use, and they had the crop cleaned off that ground by nightfall and hauled to town. By the time Karl and Calvin got back to the farm that night and family had started to arrive, the kitchen was full of hams and casseroles and pies, and neighbors were takin' care of things like they always do. As much as they can, least-wise, when something like that happens.

Three days later, they put Martha Goehner in the family plot just behind the church there with Karl's folks and his two brothers and two babes that never made it out of childhood. The ground around the church was full up with cars and pick-ups for the service cuz there weren't many for miles around that Martha didn't know or wasn't related to. The church pews were full and they were packed in the basement even, on folding chairs, and standing out on the sidewalk. His sisters led Karl around, and he smiles and shakes hands and nods to the "Sorries" and the "God bless you's," but he weren't much there, just a goin' through the motions. The church and the Lord took care of everything else.

It was gonna be a load to bear for that man for quite a while. There was family around for a long time after, keepin' Karl company, but he was a good long time gettin' over his loss. The rest of us, we get to go back to gettin' on with our lives. The old folks, they pass away when it comes their time. It ain't like an accident, or a war, or a storm that takes someone before they should be called. The old folks, they had their lives, and all you got to do is look across the land to know the score. Like I said, there she was up to her knees in the harvest, and Martha Goehner was never one to sit on the sidelines, and she always put everything she was into it. We just go on into extra innings from here, and what folks like Martha leave behind sure shows how they played the game before they left it. And out here, that ain't so bad.

CHAPTER THREE: ON THE EDGE

Even after a month, the question was still there— How could she be gone like that? A woman so sturdy and single-minded, I was sure she would see us all to our graves, dig the holes herself, and say the benediction as she shoveled us over. But she was gone, like a one-day wind, like a season, like old times—a force of the moment that you can't believe can bear on you so; a storm that can affect you forever afterward; a broken link in a way of life that just can't be anymore.

Poor Uncle Karl. I had recently lost part of a finger. Karl lost half of his life. The family lost a major organ in its body, and we're still trying to recover our health.

So much family came in as soon as it happened. Aunt Sophie and Uncle Eric, Davy and his soon-to-be wife, were here at the farm by the time I brought Karl home from Tyghe that night. By the funeral, three days later, cousins and aunts and uncles I hadn't seen for years had flown in or driven out—from Idaho, California, Washington, D.C., Colorado.... Mom and dad, of course, and my two sisters. It was like old reunions at Christmas or Fourth of July in my youth, when everyone would gather— probably at Aunt Martha's calling.

After three hundred people saw her buried in the family plot behind St. Luke's, the ladies of the church served the Goehner clan a pot luck feast in the church basement. There was so much catching up to do, picking up on conversations and questions cut off ten and fifteen years ago. Laughter and hugging and remembering and simply rejoining. Family brought back to life by death. We were all there trying to fill in the suddenly empty space where Aunt Martha should be.

I went through the food line with Davey, listening to him joke about cattle prices and broken-down hay stackers. As we filled our plates, we came down to the desserts—a table full of cakes and fresh pies, brownies and fruit cobblers. Davey stopped in his tracks, staring over the sweets with mock shock.

"Look," he said. "No cherry cheese cake. Now you know she's gone. No more cherry cheese cake ever."

It brought sad laughter out from the cousins around us. Cherry cheese cake was always Aunt Martha's contribution to family pot luck. Growing up, we had eaten enough cherry cheese cake at feasts and as leftovers afterwards to sustain a forest of family trees. That dessert defined the family dinner. Many of us as kids had been enlisted to pick and pit, to bag and freeze cherries under Aunt Martha's supervision. We had milked the cows for the cream and gathered the eggs, had helped carry it to the table and served our siblings and cousins giant portions unwanted and taken for granted the sweetness and blessing too common to be remarkable anymore.

Until now. No more cherry cheese cake, and who feeds the family now? Who devises plots and reasons to get the family gathered? Who shows us the way and the values to live by? Who points out our place? Aunt Martha did all that, and we let her, however much we pretended that it didn't matter or wasn't needed.

We were all gathered there, rejoining, filling in the empty space because Martha Goehner was no longer there to do it for us.

Mom and Aunt Sophie stayed here on the farm for a month after the funeral, taking care of their brother, doing our meals for us, seeing to Martha's gardens and going through her things with family—eight decades of clothes and jewelry and household goods and trinkets and junk never thrown out, always bound to be of use to someone some day, now simply left behind by the dead. So many people came and went—family and neighbors and old friends. Mom and Sophie regulated Karl's company, saw that he ate and slept, listened to him talk about her and let him cry over her, tried to buffer him against the sudden burden of loneliness for a while.

Besides his sisters and family, Karl had his faith. What comfort that offered, he took, trying to get on with his life. He knew he'd be with her again soon, in their daily devotion, their spirits one, their lives whole again in the Lord.

Thankfully, I had the farming to go back to—my own personal place to go, to spend the time and thoughts. Neighbors finished our harvest, of course, but I went back to milking and fencing and to the summer fallow, going over the good ground on Old Moe, watching the hot August sky blister with boiling cumulus in dusty air too hot and dry to carry rain. The horizons, where the rest of the world raged, remained distant and danced in the heat waves. I rode across the land, watching the ground being turned over behind me, thinking about faith and comfort and death and companionship lived and lost; thinking about what people do with their lives and what they believe in and why and what they live for; thinking about history and movements and causes lived, lost, and won; thinking about what one person's life contributes to the whole, what one life can produce. Just thinking, like always.

The farming gave me some place to be while adjustments took place, gave me something to tend and the private and personal chance to produce something clear and simple and natural. It's decent labor, and Aunt Martha would have—did—approve. In fact, I was closer to her out there on the ground than in the house in mourning and rituals with family and friends. If she were anywhere for me, she was standing out there on the edge of the field, checking my work, making sure I was saving moisture, making sure it was done right, sure that I appreciated the importance, making sure I was staying busy.

Uncle Karl, of course, didn't want his personal tragedy to obligate me, and he, if anyone, knew that I was more of a reason for prayer than an answer to it. "Like I told you before, Calvin, you got something to be doin', then you go ahead and be doin' it. There's plenty who would do the farming, and since I won't be workin' for AgCo no more, I'll maybe get back to some of the farming myself. And you know, there ain't much of a living to be made from this old place."

—No, no living at all. We'd gone over that a time or two also. It's strictly subsistence on ground finally paid for, working with old equipment, keeping needs down and wants simple. Not much here but time and freedom and space. Could I live on just that? I could with Uncle Karl's help.

But besides the fact that part of me was now splattered over this place and never to be found and taken away again, it wasn't as if I had some other, definite place to go. I was just going to go, like most everyone else, on down the road. I'd stay. He said that it seemed that we could stand one another's company well enough to work things out.

Aunt Martha would have approved of this, too, I think, and even came as close as she ever could to telling me so the day before we started her last harvest. I had been surprised more than Karl that she would want us—she and I—to try and do the harvesting by ourselves instead of hiring a neighbor's son to help or a kid from town. I brought it up after supper that evening after Karl had gone to bed, thinking she might feel better knowing she had at least two of us incompetents to handle one job while she handled hers and took care of Karl, too.

"'Course if we get in a bind, we could ask the Peters boy to help out," she had said. "But God gave the harvest to us to do, and I don't mind." She was washing dishes at the kitchen sink, and paused long enough to look at me over her shoulder. Then she looked back out the window toward the elevator in Tyghe, gleaming pink in the late summer light. She said, "I got faith in you, if you got faith in me," and she went back to work on the dishes.

I said, "Well, if He gave it to us to do, I don't mind either. Just might take us some time."

"That's fine," she said, and it took us the rest of her life.

...And I did stay a while longer, farming and losing myself in what was left of the softball season. We were still playing good ball. I had played two weeks already—four games—with no left index finger. The glove felt awkward, and the pocket seemed as huge as a cave. Even though I kept the stub taped to my next finger and tucked in its sleeve, I took throws that stung the tender nub and sent electric jolts up through my shoulder. But holding the bat was the major change. I had to keep the half finger a touch off the bat handle or the jolt of the ball hitting the bat shocked and numbed my grip. I never had much bat power, and my swing became an even quicker, briefer punch at the ball. I stroked for singles through the infield holes and ran the bases hard to rattle the other team. And every time I swung, I relived the accident and said to myself, be careful, survive.

With a chance to tie for first and top tournament seed, we'd all focused on playing well. We wanted to win and play at the top of our game and make Rolf's sweat and crack with pressure. Looking forward to the end of the season tournament, being there and working hard at executing the art of the game was a blessed diversion for me, made it easier to live with all the other. I pumped my energies into the play and burned off the fires that I could. And no matter what calamity of the spirit around us, waiting, it was good relief to get in a game, play well, and win. So pure and simple and lost in the moment.

Because we'd been winning, the league rivalries had heated up, and more and more people drove over to the field to kill a Sunday evening, sipping beer and letting the kids run free. They would watch the games and honk for friends and good plays in the field and run into people they knew and talk for a while. I'd drag Uncle Karl along to a game some nights. I'd play ball, and he'd be around good company. We were getting by, enduring.

It lasted until that final game. The day's roiling cumulus were massing and colliding in the west when I came out of the summer fallow that afternoon. There were no deep violet curtains of rain yet below them, nor any lightning to see, but the thunder had been rolling in like far-away artillery roar. Sometimes there was a loud cannon crack and a bouncing echo that faded across the tableland toward the river valley. The day's light faded earlier than usual. Karl said the air was too dry for rain. "Just the veil of tears," he said, the showers that the dry air soaks up before they ever reach the even drier ground. We rode in, watching to see what the weather would hold.

Mike McCormick's lyrics/

No matter what game I'm watchin', it's still that season's last one that I remember. When I come drivin' in from my place, I could already tell it was gonna be one hell of a night. The old lady was mad and not talkin' cuz I didn't tell her we had a Friday make-up game. I told her she could bring the kids and come on— everybody does, but she'd rather sit on the nest and pile it up against me that I wasn't stayin' home, too.

I left her broodin' over the kids and got outa there, but outside, the thunder was really slammin' and the cows were spooked and stampin' in the corral. I penned 'em in away from where the drywash swings around, so in case it'd rain like we need it, they wouldn't be standin' in runnin' water. But it didn't really feel like it could rain. Just the sky soundin' off like dynamite or bombs—loud ker-cracks! and then that slow, lazy rumble down the valley.

So I was late anyway comin' in, and I stopped at Mel's station to see if Buckwheat was ready or gone. But it was Mel there, and he said Bucky took off with some vet who blowed in on a motorcycle some middle of the afternoon, and they were long gone to drink beer in Ogallala. I was thinkin' what you'd expect: Shit! Buckwheat won't show. Timo will pitch, throwin' things in a tizzy just when we need to win one. Somebody's gonna have to play an unfamiliar position. Batting order changes. All that. God! I had it bad as Thompson comin' down to the end of the season there.

Comin' in toward town then, I picked up the police channel on the CB, and they had a little man hunt goin'. Some kind of rumble in the Holiday Inn parking lot and people runnin' for it. It sounded like all out-of-towners. They had two from Louisiana in the hospital, and from them, the names and descriptions of three others. Plus they were lookin' for one or two more. They all took off on motorcycles or ran for the riverbed to hide, and they had county law and state patrol and the Ogallala police chasin' 'em down. Sounded like somebody was gonna teach those boys some manners.

Then, when I crossed the tracks and pulled up to the highway, here come Crighter flashin' by all sirens and lights, headed toward Ogallala to join in the glory. And old Boar's right behind him in his pick-up with that little orange county roadwork flasher blinkin' on top—the deputy's good old gun hound and one-man militia in action.

By the time I pulled in at the ballpark, the lights were on on account of the clouds rollin' in early darkness. There were already quite a few cars parked around the diamond, partly because it was Friday night and there was nothin' better to do, and partly because we were winnin' and people wanted to see what would happen. The other team—firemen from Keystone—were out catchin' flies, and most of Mercy's was there stretchin' out and warmin' up.

I was lacin' up my shoes, still listenin' in on the CB when a call comes in, disturbance in Revere. I thought, Jesus! is there a full moon tonight, or what? It was a complaint that some drunk was ridin' his motorcycle through people's yards and gardens. Phoned in from the Charles Collard residence. I had to grin at that—old Chuckie, big Ogallala banker, too good to play on a Revere team, and he can't make an outfield throw to home to save his soul. Couldn't back up our outfield even if we wanted him, and too damn important to do business in Revere. But he sure likes livin' in his new little mansion on the edge of town where all us low life can watch on. So someone's doin' hit and run on his daffodils, poor guy.

I yelled over to Thompson sittin' on the bench, makin' up the line-up, "What the hell's goin' on tonight? The county's like a zoo," and I started to tell you guys about the police call. Then we could hear ol' Crighter's siren comin' back this way. That gets everybody around the ballpark cranin' and starin' to see what the action is. Crighter fishtailed onto Main Street about sixty or so, not givin' a good goddamn about kids or old folks or nothin', just goin' bat-out-of-hell down Main for full effect. About that time, just north of the ballpark, you can hear a motorcycle revvin' up, shiftin' gears, and buzzin' down the dirt streets.

For about five minutes it sounded like cat and mouse through Revere, Crighter's siren and flashin' lights through the trees and the whine of the pipeliner's bike bouncin' off the houses. Some folks around were even cheerin' for Crighter on account of they're scared and tired of what's been fallin' off the Interstate these days—losers and drug addicts and trouble-makers, and people like them that killed the Siever boy just a couple years back or that bank robber killin' those folks in Big Springs in the fifties.

Pretty soon, folks even want the likes of Crighter to get back at some of them for once.

Well, the ballpark was pretty buzzed up cuz everybody was tryin' to get a glimpse of the action. About then, here comes Boar in his pick-up. He come off the highway onto the road just on the west edge of town. There's the left field fence, then a stretch of vacant lot and that row of elm along the road, and then Hansen's field across it. Just down the left field line, ol' Boar set up his roadblock like he had this end of town covered, his pick-up turned cross-wise in the road with the lights out and him with his sawed off twelve gauge standin' behind the hood like he's the cavalry's last outpost.

Then damn if we didn't hear that motorcycle streakin' across the north edge of town, goin' west, and take a left onto ol' Boar's road. Crighter was just behind him, and then you could see the bike's light flashin' as it flew by the line of elm, roarin' and pickin up speed till its headlight caught Boar's truck in the road. There was a hell of a squeal and scrapin' sound as that bike went over on its side and slid across the gravel towards Boar's pick-up, throwin' up sparks and rocks. It crashed under the pick-up's lefthand door and the gas tank exploded, and everyone cringed back. You could see old Boar come waddlin' down in the ditch with a hand on his hat and one on his gun. He fell down in a little puff of dirt as Crighter's patrol car come screechin' up, then he got up and scrambled back on the road, pointin' toward the cornfield.

There was another clap of thunder like a cannon and people screamed and ducked like a war was on. Everybody was spooked and confused, and Boar's pick-up starting to catch fire good now. People all over the ballpark were gawkin' and talkin' together, kind of hypnotized by it all. Crighter got his patrol car turned so his brights showed on the cornfield right at the corner there where Hansen's lane turns into their yard. You could hear other sirens comin' then, too.

A bunch of us was standin' around the bench watchin' and goin', "Can you believe this shit?"—Timo, Thompson, me, Calvin, Smokey, and sometime toward the end of this, Tommy showed up, goin', "What the hell's goin' on?"

Thompson said, "Well, the delay will give Buckwheat time

to show up. Where is that guy?"

I said, "He ain't comin'," same time as Mercy says, "He ain't comin'."

I told him about Buckwheat not bein' at Mel's, and Mercy said, "Oh man, I seen him at the Holiday a coupla hours ago. Him and this other guy got into one hell of a fight with these pipeliners. Over Vietnam and shit. They hurt a couple of them real bad, and Bucky took off on one of the motorbikes just before the cops got there."

That's when you yanked me by the arm. "Collard's that banker for Buckwheat's old man, isn't he?"

Before I could grunt yeah, you was up to full speed for the left field fence, yellin', "Crighter, you son-of-a-bitch! Cri-i-i-ghter-r-r!"

You had wheels, man, and took that fence like a deer, but there weren't none of us too far behind. We were comin' through the tree line, and you was just down into the corn when we heard Buckwheat yellin' something Vietnamese, then Boar's one scream, and the shotgun went off.

CODA

late-July, 1990

     I never needed other voices or the sound of the wind to revive that scene. Never needed notes to remember because it's always been with me, just under the surface of everything else in my life that's happened since. I wasn't listening then to an old teammate's recollection, but looking beyond his shoulder, over the left field fence and across the road, into the darkness of the field where it happened, where I crashed into the cornfield, tearing at stalks to let the car lights in among the leaves and shadows, trying to yell Crighter's name again, but only screaming out a panicked howl.

     About fifty yards in I found them. Buckwheat was a mass of blood and guts from his chest to his thighs, so sickening and sad I still see it in dreams. I felt the heaves comin', but I caught it in my throat and knelt down beside him and lifted his hot, wet head in my hands.

     Crighter stood there over us with his gun still hanging in his hand, shaking it like a leaf. People came in yelling and crowding around. More police cars came crashing down into the corn, throwing rocket-glare light in on us. Brownie and Lox came over and covered Buckwheat with their jackets, and the cover soaked blood black like a sponge. Others backed off, crying out, yelling for help.

I thought he was dead, but Buckwheat opened his eyes and said, "I'm hit."

I tried to say, "I know. We're getting help," but the words came out in a bawl.

"Medic," he muttered, choking on blood. He looked toward me and asked, "Regulars or V.C.?"

I found my voice, said, "Regulars. They were regulars."

"I knew they would come through here." He coughed up some more blood, then said, "We get any?" and held up the bloody K-bar in his trembling fist.

"Just one," I said, and pointed straight ahead of Buckwheat's eyes. There was the Boar in the next furrow between the rows. Someone was rolling him over in the spotlight of the sheriff's car, and his mouth was slung open in a frozen scream, his one good eye staring off hazy and blind now just like the other one. There was a huge black gash across his windpipe and the jugular, clear to behind his ear, and the whole side of his huge, round body was soaked in blood and caked with mud. The shotgun was tangled in his legs.

Buckwheat stared at him a long time, glassy eyed, then he said, "That's Boar."

"Yeah."

He looked up at me then and focused, said, "Still watchin' 'em die."

I tried to say, "Yeah," again, but nothing came out.

"It gonna rain?" Bucky asked.

I whined, "No," and Buckwheat said, "That's okay," and that was all for John Van Anders. He was gone, too.

Buckwheat was gone, and so was most everything else, especially the spirit to continue. End of the season, end of a way to endure, end of a life. There would be no more of Buckwheat's solos from the rim of the tableland, no more games that mattered, no more journal notes, until now.

I survived another winter without his company, living on late-night drunks and a soddened sense of impending duty to Uncle Karl and the farming to come in the spring. I played another season of ball in Revere, but even with ten men on the homefield and four or five more on the bench, something was missing, and everyone felt it. The game had changed because the players and their positions had. Still, we played, and played to win. Like Buckwheat did.

After games, most everyone would head out to McCormick's for beer and food and sideline lyrics, mostly about Buckwheat. Everybody missed him. He always lived up to the story. Always had lived up to everything. Even when the story didn't live up to him. I didn't want to listen or remember anymore, and I'd slip into my own thoughts, my eyes would wander, and there would be Karen, distant and busy around her house in ways she was needed, a new baby in her arms. Feeling her avoid me made the coming winter feel like death.

Uncle Karl understood, without details or explanations. He said, "You seen this place from here long enough. Go see it from some other place for a while." I did, and awhile gone turned into a year, then two, then more.

Karl hired an Alford boy to help him farm with his old machinery for a couple more years, then he decided to rent out his ground to another neighbor's boy. In the fall of 1980, Karl finished drilling wheat, locked Mrs. Harris and the Speckled Pony in the shop, walked across the yard to the house, and collapsed with a stroke.

Too slight to kill him decently, it merely left him senseless and silent. His daughter came for him and had him put in a home in Washington, D.C. where she could look after him. I went to see him there once, and we didn't know each other. I left again and kept moving.

—Right now, I can hear Buckwheat solo, "Just like them other assholes, asshole. They ain't got a fuckin' clue where that damned highway goes. All they got goin' is wheels, and nowhere to go on 'em."

—And I stayed away until Uncle Karl's "official" death last month, his memorial service and interment beside Martha in the cemetery behind St. Luke's. Came back to bury him, to mourn him, and to remember. Came back to listen to the wind and take care of unfinished business, unfinished life. Came back to see whose sons played on the homefield now.

Tonight I stood behind the backstop, listening to Mike McCormick and Tom Mercy—they call him "Teetering Tommy" now—and watching Thompson, cursed with only daughters, coach everyone else's sons. Like the last time I rode into town, a stranger in the Speckled Pony, they shook my hand and caught me up on history and old stories.

Buckwheat once said, "Them two would die of laryngitis. Hell, you can't take a shit in this town without them two got a story about what color it is. The coffee shop and Cody's would go broke if those two didn't come in there to tell folks the news. Fuckin' town criers. They're worse than the Christian Ladies' Aid Society. They'll probably know you're dead before you do, and the whole damn town'll be disappointed if you don't live up to the story."

If they say much about Buckwheat these days, it's to be glad that at least he wasn't alive to see his father's farm taken over by the bank, a farm that took three generations of Van Anders lives away from them before it became just someone else's rental property. His parents moved to town, and Jerry got a job for a while at Newcastle's station. He couldn't keep it and finally retired. Drinks too much now, like his son did.

Sandy moved with Buckwheat's kids to Omaha. Buckwheat's mother wanted them to stay around Revere, but Sandy had had enough of Buckwheat's life and wouldn't even name the son he never saw after him. Who can blame her? She found work, found a guy who isn't Buckwheat, and has done better than survive. But she lets the boy come back each summer to live with family and play ball in Revere, her one concession to Buckwheat's past.

Tom Mercy never had to move, but his parents did, to Arizona—more of those forced to move out, move on, get up on the Interstate and fade away. They used to return in the summer, too, but are too old to travel now.

Thompson's wife finally divorced him and sports and moved to Colorado with his daughters, much to his relief. He sells insurance now with Chub Chatman. Smokey Johns is retired. Brownie never comes back from Wyoming anymore. Timo married a nurse and spawned another generation of Ramirezes to rile the neighboring towns. McCormick has stayed, holding on to the family place, still holding his old job to survive.

Meanwhile, the sons play ball on the homefield.

I listened and remembered and looked out across the game going on, but I drifted into the same thoughts I'd had during the last games I'd played there: Is she here? Will I be around her?

Then the pitch of McCormick's voice changed and brought me back, saying, "Recognize this lady, Calvin?" Slipping under his arm to give him a hug around the waist was the young woman I remembered—same thick, straw-blond hair slung in a tail down over her shoulder to her breast; same bluer-than-sky-blue eyes, sparking in the bright lights of the field; same fine lines of face and lithe body. McCormick was saying, "You know this old guy?"

She gave me a beautiful, unblinking look into the eyes as my heart thundered in my ears. She smiled and shook her head as Mike snickered over her embarrassment, but she only let him play his game for a moment. "Mom said, if people are coming out after the game, you need to go to Cody's," she said, turning her eyes up to Mike's.

"Tell her I'm gettin' to it," he answered, and to me he said "Hey, come on out to the place. The usual folks are comin'. They're gonna want to know what you been doin' and what you're gonna be doin' so they got something new to talk about."

"Well, I'll tell everyone when I know, but I should be getting back to the farm."

"Hell, what for? Mercy, make him come," he yelled over his shoulder as he moved off toward his pick-up with his arm around his daughter's shoulder.

The ball game had finished somewhere during the conversation and daydreams, score unknown. Two other teams were taking the field to warm up, and the crowd was changing. I moved off toward the old Speckled Pony, parked near the fence down right field line. I'd spent the days working on the old pick-up while waiting for the farm auction and asking myself an old question: What am I doing here? As I moved toward the old truck, each step felt like a step back in time. I came down the line of parked cars, hearing Buckwheat again in my ears: "Don't be messin' with that Nebraska Virgin stuff."

I turned in between the pick-up and the one parked next to it. She said, "That's some pick-up," and stood there smiling, moving a wing of grey-blond hair away from her fine, glistening eyes.

"It gets me where I want to go."

"At least you won't lose it in a crowd."

We moved to each other and embraced, and I held her tight for a long time, feeling her slight tremble against my chest. When she gently pushed away, we smiled again and went through the formal amenities. Her eyes, clear and soft, said a thousand other things. The smile wrinkles were deep around her mouth and eyes and accented her beauty. In jeans and T-shirt she was farm-labor lean, still tall and strong and radiating life.

Finally, I said, "You're even more beautiful than your daughter," and even in the shadows of the night-lit field I could see a blush rise up her slender throat.

"They grow up fast," I added, cutting the silence short. "I watched your son play tonight. He's a good-looking kid." That was why we were there facing each other.

She looked to her feet, then back to my eyes. "You never gave me the chance to tell you."

"I know," I said.

"Michael isn't yours."

"I know," I said again. I had looked beyond the traits I had wanted to see to notice his father's lazy stride, the voice and personality. "I wanted him to be, though."

Then she couldn't look at me.

"You've raised a beautiful family," I said, and she beamed a full smile of pride and love, and the light flashed off her wet eyes.

Finally, she asked, "Are you coming out tonight?" No fear hidden in her voice, no desire.

"Probably not," I answered. "Maybe another time." I opened the pick-up door.

She asked quickly, "How's your hand?"

I held up my left hand, wiggling the stub of my index

finger. She took my hand in hers as I said, "Still missing a part, but getting by."

Looking at our hands without seeing them, she said, "There have been times I've wanted to tell you...." but she couldn't finish it.

"I know," I said. "Nothing much changes." I got into the pick-up.

"Nothing much changes," she echoed.

We said good-bye then, I backed out, and left the field of play.

On the way out of Revere, I stopped at Cody's for a six-pack of Miller and drove up on the edge of the tableland. Parked off the road where I could see back down into the river valley, got out, and opened a beer for Buckwheat and one for me. Sat his beside me on the tailgate of the Speckled Pony, and drank to us.

The ballpark lights are still on in Revere, blazing like a jeweled crown above the dim, twinkling street lights and the dark forms of the trees and houses, the elevator and the main street businesses. The tree-lined river is a long, black shadow in between, and just this side of it, the east-west glow of lights marking the Interstate runs toward the lights of another town and on beyond to the stars.

North across the dark valley, I can see the single lights of invisible farmsteads on the other tableland between the rivers. One of them is the Van Anders' place, though I can't pick it out over the black distance. Not far from it, we used to drive to that point and look out on the valley and all those people going nowhere so fast.

I've been gone a long time, from something that matters. If it matters, it can't be abused or abandoned. It can't be savior or saved either. It's there to be tended, like the ground, that's all. You decide if it's worth the work and try to survive the seasons, and any harvest is hard-earned. It's a harvest of heart and hands and weather wearing on the soul.

So I think about these things and share a country-night beer with a dead friend, listen to the windsong, the voices, stir across the dark fields. Maybe I'm Buckwheat's harvest, such as it is. And Uncle Karl's and Aunt Martha's, too, such as it is. The summer season comes on. I can smell it in the new, open fields around me in the night under a canopy of incredible starlight. The work lies waiting. So I pour Buckwheat's beer out on the ground, get in the pick-up, and head home. I can hear Buckwheat again, his solo over the roar of the wind at my window, "No sale! No sale!"

About the Author

Robert Richter is a semi-retired dryland wheat farmer in south-western Nebraska, where he lives with his wife on the remnants of a family homestead. They have two grown children. His essays and stories have appeared in *Bloomsbury Review*, *Prairie Schooner*, and other magazines and anthologies. Richter is the author of three previous books: *Something in Vallarta*, (fiction), *Windfall Journal*, (poetry and prose about farming on the American high plain), and *Plainscape*, (a regional history). He is also an ex-expatriate and a frequent traveller to Mexico, to where he also conducts guided tours. In 2000, Richter won the Master Writer Award for his non-fiction from The Nebraska Arts Council.